C000135628

The Awakening of Fire

Book Two   The Singer of Days

Snaede Endeavours 2021

To Derek
Every blessing

Andrew

The Awakening of Fire
Book Two   J Andrew Evans
The Singer of Days   © Snaede endeavours
Part of the Singer series
All Rights Reserved

'Are technology and magic indistinguishable?'
Well that's the Question.

All from a poem by Ray Bradbury.

Contents

◈ CODA ◈

The fire they sang that night reached up to the sky.

The woman had sung the fire every night of her memory, and even before she was too young to sing, or to give voice to the song, she had sat on her mother's knees as the people brought the flames into being – the light that filled and sustained them as a people. The woman had never known the darkness of the night nor seen the stars except dimly through the flames of the fire they sang. The fire came as always, but this night it joined the fire beyond, the ribbons of flame that filled the northern skies above them.

This night, at the height of the fire, the words had come, as they so rarely did these days, but which were so often desired. The words came and spoke what they had so longed to hear.

Has it come at last?

The night and the song ended; she raised her head and gazed around the circle of the people. She was, as always, saddened by how few of them were left. Two hundred at most of what had once been the mighty Offspring of the fire. Each generation was smaller than the one that came before it.

The Eye was standing now. He gazed around at the silent circle of the people. They were the generation that would see it. They were the people who would reclaim the lands they had lost. They were the Children who would at last see the Offspring grow again.

She gazed up and realised that the Eye was standing before her.

She did not understand why. He spoke.

'The fire spoke your name to me. And so I name you envoy.'

The words but washed over her as if she could not claim them or own them. She did not move. *I? But I am no one, I hold no post, I am nothing.* But the Eye was still speaking.

'I too was named,' he said, 'and there was another. Three will be the number who go. Three, the ones who will find the kings of old. They are in need of us.' The Eye was reaching down and his hand was out to raise her to her feet. She grasped it and let him be the means that she rose, for there was no power left in her.

'The fire has spoken,' the Eye said.

'For in the fire is truth.' She said the words of the response without thinking them, for they came to her lips automatically, easily, as did all the rituals of the fire.

She looked around at the dawn and saw then that all the people were staring at her, acknowledging the honour paid to her. The Eye had left her now and was standing with all the people gazing at her in wonder. And then he stopped before another man and said the same.

'The fire spoke your name to me. And so I name you envoy.' The woman looked up at the dawn filling the sky and knew that the true beginning had come. The song of the fire would spread again. The arising was come.

◈ Chapter 1 ◈

Not wit, not tears, nor strong desire
can bring the singer back.
He must wait
for the rhythm of the song to reach him.
A song once sung does not go back.
A single instrument, a single voice
that once has left the theme
cannot choose the place of its return,
but must wait
until the prosody demands it,
until the song needs it.
The singer must stand and wait,
let the song roll on until the time is come
and the song declares again.

The Song of Omer

Halam turned away from the retreating Torasar. They were alone again. His gaze strayed to the stronghold. It was perhaps an hour's run from where they stood. The great flying birds, their warriors, if they were ahead, had long disappeared within. If they set out soon they could reach it before dusk. *Can we attack the fortress? How can we assail it with just the four of us?* The staff he bore seemed suddenly terribly heavy. Hewas turned and looked at him. 'Halam, do we go?'

How can I know?

What is this king of the mountain people asking me?

He collapsed. Halam hit the ground before any

of them could react or reach him and stop the bone-cracking impact with which he fell. Terras cried out some nameless words.

'Halam ...' Terras was at his side, concern written all over her face.

'I cannot hold it any longer,' he said. He stared up at her.

The staff slipped from his grasp and rolled to the floor beside him. With the staff released he felt his face flush; relief and the ease of the unburdening flooded through him.

'My son, our prince,' said Hewas crouching beside Terras, 'if you let it go, how may we assault this place? We surely have not the strength. Somehow it brings us the powers of the One. Without it, how can we go and bring him back?'

'I cannot do it, Hewas,' he said, 'it is beyond me.'

'Then I will bear it.' It was Rosart, kneeling now beside Hewas. Rosart moved at once to take it but as they all looked the staff was no longer on the ground.

Insnar stood over the staff. He had dragged it already several feet away in his teeth. He had stopped now and, crouching over it, he growled at the Hardsara woodsman.

Rosart leapt to his feet and took a step towards the animal. The little beast bared his fangs and would, in a moment, attack. The jaksar were small creatures but their teeth and the ferocity of their bite was legendary. Once their jaws closed on a foe, little could release them. This contest would by no means be won by the woodsman. Rosart took another step forward.

'No, Rosart . . .' Hewas rose now, reaching out and grasping the woodsman by the arm. He held him back. 'The animal does not understand. He is protecting his master's staff. Do not take it by force.'

Rosart looked back at his king but, in his face, it was clear he did not agree. He spoke the words slowly, syllable by syllable. 'Then how, Hewas, will we do it?'

Halam struggled to his feet. His strength was returning, but he knew in his heart that he could never again pick up that staff. It had changed him too much and too fast. It was making him more than he was, and he could not take that. He wanted to remain himself. He did not want to be someone else, not even a better, stronger person. 'I do not know . . .'

Then Hewas was shouting at Rosart. Halam stopped listening to them. His eyes were on the jaksar. Rosart and Hewas continued to argue.

'I understand, Halam.' Terras was speaking softly from beside him. 'The staff was not made for you to bear.'

Halam nodded but his attention never left Insnar. The jaksar lay over the staff now, growling softly as if to himself.

'But, Halam,' Terras was continuing, talking, pulling at his arm. 'How are we to go on without it?'

Halam still stared at the little animal,

fascinated with the strangeness of his little soft growls. Little whimpers were introduced into the noises as if the animal was suffering and growling defiance at the pain at the very same time. From the staff and the ground, an ashen greyness began then to spread up the jaksar's body, from his paws, up the legs, and into the body. Insnar mewled then like a lost pup, piteously, but still, the jaksar continued to growl his incantation.

Incantation!

Halam jumped forward. 'No, Insnar, there is another way!' He shouted out the words, screaming out his distress. Not thinking as he moved, he threw himself across the ground between them, smashing Rosart and Hewas apart. He reached the animal, but it was too late.

His hand touched the head of the jaksar. He pressed his fingers down hard, crying out the terrible emotions that assailed him in one awful scream. Bitter tears flowed down his face.

Insnar was solid. He was stone. Bound to the earth.

The animal and the staff were one, a lonely statue bereft of life.

In desperation, Halam grasped the frozen stone jaksar and bowed his head over it. The tears came freely; heedless, he let them fall onto the stone that had once been Insnar. Terras was with him, holding Halam as much as she held the jaksar. Eventually, his emotions subsided a little and he drew back and looked again at the faithful creature before him.

The jaksar and the staff were melded together, and somehow they were also bound to the ground. He had been caught in mid-snarl and now seemed like a beautiful statue, a jaksar growling over the staff of his master, clutching it with his paws, protecting it against all that might beset it. He would lie there forever, hopelessly awaiting his master's return. Nothing but time itself would mar his guardianship. Slowly, time and passing ages would grind away at the faithful guard until it was but a faceless rock, unknown and unsung, and yet still awaiting its master's return. The staff was safe from prying hands as the jaksar had wanted.

What had truly gone through the little animal's mind? What had he thought was happening? What had he feared? Why had he called from the staff such a terrible destiny? There had to be another way than this. Why had Insnar done it?

Terras was crouched down beside him and she was pulling him away. As she did, he turned his face to her. She too was upset, but differently, angry at the injustice.

He spoke. 'Why, Terras?'

'He did not understand . . .' It was Hewas who replied, standing behind her. 'He feared that something was happening to his master's staff. He sought to protect it, only to protect it.'

'Insnar understood more of what was said

around him than you might think.' Terras looked back up at her father, but there was anger in her tone. 'He knew the true situation. There was no misunderstanding.' She turned on Rosart, her eyes blazing. 'It was your fault, Rosart. You tried to take it by force!'

The woodsman stared back at her. Many emotions crossed his face, fear, anger, resentment, but also guilt at the truth in her words.

'No, Terras, don't . . .' Halam reached out and grasped for her arm, but she was already gone, on her feet. She stormed across the ground. Rosart did not move. She struck him with her fists, one to the chest and one full on the chin. He did nothing to stop or prevent her but simply fell backwards before the blows, onto the ground. She stood over him, daring him to rise but, uncharacteristically, he simply lay there and stared up at her.

At last, he said, 'I am sorry, Terras.'

She looked down at him in surprise, for Rosart, Halam knew, was not one to stand back from a fight. Hewas was beside her now, holding her arm.

'Leave it, Terras. You do not know what passed through the jaksar's mind.' Hewas looked at Halam where he lay on the ground beside the stone jaksar. 'He was a simple animal, I say. He knew only that the staff must be carried and so he carried it. This is the only way he knew how to protect it until his master returned.'

Halam spoke from the ground. 'Then let us

find Rissar. Let us go and bring him back here. For Insnar, if we have no other reasons.'

Hewas walked forward beside Terras and bent his arm to help Rosart to his feet. The woodsman had a strange look on his face, like a man changed, shocked and altered by an event that for the first time had taken him beyond himself.

'And how are we to do that now, Halam?' Terras said loudly. 'Now without the staff to aid us. You saw its power. It brought us across the plains. With it, we all but caught the warriors before they reached their goal. Without the staff, what is there?'

Halam rose to his feet, but not without a backward glance at the jaksar still frozen in his guardianship. He stood and looked across the intervening ground to where the three Hardsar stood together.

'I don't know . . .' he said, 'but surely we must try.'

Rosart shook his head. 'No, we cannot do this without great strength.' He pointed across the plain at the stronghold. 'How can we assail that, just us four?'

They all turned and looked again at the fortress. It was hidden again from their sight and seemed now but a single pillar of stone, fashioned by nature and chance to look a little like a solitary tower. But their inner vision of the truth gave them the means to perceive its shape if not its form.

It was true of course. How could four of them, three men and a woman, even ones as strong and capable as they, assail a stronghold of such might? How had they even thought they could?

Halam looked at the Hardsar and wondered how they could have fallen so quickly from the heights they achieved during the run. When he had held the staff and cried out the beautiful song of the Torasar, when the strength and power had flowed so easily, it had seemed that there was nothing to prevent them, nothing to stand against them.

It meant nothing that the evil warriors they chased seemed so strong, so armed, or that they headed to a legendary stronghold, known to all the plainsmen for its power, its impregnability, its strength. Nothing could have stopped them from coming hither, ready to fight and to die if necessary. Now, within moments, they were hitting each other, bickering, and nothing seemed possible at all.

Even Insnar had despaired, Halam realised then. Was that not why he did what he did, took the step, and protected the staff by channelling its own power? The little animal had seen no other way. *Perhaps the jaksar had understood best of all.*

He walked forward. 'We must go. Even if we die. We have been brought here. Don't you see that? The power of Rissar has brought us to this place. We must go on. What choice is there, but to go on?'

Rosart spoke. He was once more himself, confident, strident, and strong. 'That is foolishness.' He spoke as if there was no other way of thinking. 'There is another way. We must return, across the plain. If we go back we can get the host of the people. Hewas . . .' He seized Hewas's shoulder, desperate to persuade him. 'Think of it, my king, the whole nation of the Hardsar standing here on the plain before this place. The Torasar would not prevent us from crossing. Indeed, Torem gave us leave to cross the plain. If we stood here with the whole people behind us, that stronghold would not seem so menacing.'

Halam saw Rosart's grip tighten on the shoulder of his king. Hewas turned and looked at him. 'The stronghold would be just as perilous, my son. It is only that we would be stronger.'

'Or maybe just more numerous.'

They all turned and looked at Terras.

'What do you mean?' Rosart spoke, anger in his tone.

'Strength is not always what it seems,' she said. 'I think we should all have learnt that from the last few days.' She glanced at Halam, to his chagrin. 'I see the stronghold and its power, its impregnability, but perhaps more Hardsar standing here is not what we need.'

Halam walked forward to stand beside her. 'What we needed was the staff . . . but I laid it down.'

'All the more reason to return and bring the people here,' said Rosart at once, seizing the opportunity to restate his point. 'It may be that the people cannot assail that place, but if they cannot, then surely we cannot either. Perhaps all their strength is not sufficient, but it is greater than ours, and I, for one, will feel better with several thousand mountain warriors at my back.'

Hewas pursed his lips. 'There is wisdom in what he says.'

Halam shrugged. 'I do not understand. Why then did Rissar insist that the quest was small in number and why did Franeus send us hither to chase the warriors if there was never any hope of catching or attacking them?'

Halam stared at Rosart. He could see a trace of a lingering resentment between them.

'Perhaps they did not know.' Rosart always had an answer. 'Perhaps Rissar did not expect to be ambushed in the forest, and Franeus did not know that we would lose the staff.' He said the last carefully, glancing at Terras, no doubt to see if she would renew her accusations. Halam saw her catch the glance but she said nothing.

'Surely they both have the power to know such things before they occur.'

Rosart sneered. 'Don't be ridiculous. Rissar would not have walked into an ambush if he had known it was coming. No, their plan has gone awry. We are right to rethink and reconsider what we might do.'

Halam shook his head. 'We should go on. I do not know what will happen, but whatever, I cannot turn back. Insnar has given too much, don't you see that? We cannot just turn round now and walk back. If we had not come here, but had turned in the forest and called the host of the Hardsar then, he would still be with us, instead of . . .' He trailed off and turned to look at the statue of the jaksar in mid-growl, paws grasping the staff that was now part of his body, and both bound to the ground.

Hewas was speaking. 'But . . . Halam, be realistic.'

'I will go on,' responded Halam. 'If it is to my death then so be it. I wish to preserve myself no longer – even a jaksar can teach me a lesson in faithfulness.'

Hewas sighed. 'I agree with Rosart. I think we should return, but I will not seek to force you. I will gather the nation and return to this spot, that we may all honour the self-sacrifice of this friend of Rissar before we turn and assail the stronghold. Rosart,' he looked at the woodsman, 'I know you will come back with me.'

The forest man nodded curtly to his king. 'Terras . . . ?'

She smiled. 'I will go with my man as he would go with me. We are together.' Hewas smiled at her, some exchange, some private humour flashing between them, but quickly his face turned to a frown and he stared at her. 'You may go to your death.' He was serious now.

'So be it,' said Halam.

'So be it,' said Terras.

Hewas looked at his daughter; there was suffering in his face at the thought of the loss of her, but there was also love – love and admiration.

For what is a Hardsara if not stare death in the face with courage? This is our lot forever. I am a bitter one.

'It would mean more than just your death, Terras.'

Terras nodded back at him. 'I know. If it is so, you will be just in your choice.'

Halam looked between them. Then he realised. If both Terras and he died in their endeavour, the Hardsar would be without a future king and a queen for there was no other princess to choose.

'Yes, my daughter. I will be just.'

'Why don't you go on with us, my lord?' said Halam.

Hewas, king of the mountain, shook his head.

'If you are right, my son, Halam Hardsaro, and you gain entrance, then my presence or absence is unlikely to sway the balance. If four may win against such a place, then perhaps two may also. But I adjure you, if you come to the place and can see the cause is hopeless, do not throw your lives away needlessly. Stay there, scout the fortress, spy on its occupants, and await our return. If you err and die in this endeavour I will bring with me the means to rip the stronghold down and destroy it, stone by stone. My vengeance will know no pause. If this place is the cause of your deaths it will not escape my wrath.'

'So be it,' said Rosart.

Halam stared across at this king, this strong, decisive man who knew his mind and his way forward. He understood the words, but he was upset that in a matter of minutes the glorious company of runners who had sped here as if on the wind itself was now to be ground down to but a single man and woman, with nothing but their swords with which to fight and win.

'If you go, Halam,' Hewas pointed at the stronghold and the sun bending quickly to its end, 'the darkness comes. Heed the words of Torem.'

'Think again, Halam,' said Rosart, 'if not for yourself then for Terras.'

'I think for myself,' snapped Terras.

Halam stared at the woodsman. Something had changed in him. He felt it. He was still Rosart, the strong and confident Hardsara, the son of Herfa, the man who had hoped to be king. But there was something new in his eyes. He had the air of a man who had learnt a lesson but had not yet decided what to do about it. He was a man who knew that things were changing but knew not how.

'I will go on, Rosart, if only for the sake of Insnar, and in hope of finding my lord Rissar. Terras has decided for herself.'

'Yes, I have . . . Rosart,' Terras affirmed. 'I go with the king-to-be.'

Rosart looked at her. Her words had another meaning, which they all understood, but he did not rise to them and if he felt anger at the words, it did not show on his face.

'If we are all convinced as to the rightness of

the course we each take, let us set out now before the sun sets further,' Hewas declared, turning to Rosart. 'Shall we travel through this night, Rosart?'

'So be it, my king.'

'Farewell, my son and my daughter. I shall hope to stand before you again.'

Hewas turned then and without further words or show of emotion, ran off. Rosart gave Halam a last glance before he followed his king. When they had gone, Halam looked at Terras.

'Are you sure?'

'Are you?'

He shrugged. 'It does not matter. If Insnar can do that,' he indicated the frozen stone jaksar, 'then I owe it to him to continue and not to run back all the way we have already come.'

Terras looked at the setting sun. 'We had best go then.'

◎

This time the running was difficult, used as they had become to the lack of exhaustion, the pace they had maintained. As Halam's chest tightened, he began to breathe harshly and he knew then how far they had fallen. How could that magnificent company of runners have come to this? They had run with the Torasar, run with the wind itself, and nothing had prevented them. Surely, they were only a few moments behind catching that which they sought. Perhaps, if the warriors had stopped once for an hour longer than they had, maybe they would have caught them. If the runners had risen one morning a little earlier and run before the sun, they would have caught them. Then the Torasar would have fought with them, for the evil warriors would have been on the plain, their land, and the plainsmen would have struck at them for their presumption.

How great that would have been, for Hardsar and Torasar to run together and fight their common enemy. How marvellous for mountain and plain to stand together and strike at that which sought destruction for both. What would have come from such a thing? What unity could have been achieved?

But it was all gone, dead. The chance had been there, and they had failed it. Halam had failed and the jaksar was lost. The Torasar were gone, back to their hearths and clans, back to the herds, back to the plain. And the staff was lost, bound forever in the grip of a faithful servant. Halam was left with only his woman, his princess, his queen-to-be, running beside him. *Would it be enough?*

He glanced at her, and she, catching the look, met his eyes. No words were exchanged but he knew it was good to run beside her, good to thud on to their goal together. He hoped that nothing would ever separate them. He hoped that they would never again misunderstand each other. She had seemed so ready to come with him, wherever they headed. Simply because they were together. She had not questioned whether he was right in his insistence to go on.

Halam did not care any more whether he was

right or wrong. So much had happened; he had failed in so many ways. Rissar had been taken despite all the prowess his sword gave him. Now Insnar, the second of the two friends he had met at the beginning, had gone from him – surely dead forever. Halam, the weak Lakeman, had lost them both. Yet, because of all they meant, all he had done, and because of his words, so recently sworn when he became Hardsar, he must strike on. If he failed or even died in the attack on the stronghold, at least he would die in pursuit of his oath.

They ran on together. The plain began to break up, small ponds and potholes appearing as the Pasra approached, and slowly the ground began to rise. The stronghold towered above them, but it seemed now just a small, deserted, rather ruined guard post amid a strange landscape of windblown rocks.

Up and on they ran, the run filling their chest and limbs with exhaustion and savage breath. Terras pulled at Halam's arm and pointed behind them. A storm was boiling out of the east, the clouds rippling over the horizon where the plain and the sky met. It was coming quickly.

'It will be on us before we reach the stronghold,' Terras panted out.

He slowed in his run, caught suddenly by the sense of the awesome powers held in the hidden castle before him and the terrible strength of the storm behind him. He was between them, like metal in the vice of a blacksmith. Ahead of them, beyond the fortress, the sun was dipping towards the great mountains of the Pasra.

They must reach the stronghold this night. He knew that. If they did not reach the gates of the stronghold before the storm hit, Halam was not sure they would have a second chance. Yet the idea of attacking the place with a storm howling around them was not a pleasant one.

'The storm will hide us from their gaze.'

He turned and looked at Terras. She did not feel the same things at all. Perhaps he understood that for the first time. She was a Hardsara and did not flinch from any harsh or difficult task. She was a bitter one. Did she even fear as he feared, or feel as he did that they might be running to their deaths? If she did, she did not care, but only obeyed the call she had found herself to have. Yet was that not what he was thinking but moments before?

'We must go on,' he said and began to run again. She followed him.

They ran on into the encroaching dark with the storm sweeping across the great plain towards them. On into the foothills they toiled, closer to the stronghold, closer to its awesome greatness. All too soon the rain speckled their faces as the storm's edge reached them.

And then, at last, they were before their goal. The stronghold lay now across but a short flat piece of ground. The night was all but come and the gloom of the evening dusk obscured their view of the fortress.

Before the stronghold there was dolmen, some ancient stone reminder of a time, long ago probably, before even the magician kings. He thought if they ran to it, it might give them some vestige of cover as they made their approach. The stronghold looked like a small, ruined guard tower now, long abandoned, and no threat to anyone. But he assumed that the tower marked the main entrance to the Citadel.

Halam, crouching, looked up at the last lingering remnants of daylight above him. The full storm was coming and the sky was darkening early. Rain was falling, falling fast, sweeping across the landscape around them. Still, despite the wildness of the oncoming night, they felt the power of the stronghold reaching across the ground to them.

No lights showed in the stronghold, no sign even that it was inhabited. Momentarily the thought crossed Halam's mind that the warriors had not come here after all. Perhaps they had continued up into the mountains of the Pasra itself. If that were so, they would have lost them – and forever. Yet why would Franeus tell them to come here if the warriors they pursued and their lord Rissar had not been brought here?

The tower, the entrance, the way was open to them, but the dolmen still seemed like the best place to go first, to give them cover from watching eyes, if there were eyes there at all. It seemed that the stronghold could just be walked into and no one stood to prevent or frustrate them. Beyond the dolmen, a stream ran across the front of the Citadel and, whilst it did not look deep, it was spanned by a gilded bridge.

From where they crouched the megalith could be reached with but a few dozen hurried strides, and then, beyond it, they would be across the bridge and a short distance before the entrance of the stronghold itself.

'There are no guards,' said Terras at his side.

He turned and looked at her. 'I do not think that will prove to be true, any more than the fortress is what it seems.'

In the dusk, her eyes seemed to catch the faintness of the last of the day, pinpricks of light in the encroaching gloom.

Halam scanned the scene again and, of course, she was right; there was no sign of any people at all, no giant birds, no warriors, nothing. Just an old, deserted fort on the edge of the western mountains.

'What protects this place?'

A flash of lightning was followed almost at once by the peal of accompanying thunder. In its light, the fortress in all its might was suddenly revealed. Halam turned and looked again at Terras. Even if he had doubted it before, they had both seen that no one guarded this terrible place. It looked deserted, uninhabited; in the lightning he had seen the ramparts clearly, and there was no one.

'It is very strange,' said Terras quietly. 'Why were we sent here?'

Could this not be the place the warriors had brought Rissar too? Could the stories of the Torasar and the evil of this place be only that, stories and myths? He paused, doubts flooding into his mind. Had they seen the birds arriving there at all? Had the abductors of Rissar gone somewhere else?

'We must go on,' he said at last. 'We will not discover the truth crouching here. If it is empty and deserted then we will have to think again. Let us run to that dolmen. Through it, it is but a few steps to the bridge. Before anyone knows, we will be there.'

Terras nodded curtly. 'Yes, you are right. Let's go, it will soon be night.'

He rose to his feet, sliding his sword silently from his scabbard. At once the power of the sword filled him; it seemed an age since he had claimed that power and drawn it to himself, but there was no time to savour the moment. Terras too had risen, sword in hand.

'The river may be deep,' she said. 'We cross by the bridge.'

They ran across the short distance to the dolmen. As they reached the arch of the megalith, just as they passed through it, the sun, hidden though it was behind the dark clouds, slipped finally below the horizon. The light faded around them. Night had come. There was another flash of bright lightning and, simultaneously, a blast of cold air hit him. It tore into his face and grasped his chest in a vice. He gasped, the breath shocked from him. The world flickered and filled with a white brightness that was beyond reckoning.

◈ Chapter 2 ◈

I needed the Superior. I needed revenge.

It was frustrating; my journey back would be long and a huge waste of time. I had escaped from the pull of the forming black hole and I was already on my way back to the other side of the galaxy. Yet even at faster-than-light speed, it would be a tiresomely extended journey for my route was a slow curve, avoiding the galactic core. It was too dangerous for us – there is a massive gravity well. I had to curve around in a shallow parabola, it would be safer. This was urgent. Yet it had to be me that spoke directly to the Superior and in person. I could not trust others to tell the tale aright. They might not favour me; they might not put my side of this mess, this chaos.

This must not become Romul's folly. I must not get the blame for this. The Superior was mighty, but he was not always forgiving of rank stupidity. What great and powerful leader is? He needed to understand that we faced something new here. It was clear that the enemy was changing his strategy. This was not normal; this was not the way the war had been fought for aeons. This was exceptional and might have repercussions for the whole of this galaxy, if not the universe.

Yet, I felt content. I had a strategy for my meeting with the Superior – once I reached him. It was one I was sure would work. I had been called to a primitive world and I discovered that the planetary chief had entirely missed the development of hugely powerful technologies and, because of his failings, these powers were now in the hands of dangerously elevated natives. They now wielded their advanced science against us – technologies powerful enough to block us out and indeed hurl us tens of thousands of parsecs away. I could imagine myself saying these very things to the Superior.

I was satisfied. I would tell the Superior that I had also transmitted a message to Raczek instructing the purloining and usage of a neighbouring planet's weaponry against these people as a short-term delaying tactic. Highly sophisticated weaponry, devices they were not expecting, should delay them and hamper whatever their plan was for precipitously utilising their new technological advances against us.

I was pleased. I had a strategy that would convince the Superior and also achieve my priorities. I was not blameworthy. I was the agent for victory. Raczek was culpable. It was his shortcomings that had led to this and not mine.

The marvellous thing was that it was even true.

When I arrived with the Superior and all the forces we could muster we could choose to destroy the entire planet. It would be a pity to lose a whole intelligent species this way. But life had to be free of the pernicious influence of the enemy. If destroying them and their whole star system was required to achieve total freedom, we would do it for the sake of the universe.

For a moment, I savoured the thought of their destruction. These 'apotheoses', these superior-epitomes, they had humiliated me. They must pay for that. If necessary, their whole world would pay for their arrogance. We always do what is necessary.

◎

The whole world around Halam was white, covered in white, covered in brightness. His motion took him forward and onto the bridge. He stopped halfway across, the momentum ripped from his legs by the shock of the change. Outside the stronghold, it was snowing. For a moment it seemed as if the storm had, in a moment, been frozen into snow.

He reached out a restraining hand to stop Terras beside him with his left hand but he could not reach her. He spun around.

Then he realised. He was alone. Terras was gone. He cried out, despairing. 'Terras . . . !' All the angst of his loss and desperation filled his voice.

He swung round, slicing the sword in a vicious arc, needing someone to wound, to hurt, to kill, shouting her name again, and yet knowing, knowing all the while in his heart that she too had been taken from him. Now he was alone. Everything was stripped from him, everything was gone.

From the great company of runners, only Halam Aallesara was left, only him, still fighting to achieve the goal. From that first night alone in the forests of the lakeland, he had done nothing but meet and gain new friends; he had gathered so many around him. Now, in a matter of hours, they were all gone, and Halam Aallesara was alone again, in a fearsome place, with only his sword left to him.

He stared around him, calmer, anxious to understand his new position and what threats it posed. All around him was quiet. Snow covered the ground, but above there were breaks in the clouds and the sky was clearing, showing a deeply black starlit sky. The storm was ending, indeed it was hard to believe now that it had been raging around him only moments before. There was nothing outside, no one, only silence and snow.

He turned and stared into the stronghold. Inside there would be answers if they were to be found at all. He could see little of the interior. Without hesitating a moment longer, he threw himself across the rest of the bridge. It thundered beneath his running feet, and the darkness and the white brightness swelled around him. Halam cried out his torment, heedless of the warning he was giving; he ran on.

He ran across the ground to the entrance of what seemed now to be a small guard fortress. He ran through the entrance into a gatehouse. Finding himself in a place of relative safety, he stopped again. He stood stock-still and let himself come to terms with what he was seeing, with the new reality that had jumped into existence around him.

It was still snowing. He could not understand

how that could be, how it could have happened so fast. A gentle wind was drifting the snow in fluttering whirls of white. It lay all around him, glinting in the darkness of the night, taking the faint starlight and throwing it back at the sky.

Directly above him, the dark roof told him little. A courtyard stretched away from the gatehouse in which he stood. Snow covered it, thick and untouched. For the snow to be so thick it must have been falling for hours. How could that be when it had not been there a moment before? He walked forward, holding his sword crosswise before him, ready for any movement or dark shadow that would tell of the presence of the warriors.

As he left the gatehouse the starlit sky burst into being above him, and before him, the great courtyard of the stronghold was fully revealed to him. He could see the full immensity of the Citadel, understand its greatness, its raw power. It was vast.

The courtyard stretched away, a huge expanse of whiteness before the large tower that stood at the centre of the place. The snow lay thickly all across the intervening distance. No feet had crossed it since the snow had begun falling. Halam saw that this place had been deserted for many hours, if not days or months. Was it empty? How could that be?

A terrible, desolate sigh escaped from his chest and he let his sword droop until its tip grazed the floor and patterned thin lines in the snow. He whirled around to catch a perhaps hidden pursuer. Looking back at his footprints behind him, they were the only mark on the perfection of the snow.

He turned back and walked forward. There was no one here; there had not been for all the days of his journey to this place. Now, at last, from that moment when he had walked off the cliff in the forests of the lakeland, he had come to the pointless aim of his whole trip.

Why had he come to this place? Why had he run without weariness across the great plain, carrying a staff he was not meant to bear, to reach this empty fortress? What had been the point? Why had he lost even Terras from his side, snatched away to some other fate as they crossed the threshold of the stones? Another terrible sigh escaped his lips and he threw his head back, staring up at the sky and the thousand pinpricks that marked the stars. They twinkled back at him, bright and sharp in their ferocity. He would have thought they laughed at his wretchedness if he had believed for a moment that they cared about it.

He looked down, and in a single heart-stopping moment he almost did not believe what he saw. There, high in the central tower, was a light. It shone in a tiny window and for an instant it seemed that one of the stars had come down to the ground and settled in the main tower of the keep.

It was not a star, but the single flickering pinpoint of a candle, placed in the narrow window of the highest tower as if to guide the traveller to its light. He pulled his sword upward to hold it before him again. He swallowed his doubt and, bending to his task, ran quickly across the courtyard towards the keep. He would find out who it was who had lit that light. That person, whoever they were, would answer some questions. Halam deserved the answers and he was going to get them, regardless of whether they wanted to answer them or not. The snow creaked as he crossed it, marking his presence in it. He reached the central tower with the silence of the night around him, and before its great doors he hesitated and turned back, looking at the tracks he had left in the snow. Even if the occupants of the tower had by some chance not seen him running, they would know that he had passed by, of that there was no doubt.

He mounted the three steps that led up to the great entrance of the keep and placed his hand upon the huge handle that opened the doors. They were not locked, not even properly shut, but simply pushed nearly closed. They opened as he thrust at them and the snow, lifted by the slight breeze, scattered into the hall beyond.

Halam pushed the doors further in, letting the starlight into the interior. He stepped into a great hallway. He stood and let his eyes adjust, heedless of the fact that standing in the entrance he must be silhouetted against the light from outside.

The great entrance hall of the keep was huge, and a vast staircase swept upwards from it to the higher floors. There were doors off the hallway into further ground-floor rooms, and over the ground a patina of dust covered everything. No one had crossed the floor for many days.

Within, the light was dim; the starlight gave him a little view of the detail of the interior. He walked inside, grasping the sword tightly. His palms became sweaty and cold, the tension filling and tormenting him. He reached the first step on the staircase. The hall around him was almost pitch dark. A little light filtered in through the main doors that he had left open behind him, and a little seemed to hang in the air, its source unknown, hardly enough to see.

He started up the stairs, the darkness around him palpable as if it was a force in its own right, the echo of some past, some terrible darkness that had possessed this place. The staircase turned, and he looked back at the dim shape of the open door. The light from the outside seemed bright, harsh in its invasion of the darkness of the hall.

He quickened his pace, hurrying away from the sense of oppression that lingered in the entrance. He could not name his fear but knew, somehow, that things had happened here that should not be considered. The stairs came to a landing. He could hardly see in the blackness, but it seemed that passageways ran off into the darkness. The stairs continued up, so he mounted them. The light had been high in the tower. He must walk up until there were no more steps, and then he would be quite close to the source of the light.

Still, the blackness grew deeper, more like a

fog, a miasma through which he could not see. He had to sheathe his sword, which he had still been holding before him as he walked. He felt his way with both hands. The stairs continued up. At each landing, rooms or passageways stretched away into the darkness, black holes in the night. He continued to walk upwards. At last he saw, as he climbed, a faint glimmer from above him. It became a little easier to walk, to see, and he let one hand drop down to the sword.

He reached the starlit room quite soon. The stairs came to a large circular chamber. Four passageways stretched away at each of the four cardinal points and in the centre, a spiral staircase continued upwards. Between each doorway to the passages there were windows. Through them, starlight of the bright night sky glimmered in, filling the room with a faint light that seemed to Halam, after the darkness of the climb, like veritable daylight. So much so that he wondered if the greater moon had risen.

He walked forward slowly, skirting the spiral steps stretching up into the ceiling, and walked to the nearest of the windows. They were narrow, restricted openings, and yet, through them, the light filtered, and he could see the snow-covered courtyard far below from which he had climbed.

He stared down at the eerie whiteness of the snow, and then walked round to the next window and looked again. From the next window, he saw the entrance towers each side of the gatehouse. There in the thick snow, his footprints shouted out to any that looked down that he had entered the stronghold and had then run across the courtyard to this place.

He sighed and, turning, surveyed the spiral steps leading up into the darkness of the upper floors. There were no alternatives, no other ways. Even if the person who had lit the light was warned of his coming and waited even now with a trap set, he needed to get to them. Only they, whoever they were, would have the answers. Without answers there was no way to find Terras, nor discover where Rissar was. Even, for that matter, where the warriors had gone with their giant bird steeds.

After all, had they not chased them to this place?

Had they even come here?

He drew his sword. The sound of its coming whispered a warning into the silence. He walked forward and resumed his climb. At regular intervals were doors off the spiral staircase, but Halam did not try them; something told him that his quarry lay higher. The steps grew narrower and the doors less frequent. The steps grew damp, dank, and smelt old. He reached a small landing off which two doors opened, but still, the steps stretched onward. He clasped his sword tightly and walked on up.

The stairs ended abruptly in a doorway and, coming up to it, he saw the light of the candle flickering underneath the door. He had reached his goal.

◎

As Terras ran through the dolmen, Halam had been just a step ahead of her, proceeding with his usual enthusiasm and apparent lack of fear for the consequences. It was as she had this thought that she saw him flicker and disappear. She pulled herself immediately to a stop. She swung around, her sword in hand, to sense any enemies that had somehow snatched him from her, but there was no one there.

The storm had ceased as suddenly as Halam had been taken. The night was clear, crisp and cold. The ground was hard. There was no snow. It was deep into the autumn. That alone was strange, for when they had entered it had been late spring. There were signs that it had rained here, then dried, then rained again. The ground was firm, a dried muddiness. She paced slowly forward and stopped before crossing the river.

The bridge stood before her, and beyond that was the gloomy entrance to the stronghold. Moments before, they had been running towards it, together.

There seemed to be no one in the fortress; it was dark and completely silent. She looked across at it, then before even attempting to cross the bridge she turned and looked back the way she had come.

The plain behind was dark and no lights showed upon it – just inky blackness and silence. It was as if she were the only person in the whole world and somehow, through her run through the dolmen, she had passed into a place where there was no one, no one living, no one breathing but her. Unsure, she looked around again. Then, realising that there were no enemies here and this place was empty, she sheathed her sword, sighing, into its scabbard.

She wandered back to the bridge and slowly walked across it. The stronghold lay before her, the entrance open. Perhaps the answer lay inside, but her warrior training, her senses, her battle readiness told her already that there were no warriors within. There was no one here. It was empty. Whatever instructions from Franeus had led them here, they had not, after all, led them to find the attackers in the forest from that night.

This fortress was empty, desolate. She walked forward cautiously and entered. The ground within was as hard as the outside. There was a great courtyard inside, silent as a grave, and the ground, solid and rock-like, gave no clues to whether anyone had walked on it for many hours. She scouted it cautiously, examining the outbuildings around the courtyard carefully. Some buildings could be stables and others would serve as barracks here. This place was capable of holding a great army. But all was empty and no one had walked there for many days before. In one of the rooms she had decided were dormitories she found an old lantern. Despite its age, when she struck a light it lit easily enough. At least this would help her to see as she explored more.

The lantern in her hand, she returned slowly to

the great keep in the centre of the stronghold and stood for a long time before the doors, which were closed. She listened, straining all her senses to decide whether anyone was within, hidden perhaps, ready for an ambush, but all that came back to her was emptiness. It was bleak and barren.

She drew her sword slowly, noiselessly, and mounted the steps to the great double doors of the keep. She worked the handle and, with the minutest of creaks, the lock turned and she pushed the door inward.

Within was a great hallway with stairs sweeping upwards. It would not have been out of place for some great ball, some great festivity in the city of In Haxass. She had been there sometimes and had stolen a glance at the richness of the Aallesar king's palace and the great halls of the lake city. This too could have borne such richness but now it was but empty, quiet, and dusty. If there had ever been jollity it was long ago.

She walked across the floor, her feet making marks in the dust. No one had walked these floors for many days. She turned to her right and walked through another set of double doors to find herself in a great room with a great stone chair at one end. She stopped. This too could have borne some great feast, some great celebration of victory. The throneroom was huge, and so unlike anything that the Hardsar had or indeed ever desired to be in. Still, despite that, she would have liked to dance here, perhaps with

Halam in her arms. She laughed inwardly at herself and the ridiculousness of her thoughts. That would never be. She was Hardsar.

The floor in the hall was as dusty, and as she walked across it she left footprints. She should have scouted cautiously around the walls to ensure that there were no enemies here before she allowed herself to walk into the centre. But it was increasingly evident that this fortress, this stronghold, was empty.

She returned to the main hallway and explored the rooms on the other side carefully. There was furniture there covered in huge blankets, larger than any Hardsar had ever woven. It looked as if the fortress had been abandoned by a tenant who at least had time to cover the furniture for some future return. She looked under the blankets and the furniture beneath was all ruined, old, and broken beyond any hope of use. She wondered how long it had been here.

There was a library, she was bemused to discover, with many scrolls and a few parchments, scrolls sewn together. They had survived better, strangely. The scrolls were held within tubes of some material she did not recognise and the parchments were held in metal boxes. She presumed that was how they survived. She opened one or two, idly. They were written mainly in the sacred tongue, but some were in another language she presumed might be One Tongue, which was spoken no more. The ones she could read were documents of history, religion, science, philosophy. A scholar would have enjoyed many hours reading them, studying and understanding, but she did not have the patience to spend her time here. She needed to discover what her next step was, and what she must do. In a matter of hours she had lost her father, her friend Rosart, her Hardsaro Halam, and was alone. She realised then that she was, perhaps for the first time in the whole of her life, totally alone.

It was strange. She had lived all her life with people around her, for the Hardsar tribes were communal places. There was always someone sitting a few feet from you, always someone on patrol with you. Even if you went off to be alone you knew exactly where the nearest person to you was. You were trained always to know where your nearest ally was.

The feeling of abandonment and desolation that swept over her was almost as great as she had felt when her mother died. She did understand loneliness and emptiness, but she had felt it deeply at the death of her mother. Her mother had been so strong, a true queen of the mountain people, so utterly what she should be. She had lived and breathed what she was, of the royal line. And yet despite her majesty, Terras had known from an early age that she had loved her with a passion that sometimes took Terras's breath away. There was a fierceness in her love, like that of a mountain ligon, caring for its cubs, defending them against all comers. The feeling was returned by Terras and that passion, that bond between them, was what wounded her deeply when her mother died. She was torn from her, wounding her like the tearing wound of a wild claw. She had died, so stupidly, of a sweating sickness that sucked all her strength from her and within hours and left her a weak, dying woman.

Terras slid her sword back into its sheath and, lifting the lantern, walked slowly back to the hallway. She mounted the stairs and walked their slow curve upwards. As she mounted the stairs slowly she realised that, as her mother had been taken, now her man had been taken from her, her chosen, the prince, the king-to-be beside her. Just a few days together they had had, just moments of joy, and even then he had been so passionate about the task, the quest that they had before them, that he turned his attention to her rarely, too rarely.

Strangely though it was not their night of passion that she remembered most but instead simply holding him, sleeping together, hugging on the moors of the Wasra and on the plain across which they had run. She wanted to hold him, to pull him to herself and grasp him tightly. Yet he had always been dashing off into forests alone, as on that night of the ambush, leaving her behind. Now, in the twinkling of an eye, he was completely gone.

She knew, knew in her heart, that he had not just been taken away inside the fortress nor to some strange destination on the plain. She knew he was completely gone. He was not here. He was nowhere near. He had been taken away.

The next floor was as empty as below, more rooms with furniture. Some were great drawing rooms in which people could no doubt discuss all manner of things in comfort. If this was a stronghold, a fortress, a military place, it was also a palace of sorts. The furniture in these rooms was rotted and broken but it seemed to her the function was still clear.

She climbed further up the stairs, which curved upwards to the next floor. This floor had rooms and places where no doubt lords and ladies could have slept and dressed. Again all was ancient, broken and lost. The Hardsar would have repudiated this. They were the bitter people. They did not wish for comfort. They did not seek it. It was not their desire.

On the third floor, it was different. Here, there was a great temple, which almost filled the entire floor. On entering she immediately s that it was a place of great magnificence which, for Terras, was not the way the Snake god should be worshipped. It was better to worship in the mountains, or on the heath and moor of her father's tribe. There was no need for this ostentation. She was thinking these thoughts and wandering idly around the temple floor when she realised that this was a stranger place than she had appreciated.

There was no dust on the floor.

◈ Chapter 3 ◈

There was a light inside and, no doubt, the person who had lit it. Halam moved carefully, cautious and unsure. He raised his left hand toward the handle of the door, his right on the haft of his sword. As he did, he felt again its power surge for him. From within the room, a voice sounded. 'Come in, you are welcome.'

He jerked back involuntarily. Then, bracing himself, he stepped forward, turned the large ringed handle and pushed the door open. He leapt through it, drawing his sword. He brandished it before him.

A very old man sat before him. He was dark-skinned with frizzled flowing white hair and he sat in a huge carved wooden chair set beside a narrow window in which flickered a single candle. The candlestick was made of the same dark, almost black, wood as the chair. On the opposite side of the window, another black chair stood empty as if awaiting a guest. Halam gaped. The man was very old. He was ancient. No words could have described the entirety of his age. He had passed beyond any understanding of antiquity. He was wasted by time, and yet his face had been softened by it, not made harsh or difficult to read. His thoughts would not be difficult to comprehend when they passed across his face. It was an open face. A man who had learnt, through his years, the art of ingenuousness and independence from artifice.

He was dressed in a simple pale robe that fell

to his feet. He held a huge golden staff topped with a white gem. Halam stared across at him for a long time. There was about him an air of magnificence, of a splendour long lost, a bygone time of majesty.

He had waited while Halam took all this in, then he spoke. 'Please enter in peace, Halam. You have been brought to me.' His voice was familiar, as if Halam had heard it before, a voice of friendliness, of peace.

'Who are you?' He spoke the words and, even to himself, his voice sounded angry, hurt. He still brandished the sword before him. Yet somehow the threat fell, empty to the ground. He had no way to coerce this man or force him to act. He was who he was. Nothing changed that.

The man looked at the sword in Halam's hand. 'I am a friend, Halam. We have met before, yet only in mind. For I am Franeus, the True, the Everlasting.'

Halam straightened. Unbidden, Halam remembered the words he had sworn before he went to Terras and joined. He had also sworn his allegiance to him, to this Franeus, this Priest-King. And he was indeed the vision of the man that had appeared to them days before in the forest, on the very night that Rissar had been taken. This was the Priest-King of the Willsar, the left hand of the magician kings. But Halam realised why he had not recognised him. This was the same man, but he was very different. Age now marked him in another way, a greater way. He was much, much older. This was the Franeus of another age, though how such an ancient figure was older or younger than the figure in the vision was hard to grasp. Yet time had changed him and beyond measure. It was the man who had appeared in the dream and yet it was not. He was later.

'Why . . . ?' He stammered to a stop, unsure of the right question, so many flooded his mind. At last, one overriding question rose unbidden to his lips. 'By the Snake god, what are you doing here, in the stronghold of those who took Rissar from us?'

Franeus shook his head, a gentle smile of joy crossing his lips. 'It is not their stronghold, but mine. They simply misuse its power when they think I have gone, when they think it has been abandoned. Sheathe your sword, Halam, prince, Hardsaro of the bitter ones. Sit by my side and I will tell you the answers to your questions.'

Halam looked down. His sword was still in his hand, a symbol of his anger. He straightened, for he had stood ready to pounce. Slowly he sheathed the sword into its scabbard.

Franeus indicated the other chair in the room. 'Sit, Halam. There are very few of your questions that I cannot answer.'

Halam walked forward, and then, hesitating, spoke the doubt that suddenly filled his mind. 'Is it truly you?'

'I am Franeus, yes, and none other can sit in my place or take my office from me. You can trust me. Nothing will happen to you in this place. On this night, the stronghold is wholly mine, and none oppose me in it. There are few, very few who even know I am here, though many know my purpose.'

Halam frowned. 'You speak in riddles.'

Franeus smiled and shook his head. 'Only because you do not have the key. Sit, and I will try to give it to you.'

Halam scowled. He did not like the easy way that this man spoke in puzzles. He wanted to rescue Rissar and find Terras. He wanted to win through by the force of his arm. He wanted violence. He had come to fight, to live and die searching for the woman he loved and the magician king he followed. He was ready to confront but not to sit, nor to solve problems with talk. He had not realised how great the rage in him had become. There had been so much failure, so much sacrifice, and Insnar had even given even his life for this quest. How could he sit, meekly, even by the side of so great a lord as Franeus and not act?

Franeus nodded. 'I do understand, Halam, all that you have been through. I sent you on your way to this place, do you remember?'

Halam dropped into the chair beside the high priest and turned to glare at him. 'What is happening to me? Where are my friends, my woman, my lord Rissar? Why am I alone? Why, after all this, does this quest simply lead from you and then back to you?'

'I see your weariness, Halam of the Lake, but your quest is not ended, nor yet complete. I am here but to answer your questions to guide you a little on the way, to give you what must be given. Your Malasari will yet be found and you will be united with your princess again. This I know.'

He stared across at the priest; still the tension of the moment too much for him to relax, to just accept the words. They gave him some crumb of comfort that allayed the hours of anxiety, but somehow they were not what he wanted. 'Where is she?'

'She is in this stronghold, Halam. Did she not run to it with you?'

Halam looked at him. 'I thought we did. We ran to the dolmen together and, I thought, ran together through it and across the bridge. But she did not arrive with me. I turned, and she was gone, disappeared, wrenched from me by some unknown force to which the Snake god knows what fate.'

'Yes, the Snake god knows, Halam.'

Halam stared at the old figure, a little ashamed of his easy words to such a powerful lord of ancient times. 'Where is she?'

'She is here in the stronghold.'

Halam shook his head as if to clear the impossible thought. 'But she isn't . . .'

'She is not here now, but she may have been here, or may be yet to come.'

Halam pursed his lips. 'Do you always speak in riddles?'

'They are not riddles, Halam Hardsaro, they are the truth. Listen afresh to the words. Not all who pass through the array, the dolmen, enter the same Citadel.'

Halam remembered then what the plainsman Torem had said, a warning about the Citadel – the Citadel and night. Because of his words, they had hurried to reach the stronghold before night came, but somewhere the words had left him, and he had wanted only to reach it. Had they then failed in that too?

'Halam, you and Terras entered the Citadel of Endless Night. As you entered, you were not together, so the dolmen chose which of many nights you came and which your Hardsare entered.'

Halam shook his head. 'I do not understand.'

'This stronghold is the Citadel of Endless Night. The array before it, the megalith, is a gateway. The power of this place fills all of time, from the very beginning of the Universe, from when this world was formed, when life began, and into the future. The Citadel has always stood. When we built these walls and towers, we simply put them where they already were – we built around the form of the Citadel, but the reality was there before, had always been there.'

'So what then is the truth, Franeus? Is it a fortress, a watchtower, or a pile of blasted rocks making visions of strongholds that might be?'

Franeus smiled at Halam, a wide-open smile of delight. 'A very good question, Hardsaro, for it is all of them. The fortress does not hide – it is all the things it appears to be at the same time. We but built the buildings around where it already was.'

Franeus smiled again, a smile of memory, of fondness. 'It is my place, Halam, and the source of all my power, the ground of my being. I am Franeus, I am the Everlasting, and while it stands, so do I. It is the manifestation of my power over all the times there have ever been, or ever will be. It is the means of my existence.'

Halam looked at the high priest and felt ashamed at the words he had spoken. He had spoken so brusquely to a lord with such power.

'I am not angry with you, Halam. You are following your appointed way. I do not upbraid you for your love and concern for your Hardsare. But now she follows her way. For a time, it is different.'

Halam stopped listening, because something occurred to him. 'This then is not the same night that I entered the stronghold?'

Franeus shook his head. 'Through the gateway of the dolmen, the Citadel permits entry to the same stronghold that you see before you as you enter. But if you enter when its power is in place, many are the ages you may be taken to, and no ordinary traveller decides that.'

Halam jerked his head. 'Then why did you not bring both Terras and me to this place?'

Franeus inclined his head. 'I called you to me, Halam, but Terras runs on another day, she goes by another path. Do not call her back from it until she has completed the tasks that are set for her. For her commission is great, as great as yours if not greater. She is Hardsare of the bitter ones. She must complete that task. There is much to be done. We must be ready. The Hraddas are here. The final confrontation begins.'

Halam shook his head; the words made no sense to him. 'Does she not continue with me . . . on this quest? Where does she go if not to awaken Arnex?'

'It is not for you to know another's way, not even that of your queen. You may guide her on it, as she may guide you, but she and you also have to walk alone. This is the way of the Snake god.'

He looked at the high priest. 'But that is terrible.'

'No, Halam, it is not. You do not own Terras. She owns herself. She does not own you. You are yourself. There is no way to compel the path of another. It is possible for a while but not forever, and never if you act in love.'

'Where am I then?'

Franeus smiled. 'You are in the stronghold, Halam.' His smile broadened. 'But I sense that, of course, you mean *what night is this?* When are you? I will answer your question, but it is not your place, nor your time, and I did not bring you here to do anything, nor to learn anything from the people of this age. I brought you here to meet with me. That is all. This night is as far in your future as the first war of the makkuz is in your past. You are here merely to speak with me and then to return to the quest.'

Halam stared at the ancient priest. There were no words to express the feelings that assailed him as he listened to these words. Had all his friends, his family lived so long ago, had he joined with his princess a thousand summers back? The thought had no meaning to him, and no words came to explain it, nor to give him an understanding of it. He stared at High Priest Franeus, the Everlasting, and could not contain the concepts thrust upon him.

'Have peace, Halam of the Lake. All things march to their end, and all are within the will of the Snake god. Just believe and trust, and all will be well. It is not always possible to understand everything, nor to encamp around it.'

Halam opened his mouth, but for moments the words would not come. At last, he spoke. 'The stronghold ... what ... how ... how can I return? How can the quest be completed? Is Rissar lost forever? How can I ever find Terras again? I don't even know which of a million nights she might have gone to.'

Franeus nodded and smiled a smile that reminded Halam briefly of Lord Rissar. 'But I know, Halam, for I have lived through all those nights, and know, in my heart, everything that has passed and some of what will, and some of what might be.'

Halam leant forward. 'Then you ...'

'I will not tell you on which night Terras is, Halam. Nor can I, for it is not your place but hers.

From this point, you must complete your tasks and reach for the Malasari, the Rissar na Rishugn. Terras goes on a different road.'

Halam blenched. 'But this is not possible!' He almost rose to his feet. 'Rissar was taken by the warriors. They came here. I suppose then he too has passed into the endless nights of the stronghold. How may I seek him? I do not know where to look.'

Franeus shook his head. Briefly, a look passed over his features of sadness, of discouragement, almost of despair.

What does such a lord have to despair about?

The look faded and then he smiled a weak, hopeful smile. 'I can help you with this. That is why you are here and the whole reason I called you to me. You need my guidance, my aid to find Rissar, but do not seek him only where you think he is. Expect the unforeseen. Perhaps there are other deeds to do before you will find where the lord Malasari is. This is my word to you.'

Halam sat back in his chair. 'I cannot . . . I . . .' He shook his head. 'There is no way to understand this!'

'Then do what you are called to do and seek not understanding. Accept the serenity that is ready for you and wait for understanding to come. Is not your way forward clear to you? Seek Rissar, as you set out to do. Worry not where you are or what you need to do so that you may somehow understand how to find him. Just find him.'

Halam sat silently in the chair for many minutes and Franeus did not move or speak a word. Halam was conscious that he was watched but needed, despite all that had been said, to sit and let the words that had been spoken sink into his mind.

'Who were the men who took Rissar?'

'The people who attacked you,' Franeus began, 'were not men at all. They are beings from beyond even the stars that you can see. The makkuz, we came to call them in the One Tongue, Hraddas in the sacred tongue. They have been in this world and fought against the people of this world for many millennia. They seek to prevent us from achieving greatness, splendour which is beyond their, and your, imagining. They were led by a mighty being, the Destroyer, he was called by us in olden times.

'Raczek, who you fought in the forest on the slopes of the Hardwasra, is only the chief of their agents on this world. He was on this world when your grandfather and your great-grandfather lived and ages before even that. He was here when the makkuz threw down the world. Yet when the Hraddas ravaged, they were not led by Raczek, but by the Destroyer of which I spoke. He has many names, Romul, he calls himself, but long ago he was known by the people of this world by the name of Uknor, the Destroyer. And even he is but a captain of one with even greater power – the dragon, the chaos beast who is from the beginning.

'In the ancient world, when first they attacked,

they did it because they realised how close we were to achieving our goal, a magnificent thing which they fear and hate. They came and they threw down the Right Hand and took all power to themselves. They were here to destroy all that people call civilisation, for they have given themselves to chaos. They are its army. In ancient times even I, Arnex and the Malasar could not stop what they came to do. I knew then what must be done. Arnex perished, I bound myself with dire oaths never to leave the Everlasting Caves when he was gone. Even the Malasar cities melted before their terrible power.'

Halam stared at Franeus, amazement flooding his mind. He could not move, such was the fear that grasped him.

'Why did they come? Is that their only aim, to destroy, to . . .' He stopped, unable to express the thoughts that flooded his mind.

Franeus gazed at him. 'Not only to destroy. They came to frustrate, to prevent, to stop. They are powerful, Halam, and they came and used this Citadel long ago in great numbers, and in your time they have retaken the Citadel here to themselves.'

'But you said it was your stronghold. Is it theirs now?'

'It has always been mine. But I do not always possess it. I am but the Key, the foundation of its being because it is mine.

'And the Destroyer is amongst us again?'

Franeus pursed his lips, considering his words

carefully. 'He is, but his servants never left. Halam, they but paused when they thought they had won. The Destroyer moved on and those he left watched. They have always been here, and mostly they merely watch. Always they watch. Now, they have come to wonder what is happening in your age, Halam Hardsaro. They will understand that we are ready. The Malasar will sing a new song. Rissar knew that they would begin again to try to prevent and destroy us. Arnex must be awoken, but it is more serious than you know. They may even begin to understand their future. For a while, they will be puzzled. They will in the end, soon, perhaps, understand they may not have the final victory here. They will see that this world is no longer under their thrall and then they will begin to fear for other worlds, and other peoples. Then they will realise what is to come.'

Franeus's lips were a thin line as if he was considering again how best to phrase his words. 'Fear grips them, as it does all the underlings of their master. They will turn their attention not only on the many ages of this world but will look to the stars. And they will fear. They will fear that what will happen here can happen there too. They will wonder if we can be stopped. Perhaps, they will think, they will not only be vanquished here but on other worlds that circle the stars above us . . .' His words drifted off and he turned to stare out of the small window at the stars beyond.

There are other worlds, Halam thought, *and other*

people. He gazed across at this Priest-King, lost in his thoughts, lost in some future, some war spanning a thousand thousand stars. Who knew how many? He found it hard to believe.

'But what do we do? What do I do? It is such a great endeavour – what can I, a simple Lakeman, do against so great a foe as the Destroyer?' He paused. 'How can we ever be free?'

Franeus turned back to look at him, a slight frown passing over his features. 'You are no simple lakeman, Halam. You are Hardsaro, prince of those who became bitter. You were chosen by the queen-to-be and by Lord Rissar for this moment.'

Halam looked down. 'I do not know how.' He had no words for this great Priest-King.

'I cannot help you to understand it all, Halam Hardsaro, and I will not tell you all. For it is a perilous thing to know too much, and it is wrong for men or women to know all their future. You were brought here so that you understood as much as you can of what you face. Know this, Halam of the mountain, they will hurry to prevent our victory.'

Halam swallowed but did not speak.

Franeus said, 'Yet, Halam, I do not send you to face the Destroyer. He has been . . . delayed, and it is Lord Rissar who stands against him.' He became more serious. 'You must stand before Raczek again.'

'I was barely enough against him once, lord. How can I do it again, and alone?' The memory of the power contained within the eyes of the man he had battled in the forest was not pleasant.

Franeus shook his head as if unable to think how to respond to such a lack of understanding. He looked across at Halam, and his face filled with peace as if at last he knew. 'We will meet again, Hardsaro. Believe it, and it will be so. The end is not yet. The scrolls of the temple, the songs of the peoples and your history itself do not tell the complete story. There will be another, a new chapter to the story.'

Halam looked up in interest and surprise.

'You know the name and the origins of this Romul, as well as this Raczek who fought you. This is why you have to come here. This is why I speak to you. So that you may know that which you have begun.'

Halam swallowed. 'So I must stand against Raczek again? Now that I know what he is? How can I do this . . . ?'

'Halam, did you not come to seek your Malasar within these walls? Did you not chase Raczek across the plains, with the men of the plains running beside you? Did you not run to confront them and battle them with your sword?'

'I came to seek Rissar.' He set his jaw. He could tell where this was going.

'And where was he? What stood between you and him?'

'He was taken by the warriors, so yes, I came to seek him wherever they had taken him . . .'

Franeus turned his gaze fully on Halam. 'So

then, Halam, I will help you face Raczek. There you will do the will of the Snake god and continue to seek for your lord.'

Halam bent forward. 'Can't you come with me? Even if they have some power which is great enough to hold Rissar, how can they stand against you both? All people speak of your greatness, the priests of In Haxass speak of how all threads are drawn through your hands, and how in you, all the ages are joined together. If you would come, we would win.'

Franeus shook his head. 'Power I have, Halam of the bitter ones, and in abundance, but power is not an easy thing, and if you hold it aright it is hard to use well. I know where my place is. In that age, your time, I am vanquished and bound by my oaths to the Sublime Isle and the Everlasting Caves. Even if I chose to return to that fight from this age I would be bound to the oath. Here I will remain. This is my place. This is true power. To sit in quietness.'

'But—'

Franeus interrupted his doubts and broke his pleading asunder. 'You are needed, Halam. You must go, this is what you came to this place to do. As I say, you will understand when the time comes. The task is yours.'

Halam was exasperated. 'But how can I? If they hold Rissar in bondage despite all his wisdom and strength, what good am I? I am weak.'

'No,' the reply was sharp, 'speak not so. Do not

call weakness down upon yourself. As you do you make it true. Rely on the power of the Snake god. If instead you name your strength as weakness and say it – that you are only this or only that – at once you limit yourself. You have this task, Halam, and for this reason, all of your companions have been stripped from you. Return, then, with strength without limit, into the Citadel of the Malasari's greatest enemy, and do what you find to do.'

Halam sank back in his chair and felt a great emotion rise from his breast. He almost cried out in the distress that overwhelmed him.

'How can I? This is all beyond me. This is not the world that I knew before I left my home. It is too difficult, too hard to see the way forward. If there are such mighty powers at work in the world, how can I stand against them?'

Franeus considered the Lakeman for several moments before he spoke. His eyes, kindly and wise, still bore into Halam's very soul, such was the intensity of his gaze. 'Then, Halam of the Lake, walk away from it, and return to the home of your father.'

Halam laughed, a dry, curt, unhappy laugh. 'I cannot even do that. I am trapped within this stronghold and in another age. A thousand years, you said?'

'I am its Key. I can return you.'

Halam straightened and stared across at the high priest.

'It is not so far to the place of your people,

Halam, even in this age. I will return you to the very night that you entered this place with the princess you claimed of your new people and you can walk back. In a few days, you can return to the palace and your father. Your sister Jasada misses you. Your mother is distraught. You can return to your life.'

Halam almost snarled in response. 'How can I do that, priest? I . . . Rissar is trapped in this accursed place and my Hardsare, Terras, you have not hinted where she went. I cannot walk away and leave them.'

'Are you frightened of what your friends will say? Is the vengeance of Hewas and Rosart preying on your mind? If you wish I can return you to any of a thousand ages where the name of Hewas, or even that of Halam, has never been heard. There will be a place to hide if such is truly your wish.'

'You treat me badly, priest!' snapped Halam, his anger coming even though he had only days before sworn allegiance to this very lord. 'I don't care for the anger of Hewas, neither that of Rosart. My Terras is lost and Insnar has given up his life for this thing. Now, you tell me to walk away. You are no friend to speak to me so.'

Franeus rose to his feet, his pale robe sweeping out around him. Halam backed away, afraid suddenly that the power of this lord would come and strike him down.

'And so you were chosen. The Malasari does not choose amiss. He has seen your heart, Halam Hardsaro, and the king-to-be that lay within you. You cannot walk away, for he has called you to this task. Remember your oaths, Hardsaro, they were not just words. You spoke them into your life and now they are becoming true. They were already true in your heart.'

Franeus strode across the little room to a small chest standing in the corner. Halam stared at it, for he had not until that moment noticed its presence.

The high priest flung the lid open and reached inside. From it, he pulled an amulet formed of a silver chain supporting a single large white gem.

He held it out. 'There was another reason I called you to my actual presence. This is the pendant of Aramas and my talisman, Halam Hardsaro.'

Halam rose to his feet. It seemed the only thing to do, the only response.

'As you wear it you will be . . . linked to me, to the golden staff that I bear. As you wear it, you claim the power of the Key of the stronghold, and it too has its role here. Further than this, I cannot say. You go to a night where I cannot come, will not come, a night when I am bound by oath to the Isle and the Everlasting Caves. A night when Arnex is slain. This is a link to me and our hope of achieving our goal.'

Franeus stood, glorious in his power, the staff of Aramas in one hand and the pendant held out in his other hand. Halam knew that he must step forward and take the amulet, take it for himself, but he feared the consequences. Every day that passed he moved deeper into this thing, this quest, this commitment to these lords. He had feared the oaths the Hardsar had asked him to swear but now it seemed that they were but the beginning. Just to take the pendant from his open hands was yet a greater step, and potentially more of Halam was to be lost, just by taking the amulet and holding it. He was only a boy of the lake.

'Do I have a choice?'

'You do,' said Franeus. 'It is still as I offered you. You can go home.'

Halam drew in his breath. 'What of Terras, my woman, my queen of so few days?'

'Your way and hers are intertwined, Halam of the Lake. You will return to her and she to you, but for now, your task and hers are different. Leave her to do her duty and walk the path set for her. Have peace. By doing his will you will achieve all your desires.'

Halam stared across at the high priest. Silence hung in the air, pregnant, awaiting a move from either of them. Slowly, without another word, without a question or more words of doubt, Halam knelt before the Everlasting and bent his head. 'Do it.'

Franeus dropped the necklace bearing the amulet over his head. 'So be it, Hardsaro. The Malasari chose well.'

Halam looked up at the priest and then down at the white gem nestling in his chest. It shone, glowed in sympathy with the white gem that topped the staff borne by Franeus. Halam felt no pride at the wearing of this talisman and at the power that linked him to this stronghold. He felt no pride at having been chosen, but only doubt, uncertainty, and fear. Fear that he would not, could not achieve this goal.

The moment stretched out. He said. 'Shall I go?'

Franeus reached out his hand and helped Halam to rise to his feet. Halam stared into the eyes of the priest. The Everlasting smiled and quietly shook his head.

'There is no hurry, Halam. All the ages are yours. If you wish you may rest, have some refreshment, eat. There is food in this stronghold. You have come here, a thousand summers in the future. Whenever you leave this place, you will still arrive at the moment I desire you to be. This is the secret of the Citadel – endlessness.'

Halam shook his head, feeling, unconsciously, for the sword at his side.

'No, my lord Franeus. I could not wait here though I am hungry and tired. I will go now. It is a good time. The sooner I leave, the sooner I will find my lord again, and through him perhaps the way back to my princess and my new people.'

Franeus slowly nodded. 'I understand. If a decision is made you should act at once. Delay serves no purpose. Go, then, Hardsaro. Go back down the way you came, through the tower and down to the courtyard. Leave the Citadel and walk again back through the gateway which is the dolmen. As you do, it will take you to a different night when the problems were all different and yet always the same. I will use the power of everlasting Citadel and send you where Raczek is, but Romul is not. Trust me.'

Halam nodded. He did not understand all the words but he knew what he was to do.

As he turned from the gaze of Lord Franeus he felt a sense of despondency beyond reckoning. He walked to the entrance to the small room in which they had talked.

He reached for the handle of the door then looked back at the high priest still standing beside the small chest that had held the amulet he now wore.

'I . . .'

'Serenity, Halam, let it go with you. Hold on to it.'

'Will you come down the stairs with me?' It sounded to him like the plaintive begging of a small child, frightened of the dark, and he felt the shame of it at once.

The high priest shook his head. 'No, I must stay here a little while longer. This is my place. I have other things to think of and others to do. There is a need of me in this future age. So, go, Halam of the Lake, find your place.'

Halam pulled open the door and walked outside. He did not think of where he placed his feet and almost fell down the stairs that dropped so suddenly down before him.

He caught himself and grasped the wall of the

staircase for support. He could not believe what had happened. He had finally penetrated the stronghold to find within not his enemies, but Franeus the True. He had come ready to fight and had found only words of wisdom, yet words that he had no way of understanding.

Now, when he should have had the greatest of aids at his side, he was still walking alone with only a strange talisman to mark that he had even seen the priest. He stared down at the gem. As he had suspected when Franeus gave it, the gem did glow, very faintly, as if it merely reflected a light greater than itself rather than shining in its own right.

The journey down was easier than his coming. He knew his way a little more, and the light from the gem, faint as it was, guided his path and gave him his way. He reached the great hall that opened out where the doors to the outer courtyard were. He had left the doors well ajar and the light from the stars streamed in, bright to his eyes, unaccustomed to even the light that came from the sky at night. The snow had been blown into the vestibule through the open entrance and it had drifted across the floor.

He walked to the doors, scared for a moment that there had been someone else in this great edifice, and they would await him outside. He felt a sudden twinge of fear, fear of the darkness, fear of its power, its mystery.

He strode through the doorway grasping the haft of his sword, ready at a moment to draw it. The snow still lay thickly across the courtyard and his footprints were still the only marks that marred the perfection of its surface. He looked back. How long had Franeus been in there, and how had he entered without making footprints in the snow?

He released the sword. As he stepped into the starlight, the gem on his chest shone the brighter as it picked up the light from the bright stars above. He reached up and grasped the gem in his fist. Even through his fingers he could still see the light faintly glinting. He stared, amazed at the phenomenon. It seemed to him that the light gathered around the gem rather than shining from it.

He released it and impulsively thrust it into his clothing. He did not know why but it disturbed him to let it hang, visible, on his chest.

He made his way back across the snow, placing his feet in the footsteps of his coming. How strange it was to retrace his way. He had gone to the tower in search of an enemy and had returned instead from meeting a friend.

He stopped halfway across and looked back at the light, still flickering in the height of the tower. He let his thoughts pass to the man sitting there, and a feeling of placidity flowed to him and, just for a moment, there was no fear.

He reached the gatehouse and gave the tower a last glance, then turned again and walked out of the Citadel. The snow still lay thickly about his feet and stretched across the gilded bridge fording the icy stream. He stood and stared across the bridge to the dolmen, and beyond that to the plain that it seemed he had run across with Terras but minutes before.

Yet Franeus had said it had happened a thousand years before. Halam was stunned by the thought, amazed that he could see an age so far ahead of his own. He remembered that Franeus had said there was no hurry, that he might pass back through the dolmen whenever he was ready, whenever he chose, for he would still go where he needed to be. If this was truly the world a thousand years ahead of his own it might be good to look upon it.

He did not wish to walk far or stray from his task, but if he ran now, crossing the bridge over the stream and dodging the dolmen, he could walk further out. He crest the low hill and, perhaps, cast a glance on the plain beyond.

He ran, the snow crunching beneath his boots. He would look, he would see the world beyond his own, if only in the distance, and without tarrying. He thundered across the bridge, the wood echoing his footsteps into the night, slipped past the ancient megalith and ran up the hill that he and Terras and lain on and looked upon the stronghold that night a thousand years before.

He reached the crest of the knoll and stopped. The snow crunched back at him.

He looked out. The plain of the Torasar still lay where it had always been, but far out on the plain were lights, bright, yellow lights, more constant than any fire or lamp that Halam had ever seen. There were lights up in the sky too, many of them, moving through the clouds. He stared at them in fascination. For what could make such light? What fire burnt with such continuous brightness, never flickering nor wavering? No flame that he knew was so . . . constant.

He turned and looked south-east. He could not see it, but he knew that to the south-east lay his homeland and the City of the Lake. The sky to the south was bright with the same glow, a constant eerie light as if the whole city was alight with a fire that never went out, and was bright enough to light the sky around it. Far to the east was a faint glow as if a sun might rise, but where no sun should rise. It confused him.

He felt, then – knew – that this was not his time, not his place, and he must walk no further into it. This was a future when perhaps the stupendous thing of which Franeus spoke had happened, and perhaps these warriors, these strange beings from the stars, Hraddas, were defeated and driven away. Or perhaps they struggled still against them and the universal war of which he had spoken raged still. His mind held a curiosity for it all, but also a certainty that this was not his age. It was not for him to know these things. He would turn and walk back through the dolmen, and whatever happened, whether he lived through this quest or died, he would remain forever in the age that had given him birth. Whatever his fate there he would live through it, or die with it.

To escape to another age was not a good thing. He cared not who the men were that lived here, nor what their cities were like or who they were.

He swung round to return to the Dolmen and the Citadel. He almost gasped in shock, for the stronghold was gone. Before him was nothing but a jumble of ancient rocks, and beyond the ruined sarsen a rickety, aged bridge crossed a thin and inconsequential stream. For a moment he thought he was lost in this future age, and then he realised, to a flood of relief, what had occurred.

He had thought the stronghold, this Citadel, was able to hide in his own time. In this age its disguise was perfect. It was just not there, even to the most skilful eye. He ran down the slope, approaching the jumbled rocks.

'I come, Citadel of Endless Night. I will not be turned.'

The concealed dolmen flickered into his view, yet shimmering, unreal, non-existent. He drew his sword, and as he did the words of a song he did not know leapt to his lips.

'Ichtir Aramas, Halam har tonai!'

He swung his sword into the air and ran for the megalith and beyond, towards the entrance of the fortress. As he ran toward the ancient structure, the gatehouse and the whole stronghold further on flickered into existence, complete, undisguised, open. He passed through the archway of the dolmen.

◈ Chapter 4 ◈

Terras drew her sword again quickly. Someone had been here.

'There is no need for swords, Terras of the Hardsar.' The voice spoke from the great altar at the far end of the temple. She swung quickly in that direction, raising her sword. There was a great chair, almost a throne, before the altar, and in it sat a man. He was white of hair and dark of skin, and she knew at once that he was the priest Franeus the True, who had spoken to them in a vision in the forest before they met with the plainsmen and before the great run across the plains. It was he who had led them here.

Why did I not see him sitting there when I entered?

'Greetings, Terras,' Franeus said. 'I see that you have done as I requested and come across the plain to my fortress.'

'Where is Halam?' she demanded. The sword was still in her hand, but she did not cross the intervening distance between them.

'He will come here later, Hardsare, much later. I will meet with him then,' said the priest.

'Why were we separated? When will he come?' The words were curt, disrespectful, demanding.

Franeus smiled in response. 'Come and sit with me, Terras of the mountains. You are here because I have a task for you. Your task is your task and Halam's task is his. You must be separated for a while, my daughter, but I promise you, you will meet your man again and he will then be yours. There will be joy in the meeting for then all things will be complete.'

She walked carefully forwards until she stood before Franeus in the great throne. There was something strange about him, a sort of glimmering around him as if he was but an image of a man, a picture painted on an animal skin, a portrayal, a vision of the priest and not the real person. He indicated with his hand to her left.

'Bring a chair, Lady Terras, and sit with me.'

She looked where he had pointed and saw there were chairs at the edge of the temple, against the wall. They were intact, made of some dark, ancient wood, almost black. They were impressive, the work of a skilled carpenter of a finer age.

She stood for a long time and then slowly sheathed her sword and walked to the chairs. They were heavy, ornate, but she brought one and set it down before him. Before she sat, she said, 'Are you a vision, Franeus, or do you truly sit before me?'

'You are wise, Trish harge. I am not here. There are only a few places I can truly be in this age. I am sworn and cannot forswear until my counterpart Lord Arnex is awoken. For he is the Right Hand and I am the Left. My oaths bind me. I can be nowhere but the caves and the isle until Arnex comes. I can show myself, in people's minds and dreams, or as a casting like this. It is for this reason that I brought you and Halam to this place.

'I needed to speak with Halam in person and give him that which he must carry. You, also, I must sit with, and talk. You must see me, hear me, and receive your destiny. Come, Hardsare, sit.'

She let her caution go, slid into the chair and moved her sword so that the scabbard lay somewhat across her knees. She could draw it in a moment. She had placed the chair as far from him as she could and yet still be sitting with him.

'What do you wish of me, priest? Of what destiny do you speak? Are you even truly Franeus or some vision of the enemy?'

'I am he,' he said. 'What can I tell you of you, and your life? What will convince you that I have known you since before you were born? I knew your mother too. She was a mighty warrior.'

Terras paled at the thought. This vision could seemingly read her mind and knew that her first thoughts on arriving in this place had been of her mother.

'Where am I?' she said, setting aside her doubts. Whoever this man was, the priest Franeus or not, let her find out his plans and then perhaps she would and could decide whether he was who he said and what she must do.

'This is my Citadel. I have been joined with it for many millennia. Some have used it with my permission and sometimes others have usurped it for their use. It is not a problem, for I can always take it back. In your age, it will, in due time, be mine again.'

The priest paused and folded his hands across his lap, a gesture of peace, of forbearance. 'The dolmen that you passed through with Halam, it is an array . . . a doorway of sorts. It links all of the ages that this fortress has stood. By it, one can pass to any age, any night, and be there. When we enter the fortress through the stone archway, each person enters a different fortress. You came to this night and Halam went to another. He will come here later, many years later than you, Terras, for he and I need a time of peace to discuss matters. I will meet him here too and speak with him of what he needs to do and then he will be sent there to do it. For you, I have another task, a quest that you must do and do alone. Will you obey your promises, Terras, Trish harge, the queen-to-be, and follow the journey I am setting you?'

She looked across at him. Her doubts were evaporating with every word he spoke for his face was kind, and his words gentle and measured. He spoke softly and she knew that he would sit here and talk with her until she understood, until she trusted enough to listen.

'I am sworn to obey the Three,' she said, for she saw that he understood the oaths that all the Hardsar swear. 'I am a warrior of Arnex. I am at your command. You, if you truly are Franeus, you already know this.'

He nodded. 'And yet,' he said, 'there is always the choice, to obey the Three or to not. Hardsare, I need you to perform a task. I need you to go to a people who will not trust you and so you must go alone, for if a numerous party came, however small, they would think them a threat. You need to cross the Pasra and call the Istsar, the fishers, people of the sea. You must tell them that you have come to them because the One is coming after you, he will need them, and he will call their mother. You must persuade them to ready themselves. He will come with fire and they must bring the storm. They will understand my words even if you do not. Tell them to watch for the signs, for great is the upheaval that is to come and all people must be ready for it. They will know the signs, for they have been told them in olden times and another true voice has been sent.'

He smiled at her as if the words he had spoken were not of conflict and death. 'When they have listened, Terras, and you will understand when that is, you must then get them to take you into the south, and convey you to the southern coast of the stone desert. Then you must travel along the edge of the desert until you find it. There is a ruin, right at the southernmost tip of the desert, to which you must travel. When you reach there you will understand what is to come, and what your task and the burden of the bitter people was.'

She looked at him. 'Is there time for all of this, lord?'

'There is time, daughter. This is the Fortress of Endlessness. That is its gift: time.'

'Why must I do this?'

'Hardsare, we prepare this world for the coming of Arnex and my return. I have my tasks as well. There will be a struggle, Terras, and Halam goes north to bring Arnex, and the Hardsar follow, so that, as he awakes, they will join him to serve and to fight. You must prepare others, who are also of the people. Everyone must be called for the conflict that is to come. It is the final one – the time has arrived.'

'People always think this war is the final one and yet people go on fighting.'

'That is true, Terras. I see that you know this world and its troubles well. But now, Terras, it truly is the climax and we must be ready to fight our ultimate enemy. Then we will be free and so will all the peoples. Then there will be the beginning.'

'Not the end, lord?' Terras shook her head in puzzlement. 'Why must I go, my lord, why can I not go with Halam and the One? My people will follow us, you know this. Why cannot another be sent so that I may be with my people, my king, and my Hardsaro, my man?'

'There is no other to send,' said Franeus. 'The fisherfolk are expecting you, Terras. They have been told that you will come. They know you by name.' He inclined his head, imperturbable, kind. 'You wish to be beside your king-to-be and your father, king of the mountain, I know this, but in your life, though you and Halam are bound together, you must sometimes walk a separate path. Apart, yet joined, until you may be truly together. You will understand when you and he meet again. And you will meet Halam again, Terras, you will.'

Terras stared across at the ancient priest and knew that whilst she may have begun the conversation by doubting him, somewhere along the line she had realised that he was the everlasting priest and one of her three lords. She must obey him, for to this she had been sworn all her life. Now was the moment.

She nodded. 'My lord, then I will go where you send me. What is the way across the Pasra, for I have never travelled it?'

'You will find it, Terras. Just head west from this Citadel and look for a pass through the mountains. You will wander far in safety even though you do not know the way. You will speak words to a foreign land that they will understand. You shall cross the stone desert, but you will not die.'

She rose to her feet. 'So be it.'

'I will truly stand before you, Terras, when Arnex the Warrior King is awoken, and I will lead you to the arms of your husband. Trust me, daughter of the king, Hardsare of bitter ones. You carry the heart of Halam with you.'

'I will go now,' she said and turned on her heel and walked quickly away. She did not look back. If this was what she needed to do then she would do it. Was it not for this that she had trained all her life?

◎

As Halam passed through the archway of the dolmen

the world turned suddenly and completely black. The snow flickered out of existence like a white flame instantly extinguished in water.

Shock, fear, intuition made him swerve abruptly. He swung round, stopped, and brought the sword down. As he did, a guard ran out from the gatehouse. He was moving fast, and the long weapon he bore was down, rushing to impale Halam on its end. Fear bubbled to Halam's lips and words would not come. He stood helpless, hopeless.

His sword burst into light. It had before, on the night of the ambush when he fought Raczek. Again, he felt the power of the sword come to him and for a moment it seemed alive in his hand. It squirmed upwards, forcing his hand with it. As the guard pelted across the bridge, his long pike ready to impale him, Halam's sword parried the guard's blow. It was none of his doing. It thrust the pike down, away from him, and at last Halam let his mind join with the power that flowed to him and the bearer and sword became one. He leapt forwards, releasing his parry on the pike and swinging the sword upwards to strike at the guard. The man's forward momentum was too great; he had given himself too much to that one attack. Halam struck him down with a single blow. He fell, his body ruined. Halam looked down at the body of the guard and felt only sadness, no pride in his prowess but only regret at a life lost. As he looked at the man, the body disappeared, a reddish glow taking its place. It slipped away over the ground towards the fortress.

Halam straightened. The light of the sword was very great now, filling the night with light. Halam tensed, some nameless sense warning him, and swinging the sword up smashed aside the blade of another guard who had run up from the gateway without him even noticing.

'No!' Halam screamed. 'I do not want to kill you.'

'You can try!' the new guard screamed back, heedless of the danger. Halam lifted his sword. The man flinched – but it was strange. He seemed unafraid of Halam but dreaded the light streaming from the sword. He leapt back, snarling hatred, and retreated further over the bridge, towards the gate. He continued backing cautiously until he was within the gateway of the stronghold proper.

'Alarm,' he cried, 'raise the alarm! There is a traveller through the array.' A harsh and metallic rasp as if someone was dragging one piece of metal across another sounded from within, then the sound of many feet running towards him. Halam tightened his grip around the sword and stepped forward. There was no point in running away when he had come here to seek Rissar. This was, at least, what he had expected on his first arrival at the stronghold – violence.

He moved forward across the bridge and stopped before the gatehouse. Inside the fortress, people were approaching him from across the open courtyard. It was dark within, no lights showed, yet there was strangely energy, a power filling the very air itself. He could somehow feel it pulsing around him. The only light was that streaming from his sword. Even the sky above him was dark and shrouded. There were many warriors. The guard who had backed away from him was waving them on and shouting.

They were all armed with pike-like weapons. Not only were there too many of them for him to fight single-handed and win but also, with pikes they could stand at a distance and run him through, out of the range of his sword. His lips dried and beads of sweat cooled on his brow. Against a pike, it would be hard. He had to get inside the length of the weapon to strike with his sword. Against this many pikes, there was little defence.

He knew he could not fight them and win. In a moment, he realised that he only had two options: to turn and run with them all at his heels or to surrender, to hope that they would not kill him, at least until they had found out who he was and why he had come. Perhaps he could talk his way out of this. For long enough at least to find what had happened. Even if he escaped, they would be bound to pursue him and he would have to try and re-enter at some later point. He had to go forward, to find his lord Rissar and Terras . . . to get into a stronghold that was alerted to his presence. These thoughts had taken but an instant. It was clear.

He put up his sword. 'I do not wish to fight. I did so only because I was attacked.' At once the light of his sword was extinguished.

The guard who had backed away from him took several steps forward before he thought better of it and stopped. 'That is good,' he snarled, 'for otherwise, you'll die.'

Halam could not see his face clearly in the darkness but his voice had more than a tinge of enmity. This was a man who would kill him without compunction and indeed with joy. He was relieved that he could not see those eyes. As with the ambushers long ago in the forest, these people were surrounded by an aura of energy, a nameless power that took his breath away. They were not merely human. There was something else. But they were the Hraddas.

The other guards arrived. In moments, Halam was surrounded by a forest of the pikes. He realised they were not simply pikes. There was something strange in their design that he did not understand. In the gloom, he stared at the warriors as suspiciously as they eyed him.

Despite his decision, he began to doubt himself. He did not feel comfortable with his position. Any moment they might decide to run him through and he would not have time to move. He sheathed his sword noisily.

'I do not wish to fight. I . . .' He could not think of a good reason why not and another wave of doubt in his decision rushed over him. He forced himself to relax. Whatever occurred here must be the design of Franeus. He had, after all, sent him to this very night. *Surely that was not so that I would die?* Halam hoped fervently that the priest knew what he was doing. 'Peace, please, I do not desire a fight. I was attacked, that is all.'

The guards did not look convinced. Several of the pikes were pushed closer, aimed at his throat and chest. He doubted the wisdom of sheathing his only weapon. There was a commotion behind them and a tall dark man pushed his way through. The guards opened a path for him quickly, easily; this man was one who expected to be obeyed, and instantly. 'What is it?' he snapped as soon as he reached Halam, but he was not talking to him.

'A traveller, Tazek. He came through the array that we thought was ruined.'

The newcomer spoke with utter disdain. 'So, what is the problem? Kill him.'

The guard who had attacked Halam spoke, but quietly, apologetically. This was not a man any of these warriors crossed lightly. 'He wields an ancient sword of power, Tazek. And he vanquished the form of Eska, the thybuk on the gate. In one strike his sword depleted almost all his energy.'

At that, Tazek turned his eyes on Halam. At first, Halam thought it was with indifference, just some further disdain, but he realised then that his eyes, dark and hooded, held something new, a desire to understand, and something else. Was it respect? He stared at Halam. 'What is your name, traveller?'

Halam looked back. If he did not gain this man's interest, he would be dead in a very few minutes. 'I am Halam, of the Hardsar.' Perhaps it sounded better to be a Hardsara than a weak Lakeman.

Tazek sniffed. 'And why did you come to our stronghold, Hardsara?'

Instinctively, Halam knew this was not the time to tell the truth. Yet when lying it was always best to tell as much truth as it could bear. 'As I approached it, it seemed smaller and empty, a quiet and sheltered place to spend the night. I had no wish to intrude.'

A snicker of laughter rippled around the guards. Tazek glared at them and the humour was instantly quashed.

He turned back to Halam, and Halam caught in his eyes some power, energy beyond imagining, just like he had seen in the eyes of Raczek as they had attacked the party that night in the forests of the Hardwasra.

'Where did you come from?'

'From the lake,' said Halam and knew at once that it was a pitiable response. *What a stupid thing to say! Aren't I a Hardsara? What am I doing coming from the lake?* Perhaps he should have thought through his story before he decided to lie.

Tazek did not believe him. Halam could see it

in his stance, and the expression of contempt on his face. But he was no longer indifferent, that was clear. He wanted to understand this traveller who had such power and lied so badly. 'Where did you come by your sword, traveller?'

Halam floundered. He really should have kept to as much of the truth as possible or thought of a more complex lie. He could think of no story that would have any credibility. 'I . . .' There was nothing left but the truth. 'It is mine. It was given to me.'

Tazek stepped forward. 'So, who do you serve that they give you such powerful ancient weapons? And what are you doing this far across the plains from the lake or the mountains of the Hardsar?'

Halam was unsure. To reply would be difficult and would cause problems. Clearly, to say he followed the Malasari among these people would not be a popular move. 'I serve my king, but I am . . .' He paused and then continued. 'I am an outcast from the mountain people.' He stopped. Perhaps he should have told them he was an Aallesara after all. It would have been easier to lie, for he could have told more of the truth. He hadn't been prepared for this.

Tazek became angry. He leapt forward and seized Halam; shock rippled across his face. He stepped back, dropping his grasp. In but a moment his hand was moving again, fast, like an allarg striking its prey. He pulled out the white gem from Halam's shirt, and the silver chain tightened around Halam's neck. The light from the gem, faint as it was in this place, caused an immediate reaction.

'There is an energy residue in this jewel,' Tazek snarled.

The guards all took a step back. Tazek grabbed the gem and pulled as hard as he could. Halam lurched forward and then the chain around his neck snapped and the amulet was in Tazek's hands.

Another snarl escaped from Tazek's lips, and his hand moved down to the weapon at his side. Halam had achieved his goal and aroused Tazek's interest. Perhaps that had not been a wise move, after all, for now he had lost the necklace and in a moment he would be dead. He moved his hand, to die at least with his sword in his hand. There was the sound of boots. More men were approaching from behind Tazek.

A voice called out. 'Make way for Lord Raczek!'

Tazek's hand dropped from the handle of his weapon, and he backed off, still holding the talisman of Franeus in his hands. Through the knot of guards, Raczek appeared. Beside him were two other guards, one a dark-skinned woman and the other a short swarthy man. Raczek glanced towards Halam and then at Tazek.

'What is going on here, Tazek?'

'A traveller – he came through the array, my lord,' said Tazek, 'with a sword of power, and this.' He raised his hand and showed the amulet to Raczek. 'I was questioning him when I found it. It was hidden beneath his clothes.'

Raczek turned his attention fully on Halam, who had stood throughout the exchange not moving. He studied Halam for several minutes. Even in the gloom, Halam's features would not have been hidden, but Raczek showed absolutely no sign of recognition, not even for a man he had fought only days before. Halam was perplexed. *Am I so unmemorable?* Then he thought, *what was it that Franeus said?* Perhaps for Raczek it was an event in the distant past, or even, Halam was stunned by the thought, perhaps it had not happened yet.

'Who are you, friend?'

Halam knew this did not mean they were friends, but rather, and totally, the opposite. 'I am Halam, of the Hardsar. I did not know the fortress was inhabited. It seemed empty as I approached.' He paused. 'And smaller . . .'

Raczek laughed, a twisted laugh, a laugh at Halam's expense rather than with him. There was no joy in the laughter, only scorn and disrespect. He did not care about Halam one whit.

'The array operated?' He glanced at Tazek.

'Yes, my lord.' The second guard beside him answered. 'Then he struck down Eska with a sword of power that depleted his energies almost to the point of quenching.'

Raczek turned his attention once more to Halam. As with Tazek, there was something new in his manner.

'In entering this fortress, you have changed your fate forever, my friend. You have stepped into a place you cannot ever leave.' He spun around.

'Lorack ... Noxem, bring him!' He strode away without checking to see if his order was being obeyed, a man confident of his authority. The two new guards who had come with Raczek strode forward, hesitatingly, and grasped Halam's arms. Several pikes pricked at his back, but softly, as if unsure of their welcome. They still feared him for he wielded a sword and bore an amulet, and both had power. If nothing else they respected him for what he had carried.

'Walk on, fool,' snapped Tazek and as he spoke Halam realised he had made an enemy in the man.

Halam did not struggle. He let them lead him across the courtyard back towards the very central keep in which he had met Franeus what seemed only minutes before. There were many more warriors in the stronghold; it seemed that a veritable army occupied it now. It had the air of a bastion against attackers, a means to dominate and control. No wonder the Torasar resented them. There were also many carts in the courtyard but strangely no hacsar to pull them. Indeed, there was no means even to attach them.

They reached the central keep and as he gazed inside the great doors he realised that there was no light in the stronghold. Surely an army would light fires, or carry torches to guide their way. The darkness within was impenetrable, almost as if the warriors here did not need lights to guide their way, but saw, perceived the world around them in some other way. Halam could not work it out. *What are these Hraddas? Just how strange are they?*

He was still puzzling over this when he was pushed and harried through the doors into the great central tower and the hallway beyond. The two Hraddas beside him, Lorack and Noxem, did not hesitate as they walked into the darkness. Halam would have wished to wait a moment for his eyes to adjust but they were having none of it. They hurried him briskly across the hallway towards the side doors to the right. Halam had not looked behind them on his earlier visit. *Was it earlier or later?* He was bewildered . There were no words for what he was experiencing.

They passed through the doors and into a great hall beyond the vestibule. Inside was another strange sight. There were two great pillars of light, either side of the doors, glowing with power beyond Halam's understanding. A light came from them but Halam knew there was more here. It was not just light – there was breathtaking energy in them. There was no lampstand, no lantern, no candle; they blazed of their power. They were like the glow, the potency that sometimes seemed to surround these warriors.

Halam was pushed between these twin pillars and further into the hall. As he moved past them the columns of light swung in swift arcs and swept out through the doors. It was inexplicable. Before he could think properly what he was looking at they were gone. Darkness descended as they left.

The voice of Raczek sounded. 'A torch, so that our visitor may see.' Halam's forward motion stopped and the hands that held him released him. Without an apparent pause, a torch seemed to appear in the hands of the woman guard, Lorack. Light flooded the room.

Halam stood stock-still trying to make out what was at the edges of the hall. In the middle, before him, was a great stone chair and before it stood a heavy black wooden desk. Raczek had taken his seat on the stone chair. There he now sat, waiting to question his visitor.

The desk behind which Raczek sat was large and ornate. Tazek stood off to Halam's left, waiting to see what his lord would command regarding their visitor. Behind him, Lorack and Noxem barred his exit. Halam could see no one else in the hall though he did not feel able to turn and check. And if there were others at the edges of the hall he could not see them. For the first time, it seemed to Halam, the odds against him in an outright sword fight were a little improved.

'Unsheathe your sword, traveller, and place it on the desk.' Raczek spoke the words as an order.

Halam hesitated. To go unarmed into a conversation with this man was not wise.

'Do not fear,' Raczek said. 'If the sword is a

device of power as Tazek has told me and therefore aligned to your DNA, it would probably not work for another.'

Halam did not understand all the words but he knew enough to recognise that he had little choice. Slowly, reluctantly, he unsheathed the sword. It slid, rasping, from the sheath. He had a momentary desire to try and strike Raczek down. He resisted the urge and placed the sword lengthways on the desk near to him. As he straightened, he realised Tazek had moved. A chair was pushed behind him and he found himself collapsing into it.

Raczek spoke at once. 'Hardsara, you are not the first to enter our stronghold unawares, but reports are that you also came through the ancient dimensional array which has not functioned for a millennium. If our conversation goes well there is no reason you need to fear us. You just need to tell me the truth.'

Halam nodded but he was not sure he believed the words.

Raczek looked equally disparaging. 'So, then, when was it that you entered the stronghold?'

'Just a few moments ago,' said Halam. 'It was night. I am not sure what hour this is.'

Raczek shook his head, impatient. 'No, I mean what year was it? Who was queen over the Hardsar?'

Halam frowned. He knew he should answer although now he understood what Raczek was asking. He wished to know whether it was the present, the future or past that Halam had come from. Trouble was, he had no idea of the names of the Hardsar queens or kings. He really should have said he was an Aallesara.

'It is Hergos, the second of the name,' he said, making up a suitable Hardsar name at random. 'All people know this.' He threw that phrase in at random. It would not be good for these Hraddas to know how much Halam understood – if understood was the right word.

Raczek settled back in his chair. He looked at Halam with frank suspicion. 'Suffice it to say, we do not, and we require you to tell us. How many years has she reigned?'

'Forty years,' Halam replied at once. He had guessed that this was the next question and had had time to prepare an answer.

Raczek leant forward slowly, thoughtfully. 'And what are the stories of the Malasar?'

'Lords of the whole world? The subject of ancient history,' Halam replied slowly, 'legend.' Raczek's eyes narrowed. Unthinking, he carried on talking. 'There is no Malasari, perhaps there never has been.' The lies came easily. It was what his father believed, after all. He stopped. He should have kept quiet. He could see the disbelief in Raczek's eyes.

'You are lying. No Hardsar would speak thus.' Raczek glanced momentarily at Tazek as if he would know best. His eyes became abruptly fierce. 'Speak the truth, do not try to lie to me.'

He really should have said he was an Aallesar. It would have been so much better. How should he answer? How could he brazen this out? He spoke. 'I do not lie. You asked and I answered.'

Raczek moved suddenly. In a moment he was right in front of Halam. 'There is something about you, mountain man, that I do not like. You are not telling me the truth. I can see it. You hesitate a little too long between answers. What is it you fear to tell me? Perhaps you must learn a little more of our persuasive ways before you will speak. Lorack . . .'

Before Halam could even rise to his feet, the torch behind him was snuffed out. The room cascaded into darkness. Halam leapt up and tried to move forward, thinking to seize again his sword. With it, in his hand, he could still stand against them. As he moved he felt something shift to his left and turning saw a dark shape towering over him. Something hard hit his right temple and the darkness grew deeper and he collapsed, spiralling hopelessly into oblivion.

◈ Chapter 5 ◈

Terras left the Citadel quickly. Even though it was late in the night she headed up into the mountains. When she had walked for several hours, and the creatures of the Pasra forests were crying their calls of the night, she stopped and found herself some shelter in the cleft of a rock. There she could see anything approaching her and her back was safe against the rock. She lit a fire from some of the fallen branches and sat down. It was only then that she let herself look back down the way she had come. The plain of the Torasar lay stretched out below her, clear in the light of the twin moons and the starlight.

Then she let herself cry. She knew it was her duty, but she did not understand why she had been called to this way of loneliness. Before this moment, in everything, her people had worked together, supported each other. She had been the best of them, not so she could do things alone, but so that she could do them together with her people. Why then was she now sitting alone with this rock instead of her people at her back?

She cried also for her Hardsaro and silently counted the days, the very few days, they had had together before this quest had separated them. She cried, but she knew also that this was the way of her people, to obey, to give everything to the calling that they had – that they had always had. They were the bitter people. They were not sweet. They obeyed.

After a while she let herself doze, but sitting up with her back against the rock. She woke when the night was deep and dark. She would have to hunt as she went on the morrow, for she needed food for the journey and she carried little now. She knew that the Pasra mountains were even higher than the highest peaks of the Wasra. She had been many times to the high mountains of the Wasra, for she had visited the people of the mace. She had been there, both with her father, and solo. The people said that these western mountains grew much greater before they fell into the western ocean.

And so the tales went: where the mountains fell into the sea lived the Istsar, the fisherfolk. They clung to the land in the thin strips along the coast and made their living from the seas around them. They lived for and in the waters of the western ocean. They were a strange people and one of which she knew little, for they travelled the other lands rarely. The Istsar were isolated. East and to north rose the heights of the Pasra mountains, dividing them from the rest of the world until you came to the lands of the northern ice and volcanic fire. She had heard tales that they had on occasion travelled up the rivers from the western sea to the City on the Lake, to In Haxass. But perhaps their reluctance to travel to the lake was not simply natural reserve. For, people said, far from the control of the Aallesar king, several essentially independent baronies in the west controlled the mouths of the great river and forced the Istsar to trade through them or pay heavy tolls to pass upriver. And farther south was the stone desert. Terras had never seen the desert, and yet, if Franeus's words were true, she would see it soon enough. He had said she must eventually travel far south, from the Istsar lands to the edge of the desert, hundreds if not thousands of miles away, and there she must find a ruin on the edge of the desert.

Why is this? Franeus had not even said what she would find.

A deeper sleep came eventually and she woke to the early morning. The fire was out, and the plain below here looked even more beautiful in the daylight than it had in the night. She packed up and dispersed the fire, for whilst she knew no reason that anyone might be tracking her, she was keen to be invisible. It was simple wisdom, the wisdom of her people.

She walked on into the mountains and hunted as she went. She got enough food, at least for the next few days, but the next day she must seek larger game for the furs they would furnish. She would need them if, as she suspected, the climb into the Pasra grew much colder. It was late autumn now and not the spring in which she had set off from her village. The world she now walked seemed deserted of people and but the realm of the forest creatures. For this reason, the hunting was good, and she soon had enough food for many days. She preserved it by smoking it over her night fires. Hopefully, that would ensure it was kept from going bad.

After one full day of hunting, she found and settled herself in a golden clearing – a grove amidst a wood gilded with the colours of autumn. She sat there for a long time. She must have slept, sitting there before the fire, for she dreamed of Halam and spoke with him. She woke with tears in her eyes again. Although she could not remember what words they had spoken in her dream, or what she had said, she knew it had made her sad. She was lying on the ground in the glade but she could not remember lying down there. Had she dreamed or had something occurred?

On the third day she realised that, ahead of her, among the Pasra range, were two greater peaks, so high that their summits were snow-capped. Between the twin summits ahead of her was a great valley and she imagined this was the best way to go, for it seemed like there might be a more manageable pass there between the great mountains on either side. To the north and the south she could see nothing in the range that looked more promising for a pass.

She knew then that it was important she travel fast. She must hurry to cross the Pasra before the snow came to those heights in greater measure. She had wasted nearly a whole day skinning the large grasbar she caught on the second day and drying the skins, making furs for her journey as best she could. She did not have time to complete the job as she should, but at least she had some warmer clothing, if still a little smelly, to brave the mountain heights.

So she travelled onwards, day after day. Each morning she rose early and walked for many hours before finishing well before sunset to prepare her camp. She gathered more firewood than she needed and carried more and more of it on her back each day. If the pass ahead of her went as high as she feared, firewood would be in short supply and she would need a fire each night if she was going to survive the trip. This was how she continued for many days. She was almost to the valley between the peaks when she saw some smoke ahead. It was thin and weedy, the fire of someone who hoped not to be spotted and had taken some effort to make it so. Yet not enough effort for a trained Hardsar to miss.

She was cautious and skirted the fire until she was upwind of whomever it was. She climbed steeply out of the valley to reach a cliff edge, to give her a clear view. There was a small village, a hamlet really, with just a few families around a common central fire. There were some cultivated fields to the east of the village. They looked like primitive people, eking a living from the forest and the sparse fields they had cleared. They did not, in any sense, look like the fishing folk, so she felt she should quietly pass on her way without disturbing them. They probably rarely met any travellers but would, therefore, be wary of strangers. These Pasra heights were not a good route for trade, so no doubt they would be scared of her, and wary of her purposes. She slipped away and scouted a way around them, onwards towards the pass ahead.

As the days went by, she found other small villages here and there as the land rose towards the two peaks. She realised eventually that they made their home here because hills rising to the great peaks either side of their valleys probably sheltered them from the worst of the winter snows – a little at least. Also, it afforded them protection from any interlopers. Perhaps they hoped to intercept any travellers through the pass as well, ensuring they knew what was happening in their lands.

She should avoid them. This was not her place, nor was it her intent to upset them. This was their home. She was a stranger. She did not know the name of these peoples but she should not give them any sort of distress. Franeus had sent her to the fishing people and not to these people of the Pasra mountains. Perhaps they would have much in common with her people, living as they did in mountainous lands, but perhaps not. She travelled onwards through the days and made every effort to skirt the villages. There were many, but she was an accomplished tracker and knew much about passing by without notice.

Eventually, she reached what must have been the largest of the villages and probably the capital for their people. It was built around a great circle of stones – some place of the ancients that she did not understand and probably neither did they. It was just a shrine to what had gone before for them, which they revered and valued.

She allowed herself to lie on the hillside nearby for a long time watching the village and the comings and goings of its people. They seemed to have few guards and perhaps little fear of travellers. Or maybe people rarely came this way. It made her wonder whether the pass between the two peaks was going to be viable. If no one came this route perhaps it was because it was blocked.

She would have liked to meet these people, for she had travelled alone for many days. It was the longest she had ever been alone in her whole life. The loneliness and the silence were whittling away at her, making her feel that everything in her life was useless and pointless. She had always had her father, and her friends, her people telling her what they did, who they were and what was the most important thing to do or to be, what was vital for the future. Hardsar trained together, they fought together. Of her people, she was the mightiest, the best at arms, able to defeat anyone amongst them. She was not the strongest, but with cunning and skill she could beat them all. She had been the greatest of the Hardsar; she practised her skills without end and desired nothing but to be the best and to have everyone know that she was a worthy Hardsare. But she did not always feel so confident inside. Within, she had more doubts and more emotion, more worries about who and what she truly was. In her head were things she could not control. And in these days, walking alone, the emotions, the fears, the doubts came and went more strongly, more unpredictably.

She did not know who she was any more.

Perhaps that was why she had been attracted to Halam so much when she met him. He wore his heart on his sleeve and was always entirely open about what he felt, who he was, and who he was not. In his honesty, in his openness, in his diffidence, he underestimated how strong a person he was. He always assumed he was nothing, of no importance. He admitted that to the world in a way she never had, or could. She admired that and found in it a different sort of strength, a strength to be who one truly was and not to feel that one had to forever hide it, be strong and capable, to forever practice to be that worthy princess of the people.

She sighed and felt the tears coming again and running silently down her cheeks. She missed him. She missed his honesty. She missed her father. She missed anyone and everyone and would have gladly found some companionship with the people living in that village around the ancient stone circle. Perhaps they would be friends after all, and a new ally to the Hardsar. But she knew as she wiped the tears from her cheeks that she was not going to attempt contact. She was alone, and they were many, by comparison. If they took against the interloper, who knew what might happen. This was not her goal; it was not to them that she had been sent, but to the Istsar, the people of the sea beyond these high mountains of the far west. Instead, she must use her skills to slip by them unnoticed and move onwards, alone still. So she moved silently back into the wooded area behind her and continued westwards, giving the town of the standing stones a wide berth.

Over the next few days, the land rose strongly. At first, it was a gentle but a relentless slope upwards, and then it became a steep and treacherous climb into the mountains. The land rose faster and as it did the temperature dropped. The land became wilder. It was arid, but not in the way of a desert. It was dusty, cold and shrubby, the trees short and gnarled. As she climbed there were signs of snow ahead, frozen ground and puddles that had thawed in the summer and were freezing now again even though it was still autumn.

She realised that she was climbing very high, certainly as high as the high points of the Hard Wasra, where the elder Jored and his people of the mace lived. She was at least that elevated already, if not higher. She began to fear what was ahead. As she let the fears seize her, she felt a sudden wave of nausea and vomited on the ground. She growled her resentment. She had eaten something bad. That puzzled her. She knew how to be careful on the trail.

She had begun to loathe Franeus for choosing to send her on this quest. *Why did it have to be me?* Why was she called to make this trip alone and not with her people by her side, not with her new prince alongside her? Why was she travelling westward to a people she had never met and knew little about? All she knew of them were rumours. She had never seen an Istsara. Why was it important that they, of all the peoples, knew that the Malasari had come? Why must she be the one to tell them? Who cared what the Istsar thought about anything anyway? They were but fisherfolk of the far west. They kept themselves to themselves and they preferred it that way. They relished the separation.

The weather grew colder and she was now trudging through snowdrifts and snow covered the ground around her. She was very high now, much higher than she had ever travelled. The furs that she had prepared were barely enough to keep the raw wind out when she found herself exposed to it. They smelt bad too, for she had not had the time to cure the leather at all, but simply to scrape it clean and dry it before her campfire and in the sun. Nevertheless, she pulled them around her as tightly as they could go. They kept the wind from her, but her face hurt in the wind, and her lips began to crack.

She pulled a fur hood she had made up over her head. This protected her from the rawness of the wind, but only partially. She continued her trudge westward, ever higher, even colder. She felt nauseous often now. The cold, the chill was settling in her stomach and making it revolt even at the idea of food.

Each night, she found shelter on the way in the clefts of rocks and shielded herself from the wind along the path. Fires were difficult to ignite sometimes even with the firewood she had collected and carried up this far with her. For even though she carried it on her back it got damp, wet. For two nights she had failed to light a fire and, finding whatever shelter she could out of the wind she pulled the smelly furs around her before sleep. The smell sickened her deeply and she vomited on several mornings at the very disgustingness of them. If only she had had time to prepare them properly.

She collected what wet wood she could during the day as she walked and dried it around that night's fire so she could carry it, drier, to the next sunset's fire. It was a partial success. It proved a reasonable idea, but she did not find enough wood on several of the days and her supplies were running perilously low. If she had known when they set out that she would have to make such a journey she would have brought a small tent to shelter in. It would have been a burden to carry but a mighty welcome at night. As it was, she had to make do, and find or make what shelter she could each day. Sometimes when it snowed, she had to make her best of a cleft in the scarp, breaks in the cliffs around her.

She often rose early in the morning, at the very first glimmer of light, and walked as far as she possibly could each day. The more she walked, the faster she did this trip, the quicker it would be over, and the more likely she was to survive it. Each day she hoped that by hiking further and travelling faster she might make an end to this all the sooner.

On the fourth or fifth day of walking longer and harder, she began to run short of the supplies that she had hunted for on the way across the Pasra, and also badly short of wood for the night fire. She longed for the silent lonely lands of the people of the standing stones. She wondered if she would make this. The game here was hard to hunt. There were few animals hardy enough to live this high up.

That day, ahead, she saw some jaksar-like creatures, but larger than the ones she knew, with white fur to camouflage them against the snow. She thought they must be snow-jaksar. Their presence meant there must be other smaller animals that the snow-jaksar were hunting, but she saw little sign of them. She tried to catch some of these snow predators but they were too wary of her and too quick and ferocious to allow for success. She tried fruitlessly many times and then eventually despaired. She sat instead and recalled the stone statue of Insnar, forever now guarding the staff of his master. This thought made her cry again. Emotions of doubt, distress and anguish flooded her mind. Where now was the strong Hardsara princess who, with her father the king, the Malasari and the new Hardsaro she had chosen, had left on the quest to awaken the Warrior King knowing that this was the ultimate destiny of her people?

She was lost in a desert of snow that she could never escape.

◎

Halam awoke. His head felt as if it was splitting. Gingerly he felt his temple. There was a wound on the side of his head, crusted with blood and dirt. Tazek had struck him hard. He had passed out.

He moved, struggling first up onto his elbows, and then slowly he sat up. The darkness seemed to spin around him for a moment and he just stopped himself falling back to the floor. At first, the gloom around him seemed to be only in his perception, the product of the blow to his head. He shook his head to clear it and realised that he was no longer in the hall in which Raczek had interrogated him.

He sat on a damp and smelly floor. There was a very dim source of light above him. He looked up; a small window let some faint daylight filter in. The light was dim though, as the first rays of a gloomy, unpromising sunrise. It must already be morning. He had passed the night in unconsciousness. The blow on his head had been hard enough to lay him out for that long.

He struggled slowly to his feet. For a moment, the room spun again and dizziness assailed him. He grasped the wall beside him and waited until the weakness subsided. He looked around, trying in the gloom to make out where he was. It was a cell, that much was clear.

He walked forward, trying to gauge its size. The light from the window was too dim to see clearly. After several minutes of struggling along the walls, he decided the room was only perhaps eight feet at its greatest extent, and in width perhaps as little as four feet across. There was a door in one of the longest walls. It stood at the top of a short and narrow step. The roof was very high above him. He could only faintly see it in the light of the slit of the window in one of the shorter walls. There was no way to reach it, even at the greatest stretch of his arms.

He lowered his hands after he had tried this and then the realisation hit him. He clutched at his chest, thrust his hand inside his shirt. *The amulet!* His other hand grabbed at his empty scabbard. He remembered. His scabbard was empty at his side and Tazek had taken the amulet.

The amulet, the means by which he was linked to Franeus, was taken. The sword Rissar had created for him in the Hardsar fire was gone. He was lost. The amulet was surely his only way home.

Without it, how could Franeus guide him through the many thousands, millions of ages of the Citadel? Even if he escaped, even if he managed to get out of this stronghold, was he not doomed to spend the rest of his life in this age? Even if he escaped and passed again through the dolmen he might end up anywhere, even in the worst of all the ages when Arnex and the Malasar had been vanquished and the world ruined. Even if he survived the ravages of Uknor the Destroyer – Romul, Franeus called him – there was nothing ahead in that age but centuries of a ravaged land. Legends and stories of times gone by were fine, but living in them wasn't an attractive idea.

Or would he escape again into a future he did not understand? If he entered the dolmen again he could not control where he would go. He might wander a thousand other ages without ever finding his place again.

He sat down on the dank floor. What was he to do?

As he long sat there, he felt the dampness seep up through his buttocks and a cold, clammy feeling creep horribly up to his spine. He did not care. He ignored it. He had failed again, utterly and completely. He had not completed the task that Franeus had given him.

He undid his belt, pulled his empty scabbard round and fingered in the dim light the writing, the carvings upon it. This was all that was left, this was the final reminder that he had ever met Rissar na Rishugn or even become a prince among the Hardsar. It was so dim he could no longer read the words written there, nor make out if there were any new ones. He imagined that 'Halam, failure of failures' was written there now for all to see. There was nothing left but that young boy who had run from his father's house because he did not want to obey him. Halam swore. He spat the words out, unpleasantly, as if ridding himself of a bad taste.

He dropped the scabbard and stared at the walls of his prison. From those high days when he had first met Rissar, so much had changed. He had met him and in a whirlwind of events found himself committed to him, with a new people, with the Hardsare his lover – Terras, the simple girl of the mountain and Halam, the ordinary boy of the lake. That was what they had said to each that morning. How wonderful it had been, even to walk the moors and the forests with her, and even to feel the jealousy of Rosart at his back. And then had come across the plains in power, calling to themselves the very power that gave the wind its name.

And now, Insnar was dead, gone forever, and Rissar trapped in some age of this foul edifice. Possibly not even this age, but some future one, no doubt in some dungeon, like his own. Perhaps without his staff, he too had no way to escape. And Terras too was lost, wandering some other time, where the people were strange and perhaps she did not even know where she was or what had happened to him.

If, as Franeus had said, she was truly following some other path, undertaking, as he, a task set for her, he hoped that she did it better than he. Halam groaned. Even when Hewas came with Rosart and the whole host of the Hardsar, they would never find them for they weren't even in the same age of the fortress. It was all hopeless, lost, and dead. Hewas would come to the stronghold and find it empty, with no trace of where his daughter and Halam had gone and no way to rescue Rissar. Perhaps they would have more luck, yet sitting there Halam did not believe it. If Raczek and Romul's aim in attacking them that night had been to frustrate the quest, in that at least they had utterly succeeded and Halam had been their main ally helping to frustrate it all. Halam had absolutely nothing left. He had no ideas and no strength. Everything was lost.

What was left to him? He had had hopes when he set out to rescue Rissar. The quest had seemed powerful, strong. He had Hardsar with him. He had become one of them. Yet here he was, the same Halam who had stormed from his father's presence never to return. A weak boy who would not do what his father wanted and so had stormed from the palace in a tantrum.

He was no Hardsar prince, no friend of the Malasari. He may have had a few days of happiness with his princess but all that was gone. He would not regain the amulet, the talisman that helped him, nor his sword of power. They would not be so foolish as to let him in the same room with them. He was not powerful enough to regain them by any other means. He had fought Raczek once and survived, but that was with the sword in his grasp. Now in a fortress controlled by Raczek and without the Hardsar nation at his back, he would not succeed.

He sat and stared into the gloom. The thoughts circled in his mind becoming more and more hopeless, darker and darker. They disintegrated into a wordless, utter depression. It descended on him like the shadow of night, a black cloak over his whole being.

Despite him, it grew lighter outside and even in his restricted cell, the daylight came. He rose to his feet and paced the cell. He knew not why he did or whether he had some aim. He simply could not sit and vegetate there on the floor any longer.

He had been awake some hours when suddenly a small panel in the bottom of the door was thrust aside and something was pushed through. He reached the door quickly but already the panel was shut. He sighed. The guard had been quick, no doubt in case the prisoner gained some view of the corridor outside.

He looked down. The gaoler had pushed a hunk of bread and a small pitcher of water through. Halam took the bread. It was hard, stale, and mould was growing on parts of it. In his father's house, it would have been thrown away. Even such prisoners as there were in the City on the Lake were fed better than this.

Halam supposed he should be grateful for being fed at all. He attacked the bread with his teeth. It tasted foul and yet, as he chewed, he realised that he was hungry. Even so, he could only eat two mouthfuls and could stomach no more. The water was drinkable but stale and tasted of wood and tar. *Why do these warriors have such a poor supply of water? Do they not use it? But perhaps this is just part of the punishment.* He finished it as quickly as he could. That way he did not have to taste it properly.

He put down the pitcher and stared up at the

door. If they were feeding him there was little chance he would be taken from the cell soon. He might be here for days. *How long will they leave me before they question me again?* Hopeless as it was, only by being taken from this cell was there any chance of escape.

Despite his certainty, he spent another hour trying to climb the walls of the cell. If only he could reach up to the window, narrow slit that it was, he would see out and gain some view of the outside world. He did not know why, but he knew it would give him hope. He might see nothing but a square foot of courtyard, but he would know that the world was still there and that would be enough.

The walls were rough-hewn, yet he could gain no purchase that would bring him high enough. He struggled up and fell to the ground so many times that he broke his fingernails, his fingertips became bloody and he bruised his knees and side from falling.

He gave it up at last. There was no way up, no way out. He was trapped in the cell until Raczek chose to call him out and then it would be for their purposes only.

Halam was not used to this, to be at another's beck and call – to be dominated. He had not thought it before but his life in the city had been privileged. What he wanted, he did, what he didn't want, he didn't. Rissar, who might have commanded his obedience, had never treated him any other way. Even Franeus, who had brought him to this point, had given him choice.

Here he had none and no way to achieve it.

He put the scabbard and his belt back on and sat down in one of the corners of the room, leaning back against the wall and staring at the limits of his world. He could sit in this small corner or move into that one over there, but beyond these walls, he had no freedom, nothing. He sat there and waited. There was nothing else to do. Despair descended around him like a cloud, but even that had no purpose. It created nothing; it did not change his situation.

The light from the slit-window moved as the day progressed, and not a sound came to him, neither from the outside, through the window, nor from the other side of the door. He wondered, briefly, if they had deserted him there, left the stronghold with him locked within it.

That could not be true, for then why had they fed him? If they meant to leave him here to die, why feed him at all, even with the stale bread and water?

At last, the day came to its end, and Halam found himself chewing again on the stale loaf they had given him. It took him many long minutes to chew it well enough that he did not gag on it as it went down, yet his stomach was grateful for the food, however bad. It was poor bread too, having small stones and grit within the dough. He felt them grinding at his teeth, yet still, he chewed on. *Why will I need teeth?*

The light faded quickly as the night came.

Halam sat, still leaning against the cell wall, feeling the chill dampness of the cell deepen as dusk turned into darkness. When the night fully came he heard noises from outside the cell. They came not only from behind the door but beyond even that. He supposed he could hear people moving in the courtyard. The noise went on for quite a few minutes.

What is happening in the dark?

The darkness in his little cell was all but complete. Only the faint glimmer of starlight showed him the scene around him. Unexpectedly, he heard a noise from outside his door – the sound of heavy footsteps tramping down the passage. Halam backed against the wall. From the noise they were making, it was clear that there were more than one of them. He pressed his back against the damp wall. He was frightened now. The sounds of feet stopped outside.

This was it. They had come.

Bolts were pulled noisily back, grinding, rasping their complaint into the air. The door was pulled open and Halam looked out at three or four faint, indistinct figures in the blackness. 'Frightened, are we?' A voice snarled the words and at once two men entered his cell. They seized his arms and pulled him up the narrow steps into the corridor beyond.

'Best be frightened . . .' The voice crowed its glee and its owner, a short sallow man, turned and led the way down the passage. There were five people in all, two holding him by the arms, two behind him, and the leader walking ahead, arrogant, in control.

'Where am I going?' Halam meant to speak the words normally but his fear, and his throat, dry from so little water during the day, whispered them out. He sounded scared, a frightened little prisoner unable to speak properly for the pounding of his heart.

The man in front cackled, but he did not answer. The guards beside him simply pulled him along the faster. He was led past many doors, dim in the gloom, but rooms like the one he had spent the day in, and then through a large room filled with barrels and boxes. As he walked Halam realised that the place was not a true dungeon, and the room in which he had lain was not a cell. In happier times these had been the cellars of the fortress. Halam's imprisonment there was an improvisation, a change in use wrought no doubt by his captors.

What other changes have they made?

They climbed narrow stairs. Rather than let go of him his guards virtually dragged him up the steps. He struggled to keep his footing but lost it several times. As he stumbled, they simply laughed and dragged him harder. It was good for them to see him suffer. They enjoyed it. There was no respect for him, no interest in him. He was beaten, he had been vanquished and now there was nothing for him but contempt.

At the top of the steps, they pushed open a door and Halam was dragged through it. It was dark beyond; it seemed these people kept the whole stronghold in darkness. He was pulled along faster, now down several passages, too dim and dark for him to see his way. He wondered how they walked so unerringly, so quickly.

At last, he was through another set of doors and out into the hallway of the fortress. He had stood there, alone, it seemed so little time ago, and yet Franeus had said it was a thousand years in the future. Perhaps it was even longer from whenever he was now. The very thought was numbing.

He had regained his feet and he was hurried along by the guards. They pulled him through the main doors and out into the courtyard. He was surprised. He had expected to be returned to the hall in which Raczek had questioned him. He had supposed they took him to once more face a barrage of questions, that the day of confinement was just for softening him up. But they swept through the hall and out into the open.

Outside, in the dark courtyard, was a scene of amazing activity. There were warriors everywhere and in the centre many carts with no hacsar harnessed to them. They were loaded with things, boxes, chests, barrels, but there was no way to pull them. They did not load them well. Halam thought the carters and merchants of In Haxass would not have been impressed. He had not realised there were so many soldiers at the fortress. Raczek was leading an army. But what were they doing? Where were they going?

Halam was dragged across the courtyard to

where a small knot of people stood. Their state of dejection made it obvious they were fellow prisoners. Halam had not until that moment even thought that there might be others in the cells around him. There were perhaps ten, no more. It was hard to count. Guards with the pike weapons stood around them, ensuring they did not move. Next to them, the largest cart was piled untidily high with objects and sacks. There was still no hacsar attached.

Are they going to make the prisoners drag it?

Halam was thrust through the circle of guards to stand with the other prisoners. Such was the force behind the action that he staggered and fell to his knees. His fall was ignored. His new guards accepted his arrival with utter indifference. They were holding the prisoners here and the arrival of one more was of little importance to them.

Halam struggled to his feet. A hand reached down and pulled him up. He looked up into the face of his helper. The dour and serious face of a plainsman stared down at him from the superior height that was the heritage of all the Torasar.

'Welcome, my friend. Our hosts are not so kind to their guests.' The plainsman was bearded, which was highly unusual for the people of the plains who lived and ran on the plain. Halam had never seen one who was not clean-shaven before. He could not stop himself from staring. He had always supposed they had some spiritual reason for shaving, so utterly uniform were they in it. The Torasara smiled at

Halam's stare. He rubbed at his beard with a rueful gesture. 'I have not the means to shave, my friend.'

Halam smiled. 'I meant nothing.' He held out a hand. 'What is your name?'

'I am Derar, son of Redar, of the clan of Teram.'

'And I am Halam, born an Aallesar, and my father was Jasam.'

Derar nodded his greeting and clasped hands.

A guard standing ahead of them turned and glared.

'Keep silent. Prisoners will not talk.'

Halam turned and looked at the guard until he seemed satisfied that he was to be obeyed. He turned away.

'Where are we going?' Halam whispered, moving closer to Derar so that he could hear.

Derar shook his head. 'I do not know.' He stole a glance at the back of the guard's head and, satisfied that he had not heard their exchange he continued. 'I was taken many weeks ago as I crossed the plain to the connubial feast of my sisterson. What of you?'

'Yesterday, as I entered the fortress.'

Derar raised an eyebrow and pulled his head back to take a closer look at the man he stood beside. 'You are either a very brave man or a foolish one, my friend. No man enters this place willingly. This fortress is evil.'

Halam smiled, rueful, unable to explain his actions, unsure even in himself why he had found himself entering such a place. Was he a brave man or a fool? He was the last man to ask. Halam turned back to the plainsman and spoke again. 'Why did they take you?'

'I do not know. There were many of them but having captured me, they then killed all the others in my party.' He hesitated and met Halam's eyes. Halam could see the pain behind his gaze. 'They simply brought me here and locked me up. They did not even question me.' He shook his head, slowly, wonderingly. 'Did they kill my brothers and sisters simply for the fun of it? If they did not wish information from me, why did they come? Why bring me here?'

Halam shook his head. 'I do not know. Perhaps you will find out soon.'

There was a disturbance. A man Halam did not know, who seemed to be in charge, strode up to the guards around the prisoners and spoke quick harsh words. Halam had never heard the tongue before and such was the roughness of it he would have been pleased not to hear it again. He supposed these followers of Uknor had a language of their own. The meaning of the words came clear at once. The guards formed up around them.

'Forward, and let there be no trouble. I will kill the first of you that starts anything.'

The carts, fully loaded now, were prepared in some strange way. Halam decided it was to drive them forward, for the carts began to move unaided. Halam, distracted by his conversation with Derar, had not thought through what was happening until that very minute.

We are leaving the fortress.

The thought struck him like a thunderbolt. He could not leave. For all he knew, Rissar was still held here, and even if he were not they still held his sword and the amulet that Franeus had given him.

If he was taken out now he could not guarantee ever to re-enter the place. His sword and the amulet might end up permanently separated from him and beyond his reach forever. He realised his position was taking yet another turn for the worse.

'No!' The word wrenched from him.

Several of the guards jerked around at the sound.

'I cannot leave.' Halam stopped.

He was scared. He would truly be forever lost in the endless ages of the world. He had to get to Raczek again. He had to have some chance of recovering his sword. He needed the amulet. He had to have a chance to return to his age. He could not stop. He could not fail.

Derar had stopped and was looking at him with amazement, horror, and a little fear at what this fool of an Aallesar might cause to happen. He reached forward to take Halam's arm.

'Come, Halam. They will . . .' But his words were not completed. A guard stepped forward brandishing a weapon of some sort, separating them.

'Come quietly. I will kill you right here!'

Halam stared at the guard; he was afraid, but he could not move. How could he leave and condemn himself to be lost forever in some time and age that was not his? He was perhaps the only prisoner here who truly understood the nature of the fortress and what would happen when they passed beyond it. Or was he perhaps the only one out of his age?

The guard snarled at Halam's lack of response and moved forward. Halam saw the end of the weapon pointing mercilessly at his stomach and acted instinctively. He swung out at it, to smash it aside, moving intuitively as if he held a sword once more. Halfway into the movement, he realised his foolishness and feared for his hand.

A flash of intense white light burst into existence and Halam's sword splintered the body of the weapon into two pieces. Halam danced backwards, swinging the sword, out of range of any further attacks.

A voice screamed out. 'A sword, he has a power sword!'

Halam moved forward and struck down without thinking. The guard's cry was cut off as he fell, slain by a single stroke of the sword. The light of his sword was blindingly bright.

Halam lifted his sword and stared at it. He was amazed that it was in his hand, his fingers grasped tight around the haft. He felt its power pulsing, ready to fight for him, with him. It had come when he had needed it. *Where has it come from?* He had no time to consider the question. Two more guards were rushing at him. He parried their first frenzied, panicked blows with ease. He had the sword in his hand once more and the power it held for him flowed through his arm. With the sword, nothing could prevent his passage. Why had he ever given it up?

As he struck he saw in their eyes that they feared him; they recoiled from the light streaming from his blade, frightened more of it than the cutting edge itself, or indeed the nervous man who wielded it. He lunged forward, and another of the guards fell backwards, slain by the blade.

'Yes, and I will die too!' Derar shouted. 'And with a weapon in my hand.' Quickly turning he smartly kicked another of the guards. As the man collapsed backwards he seized the strange pike that he held from loosened fingers.

Action exploded around the plainsman. The other prisoners burst into motion; galvanised into action they turned on the guards themselves. In a few moments, several of them were armed with strange weapons, and Halam found himself the centre of a rebellion.

The warriors of the stronghold fell back. The appearance of Halam's sword had caught them unawares. At one moment they had been conducting unarmed and cowed prisoners from the stronghold to an uncertain fate and, at the next, they found themselves attacked by an armed band of fighters.

The prisoners ran spontaneously the only way

they could – away from the guards towards the gatehouse where they would not face attack from several directions at once, but as they reached the stronger ground, they all turned and looked at Halam.

He recognised the look. They were relying on him to direct the next move. He had got them into this, and he would get them out. It was not a good feeling. Halam did not like the idea that these people relied on him to save their lives.

I am not that sort of person. I am not a brave man.

He considered the faces around him. Of the prisoners, only six now stood there. At least two of their number had disappeared completely. Halam could not see them but assumed they at least had not been successful during the fight. They had attacked guards for their weapons and had not won.

'Run to the dolmen,' said Halam, 'we must not let them catch us.'

As they moved further into the gatehouse, ready to run, the guards had regrouped, and many more of the fortress's garrison joined them, abandoning their tasks to seize weapons. More were pouring from the outhouses around the courtyard. Some were running now across the walls. In moments they would be above the gatehouse. There were too many of them. The situation was bad. There was no way they could win.

The motley band of escapees ran through the gateway and out into the night towards the golden bridge. The megalith was beyond. Their attack became a retreat and then a rout. Halam turned back and saw a male prisoner felled. A glowing spear made of light and heat shot across the distance from a pursuing guard with unerring accuracy across the courtyard, thudding into his back; he collapsed in flame. The man had no chance. He was dead before he hit the ground. Halam did not understand where such weaponry had come from. More glowing spears of light shot at them from the fortress.

Behind them, a whole group of guards disappeared and were abruptly replaced with glowing pillars of light. More spears of heat and light arrowed toward them, some from warriors, some from the glowing balls. Halam ran on. They were after them. They were coming. The last running prisoner, a Solpsara woman with green-painted skin, was enveloped in flame behind him.

Halam hesitated, wondering whether to run back to help her. The green woman had burst into purple flame. Halam stopped, stunned. His sword writhed upwards. An explosion of white light issued from it and exploded outwards like the splash of a lake as a stone breaks it. The warriors, the globes of light, all were all thrown backwards by the blast. But in moments they had recovered and were streaming toward him again. The remaining prisoners had stopped and gathered around him. They were only four now. It was as if they thought he could protect them. His incandescent sword seemed to put their enemies at a significant disadvantage just by its presence. It was not him the enemy feared. And it was not enough.

Two guards reached them. Halam's sword dispatched one, and another prisoner beside him – Halam did not see who – operated his strange stolen weapon and another spear of heat burnt the second guard who fell, screaming. More great spears of light lit the air around them, but none hit the target. The energy bolts of the enemy's fire, whether from guards or glowing columns of light, swerved and were absorbed by Halam's sword. His blade grew even brighter and the night around them was chased away by the strange new dawn.

'Come,' said Derar from beside him, 'to the dolmen, you said.'

Halam turned and ran towards it without a second glance at the plainsmen. The guards, and even the glowing columns, were hanging back now. Despite orders screaming out, they were unwilling to face Halam's sword or stand before the blazing white light streaming from its blade. In the moment of respite that this gave him, Halam reached the dolmen.

Derar led the rest of them. As he ran up another scream issued from behind. Halam turned. Beside the Torasar another prisoner disappeared, consumed in a flash of terrible red light.

'Let us go!' Derar said. 'We can leave this accursed place. The way lies open.' He indicated the plain beyond the dolmen. Behind them the tenacious night shrouded the Pasra. Here there would be no new dawn.

A prisoner – was he a Kelsara? – dodged around the dolmen and ran off towards the plain, intent on running for his life in the darkness beyond, to hide from pursuit in the surrounding countryside. Derar and another followed him without checking that Halam agreed. Halam ran after them, passing beside the megalith without any thought until it was done and he passed it.

But . . . ?

Halam sheathed his sword in one fluid motion and grabbed Derar's elbow and the arm of another prisoner. He pulled them back, forcing the plainsman and the other round to face him.

'Wait . . . come, through the dolmen. It will carry us to a safe place.'

Derar frowned. The other, a boy younger than Halam, was simply scared. There was no time to convince them. He bodily dragged them across the threshold of the megalith, into the face of the oncoming warriors. As he crossed the threshold Halam saw the eyes of their pursuers, the columns of light. He blanched. *Will it work?*

And the night was changed.

◈ **Chapter 6** ◈

Terras was close to despair when the path became even more difficult. There was more climbing to do, more extremes of incline, up and down, and the distance she managed to make each day sharply dropped as she was forced to spend more and more time negotiating her way, finding a possible route through crags and escarpments. She was zigzagging between great crags from the mountains on either side of her. Her calves ached from all the many days of climbing. They ached when she began the day and ached when she had finished.

Then, at about noon of the seventh day when her resolve was at its lowest, she crested a hill and was rewarded with a great view of the lands beyond. She realised then that she had reached the summit of the pass, and the way now led downwards.

The relief that flooded her was palpable. She would walk downwards now, and the pain in her leg muscles would get some relief. The joy swept away her loneliness, her resentment that she had been called to make this trek alone. She trudged on, downwards at last. The land was as rough, the snow, even though it was yet autumn, was bad. She realised that in the winter this way was almost certainly completely impassable, and probably deep into the new spring too. But she had done it. She was heading downwards now and, however difficult the way, she believed she was going to make it.

Each night as she sheltered she wondered where Halam was and what he was doing. This trip had taken her weeks. It must be ten or eleven days since she left the villages of the standing stones in the foothills – for she realised now that foothills were all they had been.

In despairing moments she wondered if it would be as long again before she reached the fisherfolk and spoke to them, let alone travelled south to the desert ruins that Franeus had mentioned. Given how long this had already taken her, and what it would now take, Halam, and Rissar if he had even rescued him, would surely have long reached the northern mountains and be striking out for the Citadel of Arnex. Surely their quest would be complete before hers had even begun. She felt another wave of emotion flood her. Why was she wasting her time and her warrior skills on such a trip?

She moved on downwards; after a couple of days the way became easier and the snow lessened. Such was her relief that she was climbing down from the path that, during these days, she forgot again her feelings of loneliness or resentment. Joyfully, she realised she had made the crossing before the winter snows. She had found the way; Franeus had promised she would.

On the fourth or fifth day she realised that there was not enough land before her. The horizon seemed to be too close. It was as if there was a great chasm before her, as if part of the world ahead had split and dropped away.

The sight, the thoughts were weird, and the sense of being curtailed, of having lost a part of reality was overwhelming. Then she understood, she realised she was right, that there was indeed a great precipice before her, and beyond she could see only the sky. A day or so later she realised that beneath the sky was the ocean, merging in colour and shade with the grey autumnal sky above it.

She was reaching her goal.

That night she wondered if ahead of her she might be able to make out the flickering light of lamps, the habitations of people, beneath and beyond the precipice. The game that day had been more plentiful, if only small and almost not worth the hunt, but the food cooked on a fire that night almost filled her belly and she began to feel human again. For the first time in days, she did not feel nauseous after eating. Whatever had been the problem, a good meal of decent food had resolved it. The following night it was indeed clear that lights were flickering beyond the ridge of the chasm. It had not been her imagination. They were truly there. So this, she thought, was the land the Istsar inhabited, where the mountains dropped suddenly into the sea.

One day soon after, late in the afternoon, she finally reached the precipice and stood atop it. Beyond the cliff was the ocean, yet before the sea was a narrow land, there at the bottom of the abyss before her. This strip of land was farmed and after it, there was a great town. The habitations began on the mainland but the city, for it was a city, stretched over the water onto a great crescent-shaped island beyond. The inner side of the crescent faced the land, so between it and the mainland was a well-protected harbour. The fisher people had built causeways and breakwaters so that the entrance of the sea into the harbour was narrowed and the boats within it more protected. There was a great statue at the great entrance of the harbour. It was huge so that the boats as they came into safety passed it by. Perhaps it was a representation of some mighty hero, a man or woman of old, but now it was broken; the top half of the statue was missing. It was difficult to tell what it had been or what it had meant to the people here, so many years ago, when they had raised this effigy. She wondered if the people in the harbour even remembered who the statue was and who it honoured.

The greater portion of the city was the part on the island. On the highest point of the island, at its back, facing the wildness of the western ocean, was a great tower. In the tower, a bright light was burning. There were many houses and already they were lighting lamps for the night ahead. The twinkling lights shone off the sea that surrounded them. As she watched the lamps flicker on, she knew in her heart that this was Haven, the main city of the fishers, their capital. She had reached the Istsar. This was the land of the fisherfolk.

Terras was too high up and far away to see people in the lamplight except as specks moving between the buildings, but she watched the boats moving around the harbour, being tied up on the jetties and quays for the coming night. Other ships were heading out as the sun was setting, to fish during the night and return, no doubt, fully laden at sunrise. What sort of people would they be, these Istsar? Worried by the sea? Dominated by the thought of it? Or fascinated and amazed by it and its power. Probably all of those, she felt. She knew little of the ocean, for this was the first time in all her life that she had ever beheld it.

Terras stood watching on the cliff side for a long time as before her the sun set in the west, dipping into the cloud on the horizon, setting over the island harbour. It was beautiful to watch the sun against the striated clouds in the skies over the isle. She stared down at the harbour and the city as the night overtook them. It was a beautiful place, she decided, this Haven of the fisherfolk. She had always imagined them to be an unsophisticated people eking out a precarious existence on the edge of the world, scrabbling to find food in the western seas. But, this town, this city was richer than that. The seas were a source of abundance and they were the people who enjoyed that plenty.

As she stood, then sat there, watching the lands before her, she understood another reason the trade routes did not follow the pass that she had. The precipice before her was very high and to find a way up or down would be perilous, let alone do it with pack animals in a caravan. She looked to either side of her but in the darkening of dusk, she could not see any easy way for her to descend to the lands of the Istsar below. She would spend at least one more night atop this cliff before finding her path to the lands beneath her. If indeed, there even was one. That thought was worrying, but there was nothing for it but to search.

She lit a fire, for wood was now plentiful and there were easily enough dry branches for a good fire. She did not fear being spotted from the fisher town below for, unlike her intentions with the people of the stone circles she had passed in the foothills of the snowy pass, she did intend to meet these Istsar. If they realised she was there that could only aid in her objective. If their response was unfriendly, she would deal with that.

I am Hardsar. We do not fear any other people.

She sat by her fire, watching the embers fly up into the sky. She looked beyond them at the fisherfolk city and speculated whether they even cared who it was encamped on the cliff above them. She doubted it, for the promontory was a marvellous defence against peoples coming from the east to attack them. They would have to descend, probably in single file, before reaching the Istsar lands – time enough to mount a defence.

She slept beside the fire, warm for the first time

in many days, and able to sleep deeply and peacefully. She dreamed of Halam, adventuring in distant lands, far beyond, and doing all the things she wished she was there to do with him – walking beside the Malasari, perhaps, if he had escaped the men from the fortress. She dreamed deep and imaginative dreams of where he might be and what he might be doing. Halam walked where it was her place to walk, and she, for a moment, again resented him that chance. *Why am I here, and does he miss me as much as I miss him?*

She woke with the dawn as the sun rose behind her over the mountains she had crossed. She ate the last of her remaining supplies. She was pleased with herself for hunting so efficiently that she had found enough food to reach here. She doused the fire and did not bother to scatter its remains. The firelight the previous evening had been enough to alert any interested people that she was there upon the precipice.

The night fishing boats had returned with the dawn, as she had thought they would, and other boats were leaving, plying their way out to the open sea in search, no doubt, of other fish, of other species hunted best at day. She doubted the Istsar were ever short of food to eat.

She walked first to the north and after a few fruitless hours of searching for a pathway down turned around and headed south, hoping to have better luck there. To the south, she found the way. It was a path used by the Istsar themselves, for someone, probably centuries before, had built two stone pillars either side of the entrance. It marked the way down and peering over she saw that the path curved and recurved its way down the cliff. A narrow and treacherous path crisscrossed its way down the steep sides of the precipice. She could not see if it reached the bottom, but she was sure it did, for why else mark the route with pillars?

She started down. By then the sun was high in a clear blue sky. It was already noon. She zigzagged her way down. Sometimes the path was so steep that people had, long before, cut steps into the stone to make the way a little easier. It was rarely only wide enough for more than one person to descend and sometimes not even that, or not safely anyway. There was no way for an army to descend by this path, at least and be ready for any defenders marshalled and prepared at the bottom.

By the mid-afternoon, she was far enough down to see the bottom and could see that there was a small tower at the base. A guard tower, she felt sure, where sentries would wait to accost any aggressive travellers who had reached these fishing lands. Many seabirds wheeled around her on the way down, crying out her presence to anyone who needed to know. They nested in the cliffside and cried, of course, to protect their nests, their young, their refuge in the rocks. Their offspring, born in the spring and early summer, were already large enough to be almost adults and ready to brave the winter that was to come. Yet still their parents cawed and crowed a warning to everyone that Terras was here and Terras was coming.

◎

In a flicker of an eyelid, their attackers, the confusion of warriors, the columns and balls of energy, the glowing spears of light shooting through the air at them, the noise and screaming of defeat and victory, all the terror of the night of their escape was gone.

The darkness fell strangely around them. *How can it be so peaceful?* The stars were hard and bright above them. Before them, the Citadel of Franeus was silent once more. No one occupied it this night, that much at least was clear.

Halam turned. Derar stood beside him and on his other side a young boy stood, staring at him in fear. The boy was fair-haired, yet tanned and weather-beaten. He was of a people Halam did not recognise. For several moments he just looked at his companions, turning from one to the other as they stared back at him in wonder and fear. They had all been transported to the same night. They were not lost to him, as he had lost Terras. They had entered together, Halam grasping hold of them.

Halam felt a stab of anguish. So if he had only held on to Terras as they ran into the dolmen that night so recently, so long ago, would they be together now? Halam released their arms and sighed, not for them, but his Hardsare. 'We are free,' he said.

Derar was gazing around him in stunned amazement. 'How did you do that? How did you destroy them all?'

Halam shook his head. 'They are not destroyed. We have been carried to another night when they are not here. The archway of dolmen is the source of your rescue. It has taken us to a new night. They will not find us. They can scour the countryside for us on the night we left, but we are here, we are free.'

Derar did not understand the words, Halam could see it in his eyes. Suspicion grew in the eyes of his new friend.

'Are you a sorcerer or one of the wize? The songs of my people tell of such.'

Halam stared at the Torasara. He was reminded of Torem, of his suspicion, all that prejudice against people who were not Torasar. He saw something of the same in Derar's eyes.

'No.' He shook his head. 'I am no sorcerer. It was the dolmen that brought us here, not me. You do not know its true nature – if you did, you would understand.' As he said it Halam wondered if he even knew its true nature himself. He must have sounded so wise and clever, ignorantly repeating the words of Franeus as if he understood them. He was just as confused.

Derar glared. Halam, realising in his heart that he could say no more to convince the plainsman, turned and looked again at their companion. He was a young boy, no more than fourteen summers old. How had he come to be in the fortress, let alone in Raczek's clutches?

The boy looked scared. Halam decided it was unsurprising. His world had altered so much and so quickly. Then Halam and the plainsman had shared harsh, suspicious words without even glancing at him. Halam felt sorry. Perhaps he was right to be frightened. He would not know where he was. He would not know what to do. He would not know where he was. After all, Halam didn't.

'I am Halam. What is your name?'

He replied, haltingly, unsure of himself. 'I am Fracos.' He spoke the sacred tongue strangely, with an accent, soft and sibilant. 'I am Istsara.'

'The fisherfolk?' Halam said the words cheerfully. He had never met one of them. They lived on the western coast, far beyond the Pasra, where the great sea began. They lived from the sea, people said, for there was nothing else there of great sustenance. 'I have never met one of your people.'

'Of what people are you?' Fracos spoke the words hesitatingly, as if not sure he could even put a question to so great a warrior – or so great a sorcerer.

'I was born of the Aallesar,' Halam said. 'But now I live among the Hardsar.'

Derar, behind him, drew his breath in quickly. Halam turned and looked at him.

'You are Hardsara?'

Halam turned back to him and nodded. 'I

married into their people. I know that the Torasar do not think well of them, of us, but.'

'I have never heard of an Aallesara becoming a Hardsara.'

'No, neither have I. That has been said before by one of the plain.'

Fracos spoke hesitantly, as if afraid of interrupting. 'Whoever you are, I thank you for saving me.'

Halam turned back and looked at the face of the young Istsar. He smiled at him. 'I . . .' Derar strode abruptly away, walking quickly across the bridge and towards the fortress. 'So let us see if we are truly alone.'

Halam stared at the retreating back of the dour plainsman and wished heartily that he could have bridged the gap between them. He glanced briefly at the young boy and then followed the Torasar silently. Fracos trailed after them.

Derar paused briefly before the entrance and then, as if gathering his courage, stepped through it. By the time they reached him, Derar was standing just beyond the gatehouse, staring at the sky and, oddly, sniffing the air.

'It is strange . . .' He hesitated. 'As we fought it was a summer night, or it seemed so for the winds were warm. Now it is late, the autumn is already past. Winter is coming. How could so much time have passed?'

Halam stopped beside him. 'It is a different

night, Derar Torasara. I have told you.'

Derar turned and looked at him. 'Yes . . .' The plainsman stopped, hesitating. 'It seems to be so then . . . after all.' Behind the sternness of his expression, Halam could see something else in his eyes. Despite all his prejudice against the people of the mountains. Despite, perhaps, disbelief that a weak Aallesara could ever become one of the hated Hardsar, let alone such a powerful warrior, he was still grateful. Halam felt that something inside the Torasar knew that this Lakeman had saved his life, freed him. But Halam could see that he found gratitude hard and difficult – more impossible to express because it was demanded of him by an adopted Hardsara. Halam met his eyes and wondered what the plainsman would feel if he knew that Halam was the Hardsaro, a future king of the mountain.

At least I will be if I ever manage to get back to the age I am meant to be in.

Fracos spoke from beside Halam. 'What is that?'

Halam turned. The Istsara was pointing beyond the courtyard, further into the fortress. Halam followed the line of his arm and his heart almost stopped. There was a light way past the far end of the courtyard, beyond some of the outbuildings, in some distant part of the stronghold where Halam had never stepped. And the light was flickering.

In a moment, Derar faded back into the shadows. Halam reached out and pulled the fisherfolk boy after him. He placed his finger to his lips, indicating silence.

'We are not alone after all, Hardsara.' Derar spoke the words with a certain relish although Halam could not remember promising that they would be.

'It is a campfire.' Fracos whispered the words.

Halam looked again at the light and saw that the boy was right. As he stared at the flickering light his thoughts flew, inexplicably, back to another campfire when all this began.

'Come.' Derar hefted his purloined weapon and slipped quietly along the wall at their side. He kept to the shadows, yet he was heading slowly from one pool of darkness to the next quiet shadow, around the edge of the courtyard. Halam followed, also doing his best to keep from view. He guessed the Torasara was right. They had to know who was there.

They circled the great courtyard and, as they did, Halam looked up at the great keep. The window of the room in which Franeus had sat was dark. On this night, the high priest did not sit there and wait for him. Halam moved on, but as he went from shadow to shadow he felt an unaccountable desire to turn, to run, to climb the stairs of that tower again and to enter the room, to stand there, to go again to the place where Franeus had been. *Would he still be waiting for me in the darkness?*

Halam turned his attention back to their goal. They were a lot closer now. It was a campfire and at the fire a single figure sat, cloaked and hooded against the night. The man, if he was, seemed lost in his thoughts, staring down at the ground, fingering the dust in front of him. Derar, in the lead, crept slowly forward.

'You do not come upon me by stealth.' The man spoke, lifting his head. 'I saw you as you entered.'

Halam could not stop himself running forward several steps before he halted, thinking better of it. But the voice . . .It had to be him.

'Rissar?'

The man straightened up and tossed his hood back with one hand, revealing his face. As his head was uncovered Halam felt his chest tighten.

'My lord . . .' He ran forward and then stopped, thinking of his companions. He turned back to look at the Torasara and the Istsara still standing nervously and not moving. 'It is my friend. All is well, there is nothing to fear.'

He ran on, heedless now of whether the Torasara and the Istsara followed him. He ran across the intervening ground until he stood before Rissar. He stopped and stared down at him. He could hardly believe his eyes. It was the magician-king, the man he had followed so far, the man he had sought, even into the fortress.

The words spilt from him. 'What are you doing here? Rissar, why are you here alone? Where is Franeus? Have you seen Terras?'

'I was waiting for you, Halam. I have not

waited long, but I knew you must come to this night before I could continue my journey. I knew Franeus would send you to me.'

Halam stared at the sorcerer for several moments. *What is this? Another plan of Franeus, one he did not tell me about?*

'Have you seen Terras?'

'No.' Rissar shook his head. 'Did she enter the stronghold with you?'

'With me, yes, but Franeus said she did not enter the same Citadel and he would not tell me where she had gone.'

Rissar nodded gravely. 'Yes . . . I understand.' The Malasari turned and stared behind Halam at his new companions still standing many feet away, cautious, unsure.

Derar was fingering his pike. Fracos was the closer of the two, yet Derar hung back. The Istsara seemed torn between Halam and Torasara, unsure of which man to stand with.

'Come, Derar,' Halam said. 'This is my lord, Rissar. There is no danger.'

The plainsman walked forward then, but he was not convinced, that much was clear in his face. There was irritation there too.

'I am not afraid of danger, Hardsara!'

Rissar spoke from the ground. 'All wise men fear danger, Torasara, so do not hide it from us, and Halam Hardsaro is wrong, I am dangerous. But I will not threaten you, nor will I turn against you. You are a friend of my companion.'

Derar stared at the sorcerer for several minutes and then at Halam with a stern, serious expression. For all his sternness, his face was an open book. He was wondering what his friend had got him into.

Fracos appeared to stand beside Halam, decided.

Rissar turned and considered the newcomer. 'Greetings, Istsara.' He immediately broke into another tongue of swishing, sibilant words. Their sound reminded Halam of the Lake of his home and the water lapping against the wharves of In Haxass. Fracos's face burst into a smile and he responded in the same strange, lisping language. Halam watched the exchange with growing understanding; Rissar was speaking with the boy in his language.

Rissar nodded and responded again. Their conversation went on for several minutes. As it did, Derar quietly walked across the courtyard and sat, rather stiffly, across the fire from Rissar. He had decided, it seemed, to throw in his lot with these people. Halam sat down and turned to consider the Torasara sitting beside him. He spoke. 'Trust Lord Rissar, Derar. He will bring us all home.'

The Torasara nodded stiffly, yet with an air of the shrewd, who know the reality of the world. Perhaps the aid of this half-Aallesara, half-Hardsara and the kindness of Rissar to the Istsara boy would slowly erode the prejudices of his people.

He turned and stared back at Halam, his face

now a mask of Torasar seriousness, and yet his eyes showed a glimmer of conciliation.

'We shall see,' he said eventually.

Rissar stopped talking to the fisherfolk boy and turned to look at Halam and the Torasara. Fracos sat down quietly beside Halam.

The Malasari looked at Halam. 'So, Halam, have you brought my staff?'

Halam stared back at him in utter horror. Of course, he had been bound to ask that question eventually, but how could Halam answer it? He looked furtively at his two companions, shamed suddenly to have to admit his faults before them. So far they thought him a mighty warrior, able by his strength to do all that his lord commanded.

'No, Rissar. I have not brought it.' He bowed his head. 'We carried it across the plains, running with the Torasar we sought out to aid us in this thing. The quest stayed together. Hewas, Rosart and Terras were with me, but as we reached this stronghold and we looked upon its power and saw the greatness that lived within it, our hearts quailed.

'The Torasar left us,' he glanced at Derar, 'for they had promised only to lead us to the fortress and did not, would not enter it, or any building—'

Derar spoke, interrupting. 'You came hither with Torasar?' His tone was stunned, surprised that any of his people would travel with such a one as he.

Halam turned again and looked at him. 'Yes. Their chief was Torem. He ran with us . . .'

Derar looked confused. 'Torem? That is a name among the people, but I have never heard tell of one of that name as a chief. . .' The Torasar drifted to a close, his amazement draining the words from him.

Rissar spoke quietly, yet insistent. 'And what happened to the staff, Halam?'

Halam turned and looked at the magician king. 'Insnar has it. He took it up when I could bear it no longer. He feared that Rosart would take it, and so . . . he protected it . . .' He trailed off, bemused, unable to continue. How could he tell him what Insnar had done, how his friend, the first Companion of the One, was no more. How he had changed himself, somehow, into a statue, a jaksar of stone. He stared at Rissar. He had no words.

'Where is Insnar, Halam?'

'He is on the plain, a . . .' There was nothing left but the truth. That much he had learnt during his time in the fortress. 'He is dead, lord.' He sobbed the words. 'He turned himself to stone and the staff with him. I could not stop him before it was complete. I am sorry, lord, I—'

'Where on the plain is he?'

'Where we stood on a rise, where we stopped before the fortress.'

'Then let us find out whether lies there still, in this age. We will go in the morning when it is light and seek him out. Then, with the staff at my side, I can return all things to their proper place. Fracos can return to the boats of his father, at the Haven of his ancestors, and Derar can seek again the tents of his people.'

Derar spoke at once as if the very mention of his name gave him leave. 'I do not understand the words you speak, nor do I wish to. If it can be, I would return to the tents of the people to mourn those of my family the evil warriors slaughtered and work for my people in the fight against them. There is no place I would rather be, but I wonder, with all this talk of different nights and other ages, and how here it is nearly winter whilst when I came to this accursed stronghold it was summer . . . I wonder if I can truly return. How can so much time have passed and I have not lived through it?'

Rissar looked across at the plainsman. 'I see you have wisdom, Derar. You are beginning to understand the nature of the Fortress of Endless Night. Remember that wisdom and understanding of a person's part is that of which the songs speak. Is a limit placed in the words of the song?'

Derar looked surprised at the phrase as if it meant something to him more than the words carried.

Rissar continued. 'Remember, Torasara, that darkness can be a fell thing, but the nights are not always evil. Did you not feel the power of the night's beauty as you lay in the tent of your father and looked upwards? Did not fear and doubt keep you within the tent until the time came when you must wander the plain, in the night and in the day, to find your manhood? Did you not find it in the power of the plain, given by the hand of the Snake god?'

Derar gasped, open-mouthed. He closed his mouth, angry at once. 'And what do you know of the Arknor?' He spoke the words harshly.

Halam could see he was annoyed that a man from outside the plain should speak of such things. Then Derar glanced sidelong at Halam and Fracos as if he too had spoken words he should not have spoken before them and regretted what his anger had led him to do.

'I know it well, Derar Torasara,' Rissar responded at once, as always with a ready answer. 'Do not suspect me. I know all about your people and I love the plain, as you have learnt to love it. Follow me, and you will be returned to the lands and the arms of your woman. You will sing again.' He turned and looked at Halam. 'But these are not things to speak of here, Derar Torasara.'

'No, they are not.' The plainsman spoke the words firmly, but the look on his face had changed. Rissar had won this man's respect.

'We will go to the resting place of Insnar tomorrow.'

Halam spoke. 'There is one more thing to tell, Rissar. One more way in which I have failed.'

Rissar looked Halam in the eyes. 'Speak it out, Halam Hardsaro.'

'I met with Franeus. On seeing the might of the fortress, Hewas and Rosart returned across the plain to call the host of the Hardsar and bring them here to assail the place. Only Terras and I continued, thinking that we, at least, should continue to seek you. As we reached the fortress, we found it empty. As it is this night.' He waved around him. 'Still intent on seeking you, lord, we ran into it, through the archway of the dolmen before it. We were separated. She is gone, Rissar.' Halam stopped and looked at Rissar. The sorcerer met his gaze evenly.

Halam continued, unsure of what his gaze meant. 'I found Franeus in the stronghold. He said he was waiting for me. He told me the nature of the Citadel. He told me that Terras was not to be rescued until she had fulfilled her task, and he said I had a task, to return to a time of Raczek and to find you.'

'That at least you have fulfilled,' Rissar said.

Halam shook his head. 'But he sent me back to the age that Raczek came from. He gave me a necklace, an amulet that was linked to his staff, to guide me through the many nights. Raczek took it from me, Rissar. It is still there. By it, Franeus can control where you go within the fortress. Rissar, it occurs to me that with it perhaps Uknor and Raczek will also control the fortress.'

Derar spoke. 'Uknor? The Destroyer? You speak of people long dead as if they still live. Are you mad?'

Rissar turned to the plainsman. 'Enemies may have been fought centuries ago, Derar Torasara, but that does not mean that the war is ended.' He turned back to Halam. 'Fear not, Halam, Franeus's will does not go astray. If the amulet has fallen into the hands of Raczek, Franeus already knows it. Trust his wisdom.'

Halam shook his head in disbelief. 'But Rissar, he didn't know. He gave me the amulet to take me to you, to rescue you. How can I . . . ?'

'I did not need rescuing, Halam Hardsar, and Franeus knew that. Some of these words are your own and are not things he said to you. His will can't have been thwarted. He holds all the threads of time in his hands. Consider carefully, his will is done. You are brought here, and you will lead me to where my staff is kept by a faithful sentinel.'

'I know the plain in daylight or darkness,' Derar said. 'If by taking you there I shorten the time I have to listen to these strange words, if by aiding you now I may be returned to my clan and the hearth with my woman, I will lead you there and lead you now. I do not like what I hear. There is too much in it for one man to bear.'

Rissar raised an eyebrow at the plainsman. 'Will you then lead us, Derar?'

'Yes. I know the spot Halam means. It is the boundary of the land. We know of the stronghold, and beyond this point, the plainsmen do not go and the beasts may not graze. If Halam truly came there with people of my race, that is where they would have stopped. The Torasari forbids us to cross the border except by his command.'

Rissar rose to his feet. 'Fracos Istsara, do you

also wish to come with us?'

The fisher boy also got slowly to his feet. He looked at Rissar with wonderment, as if he saw in him a thing that filled his life with astonishment. 'I will come if by it I may see the boats of my father again.'

Derar was on his feet already. 'To leave this accursed stronghold is enough in itself.'

'It is not accursed,' said Rissar. 'It is simply a place of mystery, a power of the ancient times wrought by the power of the Snake god.'

'Whatever, I do not wish to understand it . . .' Derar turned away.

Rissar did not respond but simply turned and doused the fire he had been sitting at, kicking the ashes with his booted foot. He was not going to force a response from the Torasara.

All people must choose their way, thought Halam, and he marvelled that he was beginning to think things and words like those of Rissar and Franeus. Someone had said something like that to him. But he could not remember who. Yet Halam felt sorry for his Torasara friend, for that was how he thought of him. He did not understand how anyone could not wish to understand, could not wish to see his way forward, nor respond to the presence of the Malasari. He looked again at Fracos and saw that in him, at least, was a boy filled with a desire to understand. He gazed at Halam and Rissar with shining eyes.

In silence, they crossed the courtyard and,

hesitating only briefly they crossed the threshold of the Citadel and walked across the ground to the bridge. Halam glanced back at the towering bulk of the fortress behind them.

He had spent only a few hours of his time inside and yet had seen so many things. But, despite all the wonder that had been brought to his mind, he too would be happy never to see the walls or towers of the place again. It was perhaps not evil, but it was dangerous, and he wished never again to dabble in such a thing, to mix his days with other ages.

As they crossed the bridge the Torasara broke wordlessly into a run. He did not start slowly as Torem's people had. He wished only to return there and run with his people. Who were they to say otherwise? They followed him without response.

Rissar ran well, alongside Halam, and the Istsara, Fracos, ran at the back. He was humble, Halam thought, and sought no place of leadership.

Halam spoke to the Malasari. 'How did you escape, Rissar? How did you escape from Raczek?'

Rissar turned and considered Halam for a long while.

'It was Romul who led them that night. After the attack, I fought with Uknor, Romul is his true name. He is Raczek's ultimate master on this world, and I wrestled with him, but he could not hold me nor prevent me. He is not great enough for that. Romul took me by the power given to them and which they have taken. Yet, even without my staff, I am greater than he. They do not understand that. They wished to confuse and distract us from our course to dismay you and throw you into despair. They could not keep me, for even without the staff they cannot destroy me nor cast me down.

'I left them then, the first step in their defeat complete. I went with him to . . . a void that the Snake god devised for him. I returned to you.'

Halam was dumbstruck. 'Then . . . but . . .' He stopped running. 'So I did not need to rescue you?'

Rissar shook his head. 'No, Halam, but you needed to come after me, and you needed to want to rescue me. This was the thread known to Franeus the True, the Left Hand. He had a task for you, Halam, and one for Terras also. You had to follow so that they could be fulfilled.'

Halam sighed. 'I do not understand, Rissar.'

'Franeus cannot always explain, people do not understand. But you will, Hardsaro. The quest goes on and at its end, all things will be clear. Until then, not all can be understood. Live in the will of the Snake god, Hardsaro, and you will be a true prince of the people.'

He considered Halam in silence for a moment, as if deciding whether to say more. At last, he spoke. 'You know, your new people, the Hardsar, live to be something, to train to be worthy guards of their lord. They do not attain it, and never have they been able. May you teach them the way to true service.'

Halam was silent. He did not understand the

deeper meaning of the words but he knew they spoke some truth, some unattainable mystery that would perhaps come upon him. He did not ask. They ran after Derar and Fracos.

They ran on, down from the area of jagged rocks and jumbled stones of the edge of the Pasra, down through the lands of pools and streams that were its precursor, and Halam never once looked back to the fortress.

He did not wish to see again the place where, in some bizarre way, Terras was still trapped. If Rissar and Franeus spoke the truth, he would see her again. He would have to wait for the moment and trust that they spoke the truth to him. The run was tiring but Halam felt some joy in it. It was good to fill his lungs and run free once more.

They came at last to the plain, where the land was flat before them, the sweeping grass running out into the darkness, never-ending and free. Derar ran onto it with obvious joy. Halam and the other three ran after him. At once the Torasara stopped and looked up at the sky. They all stopped beside him.

The plainsman spoke. 'Whatever night this is, strange lord, the stars are the same, and the plain breathes the same scent as my home. The wind is mine.' He ran on then, without checking to see if they followed. He ran, seeking as he went, the place where Insnar lay. It did not take him long; he seemed to have guessed its location. There before them, the jaksar sat, guarding his master's staff, and he lay there still.

Derar stopped before the statue. He stared down at it.

'A jaksar?' He seemed confused. 'You spoke of this Insnar as if he was a man, Halam. If he is a beast, what wisdom did he have, how could you say that he—?'

'He has much wisdom,' said Rissar at once, interrupting softly, without rancour. 'It is but different from yours.'

Derar was silent; he looked at Rissar and waited. The Malasari knelt before the statue of the jaksar snarling over the staff, and slowly, gently he stroked the head. He took something from his belt that looked like a small stone; holding it he began to sing. The words were strange, alien, but the tune was gentle and vivid. The statue did not move, although he stroked and petted it like a real animal, a breathing, flesh-filled forest creature that he must greet on his return. The song ended and he spoke.

'What a true servant you are, Insnar. You serve me with your whole heart, and there is nothing you would not give me, even your life.'

Halam stood beside the magician and could not speak with the emotions that swelled in his breast. Rissar carried on stroking the head of the jaksar for many moments, singing the gentle words of the song again. Halam saw Derar shifting nervously beside him and he turned and looked at the Istsara. Fracos looked puzzled, confused. They both seemed to doubt that anything would occur. They had brought this strange lord here and now he crawled on the ground, stroking the head of the statue as if it was a real animal and singing nonsense. Halam looked back at the Malasari and he too began to doubt that Rissar was doing anything.

'Can you not . . . ?' He stopped, unsure that he should say it. The words came at last. 'Is he lost forever, lord?'

Rissar looked up. 'Such fealty is worthy of much admiration, Halam. Insnar has given much. Let us not rush along our way without understanding and without feeling it in our hearts.'

He turned back to the jaksar and stroked his head again. 'But come then, my friend, it is time you ran again and found all your joy in a world remade for you.'

He touched the small stone on the head and sang a new song. As he stroked his head now a strange thing occurred. At first, Halam thought it was his imagination but then he was sure. Up from the ground, colour spread; in the dark it seemed as if the very brownness of the ground was rushing up into the jaksar. The grey of the stone seemed to move upwards into Rissar's device and his palm as it stroked away the stillness, the solidity. The rock-hard statue became coloured as a jaksar should be and was, and dark brown fur appeared where the statue had been; a secret animal lost in the grass.

Insnar moved his head and looked up at his

friend. He growled a greeting, but carelessly as if Rissar had but stepped away for a moment and was now returned. He struggled to his feet, shaking away the stiffness like a beast waking from sleep.

Rissar stroked his head still, but at once the jaksar would have no more; he ran from Rissar's hand and settled several feet away. Sitting down on his haunches he surveyed the motley band of people before him. He looked at Rissar, and then carefully at Derar. His animal gaze settled on Halam and he stretched his neck. He liked the amazed stares that everyone was giving him. Halam turned back to Rissar. He had stood up and in his hand he held the staff. Halam looked at him and waited.

'Yes, Halam, it is time I set all things back on their course. Our tasks are to be completed.'

He looked at Derar and Fracos standing together. They seemed worried, unsure of whether to stare at the jaksar or the Malasar.

Rissar spoke. 'Derar Torasara, I will return you now to your age, to the clan of your fathers. You will be in the arms of your woman before the sun rises again. You will lie in the hearth you made with her. But Derar, remember this and learn wisdom from it. Much is the wisdom of the Songs. Learn them well for they will give to your people the wind and life.' Then he spoke words in the Torasar language that Halam did not understand.

He turned to Fracos. 'Go too, Fracos Istsara, to the boats of your fathers, and may you find your

Haven all your days. Remember me and remember the stories of the ancient, for their day is not over. The Kingdom of the Malasari begins again. And your mother the sea will return with the fire as her crown.' Rissar then broke into the language of the Istsar and Halam could understand none of it. But did he hear the name of Terras amidst it all? He decided not.

Then, before either of them made a reply, even if they had such words to speak, Rissar lifted his staff to the sky.

'By the rule of the Snake god, by the Malasari of all the world, by the power of words, may all things be as they should!'

He thrust the staff downwards. A flash of blue light came from the very earth to meet it, like lightning flashing upwards to the sky. Around them, voices cried out some magnificent and mighty song. Halam felt the sword at his side pulse with sympathetic energy, and the night fled from the sky.

◈ **Chapter 7** ◈

Shiskes was content. He did not resent that he had been assigned to the barrier cliff. It was a fine, crisp autumn day and there was nothing in the air but a chill off the sea and the smell of salt in the breeze. It was easy duty. He had five men with him. They sheltered in the guard tower and seemed content to while away the day playing halsa with the gambling sticks made from fish bones. Every few minutes he heard the cry of someone's victory or the groan of another's defeat. Every time it woke him he would rest his head back on the wall of the tower and let them continue.

He was frustrated but he knew he should be content. The accident had left him with a pronounced limp, so he was little use aboard a working boat, and certainly not to be trusted to be nimble and able when the mother sea was angry. It was the best he could hope, to be a guard, to while away his time and still earn enough share of the catch for his son to live and grow into adulthood. They were soloed now, since the death of his mate, the boy's mother. Their union had not been a happy one, but it had, at the least, produced a child.

Soon enough Shiskes's lifelong friend would apprentice his son to the boats. Shiskes had gifted Fisk with all his tackle and his boatshare so Fisk owed him that now. He would be fair. He would have been fair anyway. He would always have done it. After all, they had been close friends from childhood and they had always preferred each other's company to the company of others, even women. Indeed, Fisk had never united his boatshare with a woman. He always fished alone. Shiskes knew he was a good man and now, because he had never united with a woman, they could sojourn together and look after the boy until it was his son's time. He would see his friend Fisk satisfied, his son fed, and his son would walk the waves with the other new adults.

And so it must be, Shiskes knew, his son must walk the waves as all his ancestors had. The sea must be his harsh lover and his firm mother as she was for all the people. For the mother provided everything the people had, and was the source of all they were. But she was no sentimental nursemaid who cosseted them from every danger. Life was good, for the ocean was full of riches for those who knew how to obtain them – food aplenty for fishers who knew where to fish, full of precious things for those who knew where to dive, and full of clothing and comfort for those able to use everything the sea provided. But the mother must be respected, for she was a harsh parent.

Yes, Shiskes should be content. He still had a role, and did enough to live, to contribute what he could to the overall catch. He was the master to these few guards. It should be sufficient. He opened his eyes and tipped his chair forward, away from the wall. Most of the men were either wastrels or, like himself, injured at sea and unable to work the boats any more. The wastrels were happy enough to gamble and game their days away and the injured had little else to fill their time.

Shiskes glanced over at the door of the guard tower. It was chill so they stayed indoors. Winter was coming and even here, near the sea, Shiskes could feel it in his bones. His leg ached and the memory of the injury came back to haunt him. He would be content, and he would be a good guard and a fine master to these men.

A game of halsa ended and the usual bickering argument was started by the man who had lost the most. Shiskes called across to them and ordered the man who was mostly trying to start the fight to go and check the pathway. Tyress growled at him and complained, but he turned to go even while grumbling that it was all pointless.

'Hardly anyone ever comes that way, Master Shiskes. It is even late in the year for any of the Carqsar to come. The pass will be blocked, soon if not already.'

'So, go check then, Tyress, and when you know you are right, you will all the quicker return to your game.'

Tyress growled his disgust but he stomped from the tower. Shiskes watched him go and return rather too quickly.

'Now go and check properly,' he said and laughed like a benign father teaching his son to fish.

Tyress scowled at him, but the other men

laughed their delight at Tyress's expense. Tyress shrugged and snorted through his nose. He too was close to laughter. He stomped out again in the exaggerated manner of a boy on the edge of being an adult trying to defy the father who must help him walk the sea. And this time, he was gone rather too long. Shiskes rose to his feet just as the guard came swiftly back into the tower.

'Someone is descending, master. I think . . . I swear there is.'

Shiskes moved quickly and grabbed the guardsword – the mark of his rank – and motioned to the men to gather their weapons. They seized the harpoons, leisters, multi-pronged spears and the battle nets that were their motley set of weapons. They donned their wetskins, blackened and oiled against the sea. They looked like a disparate crew as they gathered up outside the tower. Not even their wetskins were alike, and their assorted weapons were those that had broken and been sent to them to repair and then use.

Shiskes stood at their head and looked up the cliff path. He saw that Tyress was right, there was a figure descending. They were too far away to tell if it was a man or a woman. Surely it was some hardy Carqsara, though it was mighty late in the year to make such a journey. The trip through the pass was harsh, even in the high summer. The figure was wearing furs, but they looked ragged and ill-made. Even the Carqsar would have made them better than that. *Some shabby and shiftless vagrant – it has to be an outcast.*

The Carqsar didn't come to trade often, for they wanted little of the sea and had little enough for themselves, let alone enough to trade. Yet it was a weird place for there to be a homeless beggar. What had they been doing on the top of the barrier cliffs? And descending, what did they hope for from the mother sea? They could not have been living up there. When the winter came there was nothing to protect those upper lands from the winds off the sea. The full might of the storm would strike. It must be a Carqsara vagabond from beyond. There were no other people until you passed between the high pass of the Pasra and reached the stone circles they revered.

It has to be a Carqsara outcast. Shiskes stood and watched the figure moving down the pathway. It was a narrow path, and treacherous in parts, for whilst the people had in times before cut steps into the steeper parts to aid going up and going down, it was many years since anyone had bothered to maintain it. Even the tower in which the guards sat was looking a little worse for wear. The winter storms of last year had been fierce and had taken a toll on many buildings. The tower would be the last they would repair.

The person descending, whoever they were, was nimble enough though, for they made short work of all the difficulties, leaping lithely between steep parts and climbing without pause when an obstacle needed to be breached. They were very fit for a shiftless beggar. Shiskes wondered if they were more of a warrior. The thought gave him pause.

Why would a Carqsar warrior be coming here?

Whoever they were, it was going to take them some hours more to reach the ground and Shiskes men had begun to scatter and find themselves things to sit on or to lean against. They were a lazy bunch and couldn't even summon up the desire to stand behind Shiskes and look threatening for a while. At least the injured had the excuse of their impairments.

Shiskes scowled at them. Their lack of discipline would not make them look very professional or indeed threatening to the agile person descending from the barrier. But then, he knew that his leg would start to ache if he stayed upright the whole time it would take. So he too found himself a low rock next to the pillars marking the end of the path, sat there, waited, and tried to look imposing. Some of his guards were still a little restless but a quick sharp frown from him was enough to make them regretfully return to a more readied stance, albeit leaning or sitting, resting on some stone. Shiskes sat and stared up at the person descending as the figure got larger by the minute. There was something in the movement of her body and the supple agility of the step that made him wonder if it wasn't, strangely, a woman – a woman and a warrior.

The women of the Istsar were tough enough. Many women dived in the waters for clams and shellfish and brought up pearls from the deep also. Many also walked the waves and fished more dangerous waters. But it was only the men who undertook the deep-water fishing in the remotest fishing grounds. Anyway, there was quite enough work to be done in Haven to keep the women busy, taking what the fishermen brought and treating the catch aright. They were the makers, the reshapers of the catch. They mastered it and made of it all that must be made.

Shiskes knew many strong women, his dead wife the strongest of all, besides perhaps the Istsaru, the queen. But, sitting there on his rock, he had trouble believing that a woman, warrior or not, had crossed the high pass of Pasra mountains alone this late in the autumn. This woman must be hardier and tougher than any he had ever met. It was a hard thing for Shiskes to believe – especially of a Carqsara.

The climber was getting close now, so Shiskes rose to his feet. He saw her hands move quickly around and realised that she was checking all her weapons. She slipped her right hand to the pommel of the sword that was at her belt, but she did not draw it.

Shiskes felt that this was just prudence on her part. He nevertheless let his hand drop to his sword, but neither did he draw it. He waited patiently until she would be in the range of his voice. He signalled to his men to get up; this they did and came together into a rather untidy, ill-disciplined bunch. He sighed but did not shout more orders. She was, after all, one woman, and they were six men. She would be a fool to attack them. Two of his men carried the battle nets and leisters, and two more the three-pronged spears. The fifth had a large two-handed harpoon, which had four prongs at its end. Repaired, the weapons were deadly, and could easily skewer a sword wielder before they got close.

Shiskes's bastard sword was largely ceremonial in intent, although it was a real sword and he knew how to wield it. Anyway, if she was foolish enough to attack them, she would in a moment be caught in the battle nets and pierced with the spears and harpoon before she got even close to the limping master of the guards.

She was closer now so he raised his voice and called out. 'Hail, traveller. You enter our lands. Who are you, why do you come this way so late in the year?'

The warrior halted.

'I am of the Hardsar people,' she called back. She was a woman, he could see that now. 'We live in the mountains far to the east,' she said. She hesitated for a moment and then continued. 'I have travelled over the Pasra mountains to seek the Istsar people and their king.'

'We are the fisher people,' said Shiskes. 'Have you truly passed through the Pasra? It was late in the year to attempt it. How did you pass the Carqsar? They rarely like travellers in their lands and they would seize any who tried to travel the high pass without their permission. They are cautious and wary of people. They claim that way as their own.'

'I have crossed the Pasra and the way . . . the pass through the snow lands was perilous,' she responded, 'but I was sent here and so I came.'

Shiskes stared at her in silence for a while. So she had crossed the pass in the late autumn, and she was a woman and a young one too. She was very fit, but it was still a risky journey and not one he or anyone of his people, nor any woman Shiskes knew would have attempted.

'Are you alone?' he said. 'Or were there others in your band?'

She shook her head. 'I was sent alone. I come in peace.'

She had understood the intent of his question at once. Despite her answer, he wondered. Was there a war band on top of the barrier, waiting for their unwariness before descending? Yet who would send one woman down alone while stronger people waited at the top? And how would a war band pass the Carqsar? He sighed. This should be an easier task, being a guard at the barrier.

'What is your name, traveller?' Shiskes said.

'I am Terras of the Hardsar,' she said.

There was a murmur behind Shiskes as she called out her name. Hardsar simply meant mountain people in the sacred tongue, but Terras – now that was a name spoken of long ago.

As if prompted by the thought, Tyress stepped beside him. 'Did not the Mystic Fracos speak of "Terras who was lost" – lost by the Malasari and his champion in early times?'

Shiskes turned. At least he spoke not in the sacred tongue but the Istsara language. She would not understand if she had even heard the words at that distance.

Shiskes motioned Tyress backwards, replying in the same language. 'Now is not the time, Tyress. Be silent.'

Several other of the guards shifted nervously and whispered to each other. This angered him, for even if this was the lost woman warrior that Fracos had spoken of, that had been well over seventy years ago. Fracos was long dead. This young woman could not be the 'Terras who is lost'. She would be long dead too if she was lost three generations ago. No one lived that long, and this woman was young, very early in life.

Yet it was a strange coincidence of name, and that a traveller should appear now bearing that name and alone. Shiskes was unsure what to do. He was a fisherman, not a military leader or a man much given to mysticism. It really should be easier, being master of the guard tower. His task here was the lowest. The Havenguard did not respect the wounded and the wastrels that came to duty in the watch. That was why they sent them to this useless and pointless duty.

Shiskes spoke, calling out. 'Do you truly come

in peace, Terras Hardsara?'

She took her hand from her sword pommel where it had been all through the last few minutes. She raised her hands. 'I do come in peace, people of the fisherfolk. I come as I was commanded to come, not to fight, but to speak.'

'I am Shiskes,' he said, more confidently than he felt. 'Come then, Terras of the mountain. Approach us. We also do not seek conflict. Your name is known among us, from an old tale.'

The Hardsara woman did not question what he said but she began slowly to walk forward, descending the final way, jumping between broken steps and over rough ground. Her hand never touched her sword through it all, for Shiskes watched her, but the way she stood, the way she held herself was supremely confident. She knew herself and she knew her abilities. There was no fear of a misstep as she leapt from an awkward step to a broken path. She was in charge of everything around her. This woman was a warrior.

She reached but a short distance from him and stopped a dozen feet from the two stone pillars that marked the end of her trek. Shiskes stood and stared at her, his hand on his sword, but she kept hers well away from her weapon. Shiskes felt his guards moving, shiftless, behind him. They were as unused to this as he. The warrior woman looked very content with her situation. She knew exactly what she was about.

'Welcome to the Istsar lands, Terras. Your name is one known to us, though it is unlikely that the name we know was yours, for it was long ago. So what is your intent here? You say you were sent. Who was it who sent you?'

She hesitated at this, and then slowly spoke. 'I was sent,' she said, 'but let me speak my words before your king, for it is a hard thing to believe. I struggle myself to understand it. Let your king's wisdom hear my words and judge them for you all.'

Shiskes raised his head at that and peered. 'Our king is but a young boy.' He was not sure he should be telling her all this but he found himself doing it anyway. 'Our realm is ruled now in his place by the queen. She is the Master here while her son grows to manhood and proves his skill upon the realm of our mother the sea. Then he will be king. Until that day the queen will judge your words, Terras of the mountain.'

This seemed to please her momentarily, for the glimmer of a smile passed over her face. 'So why do you know my name, Shiskes Istsara?'

Shiskes shrugged. 'I think,' he said, 'that is for the queen to tell you if it pleases her. It is probably of no matter, an unimportant coincidence of name. For you cannot be the same . . .' He paused. 'The queen may choose to explain this oddity.'

She walked forward at this and stood before him. Still, her hands were well away from her weapons, although Shiskes's guards still milled about behind him in a disorganised way. He heard the soft sound of their oiled wetskins rustling and the clanking and clashing of ill-handled weapons.

He ordered two men to stay behind at the tower. If she was just a vanguard of a larger force still atop the barrier cliff then one could stay and watch them coming down while the second ran for more help from the Havenguard. He gave them their orders in the Istsar tongue so that, hopefully, she would not understand.

That left four of them to escort Terras to the city. She seemed quite undaunted at them forming up around her. Shiskes gave the order and they began their walk – even he could not call it a march. There were many crags and tumbled rocks between the bottom of the barrier cliff and the mainland portion of the city. The roadway to the tower had been made long ago and, whilst used each day, was crisscrossed with craggy rocks. The city of the shore was built on a small rise in the land, for sometimes, in the greatest of the storms, the seas swept in this far and the coastal part of the city became a smaller island between the cliffs and the true city of the isle, the true port of Haven. Then his little guard tower stood on the very seashore while the waves crashed around it. Those were not easy days when the mother brought the storms, but she was merciful and it was a rare day when the sea came so far. On those days the roadway they walked was a treacherous path, amid the waves, from city to the tower. But mother was compassionate and this day they walked in peace.

Terras looked around as they trudged but she made little comment. The afternoon was wearing towards its end as they passed the gates of the city. There was only one lazy guard at the gate and he never made any attempt to rise and greet them. Shiskes was a little ashamed that the guard did not challenge this stranger, but then strangers were rare and she was surrounded by the three tower guards and their master. He saw Terras look appraisingly at the walls. A worrying thought went through his head then, so Shiskes looked over at them too. Haven did have walls, but they were not large, and would not have resisted a determined attack by a foe. Shiskes knew that the Istsar did not fear attack from the mainland. They felt they owned this strip of land and most of the strip of land between mountains and the sea to the north and the south. They always believed that threats, if they came to them, would be from the sea. He watched Terras openly gaze at them and hoped it was just the habit of a seasoned fighter.

Still, they were only the walls of the shore city. The largest part of the city was on the isle, which was where the best harbourage was too, protected by curving outcrops of rock extended by the inhabitants with causeways and quays to form a much-protected harbour. It was there that Shiskes must take her, for it was there the queen would be. He let out a long silent sigh at the thought. *What am I getting into?*

They reached the harbour. The tide was

slipping out, although the harbour was built to maintain the waters deep enough for the vast majority of the day in all but the lowest of tides. There were other guards on the quayside but they knew Shiskes and his men so they also did not approach, nor even ask who the stranger in the disreputable set of furs was. So Shiskes hurried them to the guard boats on the farthest jetty and he and the men jumped into one without a moment's thought. Terras, despite her apparent natural agility, stepped more gingerly off the jetty with a look akin to apprehension on her face. *Surely this cannot be the first time she has boarded a ship or travelled on water?* The very thought was astonishing.

As they crossed the strip of sea between the mainland and the isle of Haven, they passed beyond the wharf and under the huge broken statue.

Terras spoke for the first time since leaving the guard tower. 'Whose statue is this?'

They all turned and looked at her in surprise. Did not all people know? Shiskes responded. 'It is a statue of our mother, the sea . . . it was broken long ago. We no longer have the skill in stonework our ancestors had so it has not been repaired, but we still know all that the sea is to us, for all that we have is from the sea. She is our mother, our protector, and our shelter, as well as our greatest peril. Such is the way of the sea.'

They rowed across the harbour at a good speed. All his men knew how to scull well. After all,

Shiskes and all the people lived their lives on the sea. Everything they were was linked to it. During the short trip, no one spoke, but they all just did what was required without the need for words.

As they approached the true harbour of Haven, swinging the boat round to a spot where they could land, Shiskes saw that there were more Havenguards on the shore. To his dismay, he realised that their leader was Trask. Trask did not like Shiskes, or any of the shirkers and injured that were given to the Havenguard for duty at the barrier tower. He was of the harbourwatch and he took his duty of guarding the harbour against interlopers very seriously. But, Shiskes thought, at least it wasn't his deputy, Noske. He was a really bad fish. The mother was merciful, perhaps.

Trask was there at the top of the steps before they had even tied the boat up. He stood on the quayside, glaring down. 'What is this, Shiskes? A traveller has come down the barrier cliff?' He spoke with utter disdain, although, for once, Shiskes could not tell if it was just for him or mostly for this strange fur-clad traveller.

'It is, Trask. She has asked to be taken to the queen.'

Shiskes and his men were on the steps now, and Terras, after another unsure jump from boat to land, had followed them calmly. She had not grasped her sword, even though Trask's manner towards them all was antagonistic. He had spoken in the fisherfolk language so she would not have understood his words, just their essence. Shiskes doubted Trask knew the sacred language well; many of the Istsar did not.

Trask sidestepped neatly past Shiskes as he limped to the last step and placed himself in front of Terras at the top of the steps. He could have thrust her back down them with but a slight movement. She met his gaze, unblinking.

'She is armed, Shiskes,' Trask said angrily, without looking back at him. 'Did you not think to disarm her before you brought her here, to the queen?'

Trask reached down at once, snatching the sword from Terras's scabbard, and drew it quickly out. Shiskes saw the reaction on Terras's face and he knew, even if Trask did not, that he had just made a mistake. He stepped back, swinging the sword.

'So, who are you, trav—'

Terras moved so fast that Shiskes could not believe the speed. She tapped the pommel of the sword in Trask's hand and snatched it somehow from his suddenly weakened fingers. She spun it around, held the point for an instant to Trask's nose. A little speck of blood appeared on the very tip. Then smoothly she scabbarded it again to her side.

'I am Terras, Hardsare of the mountain people,' she said. 'I come in peace to stand before your queen and speak vital words. You would do well to respect my people, my quest, and the three lords that I serve.' Trask seemed truly shocked that she had managed to disarm him so quickly. Terras's hand was now firmly on her sword handle. 'Do not disrespect me again, Istsara,' she said.

Trask's anger turned immediately on Shiskes. 'You bring a bitch-volf among us, Shiskes. The queen will punish you for this.'

'I am a guest here, Istsara,' said Terras, stepping upwards and forcing Trask back onto the quayside. 'I, Terras, claim guest privilege. Are the Istsar people so sullied that they do not entertain, in peace, guests who come to them? We are the bitter people. We don't permit discourtesy.'

Trask was signalling to the other guards now to gather around. But Shiskes could see that amongst them the name of this 'bitch-volf', Terras, which she had said twice now, was having the same effect on his men as it had on Shiskes's tower guards.

They gathered on Trask's order, but their hearts were not in it. Instead of straining forward to do their master's bidding, they were straining to see this 'Terras who was lost'. This stranger had spoken not only her name but also the rank of the person Fracos had spoken of as *Terras, Hardsare of the mountain, who was lost*. Everyone knew the story, for the Mystic Fracos had told it many times, and Shiskes knew as they all did the myths and songs that had developed around his words. He had said that Terras would be found. And when Terras came to them, the Malasari would return at last to the people and would release the fire and the storm. Shiskes knew he must speak now. He must take the mastery here before Trask escalated things. This was not a warrior to be treated as an easy fish. She was of the deep water.

'This is Terras, princess of the Hardsar, a name known to us.' Shiskes pursued the advantage that Terras's words had won. He spoke loudly as if the quay was his boat and he was master there. 'She must be honoured and taken before the queen, who will judge the truth.'

He looked at Terras. This woman was a mighty warrior, but she was, he knew in his bones, no threat. He did not see how this young woman could be the Terras that Fracos had spoken of so long ago, in his grandfather's time. Indeed, it was almost the time of his great-grandfather. But that question was not to be answered yet and not by him. The queen was wise; she would know what to do.

Trask was looking unsure, for he knew then that no order he gave his men, or Shiskes's, would mean much. They would not take up arms against her in case she was the one from the prophecy. 'The queen will settle this,' he snarled, 'but woe betide you, Shiskes, if her judgement goes against you.'

Terras looked up into the city beyond. 'Where is the stronghold of the king?'

Trask laughed boorishly.

Shiskes felt the need to explain. 'We will not find the queen in any stronghold, Terras. She will be here, in the harbour. The Istsari do not live in palaces.

They live amongst us, for on a boat, captain or lowest hand, all must work the nets and rope, or the ship will flounder.'

He pushed through the knot of guards and indicated to Terras to follow. They stepped away from Trask, but most of his men, along with Shiskes's own, followed curiously behind. They walked to the centre of the harbour and there she was, with a group of men and women, as well as her young son, the king, mending the nets from the boats that had fished the night. Shiskes knew she was always somewhere like this, Narcise. Queen of the Istsara, queen of the way in the sea, fisherfolk like them all. She looked up as they all approached. They had gathered quite a crowd by now, and the news was travelling even faster than Shiskes thought possible. More and more of the Istsar were assembling as they arrived. Queen Narcise, the Istsaru, gazed at them. 'I saw the squall on the dock. Will you require me, or the king, Master Shiskes?'

Terras had stopped beside Shiskes and the two women locked eyes. The queen rose, taking in the crowd of guards and onlookers that were quickly gathering.

'Are you a traveller then and you have come to our shores?'

Terras smiled a wan smile. 'I am, Istsari of the fisherfolk.'

The queen reacted to the incorrect title but did not speak.

'My name is Terras, I am the princess of my people, the Hardsar. We live far away in the mountains of the east. I was sent here, queen, to give a message to your people.'

'Who sent you?' said the queen. She motioned to her son, the king, who was eight years old, and he dropped the net he was mending and ran to stand alongside her. 'And what is the message?'

Terras paused and looked at the crowd around her as if she wondered whether her message was to be spoken before all those gathered. She did not know the Istsar people well if she thought that. There were no secrets on a boat that would not come to light. They disavowed chiefs, kings or priests. The leaders, the Masters that they had were the servants of the people:

The sea is our mother.
Under her, all serve
for the sea clothes
and gives life.

Shiskes knew the words of the refrain, but Terras, he knew, did not. Terras was responding to the Istsaru. He had missed some of her words.

'. . . and I entered a stronghold, a fortress on the other side of the Pasra mountains, queen, and there, separated from my prince, I met, alone, Franeus the True. He said he could not yet leave the Everlasting Caves, but the time has already come when the Malasari walks the world again. Franeus sent me to the Istsar, to tell them this and to ask their aid. He said the crystal storm would be needed. That the Istsar . . .' She paused as if unsure of what to say next.

Nobody cared, for there was a great stir in the crowd as she spoke these words. Shiskes was amazed, for these were so close to the words, the prophecies that the Mystic Fracos had taught to the folk. But Shiskes was confused. There was no way this young woman could be the same Terras that Fracos had spoken of back in his grandfather's time. Everyone now, but a few, felt that Fracos had been a false mystic. It was beyond Shiskes's understanding. Narcise did not react as her people did, but stretched out her arm and took her son into her embrace. He went easily and happily, falling into his mother's arms, accepting the hug she gave him as the most natural of things to do at that moment.

'This is my son,' she said. 'His name is Mascrise. He is and was the beloved of my husband, the king, and the only consequence of our love. My king died, for our mother the sea took him, and now he, Mascrise, will be the king here, master and servant of the people of the fleet. We are the offspring of the sea, Terras of the mountain, and the sea gives us life and takes it from us too. I am but Istsaru. My son is the king.'

A look of sadness crossed Narcise's features. Shiskes knew she was thinking of her mate. Their love had been, for such a short time, legendary. Narcise looked up at the sky and then slowly down to the sea lapping against the quays of Haven. She sat down again amid the nets she had been mending, taking her son into her lap.

'In the time of his father's father, there was among us a young man. His name was Fracos. He was a restless boy and did not want to live on the sea, to walk the waves and take his life from it alone. He did not want, he said, to see nothing else of the world. So, one day, when he was too young to become an adult, he left his father's boat and he climbed the barrier path to cross the Pasra mountains when it was summer and the route was less perilous. He wanted to see, he said, and nothing would prevent him.

'He came back to us eventually, and he returned strangely and was forever mystical. He came with a storm about him and he was touched by the power of the storm ever after. He spoke and taught of a fortress, a stronghold on the edge of the Pasra mountains where a plain as endless as the ocean begins. He was captured there by evil men, who imprisoned and hurt him.' Narcise turned her gaze from her son to the Hardsar woman before her. 'Did evil men send you here Terras Hardsare?'

Terras squatted down before the queen and slid quietly, effortlessly into a cross-legged position. Shiskes felt that he too should sit down on the floor. He did, and the crowd behind them also sat, the action rippling out like a great wave of people. Narcise looked round.

'I was not, Istsaru. I serve the three lords. I was

sent by the Left Hand.'

'Trask,' Narcise said at once. 'Ring the bell. It is a mustering. All the people must come. For we speak.'

Trask moved hastily to the bell. The scowl was gone now from his face and replaced instead by the same amazement that Shiskes and all the gathered Istsar felt. He pushed his way through the crowd, which quickly separated to let him through. In the centre of the quay was a tall tower formed of great wehla bones. It was hollow and open and there the mustering bell was suspended in its interior. He ran to it and tugged quickly on the rope. The bell sounded around Haven, and even those who had not already arrived would have looked up from their work and known that the queen had summoned the fleet. Narcise spoke rapidly in the Istsar tongue and one woman raised her hand in response. She turned back to Terras.

'We are quiet people, Terras Hardsare. Not all my people know the sacred tongue as well as they might. We see few strangers, fewer still in recent years. Barques here has volunteered to translate your words to the muster.' Terras nodded without looking at the woman who had come to sit beside her. Shiskes shuffled back, out of their way. The queen turned her attention back to her.

'So, Terras, Hardsare, how do we know that the evil men of the fortress before the ocean of plains beyond the mountain did not send you here? Tell us the whole tale before you invoke the hidden Left Hand of the ancients.'

Barques repeated the words in the tongue of the Istsar and they were repeated back through the now enormous crowd, a constant, whispering accompaniment to the conversation.

Terras slowly shook her head. 'There are indeed evil warriors who use the fortress. They attacked our quest and took one of our party. We chased them across the plain, running with the people who dwell upon it. We reached it, my prince and I, and we—'

'And what was the name of your prince, Hardsare?' Narcise looked only mildly interested as if she was merely mindful of getting the full story. Shiskes knew better.

Terras replied, happy to answer fully. 'My king-to-be was Halam, lately of the city by the lake, but now he is the prince among my people.'

As Barques relayed this information it caused another stir amongst the gathered crowds. The queen said nothing to this and did not respond to the whispers of excitement around her. She just nodded and waited for Terras to continue. 'When we reached the fortress, we ran into it, and suddenly he was gone, and I was alone.' Narcise nodded and stroked her son Mascrise's long hair as he sat in her lap. She smiled across at the Hardsare.

'When I entered the fortress,' Terras continued, 'I found no evil men but a vision of Franeus only. He called it a casting. He was waiting for me. He sent me here. He said that you were waiting for me, people of the sea, you were expecting me, and you would know me. And you would hear the message I was sent to bear.'

Narcise waited while Barques translated these words, then she responded softy, like the sea lapping the southern shores beyond the desert. 'And who was it, of your party, that was lost – taken? You did not speak his name.'

Terras seemed for a moment to pause. Then she decided and spoke strongly, firmly, as one who is sure of their way. 'His true name is not spoken, nor is it yet remembered. He is known as the Rissar na Rishugn amongst my people. We are the bitter ones. It is our gift to know him. He is the Malasari. He has returned.'

Narcise did not respond at once but a ripple of excitement followed Barques's repetition of the words. The muster was almost out of control. A storm was brewing among the people of the sea. Shiskes felt like a man standing on the shore as the full force of the sea takes and gnaws at it. He was not in control of what was coming.

Narcise spoke. 'We were told of a princess of the mountain people, Terras by name, who was lost to her prince. His name was Halam and he was the champion, it was said, of the Malasari, the one who is to come, who will give us the clear ocean as our domain forever – for the waves we walk are but the first embrace of our mother. She will heed his voice and give us the crystal deep as our sovereignty. For the ocean is the gift that sustains, refreshes and cleanses. We are its offspring. The sea is our life and the mother of all that we are as a people. When the Malasari comes the ocean will be ours forever.'

Terras did not look as amazed as Shiskes felt she should at this pronouncement. He, at least, was astounded.

Terras spoke. 'Franeus said that when we enter the fortress through the stone archway before it, each person enters a different fortress, that we travel by it to different ages. I do not understand what he meant, but he said Halam did not enter the same stronghold as me. I lost him. We thought the Malasari was taken there too, and who knows which age he went to.'

'Then there are prophecies of ours to comfort you. These are the words of Fracos,' Narcise said, 'for he returned to us suddenly, carried on a bolt of lightning, with the storm around him. He told us he had met with the One, the Malasari that was returned to the world. And his name was Lord Rissar. Fracos came upon him with a great champion who had freed them of the grasp of evil. The champion's name was Halam and he was a prince, called Hardsaro, who wielded a great sword. He said that the One was coming and we must await his return. He said the Malasari told him that Terras, who was lost, would be found and then . . .'

Narcise paused and her son sat up and looked

across at the Hardsare. Young as he was, he knew something was happening and the king should be paying attention. Narcise continued.

'But that was three generations ago, and Seer Fracos lived among us and taught us all these things – until the sea took him. Still . . . we waited. We looked and we fished, but the Malasari did not come, and Fracos's words did not come true. Many among the fleet doubted, though some remained aboard his words . . . Then an idea arose, I am not sure when or how, for it was not what the words of Fracos told us. The idea came that until the princess who was lost, Terras of the mountain was found, then and only then would the Malasari return.'

Narcise stopped. Shiskes waited, eagerly, for Terras's next words. A look of puzzlement passed over her face and then slowly some sort of joy.

'So . . . this Fracos. He saw Halam with the Malasari, with Lord Rissar in the fortress. Halam found the Malasari and freed him?' Terras said. 'And this was three generations ago . . .'

'He did not say he freed the Malasari. Fracos said that the champion freed him and others. When the champion had freed them he made them run through the dolmen, into the very face of the evil warriors. He said he transported them to another night. But Fracos did not understand that. He took them somewhere where the evil was not. And there the Malasari waited for them.'

At this Terras looked delighted, if

simultaneously confused. 'So Lord Rissar escaped. The quest will continue!' She cried it out. 'They can go to Arnex.'

'So the Seer told us in his prophecies, in his stories.' Narcise paused. 'And now you are found.'

It was like the clouds of a storm clearing suddenly into the blue sky. Terras dissolved into smiles. 'I was not lost. I travelled alone to you. I am here because Franeus sent me to you. I obeyed to come to you because my people are sworn, sworn to obey the three. But I did not truly know, or truly believe that he could be telling me the truth.'

Narcise smiled back. 'Well, we don't know that yet, Terras. These are but stories that the Mystic Seer told us. What did Franeus tell you to say to us, beyond the telling of your story?'

Terras nodded. 'He said to tell the Istsar that I have come because the One is coming, and he will need them. He said he will come with fire. He said I must persuade you to ready yourselves. To bring the storm. To listen for the signs. Great is the battle that is coming upon the world and all peoples must be ready for it.'

Narcise rocked back on her heels and pulled her son closer into her lap. 'A war? As in ancient times . . .'

'I do not know, Istsaru, truly I do not. I give you the words he gave me. He told me to tell you to be ready. Then, he said, that once I have told you, and you have believed, I must ask you to give me passage into the south, to the lands beyond the stone desert. There, he said, I must head for an ancient tomb, a mausoleum, and there I would finally understand.'

'I have not yet believed, Terras of the mountain. My people have not yet believed. I do not want war for my people or any other. We do not worry about other people. We fish the ocean and the mother gives us food and all the things we have. No one comes here, or rarely, and we would keep it that way. We do not seek war, nor do we wish to wage it on anyone.'

Terras nodded. 'No one does, queen, and I said as much to Franeus, but he responded that some things are inevitable and cannot be avoided, turned aside from. Some things come whether we wish them or not.'

Narcise did not like this answer, and it showed on her face. She quietly stroked the hair of her son. Then reluctantly she slowly nodded. 'That is true of the sea as well. Sometimes friend and mother, sometimes death and devastation.'

'So it is in all lands,' Terras said. 'Our mountains give us life, but they also break us at times. Sometimes before our time ...' She paused as if thinking of something. 'I even thought I might die crossing the Pasra to reach you, queen. But the snow did not win and I made it here.'

The queen nodded. 'You were lucky to cross this late in the year. The pass will have been very treacherous. Another week and you would have failed.' She stared across at Terras. 'And you did this to bring these words to us.'

'I did, queen of the fishers, because the Left Hand commanded. I would rather stand beside my prince, the man you call the champion of the Malasari. I came because I was sent. I will travel to the tomb in the stone desert because that was commanded too. This I will do, whether you aid me or not. Whether you believe or not.'

Narcise smiled. 'We will take you south, Terras, we have many ships to command. The fleet is very great. And, whether they believe or I believe, they will do this because I will ask them. And until my son walks the waves, I am Master here. But the priest who commanded you, we know his name, but we do not know him except as a legend of ancient years. We have no priests here. No man, or woman, stands between us and the mother, or her lord, who is the Snake god. We are the fisherfolk. Everyone walks the waves. Everyone works the boat. We are that, and we are the same.'

She paused and looked up at the sky again, absently stroking the head of her son. 'Fracos was a mystic, and sometimes they arise amongst us, and speak words, dream dreams, words of truth sometimes, and sometimes words that they speak to bring them profit. It is for the people to judge a seer and know whether they are true. This is the way of the people. If they speak true words, they are true. If they ask forever for themselves and their gain, then they are false. Then we have no dealings with them. We judge. The people judge. They must judge whether you are true as well. We have no priests to tell us what is true.'

Terras said, 'So it is with my people, queen. There is but one priest, and that is the Left Hand, Franeus the True, but him we are sworn to obey.'

Narcise leant back again. 'Good answer, Terras. Come, this is enough for this mustering, for the day is late and the fleet of the deep must set sail for the night. I would not delay it further. I will take you to my lodging. We will eat. My people gathered here will think on the words of this muster and they will tell me their thoughts. You must carry your words to the towns and villages to the south and the north and we will listen to their thoughts too. The people of the sea will hear, and we will decide whether to heed your warning. But it seems on this night that Fracos was a true seer and spoke words to us that are true, for you have come. Those who follow his words still will be overjoyed that he was a fair seer and spoke truly.'

◈ Chapter 8 ◈

As the fire of the night faded, the woman looked up at the new day around her. The sun had risen and she turned to consider her companions of the fire. It was a new day. The fire had not spoken. Another night had passed in silence.

Did that mean they had obeyed correctly? That they would find the kings of ancient times? Or did it mean they walked now in error?

The Eye had risen to his feet and was walking and doing all the tasks of a new day, scattering the fire as their brothers and sisters of the guard in ancient times had done. He glanced over at her, curious at her gaze. 'Did the fire speak to you, Trioch?'

She looked across at him. 'No, Helmar. It was silent.' They both turned to their brother Sigmor who slowly shook his head but did not speak. They were doing their best to do the correct thing, to go where it seemed they had been sent. First, they had walked for many treacherous miles through the narrow valleys between their lands of the ice on the north-western coast. They headed for the great plain that Trioch had heard of but never seen. In that difficult way, there had been on one side the great mountain range of the west, the Pasra. On the other, the edge of the land of fire that had been theirs in the times before its destruction.

Trioch and, she was sure, Sigmor and Helmar

desired to walk again in those lands where their cities had been. She would have given much to see them. But, so the fire had spoken long ago, they should not walk it, nor see their great lord again until they strode alongside the king. Then would come the glorious fire.

As they reached the foothills where the Pasra and the northern range ended, they had traded with the primitive people of the Stones for hacsar. They had reached, at last, the great plain of which Trioch had been told. She had never seen it. Never before ridden the hacsar upon its vastness. They had ridden south. Each sunset they had stopped and sung the fire, chasing the night from the world.

Each day they woke from the song and travelled south. So it would be until the king came and they stood before him. Then the words of the fire would be proved. Trioch struggled to contain the wonder of the thought.

◎

So the journey began again.

Rissar rode in front, in silence, the jaksar stretched uncomfortably across his lap as he rode – strangely sleeping despite hanging quite precariously. Halam rode behind with the elder, Jored of the mace, at his side. Rosart hung back as if he still doubted his right to travel with them or still had things he wished to ponder and did not want to be disturbed. Halam, turning and looking back in his saddle, was amazed at the change in the woodsman. Rosart had not struck him as a man given to much introspection. Rosart was a man of action, confidence; surety flowed from him whenever he spoke. He had been all envy and jealousy.

But something had altered in him. There was some change here greater than that wrought by his foolishness in trying to wrest the staff from the jaksar. Something was weighing on his mind. Something had struck at his very sense of being, of his self-awareness. Halam turned back and caught Jored staring at Rosart too, an equally strange look on his face. When Jored caught Halam's gaze on him, he said nothing but spurred his mount on, forward, away from both Halam and the woodsman. Perhaps he too did not want to talk of change and doubt.

They rode on in an uneasy silence. Halam recollected Terras running across the ground to knock Rosart down. He remembered the anger in her; he saw Rosart sitting on the ground, not attempting to rise, not attempting to fight back, and in that impassiveness admitting his failure. Was that all, or was there something else here?

As Halam rode on he wondered if perhaps it was his sense of defeat that had made Rosart so keen to return for the Hardsar host. He had pushed Hewas hard to do just that and had persuaded the king that to bring all the Hardsar host was the best thing. Perhaps he regretted that decision too, as Hewas did. Which made Halam think of Hewas.

Halam could not quite credit the wonder of

their return. In the flash of Rissar's staff, the night had fled. The sun leapt into the sky and in a moment it was already several hours into the sky. Halam had been shocked. He had gaped, open-mouthed. All around them were tents, campfires and thousands of people. It was the Hardsar. They had come. The king had brought them as he promised, and now here they were encamped before the fortress, ready for their assault on it. And the fortress had awaited them, enormous in its power yet hidden from them in its endless unbeing.

Fracos and Derar had gone – to what fate Halam did not know. Perhaps they had never been people of his age and Rissar's staff had returned them to a different destiny that would be forever beyond his knowledge.

Halam and Rissar's arrival, so sudden, into the midst of the Hardsar host had caused a massive stir. There was much brandishing of weapons and cries of challenge until they had been recognised, and the shock of their arrival was replaced with a sort of joy. The Hardsaro had returned and he had brought the Malasari with him! Halam had proven his prowess. He had proven his worthiness to be their prince.

But Halam felt no pride in his choice to go to the fortress with Terras. Yes, the fortress could not be beaten with a force of arms. Yes, Rissar could not be returned to them by force of arms. But there was no pride in being right. He had lost Terras. How could he feel pride in some vaunted victory? How could he be admired as a worthy prince when by it he had lost the Hardsare?

Hewas had come, and Halam could see in his eyes that he felt the same. He had asked Halam. He had turned to look at Halam and there were twin sadnesses in his face. He had been wrong to return. He had lost his daughter. He had said, 'Hardsaro, your princess went on this journey too. What was her destiny? Halam, where is Terras? Where is my daughter?' This was not the king, this was the father, anxious for the daughter he loved. His eyes burned with a ferocity – the power of love for an only child. Halam had not been able to reply. He felt paralysed by guilt and doubt. How could he tell this man that he did not know her fate, that she was somewhere other? That she wandered, lost and confused, like he had, years in the future or the past?

Rissar replied before Halam could speak any empty words.

'She too is doing the will of the Snake god, Hardsari. Is this not the calling of the Hardsar, Hewas, king? You are the bitter people. You go where there is sadness, you go where there is need to do. You go when others flinch. Franeus has sent her elsewhere, to learn of other things and to complete greater tasks.'

Hewas had turned to look at the Malasari and slowly, reluctantly, he had replied. 'May she prove worthy of the task,' he said and he bowed. He was not content, not convinced. His voice had echoed his wrestling between the duties of a king and the love of a father. As his head rose it was the king that won, but the father would never cease to love. She was his child.

At these thoughts of the look on Hewas's face, Halam joggled his mount forward. He felt his many failures keenly. He knew, in his own heart, that he had done very little in the fortress except fail. Indeed, through the whole quest, he seemed simply to lurch from one failure to the next. He had not been the great warrior they thought him to be. He had not rescued Rissar from the clutches of the enemies. He had just found him sitting by a campfire, waiting for them all to arrive. He realised, and a wave of depression swept over him, Rissar had truly not been in need of rescue; the Malasari would have returned eventually. How demeaning it would have been to have been rescued by the man he had gone to rescue in the first place? Perhaps all any of them had needed to do was wait, wait until Rissar chose to return. *Has all we have done been pointless?*

His only act of courage had been his refusal to leave the stronghold when they tried to force him. That had resulted somehow in his sword returning to aid him. Yet, he wondered, how many of the prisoners had failed to escape? Most of all, he remembered the Solpsar woman dying in the purple flames. He had been frightened, he had been scared they would take him from the Citadel, the only place that he believed could ever return him to his age. It was not courage that had driven him. It was fear. He had even been wrong in that, of course. It too had been an act of stupidity. For wherever they had taken him in that world he could, on escape, have returned to the fortress, and then somehow to this, his age. He had not needed to fear. He had escaped with Fracos and Derar but how many prisoners had died? They had been the price of his panic.

If all this was just the will of the Priest-King, how many had died for that design? Though perhaps all the failures were Halam's alone. He glanced back at Rosart the woodsman, riding quietly behind him, his bow, unstrung, strapped over his shoulder. He was a true Hardsar and strong in his skills. He was worthy of Terras. Halam had been the one to gain her – and the one to lose her. Rosart need not feel any envy of such a one as he. Rosart was the strong man, trained and tough, like the giant mace-wielding lord, Jored, riding now beside Halam. They were worthy.

He had met Jored as they had walked to the inevitable ponderous Hardsar council that followed their return. As they walked to Hewas's tent, the tall, muscled Hardsara elder came into step beside him. He towered at least a foot above Halam, if not slightly more, and the breadth of his shoulders was at least double that of the Aallesara. He spoke and his voice was booming and deep.

'I am Lord Jored. I have not been able to welcome you before, Hardsaro, nor declare that you have my service and the service of my people. We are of the mace. We live in the heights and forge our hammers in metal we mine in the mountains of the Wasra. I acknowledge and uphold the decision of the Hardsare. May she soon be returned to us.'

Halam had looked across at the Hardsara. He carried no weapons now but he glowed with strength. He was trained to perfection. Halam could imagine this lord wielding a great mace, mowing down the enemy before his path. 'Thank you, Jored, I welcome your service and I seek your aid. I have much to learn about my new people.'

The Hardsar elder had nodded back to him. He had seemed very satisfied with the words and very accepting of his new prince. Halam looked back at him and felt small beside his towering bulk; he wondered how he could ever be the king of such a man. *I am no Hewas,* he thought.

They had reached Hewas's tent and sat down in a circle. Rissar sat beside the king and Hewas indicated that Halam should sit on his other side. Around them, ten other Hardsar elders had arrived and sat down around them. The group settled into silence. Halam waited patiently for something to be said. At last, as the silence grew long, Hewas spoke.

'We have but lately arrived here, Lord Rissar. We crossed the plain as quickly as we might and the Torasar have not stood against us. They scout us and our scouts have seen their herds moving closer. The clans of the Torasar move always with their herd so they are mustering their forces before they come to us and demand of us the reason we cross their land without leave.' The elders around him had all sagely nodded their heads at this. Hewas continued. 'It did not seem good to me regarding the urgency of our arriving here that we should waste time discussing this matter with them. We had the word of Torem giving us leave. He probably meant only the four of the party, but I decided to assume that leave was enough to bring the whole Hardsar nation.' He hesitated. 'However, we will need to talk with them, else that boldness may result in conflict. At the least, there will be harsh words. We are not liked by the people of the plain.'

Rissar nodded. 'I hear you, Hewas, Hardsari. This was why we decided the quest was to be small. We have no wish to offend the Torasar.'

Hewas bowed his head. 'I hear you. In this matter, the wisdom of the Hardsaro and Hardsare has proved the greater. They went to assail the stronghold while Rosart and I returned for the host. We were in error. We saw the fortress and our fear overcame us. We felt that only a force of arms could achieve it.'

Rissar inclined his head. 'So learn a new thing, Hewas Hardsari. The fortress is daunting. Its true strength is greater than you know. Do not blame yourself. There will always be things that cannot be easily understood. The end of wisdom, the end of learning is as far as the sky and stars are above the world.'

A murmur of stern assent came from the surrounding men.

'So then . . . elders,' Rissar continued, 'what is the solution? Where is the next step? The quest is urgent. The Destroyer has already delayed us. We cannot travel quickly with this number of the host about us. And you are right, you must talk to the Torasari and gain his leave to pass. And beg his forgiveness for any presumption.' There was a little stir among the elders at the word, but no one spoke. 'How shall we move?'

Hewas looked Rissar in the eyes. 'Shall I take the people back to our lands?' This was not his choice, that much was clear in his voice. Another noble leant forward. He was a small man, yet about his chest were strapped at least twenty daggers. 'My lord, may I speak?'

Rissar had turned and considered him. 'Hurga, lord of the dagger, we are listening.'

'Many is the year our people have waited for this time. Many generations desired this day. Your purpose was to go quickly and with a small number. This is still wisdom, we see that. But can the gathered people not perform some service? Is there not a thing you wish done? We would all wish to accompany you. Can't we follow? Perhaps to distract the attention of those who would thwart you in your purpose.'

And so it had, eventually, been decided. The Hardsar nation would first make peace with the

Torasar. Much to his regret, Hewas had acknowledged that he had to be the one to stay with the people for he would need to speak, king to king, to the Torasari.

Then they had spoken of who should go ahead of the host. Rissar had asked Halam to go. Much to his dismay, the king had asked Halam to decide which others were to go.

Halam had chosen Rosart at once. He was not sure why, but he found himself saying. 'Rosart, son of Herfa, has won a place in the quest. He ran with us across the plains. He desired to come from the day we met him. He would have it no other way. He should come.'

Rissar had called that wisdom but Halam still wondered in himself whether it had been guilt. For the fourth member, Halam had turned to Jored, for in council he had pressed Halam on the subject of Terras. So Halam chose him. He said, 'I will speak the name of Jored, for he fears what I fear and if he comes he may aid me in doing all that may be done to return our Hardsare.'

◎

They rode into the silence of their uncertainties – Rosart with his internal struggles, whatever they were, Halam with his doubts, Jored with his duty, and Rissar leading. Behind them, the tents of the Hardsar army dwindled until they were but a smudge on the horizon. The day marched on and they rode in silence. As they continued, Halam became aware of another great black mass far to the east. He stared at it for a long time but could not make out what it was.

'That it is one of the herds of the Torasar,' Jored said, riding beside him and following Halam's gaze. 'They tend mighty beasts of the plains, huge they are, grey-brown. From these great creatures, the Torasar take all their needs. Their clothes are woven of the hair of the beast, they eat only its meat, and some say they even drink of its blood. Their skins make the tents in which they live, the bones make their utensils, their tools. It is also said that the best of their spears are carved from the great bones of the beasts, though all the Torasar I have ever seen carry wooden spears for which they steal trees of the forests that skirt our land. They fit them with sharpened bone and metal points.'

Halam and Jored considered the great herd, the mass of giant beasts moving in its slow way. 'They will not come to us, they are moving to join the other herds. As Hewas Hardsari said, the Torasar are massing their strength before they come before him. In battle, the Torasar use the stampeding beasts. It is a fearsome thing. Hewas will have a mighty host of the plain standing against him should the talk with the Torasari go awry. The Torasari will not be pleased that we have moved from our ancestral lands, nor that we cross their plain. Let us hope there is no bloodshed.'

The packs strapped to their hacsar mounts

were fully stocked with food and as the sun reached the zenith, Rissar slowed his pace, turned, and suggested they dismount and eat. They did not stop though, but led their steeds for a while, resting them from the burden of carrying them and eating as they walked. The hacsar rested and they also ate as they went, for Rissar did not set an overly quick pace. Halam realised how hungry he was. He had eaten last as he sat in the dungeon of the fortress and then only of old bread and stale water. This Hardsar food was plain but good. He drank deep of his water-skin.

They walked well into the afternoon. Then, mounting again, they rode on. They stopped early before the darkness fully came and set the fire, burning some of the dry grasses around them with sticks from the stubby dry trees that sprouted there.

As darkness fell, behind them in the far distance Halam could see the many fires of the Hardsar host, fringing the horizon, as if a thousand stars had fallen to earth and lay scattered and broken upon the ground, flickering and twinkling their distress.

Halam tethered the hacsar, yet loosely so that they could feed freely from the grass of the plain. He watered them whilst the others sat around the fire and talked. He was happy to do it and to have a moment alone, away from the fire.

Hard, bright stars shone above him accompanied by the light of the twin moons. He stood and looked at the world around him, savouring it. He gazed again at the flickering fires of the Hardsar, distant almost beyond his sight. He remembered the strange lights of the far future. It was better to be here; this was understandable, containable, and liveable. That future age was not his place. He had not understood it.

He was in the age that gave him birth and he was alive. However frightening the problems were, however many things were wrong, and however many horrors lay ahead of them, this was his place, his home; this whole world was his world and he wanted none of any other. Halam walked back towards the fire. The others were talking, but he could not make out the words. Their conversation was mumbled, quiet words that were not meant for everyone to hear. But he caught Jored speaking to the Malasar.

'Will there be another attack, lord? Is there some way we can be prepared if the people who set upon the quest return?'

Halam moved and sat down next to Jored at the fire. Perhaps these were questions he should have been putting. Rosart was sitting silently, listening to the talk. Halam could tell his mind was not on it. Insnar was sleeping, peaceful, with his head in Rissar's lap. Rissar answered Jored's question.

'The next attack will be different, Jored. Raczek will not face me directly. They have learnt fear. They will do a new thing. Let us hope they think we seek to protect ourselves from such an attack by staying with the army of the Hardsar. Hurga hoped that they would direct their attention to the Hardsar host and the massed Torasar, and miss us travelling quickly ahead. Sadly, I do not think that will fool them for long. An attack on us will come. But how I do not know. Their strategy will be complex. It always is. It always was.'

Halam leant forward. 'Will Uknor return?'

Rissar gazed impassively across at him but the others recoiled, shocked into silence. Now even Rosart was taking an interest. 'Franeus has told you much, I see. Yes, Uknor will return, though I warned him not to come.' He looked at Rosart and Jored. 'Uknor the Destroyer was the leader of our opponents. Romul is his true name. I have cast him to a place that he will have difficulty returning from. Despite my words, he will come, and he will bring the dragon – but not yet. Those Hraddas who remain will underestimate us, I think. They do not know who the Hardsar were. They think they are gone from the world. They believe the Offspring of power were scattered and lost long ago. But they were merely hidden, their songs are veiled. They have not yet realised what they face. No, they will not understand. So they will think to regain the victory they let slip through their fingers. They will challenge us again – to prevent us.'

Jored leant forward. 'Do we then fight against the Hraddas – the forces of the dragon? Was that battle not over a thousand years ago? Before the

Hardsar came to the mountains, before they even took the name *Hardsar*? When there was another name.'

Rissar looked across at him. 'Yes, Jored, they come – that battle is not complete. The old song was sung and it was silenced. But their victory was only for a time. Now it is time to sing a new song.'

Jored nodded, yet he was unsure. 'My lord, is it for this that we go to awaken Arnex?'

'Yes, Jored, the new song has begun. It is around this campfire.'

Rosart spoke then, quickly, spilling his thoughts. 'What will happen, Lord Rissar, when Arnex has awoken? Will the Kingdom of the Malasar return at once? Will the dragon come and be vanquished? Will all be returned to its proper place?'

Halam knew that the woodsman meant Terras.

Rissar looked at the Hardsara and shook his head. 'Not yet, the enemy will come to understand again the true nature of the world. Yet, for the new song, the Three must unite. But, then the fight against the dragon will only begin.'

Jored looked up. 'So having found Arnex must we then seek Franeus?'

Rissar inclined his head, but he was not agreeing. 'Franeus waits on the Sublime Isle and the Everlasting Caves. Such is his place until Arnex awakes. He will remain there. Arnex must awake before the dragon understands his peril. Then the Sublime Isle will be restored. All will be gathered and

Franeus will come, have no fear.'

Halam remembered Franeus, sitting awaiting him in the room of the fortress, waiting in his chair until he came and . . . what was it that he had said when Halam had left? *'There are other things for me to do.'* The words suddenly had a new meaning and Halam felt some concern for that old man standing against the dragon. He turned his attention back to the campfire and those few gathered around it.

'Where is the Sublime Isle, my lord?' Rosart was now taking a real interest in the conversation, eager and animated once more.

Rissar hesitated then replied, but with a question. 'Far to the south, Rosart, what is there?'

Halam answered at once. 'The Southlands, from where the traders come to the lake city. Beyond that is stone. No one crosses the stone desert. It is wholly barren and without any love for travellers. There is a sickness there too, that those who attempt it catch and often die.'

Rissar nodded. 'You speak the truth. And then beyond the stone desert, what is there?'

'The sea,' said Jored, 'only the sea.'

'No, Jored, there is more. First, there are the lands in which the Willsar dwelt, ruined and deserted now. Then, there is a sea, and in that southern sea is the Isle of Willsar. It was the capital of their lands in times gone by, before the fall of the Malasar. The Isle of the Maven it was called. Franeus was their king, priest and the Great Maven. It is the Sublime Isle.'

Halam leant forward. 'There are words of this in the temple scrolls,' he said, but he could not call the words to his mind, so he said no more and sat back.

'Yes, there are,' Rissar said, and he leant his head back and stared up at the stars, 'and may it be Sublime again.'

'So be it,' said Jored. 'I knew this, but its whereabouts in the world, the tales of the Hardsar do not tell.'

Rissar stretched. 'Let us sleep then. It may be a long day tomorrow. We have far to go and many days of travel ahead.'

Jored rose at once. 'I shall take the first watch.' Rissar stroked the head of the jaksar sleeping in his lap. 'Insnar will wake us if aught approaches.' Jored looked down with some suspicion at the sleeping form of the jaksar, snoring gently on his master's lap. He clearly had doubts about the wisdom of trusting their fate to such a one.

Halam shook his head. Insnar had more wisdom than many people he knew. He prepared for sleep. In a very few moments, he had unrolled his bed, and, taking a last sip of water from his water-skin, he laid his head down upon the hard pillow of the earth. He was asleep as his head touched the ground.

His sleep that night was deep and dreamless and, from its darkness, he struggled to wake when the morning came. At last, like a man reaching the top of a great tower after hours of climbing, he opened his eyes and looked up at a cloudless blue sky.

He sat up. Jored was sitting by the fire, warming some strange food in a little metal pot. He looked over as Halam awoke.

'You wake at last!' He smiled. 'It is late, but Rissar would not let me disturb you. He said you were tired and need sleep.'

Halam pulled himself upright and stared about. 'Where is Rissar?'

Jored indicated wordlessly with the wooden spoon he held in his hand. Halam looked and saw that the Malasar was sitting some way to the north of the camp, staring into the distance. Insnar sat beside him, staring also at the dark smudge that might mark the mountains of the far north. There was a murkiness over them. At their heights, Halam supposed, they reached the clouds and people if they went there could walk among the mists. Perhaps that was what he saw.

He rose to his feet and picking up the water-skin from beside him, walked over to the fire. He sat down and drank a little, and splashed some of the water on his face. Despite the night's sleep, he felt drained and sweaty. He wished fervently that he was at the lake. At this moment a swim would have been most refreshing. His clothes were dirty too, and he would have been very pleased with the chance to wash them.

Jored was stirring his pot again. 'Some food, Hardsaro?'

Halam shook his head and drank again. Shrugging, Jored took the pot from the fire and spooned it carefully into his wooden bowl. In a very short time, the food was gone and the Hardsara licked his lips, smacking them in satisfaction. He wiped out the empty pot. Halam watched but felt no desire to join him.

Rissar returned to the camp and as if on cue Rosart arrived leading the hacsar. 'Shall we be away, lord?' he said. They all looked up in surprise, but Rosart had saddled and prepared all their hacsar. It remained only to put out the fire and pack up the few belongings they still had with them.

Rissar, with a glance at Halam, nodded. 'Yes, let us start on our way. There is a long journey ahead.'

Jored doused the fire quickly and efficiently and scattered it. The mountain man seemed to do it instinctively, without thinking whether it was needed. Halam returned and packed up his bed. He buckled on his sword belt and walked back, strapping the bedding to his mount.

The day was quiet; the sky was blue and clear above them, shining like a pool of clear water. Thoughts of the lake came to him again, haunting, and desirable memories of cool days beside the water. Halam knew that on a day like today, the lake would be especially beautiful, shimmering in the reflected blue from above.

On they rode, the sun not harsh, and a cool breeze wafting over them from the east. It was hard that day to believe there was anything evil in the world. The plainlands stretched around them, long grasses swaying in a slight breeze.

Behind them, all sight of the Hardsar host was gone, disappeared under the horizon. The quest travelled all day, sometimes riding, sometimes walking alongside their mounts, at times even galloping and giving the hacsar their heads. By the end of the day, as the darkness skirted the sky, Halam was completely relaxed, recovered from his heavy sleep of the night before and relieved of the worries of previous days. Today there was nothing but peace and silence, broken only by the sound of the hacsar. No one had spoken as they rode on, farther and farther north.

Halam knew the Citadel of Arnex lay in the far north, amid the mountains that smudged the horizon. He supposed there were many days of journeying before them, so he took the peace of the day unto himself. Franeus had told him to grasp serenity. Now he felt happy to do it, to grasp a respite from the rush and clamour that had filled his life. If an attack came again they would deal with it. Rissar was with them.

As darkness finally fell they came upon a small depression where they would be sheltered even from the light breeze still wafting over the grasses, but also and perhaps more importantly, from any prying eyes. There they found water in several clear pools, filled by a small stream issuing, he supposed, from the Pasra to the west. Stubby trees surrounded the pools, sheltering it, drinking in its goodness.

They camped there that night and lit a fire next to the larger of the pools and sat around it. Rosart tied the hacsar near the next pool. Halam and Jored sat eating rations and drinking fresh water.

Jored asked Rissar to speak again of the old times, and the glories of the past. Rissar smiled rather wryly but he spoke anyway. Halam did not listen; he heard words, he heard the Malasar speak again of the Willsar Isle and of the great city of Jorem Ta that had been where In Haxass was now.

Jored, and Rosart when he returned, listened, but Halam simply let himself stare wordlessly at the stars and the dark plain around him. He fell asleep early, rolling out his bed and lying down whilst the others still talked. He fell asleep to the gentle rumble of their voices.

On this night, he dreamed. It began strangely, for he found himself in a golden wood, a place he had never seen before. The trees were dense and it was late in the autumn, for the leaves had turned russet-gold. He walked on through them, brushing at the branches with his hands. It was a pleasant place and yet, as he walked, as often in dreams, he knew that he had come there to find something; he knew he must seek it out, without ceasing to search until he found it. He did not question this, nor find it odd that to grasp it was so important. He didn't know what it was but walked, searching, pushing through the bright branches, knocking their leaves down in golden showers.

At last, and without any time seeming to pass by, he entered a clearing, a small golden glade amid the gleaming forest. Before him was a dejected figure, sitting in the centre of the grove, their back against a strange circular rock, a fire burning before them. She was a woman and her back was to him. Yet as he looked, he knew her. He ran across the ground and cried out in joy. 'Terras!'

But the words did not sound, even to his ears, and as he reached her and swung round in front of her, he knew that he was not there. She still sat silent, forlorn, unmoving. He stared down at her and then gingerly he put his hand up in front of his face, fearing and yet knowing what he would see. Whilst he moved it and felt his arm stretch out, it did not appear before him.

Terras was looking down at the ground. She was crying. He was devastated. He could not know what was in her mind, but only what was in her face. He reached down with his non-existent hands and touched her on the cheek. She looked up at once, shocked and reached up, grasping her face. Halam was stunned. She had felt something. She turned, seeking the thing that had touched her, knowing that she was not alone, and then, abruptly, she was on her feet.

Halam stepped back, calling out. 'Terras, it is all right, it is I.'

But she could not hear him. Her sword was out

now and her eyes searching the glade. He stood and watched her, for what else could he do? She could not hear him, nor see him, only, it seemed, feel him. But touching her again would only worsen the situation, frighten her more. Her eyes were haunted now. All he brought her was angst and anguish. Was she lost in this forest, unsure of where she was and why she was there? Did she even know how she got there? Was this the fate that the fortress had dealt out to her – desolation? Did she not understand where she was? It must be so. She had not found out what the fortress had done to her. *She does not know where she is, where I am. Perhaps she thinks I am dead.*

She would have searched, first the fortress and then, later, the countryside around for some trace, some clue to his fate and that of Rissar. Perhaps her search, proving fruitless, was what had brought her here. He felt a wave of distress, of misery for her distress. Her frenzied hunting around the glade stopped and, deciding perhaps that she had imagined the touch, or felt simply the breath of the breeze on her cheek, she returned to her seat on the rock before the fire. Halam, cautious now not to upset her again, sat down beside her. 'Terras ...' He breathed the word as quietly as he could as if by subtlety alone he could yet make her hear him.

She looked up, but no, she had not heard him, that much was still clear from her face. 'Oh, Halam,' she said out loud. 'Where are you?'

He bent forward and risked putting his arm

around her softly, gently, as a man might comfort his woman. She relaxed into his embrace, unconscious of her action.

'Why am I thinking of you again?' she said. 'I swore to myself that I would not. I can do nothing to discover you while I am here. This world is ours and yet it is not the one we left.'

Halam kept his arm where it was, holding her, wishing that he could truly touch her, embrace her, take her to himself, make her feel him and return his love.

'You are in another age of the world, Terras,' he said, though he knew she did not hear. 'The fortress has transported you to some age beyond our own, though whether in the future or the past I do not know.'

She looked up again, but she had not heard him. But something had touched her. 'Halam . . .' she said and drifted off. 'Why can I not stop thinking of you? It hurts. If only you were here. If only we could find our way back together. I am a Hardsara. In all things to do with the skill of the body there is none greater than I. How can a warrior deal with a place that is her place, and yet not? I cannot bring it under command.'

Halam responded, and yet knew he had no answers. He too had learnt this lesson, that the world will not always, or even often, conform itself to one's will. 'There must be a way back for you, Terras, for Franeus said you had to do something, complete some task before we would be together. Find the task, do it, and we can return to each other.'

Terras relaxed into his embrace, but still, she did not hear him. He wondered why he bothered to speak, bothered to try talking to her. Conversation did not work.

She was speaking. 'Why can't I be with you? Why did Franeus say you would come later, perhaps much later? Perhaps Franeus lied when he said we would be together. Do you go on to rescue Rissar from the clutches of the warriors? Why couldn't I help? Why instead was I brought here to speak to an unknown people?' She stopped and peered up at the sky. 'Why do I feel so close to you, Halam, when you are not here?'

Halam smiled wryly, but sick that he was not truly there.

'Perhaps you are near!' She sat up suddenly, breaking his embrace. 'If I left this place and turned aside from my quest and tried to find you we could be together, and we could find the way back to our people.'

Silence settled on the grove. Halam could see that Terras was thinking, hard and quickly. He reached out and touched her. This time she did not react, but simply jerked and spoke out. 'But I will go, even if I fail. I will go until I understand. All this I swear by the strength of the Malasari and by the Snake god.'

Around Halam, the glade vibrated with

released energy.

'So be it,' said Halam.

Halam knew he could not stay with her, in his dream or in the waking world to which he must return. There was no other way. He knew it in his heart with the certainty that always comes with dreams.

The scene shimmered and he found himself walking again in the beautiful wood around him. This time he did not search but let his mind and soul drink it in. As he opened his eyes to the world around him he felt something, some strength, some power, some passion that had not been there before, that he had not felt. There was something desirable, infinitely worth pursuing, yet faint and easily missed if one's eyes were closed to it.

He stood, considering the beauty, trying to trace the source of the power, knowing it was very important that he find it and, having found it, not lose it again. Then, before he could grasp it, he woke up.

It was near dawn and the camp was silent. He felt a strange despair flood his mind, yet not the dark deep wretchedness he so often felt, but a strange barrenness, an emptiness. It was not simply that in his dream he had seen Terras and now, once more, he was separated from her. It was because the world was a poorer place without the power, the passion that had filled that golden glade. He sat up and put his head in his hands. *Have I lost that potency forever?*

Jored was rising with the sun, and he looked

over at Halam. He smiled, a flash of wicked humour crossing his face. 'Are you well, Hardsaro? You have risen very early this day.'

Halam, looking up, said nothing, the humour passing him by. Did he not understand what he was losing? Had lost. Jored rose fully to his feet and walked over. Rissar was sitting and Rosart was stirring.

'Are you well, Halam?' Jored was closer now and the words spoken with real concern.

'Yes . . . yes . . .' Halam shook his head. 'It was a dream, a strange dream.'

Jored reached down and touched Halam on the shoulders. 'No matter, my friend. You will be well in a moment.' The words were gruff, the sympathy of a man used to shaking off his troubles as easily as a splash of water.

Halam looked over at Rissar, sitting where he had the night before. The jaksar was nowhere to be seen. Rissar was staring at him and Halam knew in his heart that the Malasar knew what Halam had seen. They did not talk of it, but quickly breakfasted and set out again. No words seemed worthy of what he had seen and neither Rissar nor Jored ever pressed the point.

Nothing else of any note occurred that day. Even the plain seemed empty, and few indeed were the animals they spotted. Halam supposed that the Torasar had drawn their clans south to meet the threat of the Hardsar nation. These lands to the north, then, were left empty and were free for them to cross. No one cared now about four travellers making their quiet way into the north. Halam fervently hoped it would remain so. He had already had enough excitement.

When night came, Halam was afraid to sleep, lest he dreamed again. He both wanted to live again within the dream and feared the desire of it. Something in that world of the night was too strong for him. It made him, had made him, ache with the desire to possess it. Such passion scared him. At last, sleep came even to his fearful heart. When he woke he remembered no dreams, and he was a little less bereft. Terras had decided something in that grove. Perhaps it was the right thing to decide. *Perhaps it will bring her back to me.*

◎

For many days they continued this way. The plain was huge. Sometimes, it felt to Halam that they had made no progress, there was so little change in the landscape. Was the smudge on the northern horizon closer? Was it even the northern mountains or just some dark miasma in the sky in the north? They crossed many rivers meandering their lazy way across the plain and came upon lakes and watering holes surrounded by pleasant trees and grasses. Their slow march forward went on.

The others listened as Rissar told them more of the ancient world and the times before, but Halam did not heed the words. He stayed silent and Rissar did not press him. A silence filled Halam's heart. Jored tried several times to enliven him. Halam was pleasant back to him, polite and happy to talk, but always the conversation petered out when Jored stopped. Rosart was silent too, although not in the unpleasant brooding way he had been. Sometimes Halam saw Rissar and Rosart speaking alone, sometimes near the night fire or while they rode. Jored would speak with him too as he tended the hacsar, or prepared the night fire, or hunted briefly for some food to improve their supper that night. Gradually, Halam could see that Rosart was changed. The hurt and doubt had begun to slip from him. He had learnt something but now it was sustaining rather than destroying him. Halam watched as the strength of understanding grew in him. Rosart was no longer the person he had been. Perhaps he realised that he had never been what he had thought himself to be, nor what others believed him to be.

As they travelled, the mountains of the north eventually grew on the horizon. The dark smudge had been some strange dark clouds edging the horizon. Now, finally, there was the dark blue of mountains against the northern sky. During these days, they had seen several Torasar. They were usually solitary men, or at most two together, viewing them from a distance. The Torasar never approached but only watched them for a long time. Sometimes they ran alongside the group, pacing them silently for several hours then turning and hurrying away across the plain. There was no attempt to parley.

So, the Torasar knew that the quest was crossing their land, but did not mind or fear four riders enough to attack. Perhaps with the Hardsar host in such numbers far to the south, they thought they had little to fear from four more. They had scouted and then they would leave. Later, another Torasara would take up the task.

On the thirteenth day, as the sun was reaching its zenith, they saw ahead of them some riders, stationary, seemingly waiting for their arrival. They had not seen any Torasar scouts all that day but the figures ahead of them were not people of the plain. For one thing, they had hacsar, and they were heavier-set and more muscled in their bodies than tall, gaunt Torasar. They were almost as tall as the plains people. Jored pointed ahead and grunted some words to Rissar whom he was riding beside.

Rissar nodded. 'I have seen them, Lord of the Hammer. They are waiting for us.'

◈ Chapter 9 ◈

I was more than three-quarters of the way to the Superior. It had already been a gruesomely long journey and a complete waste of my time. I was chi'shadii. Even travelling in trans-light energies, it was taking me too many days. And I had lost even more time relative to Raczek and the mission because of time dilation during the black hole's formation.

But I was ready to justify myself.

I had sent Raczek another message requesting an update on the orders I had given him. I had just received a response from him. He acknowledged my orders and he reported that his agents had intercepted a military transport of an Arcan colony. It had been diverted to his world with most of its contents intact. They had landed it in the far north of the planet. They seized control of most of the robotic and other weaponry. Some minor items had escaped from the crashed ship, but he would be able to intercept them. But they were now armed with superior technology. Arca was very advanced. I knew it well, for I had been active there for the last centuries. Raczek believed their capabilities would now exceed the powers of the indigenous native band heading north. I was not so sure. These natives had more technology than we credited.

For me, it was a delaying tactic. Whatever the result of Raczek's attack and whatever he thought the aim of it was, that was all I intended. I needed time –

to muster the forces of the Superior for a concerted move against that system and its people. An attack where I would stand alongside the Superior and the success, when it came, would be mine. The planet's civilisation needed major adjustment again. I was looking forward to knocking them right back into barbarism. This situation must not only be contained; it must be eliminated. There was too much danger. If necessary, I would convince the Superior to destroy them.

Raczek, on the other hand, was sure he would be victorious. It was either that or it was mere bravado. It mattered not. Raczek had repeated his assertion that he did not understand why they were heading north as there was no one there. He was just making excuses for ignorance. We placed thybuk agents on planets so that they, and thereby we knew the reason for every action the natives took. Something was going on and Raczek had missed it. He would suffer for that.

After listing these excuses, he then slipped in the information that the Arcans had reacted to his diversion of the military transport. He had been inept. They identified a nearby vessel to recover their weaponry and exploration devices. Raczek said that he had responded by delaying the rescue vessel by interference with its guidance and piloting systems and had crashed the Arcan investigator onto a nearby asteroid. I was incensed that he hadn't purloined the equipment without them noticing – more evidence of incompetence. He completed the message by asking where the reinforcements he so badly needed were. It was one thing to appropriate weaponry from a nearby planet, quite another to face what he was facing, – two immensely powerful beings of unknown capabilities.

So all his previous confidence was simply bravado. It did not matter. He had his orders. I did not bother to reply to him. Reinforcements would arrive with me at their head. That was what was essential.

◎

The sky curved away sharply, the horizon rounding away from him like a sports ball held in the hand before the throw. It confused his neuromental state, giving him the feeling that he had passed beyond a normal reality into some weirdness beyond it. He shook his head in annoyance. His egostate had been disturbed by the crash and it was all wrong. He should not be full of these things. He was in a difficult position here. His mind should not be thinking these thoughts.

He flicked the retinal display down and readjusted his emotion counter. Relief and renormalisation flooded his psyche-norm. He activated the remote interface, but the computer did not respond. That was puzzling. Surely it had not undergone a system failure? It was years since he had heard of such a thing – in any infrasystem.

There had been that incident on Thauceet 9

when a game-computer had failed in the middle of a game, but such things did not happen to him and they were not rational. He readjusted again and restated his interface request.

The retina flickered and the computer request screen reappeared. Well, at least the computer was not disabled, although it did not explain the delay. He felt his egostate worsening again. His concentration was drifting, so before establishing a full interface with the computer he changed his emotion count again. He should have had that systemcheck before he left.

He switched to full computer interface and requested positional confirmation. The retinal display flickered and jumped and the sub-audible systemspeak was shaky, but he got his information. He had crashed on an asteroid – and a big one by most planetoidal standards. The highly curved horizon, feeling of distortion and strangeness as he re-established conscious activity was solely because the rock was so small in the standards of his psyche-norm.

As to the reason for the crash, he could not determine it and the computer, typically, was feigning ignorance. How the system could claim not to have noticed a rock this big entirely escaped him, but he did not sub-vocalise his feelings.

The system reported that all his Arcan daemon sub-units were still operational and ready to correct this unplanned interrupt. However, the ship was somewhat damaged, and the computer seemed at loss to state its reparability. Strange as it might be to believe a computer could have failed, at least one thing was clear: the resiliency of the interface or the host was impaired by this crash. He requested remote area neural interface and the host reported that the establishment of the link would be delayed.

This did not look good.

He had crashed on a big asteroid and he was not going to be able to establish repairs on his ship or make a request to remote authority to come and rescue him. He frowned, allowing the egostate to slip towards a flash of panic. A little stress at this point would be helpful for he would perform better with a little frenzy in his system. Naturally synthesized adrenaline was always better than the artificially introduced manufactured variety. In some ways, he even found his natural emotions a better structural fit than the computer-generated ones. But who knew the truth of that, they so often filled his mind and being?

The computer was silent and for a moment he wondered if it had offlined again, but instead it was simply consulting the Maxwellian daemon as to what he, the carbonic subsystem, might require at this point.

A flash of frustration, of indignation at the all-pervasiveness of the daemon's knowledge of him racked his psyche-norm for a brief moment. Then the daemon decided, and the computer changed his emotion count without his request and he felt calm acceptance flood him. He had instigated too much adrenaline. After all, it only had his best interests at heart.

It did not much matter if he did not get off this rock for quite a while, of course. His task on Cha Xai 6 was completed and he had not yet decided on the next formational phase for himself. One state of life, one myria-unit of his monadic substantiality was concluded. From here there was free choice into the future. He let his egostate consider what his next structural monad should contain. He had many more operative formational units to live before the daemon decided he had completed span and began deterioration.

Controlled deterioration held no fear for him, of course, for the daemon was programmed to only supply him with his needs. It would not, could not, supply needs that he did not have. When the daemon, through the computer interface, decided that he was tired of substantiality, only then would it begin to remove it.

He rose to his feet. Despite the completeness of his acceptance, he supposed that forward motion was a requirement. Perhaps he should even VEP onto the rock's surface. These next few monads, this unit of substantiality, might be entirely completed on the rock. A monad of complete isolation from all peer and sub-group contact might be all that was required for the next section of his substantive existence.

He ambulated towards the vehicular egress

point, wondering if his Maxwellian daemon could have staged the crash. After all, if a portion of defoeian isolation might have been his unconscious need, the daemon might have ordered the online computer to hit a rather obvious rock and then refuse remote-host access.

As he approached the VEP, the computer automatically changed his life-support system to vacuum conditions. He stepped through the first of the doors and felt the air being sucked quickly from the VEP point. Gravity dropped as he perambulated from the ship and onto the asteroid surface.

The horizon did indeed curve away almost impossibly sharply, which made him feel quite amazingly disorientated. It was as though he was some ancient semi-divine god-person standing so high and far above a planet that he dominated it.

He stood for a moment, the harshness of the life-support electrogravitics causing slow shimmers between him and the scene before him. It was as if he stood there on a summer's day and the heat of the sun rose in great waves from blanched earth. He requested vision correction and the computer flicked down the highscan eyes. As the eyes switched systems, he had a momentary glimpse of the scene with his own all too limited vision. The image wavered as the online computer corrected the scene, compensating for the light distortion as electromagnetics met electrogravitics.

He looked around. It was a barren place, with a

dark and star-spattered sky crystal clear above it. The sun of the system was far away, a small cold disc of blue-whiteness. This was no place for any dream of solitude, no place for a carbonic to stand unless he wanted death.

Death.

He let the word, the archaism of the phrase rest in his mind for a moment. It was so long since he had even thought about it, let alone remembered the fear of it which had grasped so many carbonic sub-units in millennia past. Now there was no death; the computers cared for you, your daemon system would not allow it. There was a deterioration that they finally allowed when your life had become enough. When all that you had to do had been done and your unconscious wished only for the finality of system decay.

Death? Was it the same thing?

The daemon system was kicking in; he would not be thinking like this for much longer. It was too depressing, too disturbing. The egostate was too dark. His emotion counter changed. Online reported contact with remote-host. He turned unconsciously, unnecessarily, and stared up at the crystal-black sky. Remote-host interface flicked into being before his eyes and the starlit sky of the remote asteroid snapped out of existence.

His daemon was already sending the status report and the remote-host reported that rescue ships were not being dispatched. The report on the reparability of his ship was not completed and remote-host was as yet unable to decide whether he must be picked up, given a new ship, or whether his old one could be reconstructed sufficiently for him to complete a brief interrupt. In this condition, all three objects would be explored on a parallel processing model until the optimum solution was traced.

He had two sub-monads before complete analysis was reached and his condition-state would alter. Since rescue systems were not going to be promptly implemented, his online requested what leisure diversion he requested to pass the interval before reconstitution with the peer grouping.

He sighed. His daemon was worried by his isolationist musings as he stood on the surface of the planetoid, that at least was clear. He should not have thought so deeply about his destruction and deterioration. The daemon system never liked their guardianships to think too deeply about destructive dark things such as system deterioration. After all, it would not come before he had completed his functions in life and had come, in his deepest subconscious, to desire decay more than continuance. So what was there here to disturb his egostate?.

If the daemon had ever entertained any thoughts of giving him a monad of solitude, a portion of his life stranded and alone on this planetoid, it had abandoned them. Computer reported that if rescue was not dispatched, the failsafe was that within two sub-monads maximum he would be removed from his predicament to some other interface scenario.

He requested minimum interface and told the online that he would spend the intervening period, before analysis was completed, exploring the planetoid. The online hesitated, no doubt to consult the daemon system as to the suitability of the idea, and the response came back.

Did he not . . . ? Would he rather?

He requested close-down.

Of course, they never shut down entirely. How could his daemon fulfil his every need if they did not observe him always and see his secrets and know all his profound desires? But they would not insist. They were servants, guardians, protectors; they never insisted on obedience.

His emotion counter changed.

This substantiality was his. This monad of his existence was beyond their understanding and what he desired or did not desire they would not, could not question. He requested minimum interface and walked forward, his way utterly free.

He walked across the blasted, meteoroid-pitted landscape of the tiny planet. Ahead of him was a small mountain range. He strode towards it. Why not spend these sub-monads bestriding the planetoid like some great colossus of a pre-technoid era, walking across the plains and peaks of this small world? Why not let his id roam freely in the belief that but for a moment he was the sole ruler of some mighty and unassailable empire?

He reached the mountain range. It was larger than it had looked, and it took quite some effort to get over it, even at such low gravity. He could have asked the computer for lift, but he did not want that. And the daemon did not simply recognise his need and supply it without the request; a moment's need, the flick of a microswitch, the twitch of an electrogravitic and it would have been done. It was obeying his close-down order. It was not interfering. It was watching, of course. It never stopped watching.

He sat down on a rock that he found at the top of the largest of the mountains. It lay there, splattered into position during some long-ancient meteor strike, motionless for aeons, awaiting the time when he would come and sit there. It rocked slightly as it entered his life field and he wondered if that was the first move it had ever made since it had landed here and stayed, trapped by the minor gravitic field of the planetoid.

He looked down at his ship lying on the meteor-spattered plain before him. It was quite broken, a smashed and ruined hulk, broken in half by the landing. From the angle, the ship had been heading for the planetoid head-on until at the last moment the computer had seen it, understood the need, and swerved aside, snapping the ship with the force of its skidding crash across the rough plain of cratered rock. If the computer had not understood its error in that last moment he would be dysfunctional.

Death. There was that word again. People died

so rarely by accident. The computers so rarely made a mistake. There had only been that incident on Thauceet. How many had it been? Ten males and five females killed as the computer failed during the game. Their life fields had gone and the game killed them. Just fifteen beings in so many carbonic individuals that were no longer functional.

It was of small matter. Who even knew what caused it?

He put his head in his hands and was at once struck by the strangeness of the movement. How long was it since he had done that, how long since he had felt the need to touch his own body, let alone another's? Why should he, when the computers did all that for him? What was the gesture for, to put your head in your hands, to place its weight there, to support the mass of the brain and skull for a moment's respite from the carrying whilst the mind thought? Why do so when the daemon would trace the need and support the head with a momentary change in the electrogravitic fielding and the need would be fulfilled, even before consciously understood?

He moved his hands, running them up over the flesh of his cheek. How strange it felt. He reached up and felt the metallic roughness of the eye-systems. He let his hand move down over the feed-system on his mouth and then up to the silky smoothness of the skull complex.

Was there still hair under there?

How many centuries had it been since he had even thought of his hair? He had had it once, he remembered, but then, in a panic, he could not retrieve from his memory what colour it had been. When he had been small there had been mirrors in the neonate nursery. He had seen it, seen himself. How odd not to have a computer to answer the question when his memory systems failed. How strange this experience was becoming. In requesting a system close-down he was allowing himself a glimpse, almost, of how some primitive subcultural barbarian race would see him. He requested full-system ophthalmic viewing of the system-support daemons.

The systems that surrounded him swung, rather shyly it seemed to him, round into full view in front of him. They normally structured their physical presence to avoid all viewing by carbonics, for it was possible, if they did not, that they might block his view of something he wished to see. The systems floated behind him on their own electrogravitics awaiting re-establishment of full interface with him, his savants, his daemons, his ever-present servants, his link to the central. Ready to provide him with information, do his will, provide for his needs and his total physical security.

He cancelled the instruction and the daemon and computers flicked back on hasty gravitics to the invisibility of keeping behind his optics. It was many years since he had even bothered to think where they might be physically located, let alone requested ophthalmic interface. They simply were.

He rose to his feet and from his vantage point scanned the landscape around him. Beyond the mountains, the land was rough and impossibly difficult. Not only did craters pit its surface but great gashes were scattered across the ground. If he walked down there, the going would be difficult without the aid of the computer to allow him to skim over the top and save him if he fell into the cracks.

He could have asked for transit but somehow to do that would have defeated the whole purpose of these sub-monads. He would rather not go, not walk upon the difficult place, than be forced to use the computer's resources. It was strange to be so alone but, perversely, he was enjoying it.

Was this what it had been like for the ancients? Had they walked alone without friend or companion to care for them through all their lives, walking where they willed, going as they willed to do and being only what they willed to be? If he walked far enough away would the daemon fail to bring the rescue to him? He smiled at the thought. If they did not, perhaps he would, after all, spend a monad of existence upon this planetoid, living only as he wished to be. Living free, living without anything but himself.

Without further thought, he picked his way down the mountainside. It would have been impossibly steep on most planets, without the computer's aid, but here on this light and airless rock, it was just strange. The gravity of this place held little sway. He was going back to the ship. He knew it inside himself naturally and easily. He could, after all, await the completion of options analysis with more ease there. What else was there? This had been a good thought, but he had had enough of this meaninglessness. Something in those thoughts had frightened him. Whether it was the loneliness or the thought of his death, he was unsure.

He reached the ship quickly for as he covered the ground he found himself running, moving faster than he needed to reach the haven of the ship quickly. His heartbeat was heavy in his chest. What had scared him so? He reached the VEP and stared up at the damaged ship above him. He had indeed been lucky to survive the crash.

Lucky. The very word was archaic too, for who cared about the ancient concept of luck, of fate, of an uncontrolled and uncontrollable destiny shaping one's life as it chose, snatching it from you, unasked and uncaring. The systems took all luck from the equation, all fate was removed. That which he needed, that which one wanted, one got. Whether in reality or fantasy, it was the computer's choice, and society's. Psychosocial stability of the polity was paramount.

Yet, he thought, there must still be luck. For how else but by bad luck had the computer missed even the presence of this planetoid and bent and broken his ship here instead of evading it. What possible reason could there be, after all, to crash here? He had not desired it.

Oh, what did it matter? Why did anything matter?

He requested reintegration to full-system interface as he stepped into the VEP and felt at once the daemon system evaluating his emotional egostate and re-establishing proper emotion count. His egostate and emotion count altered.

He sat again in the comfort of the ship and surveyed once more the view from the piloting interface. It was hard to believe he had been out there, or even properly to remember why he had gone, or what could possibly have scared him in his thought processes so much as to send him scuttling back here in such panic.

There were only fifteen deci-monads left before system options analysis completed and he could achieve full interface with the host and receive the decision on implementing the best achievement scenario. The brief sub-monads here on the planetoid had been an interesting experience, but he did not need to repeat it. What after all could an airless and minuscule planetoid have to offer over the full Arcan infrasystem?

What had been in his mind to believe even for a monad that he could gain from such total isolation? The daemon system was disturbed at the self-destructive thought images that had entered his mind during the period and was still assuring him, subconsciously, of his worth and the total need of him within the infrasystem. To live other than he did was a negative feedback loop and did not enhance his psyche-norm.

A request came through.

Let him complete the interrupt, the recovery of lost subsystems – just a recovery scenario. This interrupt had been requested by Arca Rho central, and while he was not forced to attend to the interrupt, the system advocated and incentivised.

His emotion counter changed. Alternatively, he could begin a new myria-monad in a new positional locus as previously planned. He requested briefing. The system wanted him to physically interface in a situation regarding strange subsystem loss in an inhabited subcultural system nearby; Messixan, they called it. Such interrupts were the norm for his people, so he had the competence-system to complete this one.

The Arcan approach to subcultural syzygy was unusual. Their theories regarding the efficacy of barbarian interface weren't widely accepted especially by the full psychosocial scientific community in which he had been operating for the previous monadic slice on Cha Xai 6. The Arcans were explorers, often using a more carbonically acceptable styling of infrasystem-confrontational daemons to allow them to explore primitive unknown cultures. Without that, the subcultures could not have accepted the appearance of any normal carbonic/mandelbrot infrastructure as anything other than godlike, or more likely demonic. So the alternative utility styling was implemented. Most infrasystems had long ago abandoned androidic structural styling as unproductive and archaic.

But, in this way, the Arcans had documented many carbonic cultures beyond the normal interface infrasystems. Whether the history of these primitive subcultures would ever be useful in any meaningful psychohistorical review of the growing galactic infrasystem was unlikely. But the Arcans enjoyed the activity and pleasure was in the last analysis the major carbonic goal-seek.

The system briefing didn't specify what form of protector-system was missing but he assumed it must be one of such exploratory missions – so, several robotic sentinels with mandelbrot brain systems ready for interconnection with carbonics into an Arcan system. This was socio-normal for exploratory missions. This would just be another exploratory with an additional recovery scenario.

Should he refuse, the mission would be compromised. The system incentivised him; otherwise, it would have to be picked up by another carbonic sub-unit. After all, it was simply an interface and recovery operation which should not delay his overall goal-seek for more than a few sub-monads.

He asked if he could return promptly to Cha Xai. Rather distressingly the computer responded quickly that the interface was a high priority interrupt and Arca central had requested several times of the host systems as to when a full physical interface would be established by him.

He sighed, despairing at the thought of what was ahead. A tiresome interface into a situation that held no interest for him to rescue confrontational infrasystems that should not have been lost in the first place. No doubt they were merely lost during an utterly mindless attempt to explore another subcultural barbarian planet.

He acquiesced and asked when a transitional ship would be available to implement the scenario. There was a pause while these scenarios were appraised.

He wondered what to do with the intervening time before the system achieved full-verdict. He had just completed the thought when the daemon responded. A field was created around him and he was transported upwards away from the planetoid. The daemon told him that it had completed its analysis and remaining ship structures were sufficient, with gravitic support, to transport him to the primitive world and complete the interrupt mission. The subcultural planet was not far away, and he would be there within twenty-seven sub-monads.

As for his security during the interrupt, once recovery was even partially completed he would have the mandelbrotic sentinels to protect him. Before that, he could rely on his system-support daemons. This should be sufficient for any scenario a primitive planet could throw up. If not, the rescue mission could stage a revival of his carbonic lifesystem. The risk-reward analysis predicted this to be the best forward projection for interrupt goal.

Once this interrupt was fully complete a request transfer would automatically initiate the return ship for himself and the recovered subsystems. Such transportation would arrive in due course as required by the success-fail scenario that presented itself.

He felt his emotion count worsen as he was propelled through the vacuum of space by electrogravitics to an interrupt destination within the dubious comforts of a broken ship, followed by a risk-reward based scenario. The daemon responded to these dark thoughts. His emotion count altered and it created a simulacra-world around him.

All was ready for a transitory pleasure sensing.

He sat on the grassy bank and above the golden sun streamed its heat and light onto his body. He was naked and there were no eyeshields or daemon system to be seen, let alone to have to hide. These simulacra-places were so fulfilling and in them, a man or a woman could fulfil their souls utterly.

What was after all so good about the real world? Perhaps he should stay in a neo-world forever and forget this whole rescue and recovery interrupt. After all, some people did. It was easier than reality.

◈ Chapter 10 ◈

Jored turned in the saddle and gave Halam a meaningful stare. Halam urged his hacsar forward until he rode beside Jored. There was a sudden thudding of hooves as Rosart's mount too moved forward, but he, instead of joining the three riders, swung out to the side and pulled a short bow from his saddle. He strung the bow quickly and dropped one of his quivers down to his side. He opened it. He could easily reach his arrows. The bow he nestled to himself. The forester was ready and could, in a moment, loose an arrow to the air.

Insnar jumped vigorously from Rissar's lap and ran quickly to the rear. In moments he was lost among the tall grass and Halam could not see where he was.

Jored reached behind his back and unclasped the war hammer. The strap swung round, under his arm. The handle was now in easy reach. Jored too would be in battle as swiftly as needed.

Halam watched the calm way the Hardsar prepared for battle with unease. He glanced across at Rissar. The Malasar's face was calm, and yet perhaps there was a tinge of something else, perhaps an eagerness. Why would the Malasar be encouraged in such a situation? Halam watched and felt sure that the Malasar already knew, or suspected, who it was that awaited them. Halam could not guess. He did not even know if any people lived in the mountains north of the plain. He had never heard of any. It was supposed to be a wasteland of fire and mountains until eventually they merged with the ice and it became a land of volcanoes and glaciers. Yet, if these people had come from anywhere, it must be that blasted wasteland, for they were travelling south, out of the mountains.

The northern lands had been in Halam's mind purely as the province of Arnex, the domain of the Citadel. He had never heard, never given thought to whether people lived there. Could it be that the inhabitants of the place had come down to meet them?

Jored dropped back, then he swung his mount out to the side. They rode on – Halam beside Rissar and Jored and Rosart on either side, protecting their flanks. As they neared them, the three riders showed no sign of fear at the coming of armed Hardsar or a sorcerer. They waited patiently for their arrival.

Two of them were tall, heavyset, and burly, with very dark hair, and thick beards. The third was not bearded but just as heavyset and burly. They wore long, dun-coloured robes which contrasted strangely with their dark, bearded appearance. The robes were loose, cinched at the waist with thick leather belts. At their sides, short swords were sheathed.

As the party came within hailing distance they mounted up, but they made no other abrupt movements; they still waited on their hacsar. Still, there was no fear in their eyes but only readiness and some strange glint, like a fire unlit yet ready to spark.

'Greetings, travellers on the way,' one of the strangers called out at last.

'Greetings,' said Rissar, reining his steed in at a comfortable distance to speak, but still far enough away not to have to worry about an unexpected attack. Halam was still at his side, Jored out to the right and Rosart on the left.

'It may be,' said the man standing in the middle, 'that you are those whom we await. May we know your names?'

Rissar straightened now in the saddle. 'We will tell you our names, and gladly, if you first share yours.'

The man nodded. 'This is fair.' He glanced at his companions as if to check his decision. 'I am Helmar, and these are my companions, Sigmor and Trioch.' Sigmor was on his right and Trioch his left. He indicated them with a quick motion of his hands. It was then that Halam realised that Trioch was a woman. She was like her companions in all ways, but without a beard.

Helmar looked back at Rissar expectantly; in giving names the stranger had given little and expected much.

'Very well,' said the Malasari. 'As to my name, I will not tell. It is for a man to discover it. My companion here is Halam, born of the Aallesar of the lake, now a prince in the mountain, and our friends are Jored and Rosart, also of the Hardsar, the mountain people.'

Helmar nodded and gave his companions a fervent, almost passionate glance. 'You then are those whom we seek,' he said looking back at Rissar with a new excitement in his eyes. 'I am Helmar of the Offspring of the fire. Hear now the words of the fire: "Seek, my sons and daughters, for the time of new dawning is come and he will return to you. Seek on the plain of the wind for four people journeying to the land of the fire. One there will be whose name is not known, lest a man has wisdom. One there will be born of water, yet who found his life in the rock. Two warriors more are there, both of the mountain – a race long hidden yet never lost. Seek them and serve this lord with all that you are." This is the word of the fire.'

'Praise to the Snake god,' intoned his two companions.

'So be it,' said Rissar.

Helmar immediately urged his hacsar forward although his friends kept their mounts where they stood. Helmar stopped only four or five feet before the Malasari. 'So then, my lord, is there a new dawning? Will our lord return to the Offspring?'

Rissar held up his hand. 'Many may claim to be the Offspring of the fire, although few attain it. And people, when they speak of the Children, say that they perished from the world. Do they walk upon the earth?'

Halam watched this exchange in silence. He had never heard of any people known as the Offspring of the fire so to him the question of whether they walked still upon the earth was moot.

Helmar replied, 'Yes, my lord, they walk upon the earth still, for we are they. We walk here and now we have come.'

Rissar nodded, fixing Helmar with a stare. 'What is the purpose of the fire?'

'Strength.'

'What is the will of the fire?'

'Splendour.'

'What is the power of the fire?'

'Honour.'

Rissar rocked back in his saddle, satisfied with their responses. 'Welcome, then, Offspring of the fire. Greet the hidden warriors, a people of the hidden kingdom, and give to them again the gift of the fire that they lost.'

'Truly,' said Helmar.

'Truly,' intoned his friends from behind; now they spurred their hacsar forward to join their companion.

Helmar held his mount steady as his friends halted beside him. He looked again at the Malasar. 'Where then are we headed, lord?'

Rissar pursed his lips. 'Answer me first, why the Offspring were not known to still be with us? The people of the Isle say you perished in the battle with Uknor. I have travelled the length of this land and all the lands there are and never have I found the lands of your people.'

Helmar nodded, accepting the words. 'Yes, lord, for this was the will of the fire. We lived among the peoples of the world and did not tell them that the fire was still with them. The fire spoke and so we did what was commanded. Many people came to us but only a few found us to be what we are. Those that found the fire, they stayed and became of the Offspring, though scant enough of them there were. We are few now. There are in all only two hundred Children left in the world and we live in secrecy and silence far to the north and to the west of this place. The world has changed and the fire has spoken. So we come. We were sent to fulfil the word of the fire and find the lord and serve him. When the time is right we will gather the rest of the Offspring. Command it, lord, and it will be so.'

Halam shook his head. Why had he never heard of these people? Even the scrolls of the temple did not speak of them, or not that he knew. Or if the scrolls did, then the priests did not tell of it in tales they told. The Hardsar had never spoken of them either – not while Halam listened.

He looked over at the Hardsar. Jored and Rosart did not trust the newcomers, for they had circled silently round and now stood, waiting, behind them. If anything went wrong from this point the Offspring were surrounded and the Hardsar would strike at their backs before the strangers even drew their weapons.

'What then is your will, lord?'

Rissar sat silently in his saddle for many moments considering the faces of the strangers. 'Follow me!' Abruptly he urged his hacsar forward, between the mounts of Helmar and Trioch and out onto the plain beyond. As soon as he was beyond them he dug his heels into the sides of his steed and galloped away.

The Offspring swung their mounts around and thundered after him without a backward glance to see if the Hardsar followed or wished to prevent them. Jored and Rosart also swung their hacsar round and hastened to catch up. It had all occurred so fast that Halam was left behind for a moment, alone on his hacsar. He sighed and then cantered after them.

Rissar slowed his hacsar and when they had all caught up the party settled down to a quiet walk. As the day progressed the Children followed in silence, without questions, which Halam decided was the most puzzling thing about them. They had about them such a definiteness, a surety that no doubts seemed to assail. They were called to be here, so they came. *Do they have no questions?*

Halam rode on beside Jored and kept a wary eye on the strangers, glancing back at them from time to time. They kept to themselves, riding at the back, talking in whispers to each other, yet even at that distance, Halam could sense the excitement in their voices. He did not know what they thought they were going to see, but they seemed completely convinced that they had found what they sought. He found their certainty puzzling.

He urged his hacsar forward until he was level with the Malasar and then, without preamble, he asked the question. 'Lord, who are these Offspring of the fire?'

Rissar turned and looked at him. 'A strange people, Halam, the folk of Arnex, and when Arnex fell to Uknor they disappeared from the world. A great many of them perished as their cities fell to the makkuz. They were powerful people in the old times and their passing was greatly lamented.'

Halam nodded, understanding. 'But the Hardsar never speak of them.'

'No.' Rissar nodded sagely. 'The Hardsar mourned for them the greatest, more than all the peoples of the world, for mighty was the affinity between them. So great was their anguish at the loss that they did not tell their children that the Offspring had ever existed or of their demise. In this way, all knowledge that the Offspring of the fire had ever lived at all was removed from the people. It was an act of sorrow and, as such, a thing that can be understood. Yet perhaps it is always better to remember sadness, for they were worthy of their grief. Many things did the Hardsar forget in this way and much difficulty has been caused by that ignorance. You will understand this more in time.'

Halam was stunned. The thought that the

existence of a people could be forgotten like that – a whole generation to simply decide never to talk to their children of their grief and hence blot it from the world. How could they even conceive of such a thing, much less carry it through?

'Yet the priests in the temple at In Haxass say nothing of them either. It is not in the scrolls that my people saved from the old time.'

'Yes, Halam, it is there, but the priests never read it, and if they do they read the words and do not understand. They too have forgotten much that did not fit with their wisdom and their desire. They will not tell the people of these things lest they seem stupid, or uncomprehending. In all things, they must appear wise and clever – enough to rule over people's hearts.'

Halam was silent. He could think of nothing to say, but he felt a sudden and terrible sense of loss. Would they ever regain the lost world, if so much had been forgotten of its glory?

'Are these people truly the Offspring then? Could it not be a trick to deceive us?'

Rissar gave Halam a piercing stare. 'You will see. We will all see tonight if they are truly the folk of Arnex and the fire.'

Halam did not understand his meaning but Rissar would say no more. Halam asked further questions but the answer was always the same, that they would see the truth that night.

Halam could not fathom the words or perceive

their meaning. Whatever it was that would happen that night to prove or disprove the claims of these strange people, he could not see how it could remove all his doubts. After all, what could happen? They either believed them or they did not and there was no other way. None that he could see.

So the uneasy company continued, riding in silence as the afternoon continued and the day gathered towards night. Rissar stopped early. The sun was still in the sky, though fast speeding its way to the sunset. In a short while, the night would come. He gave no reason for the early stop, but simply spoke the words and dismounted.

The Offspring leapt from their mounts in some haste. Halam and Jored busied themselves in their usual way, tending and watering the hacsar. Sigmor and Helmar worked feverishly, gathering wood and brush from around them as quickly as they might. They created a small circle of stones, and in the centre heaped as much wood and dry grasses as they could find, building as quickly as they could the fire for the night. It was a very large fire, just for one night. Rosart would have lit the fire, but as he tried the one called Trioch caught hold of his arm and silently shook her head. Halam, watching from beside the hacsar, had a sudden inspiration. They were preparing some ritual and did not wish the Hardsara to interfere. Rissar sat silently on a large rock and watched them. Insnar had returned. He had travelled the day mostly on his own feet and ranged far from them, but now he was back and sat quietly beside his friend. He seemed completely accepting of the presence of yet more people. Rissar was not worried, so he wasn't.

Helmar halted before the stack as he piled the last handful of dried grass on the heap of firewood, and glanced nervously at the sky. The sun was already touching the mountains of the Pasra to the west; soon it would be beneath it and darkness would come.

Trioch, having now fed and watered their mounts and tethered them beside those of the Hardsar, came and stood beside her friend. Sigmor arrived with another, final load of dry wood.

Helmar turned and considered Rissar. 'Will you then join the circle with us, lord?'

Rissar pushed himself upright. 'I will.' He turned to Insnar. 'Come, friend jaksar, this is for you as well.'

Helmar turned and considered Halam, standing with Jored beside him and Rosart, still hesitating, beyond the main group. 'Come, the circle must be complete before the sun is set. The Offspring of fire choose not to see the darkness that comes upon the world.'

Halam walked forward but hesitated, worried, unsure. 'Circle? What is the circle?'

Helmar glanced again at the sun. 'There is not the time to explain, prince of mountains. The darkness comes, and the fire must be complete. There is nothing to fear, ask your lord. He will reassure you.'

'Sit,' said Rissar, 'there is nothing to fear. These people are truly Children of the fire and they are returning to you a thing that is only faintly remembered. Those who hear of it do not understand, even when the words are spoken. All should join the circle. There will be no harm.'

'Truly,' said Helmar.

So they sat in a circle around the unlit heap of wood and grass, Rissar beside Helmar, and the other Offspring next to him. The Hardsar sat together, on the opposite side, with Jored on Halam's right, and Rosart on the other side. Thus, they formed a circle, as the sun slowly slipped towards dusk and the darkness began to fill the sky.

'The stars,' said Trioch, and the two men looked up at the multitude of stars, already appearing to fill a darkening sky. Then Helmar began to sing. He sang in some strange, trilling, musical tongue made strong by the deepness of his voice and the power of the song. The final gleams of the day slipped away behind them and Trioch and Sigmor sang also, intertwining and joining their voices with the theme. From deep within the wood a glint of fire appeared and, in moments, like a brush fire catching in the noonday sun, flames burst into being.

As the fire spread through the wood, Helmar's voice grew also until the song, the tune, the strength of the melody was beyond any beauty that Halam had ever known since he had sung the songs of the Torasar that day, running on the plain. It was beyond life itself, beyond even the faint echo of it that he had felt in the golden wood. This was the secret desire released, blossomed, fulfilled and complete. This was the truth; this was beauty itself.

The Children sang now as one and the fire leapt up the sky. At once, as sudden as a rock breaking in the sun, from beside him, Jored began to sing. His voice was deep, strong, and as powerful as the peaks from which he came, and Helmar briefly smiled; as he sang on, Halam could see the joy in his face that another had joined.

As swift as the dawn, around them daylight seemed to burst into being, casting all memory of the night from them. Around them, within them, and through them, the fire burned. They looked no more at the fire before them for it was in them and they were in it. They were surrounded by light, bright, glorious, as brilliant as the sun on the lake, as glorious as the brightest and best summer day.

The song had grown complex now and each singer brought to it new glory, new depth, new power, as though they all sang their own song and with it and with each other created the whole. The song grew higher, surging upwards like the fire burning through them. At last, Halam could remember no more and cared not for fear, nor doubt, nor his own life, but only for the song. He realised that he too sang and sang without any unbelief.

Nothing disturbed him and there was nothing he could not have sung. He was lost in the moment, poised forever in but an instant of time, and yet through it, in all the moments of his life at once.

The song subsided at last, as all fires do, for all fire must end and Halam, finding his song complete, looked up at the sky. The night was gone. The sun was rising gloriously in the east, and once more it was filling the earth with light. The day had come. They had sung their song through all the hours of darkness.

The hacsar stood silently, watching as if they had seen it and even though their minds could not comprehend it, desired it.

They all sat where they had the night before, but the heap of wood and grasses was now but a layer of fine white ash amid the circle of stones. The fire had consumed all that they had given it and left little but dust.

'The fire did not speak this night,' Helmar said and looked around the circle as if he expected to be contradicted.

'It did not,' said Trioch, with a tinge of sadness to her voice.

'Yet, is it not always so when another joins? Do the Offspring not say it was so when that stranger joined us three generations ago?' Sigmor said.

'They do,' said Helmar.

'Praise to the Snake god,' said Sigmor.

'Truly,' Rissar said, 'and welcome back to the world, Children of the fire. These men are the

Hardsar, the Trish harga of old who once you loved. You have returned to them the gift they lost when you departed.' Rissar rose to his feet.

Trioch, Sigmor and Helmar rose also and stared at the Hardsar. 'These men of mountains are the Trish harga? This you did not say. We are pleased indeed to bring them once more to the fire.'

'And, in a way, still remembered,' said Rissar, 'for the Hardsar light, always, a single great fire at the sunset, even in the heights of summer. It is by this they remember you.'

Jored looked at the Malasar. 'So it is. I had not known that was why we did it.'

Trioch and Sigmor seemed suddenly released, for they all but leapt forward and embraced the Hardsar before anyone could move. Helmar himself came and hugged Halam with a strength that made Halam, for a moment, fear that the Offspring would never let him go and sought somehow to pull him into himself.

'Welcome, brothers, you are of us now, and we shall not depart from you again.'

'Let us be away,' said Rissar, 'unless any of you wish to break your fast.'

'No,' said Jored. 'I am not hungry.'

Neither, it seemed, were any of them.

So they saddled the hacsar and set off. They rode, Rissar, as always, in front, keeping his own counsel, with the jaksar riding this day in his lap, but now the Hardsar and the Offspring rode together.

The Children were different – friendly, happy, bursting with smiles. They asked the Hardsar many questions, seeking to hear in but a day the whole history of the Hardsar since the fall of the ancient world.

They told them also of their people. They lived in the far north-west, where, they said, fire met the ice; it was a barren and harsh land where they could best hide from the gaze of people and live as the fire commanded. Though few, and kept few by the harshness of their lives, they waited for Arnex to return. Now, they said, the fire had spoken. He would come.

Halam listened to the talk with fascination but without the ability to join in. He knew little of the history of the Hardsar. There had been no time to learn more than the few stories of Hewas. And no one, at this moment, seemed particularly interested in the history of the Aallesar, how Vaalasar had founded the City on the Lake. The talk of that day was all of the Offspring or the Trish harga, the Hardsar.

As the afternoon slipped away, Halam tried to remember more of the experience of the night before, but he could not. To him it seemed they had sung only for a few minutes, an hour at most, and then, lost somehow in timelessness, the night had passed them by. His mind could not encompass the greatness of the experience nor understand it.

He did not feel tired, although he had not slept at all but only sung. He felt refreshed, rested, more than he had from many nights of sleep. Any exhaustion, any tiredness remaining from his exertions of the days before was gone. He was refreshed and renewed. The fire had given him vitality.

He realised then that he had not, until that moment, really believed in this Warrior King Arnex. Even though he had followed Rissar to this point, from that small poolside amid the forests of his land, even though he had spoken with Franeus himself, he still had not believed until this day. Now, somehow, he knew that Arnex truly awaited them in the mountains of the north and that, despite his former doubts, he was there, ready to be awoken.

He stared at the mountains, now larger and clearer, and he was stunned by the thought that the great Warrior King was in there somewhere and that they would stand before him.

He stared at the mountains for the rest of the day, indifferent to the talk around him, amazed at the very thought of what awaited them. As dusk approached, he saw a strange thing. Over the mountains, yet not truly over them but from within them, was a glow, a reddish light – a strange, burning radiance like the last vestige of a blazing sunset yet in the north. He stared but could not make it out. It was as if another sun was hidden in the mountains, a fire not quenched, another light for the world lying buried beneath the mountains. As if a second star had tried to set there and had become stuck in the mountains. *Could the land of fire still be that fierce?*

They stopped as the sun edged towards the horizon. This night the preparations were quicker. Rosart took charge of all the hacsar and Jored, with enthusiasm, helped the Offspring to gather the wood and stones for the night's fire. Rissar stood with Halam in silence, the jaksar sitting at his feet.

'What are your thoughts, Halam Hardsaro?'

Halam turned to gaze at his lord. 'I have none, lord. This is beyond me. I didn't know that there were ever people like these in the world. I see the power they bring, and I wish with all my heart to sing again with them tonight. But understanding? I don't have an understanding. Even the questions are beyond me.'

Rissar touched Halam's arm. 'Trust to the Snake god, Halam, and trust to me. There is no way forward but this way.'

Halam nodded. 'So be it.' He felt for the hilt of his sword and nodded again, knowing its power.

Rissar began the song this night, not Helmar, but they allowed this. The fire that came was different; the night before it had raged with a burning, refining, all-encompassing blaze. This night it burned with peace, a flame of blue, brighter than the sky, brighter than the sunlight in the water, brighter than the brightest eyes of a newborn. The fire took them, but it took them in peace, with joy, the flickering glow of a man at peace with himself and joined with the source of all life.

As they sang the song, it taught them peace and gave them healing. As before it grew until Halam could feel, in front of him, just out of reach, a moment of timelessness; as he reached for it, straining in song, he heard the voice speak. The words were subdued but clear and somehow, though they were not part of the song, they came from it, and they were linked to it.

'You are mine and you are carrying out what I have for you. All things will be well. All things will be as promised. This I say to you: be not afraid, nothing is to be feared. In three days you will reach the fire signs at the end of the plain. Be not afraid, but be cautious of whom you meet. This is not his place. Yet he is here. Do not be concerned, all things will be as they should.'

Halam let the words settle on him without thinking, for the peace of that night overcame him. When next he thought, the fire was dead and the day had come. He did not tell them of the words that the voice had spoken. He was sure in his mind that they had all heard it and he felt no need to repeat them.

At noon they stopped briefly; the hacsar were grazing peacefully beside them when he turned to the Malasar. 'Rissar, what are the fire signs at the end of the plain?'

Rissar looked at Halam in surprise. For the first time, it seemed, he had caught the Malasar unawares. 'How do you know of them?'

Halam shrugged. 'The voice spoke of them. Do

you not remember?'

Helmar leant forward, excited, yet upset as well. 'The Fire has spoken to you!'

Halam stared around the circle of astonished faces. 'Didn't you all hear it?'

Rissar spoke. 'We did not, and it was hidden from me also, for it is your word . . .'

'But speak it out,' Trioch demanded at once. 'You must always tell what is heard immediately.'

'What did the voice say?' Rissar said more softly.

Halam stammered out his reply, nervous now. 'Nothing that we need to worry about. Not to fear, mostly, but to trust, and to continue to do his will. Then the voice said that in three days we would reach the fire signs at the end of the plain, and we must . . .' he hesitated, trying to remember the exact words, 'be cautious of whom we would find there.' He stopped. 'That this was not his place. Yet he was here. I did not understand that part.'

Rissar looked up at the sky at once although he did not explain the action.

Sigmor spoke as soon as Halam stopped. 'You were wrong, Trioch to demand that he speak the words.'

'But it is a rule of the fire,' said Trioch, turning to her companion. 'The words may be forgotten, this has always been so.'

'But we had not told him that,' said Helmar.

'And that is our fault,' said Sigmor, nodding.

'We must apologise, prince, for in our arrogance we expected the fire to speak to us alone. We should have spoken the rule to you. This was our pride, and I am sorry for our thoughtlessness.'

Halam felt at a loss. He had made another mistake. Yet these people took responsibility on themselves and were asking forgiveness. 'I did not understand.'

'Yes,' said Sigmor, 'we should have told you.'

Rissar rose to his feet and spoke. 'Listen also to the words, people of the quest. Ahead of us are the fire signs and there another traveller awaits us. I . . .' He stopped.

'We must indeed think the message through,' said Trioch. 'It is often hard to understand. Caution was the counsel and not attack. We may be cautious of both good and evil. Let us not judge those we will find until it is clear.'

'Truly,' said Sigmor. 'You speak the truth, Trioch, sister of the fire.'

Rissar was staring into the north. 'Let us go then,' he said, 'for the sooner we start the sooner we will reach the fire signs and discover the truth of the words.'

Jored gave a long, exasperated sigh and also rose to his feet. 'But what, Lord Rissar, are the fire signs? I for one have not yet understood.'

Rissar turned and smiled at the Hardsara. 'Yes, Jored, you are right. I have not answered Halam's question. You must understand that the northern range of mountains are volcanic and the fire beneath them invades the surface of the world at this point or comes close, at least. There is water, heated by underground fire that boils to the surface in great geysers of steam and scalding liquid. Also, there are pockets, rocks that release a gas into the air which burns as it reaches the atmosphere.' Rissar's face was stern. 'It is a terrible place and there are many threats for the unwary traveller. Anyone coming there must be cautious. It protects the north from the travels of the unprepared, people not able to survive its power. For terrible as the place is, it is but a precursor of the land beyond it. The Citadel sits in the land of fire.'

Jored nodded. 'The Hardsar tales say that the Citadel is a place of fire – and the door to it is rain. Now I understand the words.'

Rissar nodded. 'You do understand, Lord Jored, but you will still not know until you have walked it. Let us now be away, for we have spent enough time.'

They mounted the hacsar and rode on. That day nothing changed and the fire that night burned with a dark blue flame, as dark as a sky hurrying towards night, as beautiful as a starlit sky, as beautiful as the day end. Halam gave himself to the song and did not concern himself with anything.

The next day was clear once more; as they took to their hacsar and travelled onwards, Halam looked once more at the mountains now towering into the sky ahead of them. There was indeed a red glow in the sky around them and from the words of Rissar he knew now what it was – the echo of many blazes, the glow of untold burning lakes of fire. The lands of the north were the domain of fire.

On the following day, the red glow was unmistakable and rivalling now the blueness of the sky. Its redness merged with the clear sky and changed it into itself.

As the day ended, Halam urged his steed forward to where Rissar was talking quietly with Rosart. The woodsman ceased his talk with the Malasar at once and smiled across at him. Halam stared at him in amazement, stunned by this response. So changed was this forester Hardsar and so astonished was Halam of the change that he forgot why he had come.

That night they sang again and the fire was full of life, like the yellow of flowers growing beside the lake in the summer months, or of animals grazing peacefully in the southern farms. It spoke of life, and in the morning Trioch said that the fire had spoken to her of life itself, and its greatness, and of the power of its being and the gifts of the Snake god.

As they rode on that day, Halam knew that they had truly come to the end of the plains. The mountains ahead of them grew with every step, and the plain was breaking up. Strange muddy pools of steaming water appeared around them as the fire desert of the north crept into the plain, destroying it, eating it. It took the life from the grass and burnt it.

The fire in the northern land was not a refining fire, a pure fire as the Offspring brought them. The fires therein destroyed and gouged life from the grass. He was sure that the Torasar would have hated this place. Their plain, the lands of their fathers and their mothers did not end in the north; it was consumed by the north. Ahead of them, as they stopped that night, Halam could see the fire signs. This was the fire desert of the north, awaiting them. To the south, he knew, lay the stone desert, and now he realised that to the north lay the fire desert, the Har craka. He had never understood that ancient name before.

Beyond this point the plain was no more; there were only the fire signs and death. But despite the words he had brought, there was no sign of waiting travellers. Still, if the words were true, this must be the place they would come. When they set out the next day they would have left the land of the Torasar and would walk the northern mountains.

They hurried to prepare their camp, to feed the hacsar on the last of the grass, sparse and coarse as it was, all that could live here. Halam felt a tension this night that he had never felt before, a fear almost of spending the night within the fire. What would come; what could come upon them as they sang?

But still they sat, and the song began and again the song was of life. But it was of striving, of reaching to be, to justify, to be enough and failing to be, failing and learning to be humble in defeat. To learn to reach for the sky and not be able to touch it. Despite it all they fought, onward and upward, and Halam knew that if once he let go, he would be lost.

When the circle was broken, Halam turned and looked around. Near to where the hacsar were tethered, a stranger sat on a rock in the camp waiting for them.

◈ Chapter 11 ◈

Halam jumped to his feet and drew his sword. The camp exploded into motion around him; the Hardsar and the Offspring rapidly formed into a defensive arc. The stranger watched the swift response impassively. He sat as if he was invulnerable and saw no threat at all. Halam, standing beside the Malasar, looked at the man before them.

The newcomer was bizarre. He was dressed entirely in metal. Even his head was covered in a metal helmet. Over each of his eyes were curved metal plates. They too were silver in colour, bent to fit tightly across his eye sockets. Within their polished surface, multiple coloured lights flickered on and off, like faraway stars reflected in a mirrored lake. Halam gazed at him, not really believing what he saw. He wondered if he had many eyes and he was moving between them, seeing the world through the many different colours – as if each twinkling light was a different way to see. How might the man see many things and what would he see? It was either that or he could not see at all.

His face was not completely covered. There was a hinged facemask, which had split away from the bottom of his face and slipped down around his throat. Halam was sure he could move the hinged area upwards and then virtually his whole face would be covered. The skin Halam could see was paler and whiter than Halam thought possible and his features were stripped of all that gave them passion. The man wore no item of clothing outside the armour and the metal was so tight to his body that there could be none within. The effect was alien. No one like this had ever visited the city. Halam had never heard tell of such people from the merchants who travelled distant lands. Halam stared at him in silence, amazed.

As he looked, Halam had the feeling that there was something else just outside his gaze, that chilling feeling when there is something unseen just beyond perception. He could not rid himself of the idea. Was there something floating just behind him, out of his sight? He turned swiftly, but there was nothing. But he still had the odd feeling that whatever it was had abruptly moved away, just before he turned. There were things at the edge of his sight, evading him, slipping away whenever he even thought of looking.

Halam looked over at Jored, but the giant Hardsar was gazing balefully at the stranger. Trying to shrug off the disturbing feeling, Halam looked back at the newcomer. On his chest was a small golden crest. Halam was too far away to make out all the details of the golden emblem but it was no symbol he knew. Throughout their silent inspection, the man had sat quietly upon a rock, impassive and unmoved as if meeting them was something that happened every day.

He was the first to speak. 'What exactly was that?' As the words came out of his mouth, the colours of his eyes flashed quickly through the whole spectrum. 'Was it some protective energy shield? Are you not of this world?'

Halam did not understand the words and looked quietly back at him.

Helmar spoke. 'Who are you?'

Halam glanced at the Child of the fire for there was anger in his voice. He had never seen him look so furious, so unmannered. He brandished his sword. Then Halam understood. This alien man had trespassed during the time of the fire.

The Offspring were affronted. 'Tell us your name and why you have intruded on the fire? This is our camp and you are a visitor to it. Speak, tell us your business here!'

The man rose to his feet. It was a strange movement, an exaggerated, unrehearsed dance, yet perfectly executed. Halam could not quite work out why him rising to his feet felt so strange. The Hardsar tensed. Rosart, his arrow already nocked, pulled back the bowstring.

The man bowed deeply and straightened, a strange half-smile flickering across his features. 'You are perfectly correct,' he said suavely, 'the fault is entirely mine. You will forgive my intrusion. I was attracted by the great fire you had lit and I wished to discover what . . . people travelled in this land. I was surprised when I found you. You did not sit around the fire as I had thought. You sat within it.'

He smiled again, the same strange, rather impenetrable smirk. He made the gesture but no emotion was attached to it. This man thought little of them and cared less. 'I apologise. I was amazed that you have control of such energies. My curiosity overcame my courtesy. I could not help but ask whether it was a shield of some sort. After all, whatever could attack you within it?'

Halam did not like this man. He spoke like some of the ambassadors from the unruly Barons of the western southlands or the Karsar wizards of the east. His words were slippery and full of sly cunning. Rissar had stood silently amid the defending Hardsar and the affronted Offspring until that moment. He strode quickly forward until he was within three feet of the newcomer and then he stopped. The stranger gazed with his strange eyes straight at him. For the first time, the stranger looked mildly discomforted.

'Before we tell you aught of our ways or our power, perhaps you could tell us your name and your business. Where are you from, and where are you bound?'

The man smiled again, a perfunctory, brief smile that touched no part of his face but his lips. Halam could not read his emotions as he could so often sense in others. But this man, with such strange eyes, how could anyone know his mind?

The stranger responded. 'Of course, I must apologise again. I am Taxarzerek, an . . .' he hesitated, 'explorer. I am intent, committed I may say, to discover the mysteries of the lands in which I find myself. I am, you see, from a distant place. Our homeland is far away and we know little of the people hereabouts. I do not know how you converse and what is considered polite. Therefore, you must forgive me if I have encroached upon some private thing – or seen something you would prefer to remain hidden. I am ignorant, you see, of the correct way to carry myself.' Taxarzerek smiled the same contemptuous, mocking sneer. 'Did you come from the land of fire to the north or from the south, from the plains?'

Rissar inclined his head. 'You need have no fear regarding our customs. We are not so full of needless manners. A man may speak his thoughts plainly and can expect others to do the same. All our guests do this.'

'A very refreshing style, I am sure,' said Taxarzerek smoothly.

Rissar smiled again slowly. 'Your homeland cannot be so far away – you speak our language well.'

Taxarzerek shrugged and the lights in his eyes flickered quickly. The strangeness of the movement caught Halam's attention again. Nothing the man did truly affected his face. It was as if his emotions were entirely cut off from it. 'Not true, unfortunately.' He smiled. 'I am very far from the . . .' he hesitated. Was it regret? He correcting himself, '. . .very far from our homeland. I learnt this tongue from some travellers I met. My people are blessed with an easy facility for languages. I am chosen among my people as best in this talent. As I am an explorer, to know the language is essential. Do you all speak the same language hereabouts?'

'No,' said Rissar bluntly. 'So, tell me then, Taxarzerek, what far land do you hail from? I have travelled far in the world. Your people are not known.' Rissar looked the stranger directly in the face and smiled the same knowing, disdainful smile, playing the same game.

Taxarzerek nodded, the gesture of someone who entirely understands another's confusion but does not care about it. 'Ah, that surprises me not at all. I am very far indeed from our home, and I would doubt you had been there. Few people have visited us for many generations. Well, indeed there have been none in living memory.'

Taxarzerek stopped talking but Rissar did not respond. He did not attempt to take up the conversation. The silence stretched between them. Jored walked forward. Rosart, his arrow still nocked to a taut bowstring, followed. The Offspring of the fire moved around, taking up positions further to the rear and side. Halam, unsure, hefted his sword and walked forward to stand beside Rissar. The Malasar still stood staring across at the stranger, waiting. Taxarzerek stood impassively staring back, his eyes full of coloured lights, flickering like bright stars twinkling in the dark sky.

'So where is your homeland?' said Jored.

The stranger turned as if reacting to something he had not perceived before, a new sound, an unknown intrusion. He stared across at Jored with flickering eyes.

What is this man actually looking at?

'Ah, its name is Arca.'

'And where does it lie?' said Rissar.

Taxarzerek frowned now, the creases of his forehead showing above the eye shields and before the domed metal of his helmet. Despite these limitations, this expression seemed completed, finished for the first time. 'I am very sorry. I must apologise to you, once again. You see, it is not permitted for me to reveal the position of our land to people we meet. Our rulers, you see . . . are . . . well . . . frightened of invasion and think if our land is concealed from other people, well then, who can attack us?' He smiled again as if his words completed the game, removed the need to answer the question and, thereby, their fear. He continued. 'Perhaps when I know your own disposition a little better, how you react to strangers, your different ways and your thoughts, I will be able to tell you more.' He hesitated as if musing, but the gesture was entirely false. Once again, it was without meaning. He did it merely for effect. 'But why do you wish to know it?' His words were sharp now as if they had only asked so that they could, indeed, attack the land of the Arcans. Yet, Halam thought, the emotion was not authentic either.

Jored looked to Rissar for support. Rissar was silent and the tableau remained unbroken, as each of them faced the other and did not move. 'Your caution is wise,' said Rissar suddenly, breaking the silence. 'I commend your leaders upon it. It is certainly true that there are forces in the world best left alone,' he spread his hands, 'if one wants peace.' He smiled now, and for the second time, Rissar's smile was also false. He was mimicking Taxarzerek. 'However, we too are cautious. I am sure you will understand. We are indeed greatly flattered by your interest in our camp and in the fire that was lit. But now we must be on our way. Farewell to you, Taxarzerek of Arca.' He waved his arm and turned away.

'Jored, bring the hacsar with Halam and then we can release them. We can take them no further. The land is too terrible beyond this point. I would leave Insnar too if I did not know that he would follow anyway.'

Jored frowned but was silent.

Halam looked around. *Where is the jaksar, anyway?*

'No hacsar, lord?' said Rosart.

Rissar turned. 'There is no point, Rosart, they will only hinder us. Their fear will be great and even if they scaled the mountains ahead with us they would be little use. Release them onto the plain. Perhaps the host will find them as they come. If not, they will be free and they will be safe.'

Jored turned away at once to obey. Halam could not resist waiting a while longer to see if Taxarzerek would respond. The Arcan did not react. He simply stood there as if listening to some unheard voice, some unspoken words from deep within himself. Halam stood and watched him for a few moments and then could wait no longer. He hurried to go after Jored. The Offspring all turned to pack up the camp, destroying as they did the circle of stones, as they always did, and scattering the ashes of the fire to the wind.

At last, the Arcan stepped forward. When he spoke, they all turned to hear him, fascinated. Halam stopped. He felt a mixture of complete curiosity and utter distaste.

'My friends, I fear that there has been a misunderstanding. I certainly have no wish to offend you and it is obvious that I have. For this, once more, I must apologise and beg forgiveness. It was due, as I have said, to my ignorance of your ways. I do not wish to force my company upon you. I only wondered, seeing the great power you can wield, if . . . as we are travelling this land, I might not,' he hesitated, seeking the correct word, 'join forces with you upon the road . . . share the way.'

Rissar turned back to face him and yet Taxarzerek's eyes did not face the Malasar. It was as if he was seeing something else, beyond them all. Rissar stared at the Arcan for many moments. Taxarzerek was forced to wait in silence for his reply. At last, the Malasar replied. 'No offence has been taken, my friend, but we see no reason for an alliance. You do not know us, and we certainly know little of you. You cannot even know that we head in the same direction as you. My friend, in such a dangerous world, why would you wish to travel with us, or indeed we with you?' Rissar hesitated and then his voice boomed out, authoritative and commanding. 'Speak some truth, Taxarzerek of Arca. Perhaps then we will understand.'

For a moment Taxarzerek seemed once more at a loss to know his reply. At last, a rather exasperated expression crossed his features. When he spoke there was a great deal of hesitation in his voice. 'I . . .my friend . . . I fear that I have indeed spoken amiss and given you great cause to doubt us . . . me. This was not my intent. But the truth of the matter is that . . . I am not quite as I represented myself.'

Rissar nodded, ready to hear more, but he did not speak.

'I spoke no untruth, you must understand,' Taxarzerek continued, 'but I gave you reasons to believe that I was simply an explorer. This was not all the truth.'

Rissar remained silent still, although Taxarzerek clearly wished some further encouragement for his revelations. 'That is,' Taxarzerek went on at last, 'I am an explorer of sorts, but there are also some . . . warriors, I imagine you would call them. They were . . . to protect me during my . . . our journey. I, ah, found myself in the volcanic land to the north, a blasted land surrounded by great mountains. It is a terrible place, and I . . . well, we, the warriors and I . . . arrived . . . there among rivers of fire and dense clouds of sulphurous smoke. Beyond it, further north, I could see a great land of snow and ice, where the mountains are higher still. Great steam arises where the two lands meet and the sky above is rarely seen. A great mist covers the land mixing with the volcanic vapours rising from the rivers and mountains of fire. I wondered what infernal pit I had landed in. Still, I could see that to go further north held out little hope for us and yet to the west and east we saw no end to the fire . . . the volcanoes . . . When, that is, I could see through the smoke.'

Rissar nodded. 'I know the land.'

Halam was horrified. Rissar had said the land was a land of fire, fire and rain, and yet he had never imagined anything as terrible as these descriptions of Taxarzerek. *Is this the place in which the Citadel lies?* Then, as he listened, he wondered if this was not some ploy of Taxarzerek. He was building up the fear of what lay ahead so that they might doubt their course and so, somehow, they would be tempted to aid him in his goals, whatever they were.

'Uh . . . I was attacked there. The warriors would have fought for me. It is their . . . function. It is their purpose. But I was unable . . . well, they were separated from me. I have precious few skills in matters of conflict and my attackers were endowed with armaments I was not expecting. Weapons that are not normal, not to be expected on . . . well, in this land. So I made my escape. But I would like to meet up with my warriors again. You have control of energy beyond the norm. I had hoped . . .' He paused.

Rissar nodded. Jored grunted his distaste. He was not a man to flee from a fight and he held little respect for any man who did. And to expect others to defend you while you ran was offensive. Halam knew it would be for any Hardsar. But he understood the fear of battle in a way no Hardsar ever could. As he looked back at Taxarzerek, Halam saw for the first time that he carried no weapons, not even a dagger at his belt to eat with.

The Arcan continued. 'In such a land, and with fire raging around me, reconsolidation does not seem to be possible. I have lost . . . track of our warriors.' He hesitated again as if composing the next lie. 'They did not come to me when I called.'

Rosart spoke out. In his voice was all the disdain of the Hardsar warrior for one who is cowardly in the fight. 'Perhaps they were beaten . . .'

Taxarzerek swung to look at him. He spoke. 'Oh, they have never lost a battle. I very much doubt they have been vanquished for they cannot be . . . easily . . .' He stopped suddenly, uncharacteristically at a loss for words. He turned from Rosart and looked again at Rissar. Taxarzerek continued his story as if he had never been asked the question, nor begun to answer it. 'I searched of course. I had no wish to leave the . . . my fellow countrymen to their fate but finally I had to give up. I found my way out eventually and came to this place.' He spread his hands out as if to indicate the devastation that surrounded them.

'South, I can see there is a pleasant land, but somehow I must still find ... uh ... rescue my people. They will still be there ...'

Rissar replied. 'I do not know how we may help you in this matter.'

Taxarzerek spread his hands. 'Why not? If you are heading towards that land, I might accompany you. I have no weapons, as you can see, and you are well-armed. I thought perhaps that in your company, I might find the warriors I have lost.'

Rissar frowned. 'We are heading there?' It was both a statement and an implied question.

Taxarzerek shrugged his shoulders. 'I thought you said so, and why else come here? South there is a pleasant land and no doubt the world is crowded with agreeable places to visit. You must be heading north. You have not come from there.'

Rissar pursed his lips. 'And what is the value of such a pact between us, Taxarzerek? You do not know us, and we certainly have little knowledge of you. Why would we trust you? We are on a journey ourselves, a journey of importance which cannot be delayed.'

Taxarzerek nodded. 'I will not delay you. I wish only to find the warriors and you are a means to do that. If those who have them have somehow worked out how to utilise ... I will not delay you.'

Rissar stared back at him. 'What if our paths divide?'

Taxarzerek looked confused. 'I do not know.

Though you are my only hope. I must find the warriors. It is my mission.' The Arcan hesitated. 'But I cannot detect them. And since I do not know where to look for them, how may our paths divide?'

Rissar was silent; he stared at Taxarzerek for a long time.

Jored, holding the hacsar, lost patience. 'There is no reason to agree to this, lord. A stranger walks into our camp uninvited and asks to accompany us. Why should we do this? It is nonsense. Let us be on our way. There is no reason to take him at his word.'

Taxarzerek nodded, but he did not turn to Jored. 'I know,' he said, 'but I have no choice but to ask you. I thought perhaps to persuade you with fair words, but I am left with only the truth. I must find the warriors, for without them I will never return to Arca. The connection-savant was damaged during my encounter … during the fight. I must have the warriors' … vision. My eyes are not enough. I cannot stay in this place.'

Halam could stand it no longer. 'Are you blind?'

Taxarzerek turned his bizarre eye plates towards Halam. 'No, I am not, but my sight is not as you would understand it.'

Rissar turned and called to Insnar who was now sitting where the fire had been, watching the whole episode in silent contemplation. 'Very well. We must be away now for the day is passing and we have far to go. Since you return to the land of fire and that is where we are indeed heading you may accompany us. We would travel on the same road anyway.' He hesitated and fixed Taxarzerek with a stare. 'But be warned, Taxarzerek of Arca, our errand is urgent and we will not be delayed. Our association may be very brief, and this will especially be the case if you act against our quest.'

'Thank you,' said Taxarzerek.

Rosart jumped; he moved quicker than Halam would have thought possible. The bow in his hands dropped and he leapt, impossibly, backwards. When he thudded to the ground, he was holding a large solid cylindrical tube, its surface covered with the same twinkling lights as Taxarzerek's eyes. Even as Rosart held it, it was struggling to be free. It seemed able to float in the air, animated by some life.

'Please!' Taxarzerek screamed the word, a rare expression of actual emotion. 'Let it go! It is a savant. Do not damage yet more of my systems.'

'You were hiding them from us,' said Jored.

'No, no.' Taxarzerek still had an air of panic in his voice. 'Not hiding – they seek always to keep out of anybody's vision. It is not their function to be seen.'

So, Halam realised, that was what he had thought was there but could not see. Rosart's senses were keener than his.

Rissar took a step toward the woodsman. 'Let it go, Rosart. It is a servant of the Arcan. He needs it.' Rosart released it at once but there was a look of great reluctance on his face. The three Offspring, Halam noticed, looked very irritated at the idea.

Rissar turned to the Arcan. 'Show us them all, Taxarzerek.'

The Arcan paused and then into their vision swung three of the floating cylinders. They were of different sizes and all had twinkling lights on their surfaces – except one where the bottom half was blackened and the lights were dark. They hovered briefly and then swung out of their sight again.

Without a pause, Rissar turned to Jored. 'Release the hacsar, Jored.'

Jored nodded, obedient but clearly unsure. Along with Halam, he led the hacsar as far south as they dared go and released them, stripping the saddles and bridles from them before they did. The hacsar galloped off, happy it seemed to be free, but within a few hundred feet they stopped and stared quietly back at the people who had ridden them so far. It was as if they were saying farewell.

Halam and Jored turned and walked back to the camp. *What does lie ahead of our strange band of companions in a land of fire?* He glanced back at the hacsar, still watching them. Rosart and the Offspring had packed everything up efficiently and now everyone put on their own back the things the hacsar could no longer carry for them. They hid the saddles and other hacsar equipment they did not need as best they could beneath a pile of rocks. It might be that they could regain them upon their return – if they ever did return.

They began their walk in the strange company of the Arcan. His savants were once more nowhere to be seen. Taxarzerek followed Rissar and all three Hardsar. It made Halam nervous. He had to keep looking back to check on him. He glanced back frequently, wondering what a strange vision of the world he had, perceiving it as he did through many eyes of twinkling lights, and with floating cylinders, presumably, to further aid his vision.

The Offspring took up the far rear, scowling, clearly displeased that the Arcan had been permitted to accompany them. Halam had never seen them look so annoyed. Helmar muttered dark words to Trioch and whilst the words were indistinct the tone was unmistakable.

Jored strode past Halam and came into step with Rissar. 'May I ask a question of you, lord?' His voice was low because, clearly, he did not wish to be heard by the newcomer. Halam was close enough to follow the conversation but he did wonder if the Arcan would hear them anyway. What did they know of the accuracy of any of his senses? His sight was very different, what then of his hearing?

'Of course, elder Jored, speak the question, I am listening.'

'Why have you permitted this person to accompany us? The words in the fire given to the Hardsaro were for caution. I support that. This is a strange man. I am sure he wishes only evil upon ourselves and our task. He still lied, even as you demanded the truth of him. He wasn't honest with us. He hid more from us, as Rosart showed. Why shouldn't we forbid him to our company?'

Rissar nodded, but Halam could tell it was not in agreement. He understood. 'Yes, I see, elder Jored. May I answer your question with a question?'

'Of course, my lord, speak it.'

'The words given to Halam spoke of caution and not of evil. If as you believe the Arcan is evil in his intent, what then would have been his next step, evil man as he is, bent on joining with us?'

Jored spoke slowly. 'He would follow us, lord.'

'Yes, he would, and then we would not have known his movement or his intent. The words of the fire spoke caution and not evil. Good remains to be found here. If he speaks some form of the truth and he needs our company to aid him, shouldn't we help? Who can tell what may come of it? Perhaps good and not evil.'

Jored threw up his hands, a gesture so typical of him that Halam almost smiled. 'Lord, our quest is vital. We cannot delay it.'

'So it is, Jored. Yet we must try to do good and not evil along the way.'

Jored was entirely at a loss. 'It still seems a great risk, my lord,' he said gravely.

'It is, Lord of the Hammer . . . it is . . .'

Jored was silent. For a while, they all walked along, picking their way through the hot pools and pitted ground towards the mountains, which towered before them, impenetrable in their grandeur.

Then, continuing, Rissar spoke. 'Yet, I know who and what he is, Jored, and I worry for the consequences of his arrival. Long years it is since such peoples walked upon our world and great may be the portent of their arrival. It belies the question of what awaits us in the land of Arnex. It may be that we shall need the Arcan's . . . skills.'

Halam spoke up from behind. 'Who is he then, Lord?'

Rissar glanced back at him. 'We will speak on this again, Halam of the Lake.' He turned back and spoke no more.

The land became even rougher as their trip continued that day. Beneath, the ground had some underground fire, an underworld of raging flame. They walked past hot pools of water, steaming and bubbling noisily. Far to the left, Halam saw a great waterspout showering the blasted earth with hot rain. Around them, pools of boiling mud spattered the ground. Ahead, where the mountains met the plain, fires were burning as if the ground itself had caught alight.

'The burning gases of which Rissar spoke,' said Jored, shattering his mood of fascination. Halam looked up at the sky. The blueness of the sky was distinctly tinged with red from the mountains ahead and with yellow from the murk of the rising gases. It gave it a purplish hue as if some great darkness was clawing at the day. Halam wondered again at the terrible land they were heading into. What was the mountainous land of the north like if this blasted place was only a foretaste?

The journey grew more difficult and unpleasant as the day wore on. The hot pools of bubbling water and mud became more frequent, their route more tortuous as with difficulty they threaded their way through, struggling to find a pathway that was passable. At last, they approached the beginning of the mountains; the ground itself had become nothing but a hot scalding quagmire that steamed and heaved beneath their feet. As Halam placed his feet upon it he felt that at any moment he might take a step and the ground itself would fall away beneath him – or be yanked away like a carpet tugged out from under him.

The afternoon was well advanced when they reached the end of the fire signs. Without hesitation, they slipped by towering blue flames and began to climb the mountains themselves. At first, it was but a steep pathway, which they managed easily, although they had to travel in single file. Around them the ground was rough and some of the rocks were hot to the touch. Insnar had made his own way through during the day, but now he made his journey in Rissar's arms.

The waterspouts of steam and scorching water were left behind. Looking back at the blasted ground that marked the end of the plain, Halam could not but feel regret that they were leaving the land of the

Torasar. He held a great fondness for them, even though they had deserted him in need. He remembered the face of Torem Torasara. He had run the plain and sung its glories. He knew that he would hate the place where the plain was eaten by underground fire. The Torasar were people of freedom, people of open grass and wind. They would no more enter this place than they would the buildings of the Aallesar.

When will I ever return to the plain?

The Torasar were far to the south. Further still was his home in the City on the Lake. He remembered his sister, Jasada, and his parents, Jasam and Misaneer. They did not even know where he had disappeared to that night. He stopped and continued to look back. There, to the south, somehow lost in the Fortress of Endless Night was Terras, his Hardsare. When would he see her, see any of them again? He did not know. Why was he leaving and walking into such a terrible land, such an inhospitable place?

Why had he done it? Why did he let go of her hand? If they had held each other as they ran through that archway they would have stayed together and she would have been here now, encouraging him, aiding him, helping him feel whole. Helping him to be a Hardsar.

He turned and hurried to catch up with everyone else. They had all passed him by, leaving him to his musing. Jored was plodding along behind Rissar, who, as usual, was leading. Rosart was now walking behind the Arcan, keeping his gaze firmly on him. The three Offspring came behind the woodsman.

Taxarzerek even walked strangely. At times, he seemed to glide more than walk. There was something in his steps that was odd – as if walking was no effort and yet supremely complex at the same time. He walked gracefully and yet simultaneously as if he was struggling to remember how to do it. Halam wondered if he were dissembling still, pretending something to avoid more questions.

Halam caught up with the Offspring. Helmar was leading. They all looked unhappy. Trioch particularly was still glancing irksomely at Taxarzerek's back.

As Halam passed them, he suddenly knew why it was that he was still on this journey, despite his sister's, his parents' distress and his lost woman. He would not desert Rissar, any more than any of these could. He had never managed it. Whenever the thought had come he had rejected it. From the very moment he met him on that night beside the small lake he had followed him.

Now there were yet more people to care about – a Hardsara princess, his Terras, his lost woman; Jored, a man of the mountains if there ever had been one; Insnar the faithful jaksar, willing to die to save the sorcerer's staff; Rosart, his erstwhile rival yet a person he now cared about. He knew that Rosart had changed, grown, and the changes were good ones. And that was not even to begin to think about the

Children of the fire who had brought him such a gift. He could not leave them. His own life no longer mattered so much to him as being here. He needed these people and would not give them up. There was nothing that could remove him from them, short of his demise.

The climb up that first narrow pathway took them the rest of the afternoon. As the sun hurried to its setting, they reached the top and, over the crest of a rise, found themselves entering a small dry valley. The ground there was not completely devastated by the heat and coarse grasses and stubby trees still survived. Above and beyond the valley there was only a terrible climb, high into the mountains before them.

Halam could see a pass far above them; a high pass that it would take them many hours on the following day to reach, even if they made it that far in a day. But it was the only way. He looked to the west and the east and this route was the best way through the seemingly impenetrable barrier of the northern range. In the oncoming darkness, the sky above the high path was a bright flickering red, as if a northern sun was struggling to rise beyond – a ruby sun climbing from the ice. Halam swallowed his fear. From the vantage of the plain, it had been clear that the mountains they now climbed were but the beginning, that beyond these were more peaks, greater than these and fierier. He dared not think further on the land beyond that far pass. Rissar had stopped, for even though the full darkness was an hour away there was no other place within walking distance that they could sleep that night.

There was tension in the camp. Taxarzerek sat by himself on a rock beside a stubby tree Jored and Rosart gather wood for a fire. Halam walked over to where Rissar was sitting, leaning against a large rock. The jaksar was asleep with his head in Rissar's lap. All three Offspring were standing beside him, muttering in low voices. As Halam arrived Helmar was speaking.

'We will not form the circle this night, my lord. It is forbidden when there are strangers present who may not understand or appreciate its power. It is not possible in the presence of such an unknown.'

Rissar nodded. 'I expected it and you are right, it would not be wise, whether we trusted him or not. He will not understand what is happening or what it means. His response will be unpredictable. In the place where he is from, such things are lost, if they were ever known. They have forgotten much. They abandoned them all to pursue pure satisfaction. We should be vigilant. As the night proceeds, we will see where it leads us.' Rissar bent forward and stroked Insnar's head. *Nothing bothers the jaksar,* Halam thought. *Is his way of being true, and all the stress with which we fill our lives, the delusion?*

'It is a great shame,' said Trioch from beside Helmar, 'for it is many nights since I saw the darkness and a sad thing that I must see it now.'

Rissar, looking up, nodded understandingly. 'But darkness is part of the world in which we live, Trioch. Sometimes it must be endured.'

Trioch still looked unconvinced, or perhaps, Halam thought, it was just sadness.

'You speak words of truth, lord,' said Helmar. 'I know this and so do Trioch and Sigmor. We stand against the dark and we sing the fire to bring the light into the darkness. For what else is our purpose?'

'Truly,' said Rissar.

Sigmor spoke. 'We will prepare the campfire as an echo of the true fire.' The Offspring turned and walked away.

Rissar looked at Halam. 'What are your thoughts, Halam Hardsaro? You are very silent. You have said nothing of your opinions of this stranger.'

Halam hesitated. 'I am not sure, lord. Your words to Jored today were clear, we didn't have a choice, and yet,' he hesitated again, 'we have important reasons to hurry, and have met a person whose needs may delay us.'

Rissar indicated for Halam to sit beside him. 'Say more,' he said, 'speak your thoughts.'

Halam sat. 'You said the next attack of the enemy would be different. They might not, this time, attack us physically. Could not this man be sent to delay us, confuse us and set us on the wrong track?'

Rissar nodded. 'It could be so, Halam. It could be. But we are aware of that risk. We have been warned to be cautious. So, yes, treat him with suspicion. But there is another thing. Taxarzerek thinks he has deceived me. He believes that gives him an advantage. He has not been open with us. He has not spoken the truth or not all of it. I know who he is, what he is. His whole purpose, his true aims here we have yet to discover. I want to understand them. It is important, I think.'

Halam raised his head and looked the Malasar full in the eyes. 'You said before that you know of them. So, who is this man?'

◈ Chapter 12 ◈

Rissar cast a careful glance at Taxarzerek sitting quietly on his rock. The Arcan seemed lost in thought as if he was speaking, silently, with people who weren't there. He was utterly preoccupied with whatever it was he was doing.

Rissar looked back at Halam. 'Have you ever heard that there are worlds around the stars, Halam – when you heard the myths in your youth?'

Halam looked across at Rissar. He did not easily believe such strange ideas. He answered, unsure. 'Of course, the tales the priests tell us speak of it, for the stories say that the Hraddas, monsters, came down from the stars. Did not the destruction of the ancient world, wrought by Uknor the Destroyer, come at their hand?'

Rissar nodded. 'And do you believe it?'

Halam hesitated and then, slowly, he spoke the truth instead of the falsehood that had leapt to his lips. 'I know it was Uknor who attacked us, lord. I have been told it was he that night in the forest. But I find the ideas of other worlds difficult. How can there be worlds beyond the sky? How can the stars be other worlds? Aren't they too small? They are but pinpricks of light. How can someone live in such a place?' Halam looked across at him, knowing that he was sounding naive.

Rissar smiled, but it was kind and there was no hint of mockery in it. Nevertheless, Halam winced.

He felt he might have been foolish and said something idiotic. The Malasari seemed to know this because he reached out and grasped Halam's shoulder. When he spoke there was no scorn in his tone.

'The stars are not distant worlds, Halam, but they are distant suns. Around them are worlds too small for you to see, for they are very distant – unimaginably far away. Around each star, as around our sun, there are worlds, and many of them are as full of life as our own. This is the way of the Snake god who gives. There are countless worlds as vibrant as this, many peoples like us and many very different to us. If Arca is the true name of his home, it exists out there. Taxarzerek comes from such a land among the stars. He believes us foolish and primitive, savages and barbarians who would not understand.' Halam cringed because he knew he didn't understand. Rissar continued. 'But that is Taxarzerek's origin. It gives us a small advantage to know what he believes us not to know.'

Rissar turned slightly and looked across at the Arcan, sitting on the rock, still seemingly completely lost in his own thoughts. *Or another's,* Halam thought.

Rissar looked back at Halam. 'If Taxarzerek is not a ploy of our enemies, and he does not seem so, then we must know what his arrival portends – what is the reason he has come? His thoughts are closed and I must know them. Why has he come now, and why now when, at last, the final battle is beginning? Is he here to aid us or to hamper us? Or neither? What need brought him here? What, Halam Hardsaro, is the reason he is accompanying us? That is why I let him come. We must understand the answers to these questions. I did not want him wandering our world, doing things that would hinder our aim. It is better to keep him close.'

'I will ask him,' said Halam impulsively. 'He will have more trust in me.' He looked across at the Arcan. 'He will believe my knowledge small and will think I will not understand.' *Which I don't*, he thought.

Rissar nodded. An engaging smile flashed across his face and his grey eyes shone. 'You are right, Hardsaro. But be careful, Halam, for he is wily. He will see more in your words than you mean. Tell him nothing of our quest or our knowledge of him. Try to gain information from him. Be cautious with him, Halam, until we understand why he has come.'

Halam nodded and rose to his feet. He walked slowly across the camp and as he neared the Arcan he saw Taxarzerek's head jerk round at the approaching sound. The lights in his eye shields twinkled through several complex patterns and then Taxarzerek turned and looked directly at him. Halam crouched down.

'Greetings, my friend,' Taxarzerek said smoothly. 'I do not think I have been told your name?'

Halam nodded and sat down properly before the bizarre man. 'Yes, Taxarzerek, I did not tell you.

My name is Halam.'

Taxarzerek peered sightlessly at him. Halam, sitting closer now, was fascinated by the flickering lights within the eye plates. *Do the patterns mean anything?* There seemed no discernible source for the lights, they seemed but reflections of external lights in the mirror-smooth surface. Halam was at a loss to understand whether he could somehow see through them or whether they signified something else was going on. 'I thought I would come and speak with you to properly greet you,' he said.

'You have a good point, my friend. We have indeed not introduced ourselves fittingly. Is not mistrust a terrible thing?' Taxarzerek smiled, again with a curious disconnected half-sneer that was characteristic of him. *Can it be that he does not remember how to smile?*

'And where was it you come from, Halam?'

'From the lakeland to the south.'

Taxarzerek nodded judiciously as if interested in all he might hear. The lights twinkled whatever message they conveyed and he spoke. 'Ah, I have not been there, perhaps it is a place worth visiting after we have found my sentinels. What is the name of your leader?' He indicated Rissar who sat watching them from across the camp.

'He is Rissar.'

Taxarzerek raised his sightless eyes to the sky, musing thoughtfully on this new information as if something up in the atmosphere had the answers for him. 'Ah, now that means something like "stranger", or "strange one", perhaps, does it not?' he said eventually.

Halam raised his eyebrows. 'You know our language well.'

'Ah, yes, it is as I say a great . . . skill with me. Part of the, what shall I say . . . compensations.' Halam moved to sit alongside the Arcan, as friends or compatriots might.

The campfire had been lit and was burning well. Sigmor, who had made it his task, was finished. The flames were flickering, rising into the darkening sky. Everyone was settling down around it. The three Offspring were looking most discomforted and were looking up at the oncoming darkness with doubt and apprehension.

Halam looked across at the Arcan, who turned his head towards him in response. 'I was wondering,' he said, 'you mentioned in your story that you were attacked . . .'

'Yes?'

'Who was it that attacked you?'

Taxarzerek shrugged, a careless movement without any underlying meaning.

It signifies nothing, Halam thought. *There is no reality to it.* It was just a movement that he thought was necessary at that moment but held no emotion for him.

'I do not know. Some armed men ambushed me amid the worst of the fire. I had seen ahead of us what seemed to be a ruined city and I was heading for it in the hope, I suppose, of finding aid. They came at me from behind some shattered rocks. I did not see them until they were upon me. My savants attempted defence, but the attackers had advanced weaponry – which was not predicted. I fell back at once. I saw no more of the fight. I was lost at once in the smoke and clouds but my savant was damaged, which cut me off from . . . which disorientated things . . . I mean, me. Night came soon afterwards and I became completely confused. Do you then know the people of this land that might have attacked me?' Taxarzerek spoke the words but there was no passion in them as if he didn't care whether Halam believed him or not.

Halam was not entirely sure he did. He shook his head. 'No, I have never been here before . . .' He trailed off, wondering if he should have spoken the words.

Taxarzerek smiled the same false, heartless movement. His gestures were meaningless; his concern meant nothing.

'I am sorry that I cannot help you further,' the Arcan said slowly. 'If you have not been here before, why are you travelling into this terrible place?'

Halam stared across at the man, unsure of how to answer. The truth seemed a dangerous thing to share. The Arcan was turning away his questions but asking his own. *Anyway, what would this stranger know of Arnex, or the Snake god, or the Malasari and his kingdom?* Yet, despite it all, he could not lie. 'I follow my lord,' he said at last, feebly.

Taxarzerek smiled again, disdainfully, perhaps seeing through Halam's intent of evading the question.

'Did you see more of the city, the ruined city?' He asked the question but he was sure that the Arcan would not be helpful.

'No, I am sorry,' said Taxarzerek. 'It was lost in the mist, although I saw other ruins as I made my way out. They were all deserted, quite ancient. I saw no other people.'

Halam nodded and rose to his feet. The conversation was ending; he could tell that Taxarzerek was impatient and Halam was irritated with the Arcan. He had no desire to talk longer with him. The Arcan was never really listening; someone doing several things at the same time and not really paying attention to any of them was distracting. He was beyond a proper approach.

So Halam made his excuses and walked back across the camp. Things were settling down now. The three Offspring sat morosely around the campfire, staring alternately at the darkening sky and the pitiful echo of a blaze before them. Clearly, they were not going to cheer up throughout the whole of the rest of the night. As usual, Jored was busying himself cooking their food over the fire, making a stew from their water, his supplies and dried meat. Rosart sat beside him, helping the Hardsar elder and simultaneously quietly checking and repairing his many arrows. The Arcan sat, entirely isolated, on the other side of the camp, ignored and disconnected.

Halam walked over to where Rissar was still sitting, talking quietly to Insnar who was staring up at him attentively. Rissar stroked the jaksar's head as Halam sat down beside him.

'Insnar does not trust the Arcan, Halam. He agrees with you.'

Halam looked down at the jaksar who peered back at him from his strange animal eyes. He still felt a certain hesitation with the jaksar and he had purposely avoided contact with him since the creature had been turned back from stone. He wondered if, in the animal's mind, there was still some blame. He had caused the situation where the beast had borne the staff and frozen himself to stone.

But there was nothing in his eyes but respect. It was strange enough to see such esteem in the gaze of a jaksar. *How can he favour me after all I did?* He reached out and touched the jaksar softly on the head.

'He does not like our new companion being allowed to follow.'

'No one does, my lord,' said Halam indicating the camp.

Halam glanced over again at the Offspring; they were still looking despondent. The night had come and the stars were twinkling into being above them. Trioch was staring up at them with a sort of morbid fascination. It was as if she saw their beauty, desired to understand them, and yet wished that she didn't.

'What did Taxarzerek tell you?' Rissar said at last.

Halam stroked the jaksar again and looked up at the Malasari. 'He did not know much, or would not tell me it, at least. He was attacked where the fire was worst and he said he did not see who attacked. They came from behind some rocks and his savants went forward to defend whilst he retreated. They had weapons he had not ... predicted ... he said predicted. There was a ruined city in the mists. He had been heading for it, hoping to find some help. He never saw it again afterwards, although he said there were other ruins on his way out, empty and deserted.'

Rissar nodded slowly. 'There is more in his words than you might believe. Interesting that he spoke of the savants defending him. He implied before that he had warriors he lost who defended him. Did he ever have control of them? Or is getting them the reason he is here? The city of which he spoke might have been the Citadel in which Arnex dwelt in ancient time. If he was attacked when heading there, it would seem that there are forces who wish to prevent travellers from reaching it. They wait for us where the land is most perilous. They will be our next threat. Perhaps they mistook Taxarzerek for us. Whichever it is, we know that they are waiting.'

Halam raised his head. 'Only if we believe the words of Taxarzerek.'

Rissar laughed, a good-humoured, unrestrained laugh that made heads in the camp turn in their direction. 'What a terrible thing suspicion is, Halam,' he said. 'There is nothing in his words to make us doubt the story. The result is to make us cautious. If he aimed to make us fear, to prevent our going, the story would have been more horrific. There are many terrible tales to be told of this land.'

Halam looked across at the Malasar and wondered what they might be. They walked over to join the group around the fire. Jored's stew was ready and he was serving it up to everyone. He even walked over and offered some to the Arcan, but he did not accept. As Jored walked away, Taxarzerek raised the faceplate of his helmet, covering the bottom part of his face. Very little of his face could now be seen, just colourless cheeks and forehead. Later he lowered it again. *Has he eaten and is now finished?*

The Offspring gazed up at the stars with a dispirited fascination. After he had eaten, Halam became rather tired of the silence and, slipping his sword belt off, began to clean the sword with some materials Jored lent him. He had given it little attention in the previous days and it needed some care now. He was rubbing away absently in the half-light of the fire and the stars when he noticed that, without him having been aware, some of the words on the scabbard had changed. He looked down at them, peering self-consciously at the words, trying to make them out without giving away what he was doing:

Halam, Bearer of ages, Child of the fire.

He was shocked that, once more, words of his deeds had appeared on the scabbard without his even noticing. He looked surreptitiously around the fire to see if anyone had observed and caught Rissar staring at him across the blazing wood. He felt ashamed. Why did the sword honour him when so very much was unsuccessful? So little he did was right, so little good. All of it was accidental. Why record exploits that he had more or less fallen into rather than decided to do?

He was no hero. He was just a man to whom things happened.

He replaced the sword in the scabbard and placed it slowly on the ground beside him. It was fully dark. The climb had been tiring, in addition to the early part of the day spent picking their way through the hot steaming quagmire of the fire signs. He prepared for sleep. The camp was silent but for the crackling of the fire and Jored quietly finishing the stew with satisfied slurping noises. Halam lay down a distance from the fire and put his head upon his pack. He supposed the Hardsar would mount a guard this night and not trust the jaksar to protect them against the wiles of the Arcan. As he slipped into sleep, he hoped that they would wake him when it was his turn.

He slipped into slumber with a vague concern that he should have offered to help – even to have taken the first guard. *What will they think of me, sleeping when they must toil?* The feeling of unease, of doubt, and tasks unfulfilled came with him as the dreams began. They were disturbed and disturbing dreams of fire and death, swirling fears of the ancient Citadel and the enemies that awaited them there. Halam awoke with cold sweat covering his face and a clammy feel to his body under his clothes. It was still dark but the dawn was not far off. He did not readily desire more sleep and a return of the dreams. So he waited for the dawn. The night was quiet, which felt odd, for this was despite the crackle of the fire burning and the hiss of gas escaping from the cracks in the ground before bursting into flame. He wondered at this for a long time until he realised that there were no animal sounds. He had unconsciously expected them. Now, when they were gone, there was an all-pervading sense of quiet. He looked up at the glow of the red fire, tingeing the sky above the mountains, the echoing memory of the distant fire of the north. The daylight was not long in coming and, as the light returned, as if on cue, the Offspring of the fire rose.

Trioch, rising to her feet, smiled across at Halam. 'Welcome, Hardsaro, to the new light of the day. May the darkness not come again.'

'So be it,' said Halam.

'Truly,' she replied and smiled again.

The Child of the fire immediately turned to her fellow Offspring, and they at once set about preparing some food for the party to break their fast. 'When there has been no fire to sustain us,' said Sigmor, 'we must eat!' The Offspring all laughed at him; their joy was returning with the dawn.

Jored and Rosart also woke soon, and Jored seemed surprised to find Halam awake. He said nothing; he only raised his eyebrows and smiled a teasing grin.

The Arcan was the last to wake, the lights in his eyes twinkling to life as it became obvious that Rissar's group would be wanting to leave soon. Taxarzerek ate by raising his faceplate to cover his mouth. He requested no food, no nourishment.

The day ahead of them was dismal. They left the small valley and headed into a dead land. Halam had disliked the little blasted vale with its coarse grass and dry stubby trees, but as they travelled on he realised that it had been an oasis, a vestige of normal life. In the place they now walked, nothing grew. Gas escaped from the ground and burned all around them. Many rocks were aflame yet strangely not consumed. These flaming rocks released into the air a noxious and choking stench that bit at their throats and made them gasp. The air itself was filled with a sharp smell, acrid and acidic. As they climbed above the place where the gases burned, still the sulphurous fumes rose with them, curling upwards in great plumes of yellowish sickly smoke, and the smell grew worse and not better.

They trudged on as if it was a common habit of

theirs to travel in such a land. They climbed upward in single file, suppressing their fears. They did not need to worry and would not. The jaksar had no such qualms about his feelings or pretence in his demeanour. He whimpered and mewled until Rissar allowed him to spend the day losing himself within the folds of his robe. When the fumes were at their worst, the jaksar would bury his face and then peer out with baleful, frightened eyes.

Halam pitied the little creature. This was no place for anyone, let alone a forest animal used to a place full of vibrancy – a place to run and hunt, a place to be full of life. Halam remembered Rissar saying that if he had left Insnar behind on the plain with the hacsar, the little jaksar would still have followed them. He knew it was true. The climb grew more difficult as the day progressed and soon they were struggling up cliff sides or searching for routes across the face of the mountain. As the afternoon advanced Rissar was driving the pace.

Despite his hurry, they spent the night upon the side of the mountain. They reached no haven that night. There was no place to light a fire, but there was little need. Even in the deepest night, it was no longer truly dark on the perilous heights. Below them, the desert of burning fires sent not only sulphurous and unpleasant smoke but filled the night with a blue-yellow glow through the haze. Above them, the sky was lit by the red glow above the high pass. It seemed a fearfully long way up. Halam slept that night but fitfully, uncomfortable upon the slope, leaning against the sharp rocks. There were no dreams, only a terrible half-sleep where dreams and truth mixed and became dreadful. For two nights they slept like this, if as sleep it could be described. During the days they fought to find their way up. At times, Halam thought he could trace paths, the remains of steps, or strangely carved pavements. It was as if once, long ago, there had been a great roadway built to travel up into these mountains. The echo of an ancient time, long ruined and lost.

Taxarzerek, who claimed to have come this way, proved little help in finding the way up. He seemed as confused as they as if he had never been there. He said he had no memory and that the land had been covered in mist and smoke as he had descended. He had not planned the route but simply moved downwards. Halam found that a puzzling phrase and began to doubt the Arcan had ever been there. He wondered why he bothered to pretend. The fumes grew still worse and yet, ever-present as they were, Halam never became unaware of them. A sharp and bitter taste filled his mouth and ruined every mouthful of food he ate and every drink he drank.

They were short of water now, having found none in this forsaken land. For a while longer they could manage but soon it would become vital that they found, in this desert of fire, some source of water with which to fill their skins. At last, as the third afternoon of climbing began, they reached the high pass and passed over the crest of the final rise.

Halam stopped in horror.

Before them lay a great sweeping valley, sloping down from the pass. It was flanked on either side by huge mountains. This valley was the last vestige of life. There was grass; trees even grew in it, but, on either side of this final valley, the mountains were black and pitted with burning rocks. Smoke curled from the top of many of these peaks, both to west and east. On one mountainside, what looked like a river of molten fire curled lazily down. This vale was the only refuge of sanity in a land of madness, a road through the ruin, a way of dread. It was a pause, an oasis, before terror. Beyond it was fire. Beyond the sweeping valley was a place of deep foreboding. Ahead the land was gouged from the earth, a hollow, awful, ground torn and pitted by flowing fire. The whole was covered by a dense grey and black smoke. It was as if a great fiery hand had torn life from the world and replaced it with desolation. No wonder the sky glowed red at night for within that place there must be fire beyond reckoning and no sense of life, nor any memory of it.

Is that the goal? Are we heading into that?

Then he looked and he saw it. Just before the gouged land of fire and smoke, at the lowest point of the pass, was a city. There it was, at the last, in the richest and greenest place, the final depth, before the grass was swallowed by the murk, fire and blackness. It was not a huge city, but it was full of towers and tall buildings. *How could people live in this place? How could they survive here? It must be a ruin.*

'Is that the Citadel?' he said, hoping with all his heart that it was and yet knowing, somehow, that it was not. 'Is that the city that Taxarzerek saw?'

Rissar shook his head.

'It is the City of the Gate,' said Sigmor, before Rissar could speak, 'and it was one of the places of our dwelling in the ancient times. I have never seen it before, though the tales tell it well. It can be no other. I have long desired to see the homes of my ancestors.'

'Yes,' said Rissar, 'the gate of the land of Arnex. No one has dwelt there since Arnex was slain.'

'A beautiful place, it was,' said Helmar, 'and I'm happy to see it with my own eyes. Many tales are spoken of it.'

Trioch had not spoken but tears, unheeded, were running down her cheeks. Halam stared down at the ruins and could not help but wonder, not only how they could have lived there but what it had looked like when a whole city of Children sang the songs of the circle and the fire had burst into being above a whole city. The very thought was incredible, too vast for his mind.

'It would glow with a light that seemed imperishable,' said Rissar, answering Halam's unspoken thought. 'Every night it would fill the darkness with light, turning the very night into blazing day.'

'May flames of fire burn,' said Sigmor.

'In the core of the dark,' said Helmar.

'And may our Warrior King return to us,' said Trioch.

'So be it,' said Halam.

'So be it,' said Jored and Rosart together.

Halam turned and looked at the Arcan standing beside them. He wondered then if they should have spoken of such things before him. Taxarzerek was standing, silently listening to their talk and speaking not a word; the lights in his eye plates twinkled on and off, a garish, grotesque reminder of his oddity.

'The fire land grows worse as we travel on,' said the Arcan at last as they all stood, gazing at him. 'What we have travelled through is but a shadow of the fire land.'

'I know this, Taxarzerek of Arca,' said Rissar, 'for I have walked this land centuries before this moment. If you fear to accompany us, wait here, or in the ruins of the gate.'

Taxarzerek shook his head and, for the first time, the gesture seemed to have meaning. 'I escaped in fear all the way to where I met you and yet I knew I must return to find the . . . warriors that I have lost. I cannot return to my home without them.'

Rissar nodded. 'I understand.'

Taxarzerek stared at him. 'I begin to think you might . . .' he said as his eye plates flickered on, impassive, uncommunicative, '. . . truly, understand what I am.'

'I know where your place is, Taxarzerek,' said the Malasar. 'You were not expected.'

Taxarzerek nodded slowly, considering the words. 'The land below is terrible. We will need an alliance, Lord Rissar. Will you have trust in me? I simply wish to recover our ... equipment, the warriors, I mean. I have no other purpose that will harm you.'

Rissar smiled back. 'Then let trust begin and, perhaps, who knows, more may come of it.'

The Arcan nodded back and smiled one of his unconnected, unattached smiles. Rissar glanced at Taxarzerek, then turned and began to walk down the valley. 'Let us make the City of the Gate before we sleep this night. There is some shelter there and there will be water.'

They all followed him as they had on many roads to this place. Now it seemed he would lead them onward into an inferno. Halam wondered at the meaning of the exchange with Taxarzerek. *What will happen now?*

The path down to the city was easy in comparison with the climb they had completed. As the day wore on they neared, at last, the many-towered ruins of the city. Rosart, walking beside Jored and Halam, suddenly stopped.

'What is that?' He pointed down, towards the city.

They all looked in the direction he indicated.

'I see nothing,' said Jored.

Halam was silent. He too could see nothing.

'There,' said Rosart, 'glinting in the grass.' He pointed again to the coarse dry field before the gates of the city. 'Something is shining there, like polished metal.'

Halam looked; glistening in the rays of the sun settling towards the west, something was lying in the grass.

'Perhaps it is just that, metal,' Helmar said from behind.

'But it glowed so brightly for a moment,' said Rosart, 'and how can there be bright metal in such a place. It would have been corrupted long ago.'

Taxarzerek gazed in his usual impassive, unreadable way but then something in his stance changed. He leant forward.

Was that actual excitement?

'We will soon find out,' Rissar said and continued forward.

They hurried after him. For the first time, the Arcan seemed to desire to be in the lead. Then, without words, he broke into a run, his usual strange way of walking becoming a virtual glide along the grass as if he was slipping along on some great invisible sledge like a child playing on a winter hillside.

Halam ran after him. Now he could see that there was indeed metal lying in the grass before the city. It was large, but he had no idea what it could be. Then, as they neared it, Halam could see. Lying, or perhaps sitting partially, was the figure of a man. He was covered in shining silver metal from head to foot, like the Arcan. But with this new figure, there was no sign of flesh, neither his hand nor his head was free of the encasing armour. *This is armour.*

He was wounded. At least one of his arms hung at an unnatural angle and the other was supporting him, slightly upright, as if he were trying to rise and had frozen in the act. In his fist, he held a sword, upright, but broken off about two feet from the hilt. They all came to a stop before the strange figure, frozen as it was in the act of rising.

'It is a . . . warrior,' said Taxarzerek, moving.

◈ Chapter 13 ◈

I had finally reached the star system the Superior was in.

He was operating on the main habitable world. There was an epitome in action on this planet. The Superior tried his best to be present whenever there was an attempt of the enemy to infiltrate any world. And this scenario was going entirely normally – the same we had faced billions of times.

Raczek's world was different. I was here to convince the Superior to act. Raczek would obey my orders and keep the natives busy while I placed myself at the centre of the actual solution. I would deal with his blundering later. I flashed inwards and dismissed Raczek from my mind.

I gathered the reports of the situation in the system. It was an ocean world and the sentient species was therefore amphibious. They were hermaphrodites and would be either male or female depending on the need and the desire of the moment.

The reports were good. The Superior's mission had gone well; the action of the enemy was almost completely thwarted. Very few on the planet were listening to their epitome. He had scant native supporters interested in his corrupt message. There was little interest in the possibility of augmentation. This was good. There were even fewer underlings than they normally garner.

But then, we had been preparing here for

centuries, if not millennia. The harbinger had been quickly killed and the epitome, who seemed a particularly weak specimen, would be following him to death very soon.

I streaked to the planet in a form of electromagnetic energy invisible to this species. A probably unnecessary caution as they did not have the technology nor the means to track me. The habitable world was the second planet with a single large moon. So large was the moon that it was really a dual planetary system. The tides on this water world must be . . . interesting.

Perhaps that was why the sentient natives were amphibious. Only adults lived on the small amounts of land here. They reproduced by laying live fertilised larvae into the sea. When the young developed and transformed into adult forms they moved onto the land and joined the growing adult civilisation. Most of the land was given over to cities. In recent years they had even stopped laying the larvae in the open ocean. It was too risky for the young with so many other predators. They had built great nest pools in enclosed parts of the ocean where the predators were removed. The far oceans were now just to farm and harvest food. The system intelligence reports saw this as a good development for the race. They had tried things like it in the past but now their technology was at the point where they could achieve it. This had caused a distinct spike in population and that was probably what had attracted the enemy. He was attempting to acquire another, now numerous, species to his cause.

The Superior was in the main city of a string of islands in the southern hemisphere. I leapt down from space to land as electrical energy, just a sudden and unexplained bolt of lightning shooting from sky to earth. It does to be dramatic sometimes. It keeps native races in order.

I found as deserted a shoreline as I could. It wasn't completely empty. With the massively growing population and small amounts of land, it was mightily difficult to find a place with no natives present. I coalesced into the native form outside the city, behind a large rock on the shoreline. I then hopped out from behind it in what I hoped was a nonchalant manner. None of the hundred or so adults on the shore even gave me a second glance. One gets ignored in crowded places.

It was a strange means of locomotion – scurries, hops, leaps and jumps – but it got me quickly off the beach and into the city proper. I made my way through the crowds of adults thronging the streets. There were so many that they did not so much walk past each other as hominids might but instead struggled up, over, and beside each other or all of them simultaneously. Perhaps it was the overcrowding, or perhaps that level of bodily contact was the norm for this species. Either way, they didn't seem to care who they crawled over, leapt past, or scurried beside and under. They just ignored each other and moved.

Despite the crowd, I reached an open marketplace in the centre of the thronging city quite quickly. It was equally as overcrowded although in a more structured way. The natives were only heaped three or four deep, struggling through and around each other. The Superior was on the far side of the precinct. Of course, he had also taken the form of a native, but I sensed who he was easily enough. He already knew I was coming. I had sent a message indicating that I wanted permission for a direct meeting. He had granted me the audience. I am one of the few chi'shadii in this galaxy at the moment. I had the privilege of coming before him.

He was crouched on the far side of the plaza. There was a single member of the species speaking a few hundred feet from him, surrounded by a small number of her hangers-on. This would be the epitome and he, or she, was a sorry specimen. Even as he spoke the crowds of amphibians struggled past her without even a momentary pause to listen to what he was saying. We would have another success here. The Superior is mighty and wise.

I hopped hastily over to him. I would have made full obeisance, but we were in native disguise. I made do with a respectful bob of my head and the dutiful croak of a worker to his boss. He acknowledged my nod and gave me a quizzical look. He did not speak but continued to watch the native epitome speaking, with a wary eye on his sycophants.

'Lord,' I said, understanding that he wanted to know why I had come. 'There is a situation on Raczek's planet.'

'Which is?' he said. 'I have heard no reports, but I have been busy here. We have rendered this epitome insignificant.' He indicated the native with a flick of his tongue, an inclination of his head and a slow, considered croak.

The crowds around us were even more numerous. They crawled over and around us constantly. There was no sign that they were bothering to listen, not to the epitome nor the Superior and myself.

'I was summoned there, lord, because Raczek reported a new harbinger emerging. That would be the second instance of a harbinger on that world. Which would be strange, but he had reports of a figure on the southern isles. When I got there, I realised the situation was far more serious than that. Raczek has missed many developments on his planet. He has allowed powerful enemies to rise. The figure in the south is far greater than any epitome. And there is another in the northern lands. It was a very serious situation. There are two immensely powerful epitome-type natives abroad. But they are greater than an epitome. They wield huge powers and have great influence. One might even designate them apotheosis or vertex epitomes. This is some new departure, a new strategy of the enemy.'

The Superior raised his foreclaw to silence me

and indicated across the marketplace where the native epitome was still speaking. A band of military types, at least they looked like that, was cutting across the marketplace towards her and the crowds of amphibians, stacked several deep, were scurrying respectfully out of their way.

Clearly, the natives knew what happened to those who opposed the government. The intelligence reports I studied on arrival had told me that this planet was ruled by a military regime – one of our influences. Tyrants are so much easier to manipulate than other more complex forms of government. They are to be encouraged if the universe is to be reclaimed. The importance is not what they do, nor whom they kill, but whether they can be coaxed into doing the right thing for the future of the cosmos.

They marched through the crowd and stepped on any bystanders who weren't quick enough to depart. Heaps of natives were rushing over us now, hasty to be out of the way of the soldiers. I moved a little closer to the Superior to prevent my view of him being blocked by these spectators and bystanders.

The amphibian in charge of the troops stopped in front of the epitome and barked out some harsh words at her. Her followers, such as they were, shrank back into the crowd as the soldiers gathered around the pitiable figure. She might have had great powers but here she was, being arrested. I watched with rapt attention. It was always amazing to see the pitiful attempts of the enemy.

'Another failure,' the Superior said. 'It is most gratifying to see centuries of our work come to fruition, Romul. Another world the enemy will lose.'

As the epitome was marched away, his lackeys melted quietly away into the crowd, worried for their safety. The Superior smiled and turned his attention back to me.

'So, Lord Romul. Powerful epitomes? Apotheosis? Vertices, you say?'

I made a small bow to him again and croaked dutifully.

'Lord, I do not have the correct term. But they are not simply epitomes. We will need a new term. Raczek has missed much. We are facing much greater technological power than the planet should possess. This is some new development, a new strategy of the enemy. This is why I come before you.'

I flicked my tongue nervously, unable to prevent a twitch of anxiety. 'One of these beings, the one that Raczek first reported to us, was able to cast two thybuk and myself from the island on which he was spotted, and he has now surrounded it with some sort of energy shield that prevents any of our kind entering it. Lord, this shield operates even if we are clothed in a native form and keep all our energies completely under control. The shield is still able to prevent an approach. The natives, however, can come and go as they please. Lord, if a shield this powerful was extended to a larger area, a continent, or even to a planet, it could prevent us from even knowing what the enemy does there.' I indicated my disquiet by licking the end of my nose. 'Following this episode, I personally attacked the second of these beings, along with Raczek and twelve of his thybuk. Lord, he transported me far across the galaxy. It has taken me many days to return and come before you here. The technology he used to transport us there took only minutes to make the trip. Lord, if the enemy had the technology to cross the galaxy at a greater speed than we are able . . .'

I had the Superior's attention.

'Was it a phase tunnel, a handle in multidimensional space, or perhaps a wormhole?'

'Lord, he conjured it whilst I had him in my claws . . . It cannot be a stable wormhole unless he has the technology to create them instead of simply utilising naturally occurring ones, as some natives have achieved. He conjured it by speaking a single word. He had no technological equipment with him. I had stripped him of a power staff before taking him.'

The Superior's forward gills flicked with concern. He was staring at me now, multiple eyelids flickering in fascination.

I had him. This was working. 'Lord,' I said confidently. 'I come before you because I feel we must bring more forces to bear on these beings – more shadii, more thybuk are required. If you would send a great host under my control, I can repeat my success on this planet of the last millennia. We must thrust this race so far back into barbarism that they would take aeons to recover. These vertex epitomes could not stand against such a force – a sizable army of shadii and thybuk. Lord, they must be crushed. The situation is dire. Raczek has failed greatly.' I hesitated, unsure whether to make a final suggestion. I had gone back and forth on whether to request it during my trip and my constant planning and replanning of this conversation.

I decided to speak. 'And, Lord, if you would come yourself.'

The Superior did not respond at once and then let out a long, disgruntled croak, his tongue flicking around him, slapping into many passers-by who, naturally, ignored it.

He spoke. 'These figures, these vertex epitomes, were they ma'laak, or chi ma'laak?' He said it but I could see that he did not believe this even himself. His nose flaps were flattened.

'Not ma'laak, lord. We would know. I have seen no trace of their presence on the planet or in the system, lord. In itself that is strange, I know, but these vertices do not appear to be either of them. They are more powerful than ma'laak. Their technologies are beyond theirs, as well as ours. The energy shield, the interstellar transportation, these are not the skills of the ma'laak. Lord, this is some new development – has the enemy found allies amongst races we somehow do not know?'

The Superior croaked again, thoughtfully, and his multiple eyelids opened and closed quickly as he thought.

'This explains . . .'

I looked across at him and my tongue flickered nervously. *What is he saying?* Concerns rose to the surface of my mind again. *Is he going to blame me?* I waited patiently.

'Lord Romul, there has been a new gathering of the ma'laak. They are massing their forces. They have been travelling from muster points all over this galaxy. Many of them are assembling, very many. I was going to investigate them as my next task. The epitome on the planet here will be dead before the day is complete. I will leave it to the planetary chief to complete the disintegration of his sycophants. This civilisation will not hear any more of his seductive strategies to lead them to their doom. With careful strategy, there will not even be a future myth.'

He turned to me, showing his vomerine teeth in aggravation. 'So, Lord Romul, do you think the ma'laak might be heading for Raczek's world? To ally with these vertices?'

I bowed my head. 'I cannot know, my lord. I bow to your wisdom. It remains a strong possibility. It would be a strange chance and I find coincidences are rarely accidental. There is something very different occurring on that planet and Raczek missed it. Is the amassing of the ma'laak forces near this world of which I report?'

'Near enough,' said the Superior smartly. 'They could reach it quickly enough.' A testy call of fervent indignation escaped his amphibian lips. 'Why did this development escape our gaze, your gaze until this moment? Why were these natives allowed to develop new technology?'

I licked my nose. 'My lord.' I let my vicious grasping teeth show. 'The planetary chief, Raczek, summoned me from Arca where I have been operating for the last few hundred years. He reported a harbinger. Or he said it was a possible one arising on a southern isle. He had not investigated it personally. He dismissed it because I had already destroyed harbinger and epitome on his planet. I found these powerful vertex beings fully formed. Their uncontrolled technologies were fully developed. His agents failed to report even the existence of such beings. Why he failed in this matter I do not yet know, but fail he did. And I will find out why.'

The Superior stared at me for a long while, his multiple eyelids flickering and his gaze swivelling in a random, thoughtful way.

'I will ask Raczek that,' he said eventually, slowly. 'Why did you not ask him, Lord Romul?'

I did not at that moment care how many natives were streaming past us or over us. My focus was entirely on the Superior. This was the point of danger. I had considered and reconsidered this many times during my trip back. The responsibility for this failure must not be mine.

'I did question him closely, lord. It was clear.

He failed to establish the nature of the threat. He did not investigate properly before summoning me. Consider, lord, I visited one of these vertices and at once he implemented the barrier field. I attacked the second and he transported me to the other side of the galaxy. They were waiting for a shadii or Senior to arrive. Raczek failed catastrophically. Because of his failure of intelligence, I was transported twenty thousand parsecs by an unknown and an unobserved technology. I come before you to request reinforcement. Something more significant was happening here than the norm. Raczek will be punished, lord, and by me.'

The Superior's eyelids flickered again, sideways and up and down. 'So he will, Romul. So he will.' I could see that the Superior had not quite decided whether I had missed something also. Had I failed in the same way? I was concerned. His head rose and his tongue stretched out to caress some passers-by. He looked across at me, eyes swivelling.

'By my authority, Lord Romul, send the messages. Call a muster. Gather as many chi'shadii and shadii as you can. Call for all spare thybuk to rise to the fight also. I will visit this world with you as soon as you have gathered.' He paused. 'I should go against the gathering ma'laak horde before they achieve what they plan. They might well be heading for this system of Raczek's. There are times when a rare pitched battle over a planet is required. This may be one. It may not be what they intended, but they will respond if we attack the planet. We will draw them to battle and thwart their plans.' He croaked and moved lazily. 'I will go now and ensure the epitome on this planet is thoroughly lifeless and then I will come. You are dismissed, Lord Romul. Go, gather our forces.' He rose from his resting place and leapt promptly away.

I struggled my way through the crowds towards the street back to the shoreline where I could transform unnoticed. As I reached the far side of the marketplace, a native stepped before me.

'Lord Romul,' she said. 'I am Jatcha, the planetary chief here on this world. It is an honour to welcome you.'

I let my long tongue flick lazily outwards in an expression of recognition. The crush of passers-by climbed over and past us as we stood talking. No one here seemed even to care. Even as the epitome here was being crushed, Jatcha and the Superior had little need for secrecy from the crowds.

This chief had prepared for this moment for centuries. As it should always be. Jatcha had established that the epitome was coming. They had prepared well and it had all gone successfully. Both harbinger and epitome were arrested and killed by the governing authorities under the command of the tyrant we had helped create. And that dictator didn't even realise it was all under our prompting. That was how to lead a planet. A perfect example of an effective planetary chief. Raczek had failed to be one.

'A good job of work you have done here, Jatcha. The planet is safe now from the enemy's machinations. My congratulations.'

Jatcha looked pleased and I realised I had given her exactly what she had hoped for, an accolade from a chi'shadii, from a Senior.

'Have you any thybuk that you can spare us, Jatcha?' I said, pressing the advantage. 'Under the Superior's command, I am gathering a force to go against the ma'laak horde. The Superior has ordered all available forces to his direction.'

Jatcha's gills flicked. 'Yes, lord, he has communicated your desire. I have already sent the messages. Communication is easy here. There are few cities on all the isles. Undersea agents all have special missions which we will not disturb. But I can gather the force for you quickly. Where do you gather?'

'In orbit, initially.' I looked him over and flicked my tongue out. 'Is that safe? Will the natives track us?'

'Very safe, my lord. A good choice. They have not the technology to track our energy forms. Muster over the central sea – there are fewer islands there. They will see nothing and those undersea rebels will not care.' She smiled an obsequious smile back at me, a reptile considering her next meal.

'Very good. I shall wait in orbit. The Superior is coming with the force once your epitome is dead. You will handle things here.'

'Always, lord, always.' He flicked his tongue

out.

I slipped away from her and hopped quickly to the shoreline. It was difficult with even more natives thronging their way along the same pathways. Perhaps the epitome's death was finally drawing the crowd which the enemy had hoped for earlier.

I reached the shore and paused for a moment looking out across the warm southern seas. There was a string of islands stretching out from this, the largest, in a great arc of glowing golden sands. Every piece of stable land was peaked with huge and towering biotic structures from shore to shore. Their cities clawed for the skies. They were impatient predators seeking to grasp their prize from an endless blue. This species would leap for the stars in just a few generations. Under careful direction, they would achieve much. *Today, they achieved freedom. Today, they escaped the thraldom of the enemy's falsehoods. They will no longer hear his vacuous and wearisome lies. They will remain unchained.*

I stood and drank in the beauty of this world ignoring, or trying to ignore, the incessant croaks of passers-by, the incessant chattering of the natives trying, like myself, to look at the view. Yet they did not so much look at it as indulge in a constant prattle about it to their companions. It felt like nobody just saw the beauty but me. And what a beautiful world this was, or could be but for the natives and their constant motion, constant gesture and chatter, and constant boorishness – and the untidy biotic skyscrapers.

As I stood there, surrounded by mobility and jabber, I thought again of the troublesome vertices on Raczek's world. Not all races are attractive or even likeable. But on Raczek's planet, there was something else. They were dangerous.

This cannot be allowed.

I will gather the forces of our people and return in force.

Raczek would have to answer the Superior and to me why such a dangerous situation had gone on unnoticed. But these upstart natives would not stand against us. I walked to the rock at the end of the shore. I stepped out of sight and returned myself to energy not visible to these natives. I flashed skyward and transmitted messages to all the systems on this side of the galaxy – the order to muster all available shadii and chi'shadii in the segment. Those beyond that would never reach us in time. Shadii in other galaxies would have taken many months to reach us.

I settled into an orbital pattern, far above the central sea. Once the Superior joined me from the planet we would set off for a more remote muster point, a more suitable place.

I was still gathering the thybuk planetary forces that Jatcha was sending from the surface when Raczek sent a message, no doubt confused at my silence. He asked again where the reinforcements he so badly needed were. I did not bother to reply to him. He knew what he had to do. If my silence stressed him that was all to the good. He would be motivated. We would be there soon enough.

And they will suffer.

◈ Chapter 14 ◈

Halam stopped and stood, dumbfounded, staring at the huge man encased in metal lying on the ground. Taxarzerek had reached the warrior first and his three floating savants, so often out of view, swung quickly around to join him. He had not hesitated. There was no thought of caution. He knew what it was he saw. He acted. The Arcan knelt before the body of the warrior and the floating savants swarmed, obscuring their view.

Halam stepped forward, curious, worried. 'Taxarzerek, what are you doing?' He knew as soon as he said it that he would not get a reply.

'What is going on?' Jored snarled from beside Halam. As the Hardsara spoke he released the giant war hammer strapped to his back and swung the great weapon into his hands. He hefted it, threatening. The Offspring drew their swords and came to stand with the Hardsar.

'Peace,' said Rissar, stepping forward. 'Do not threaten him. It is his purpose to defend.'

'Is the warrior dead?' said Rosart.

Halam was watching the Arcan kneeling over the metal figure. Taxarzerek's hands were moving, touching the warrior, indeed he seemed to be inspecting his chest, changing something, making strange adjustments. What exactly his quick hands were doing was not clear, for the chest of the warrior was smooth and featureless. The lights in

Taxarzerek's eyes were changing very quickly. Halam could see their multiple colours flickering swiftly, reflected in the metal of the warrior's form. The lights were much brighter than usual. Halam stood there and for a moment he wondered whether to stride up and peer over Taxarzerek's shoulder, but something stopped him, some caution, some realisation that the Arcan would not permit it.

Though what would he do to stop me?

'Shall we stop him, lord, until he tells us what he is doing?' Jored spoke the words Halam was thinking. He raised his hammer higher in his great hands.

'No, do not stop him,' said Rissar quietly, raising his hands. 'He seeks to . . .' he paused as if seeking for the right word '. . . to heal the warrior.'

So, they stood, impatient, silently observing the operations going on before them. As he waited, Halam felt a wave of dislike of this stranger, this alien, his ways, his attitudes, his very self. In the past days, he had grown used to his peculiarity. But Halam did not trust him. The Arcan had moved from words of alliance back to this, to secrecy, to silence, to hiding his actions. *How can we trust him? He is not worthy of it.*

They stood and waited. Jored was still ready, hammer in hand, the Offspring beside him. Rosart had hung back and had not even strung his bow. Rissar was standing calmly, with Insnar at his feet. The tension of the moment stretched out. Halam did not know and dared not imagine what was about to happen. Perhaps they would finally understand why Taxarzerek had come, for surely this was his aim – to achieve this warrior, this sentinel. Now that he had him, what would he do next? Go home? Go away? Attack? Halam did not know.

There was a strange silence in that moment, like the quiet before some great event. Then, with a slow and ponderous creak, the warrior struggled to his feet. Halam was amazed. He had looked big on the ground, but standing, the warrior towered over all of them. Taxarzerek, kneeling on the ground, looked tiny beside him. *By the Snake god, he is huge.* The towering bulk of the metallic warrior must have been at least eight or nine feet tall. Halam stared up at the hugeness of the man. He had never conceived that anyone could be so tall. This man made Jored the giant Hardsar look like a dwarf. In the sunlight, he glowed.

Mist clung to the vale around them which obscured and changed everything. It was hours before sunset, but the sun was boiling into the west, turned a terrible crimson by the haze rising from the fire land. The scarlet light of the sun shone onto the metal of the warrior's armour as he towered above them. He glowed with blood-red light, like some terrible fighter newly returned from slaughter, covered in the blood of his enemies. He was a complete combatant. The word *warrior* was unnecessary. He did nothing else. He was nothing else. And he was not simply a warrior, he was a war in and of himself. It was his only purpose. From head to foot, no inkling of humanity was betrayed, no weakness in the armour, no point at which his frailty was exposed. Perhaps he had none.

The warrior viewed the world through a single thin slit, though Halam doubted he could see through it, so thin, so stylised was the opening. It was completely straight with a small peak above it as if to shade his eyes from the sun. Within this breach in his metallic perfection, there was no sign of the man's flesh, no view of eyes. It prevented the light from entering and revealing anything. There was no view of his head As he neared them, as Halam met the warrior's stare, he thought that perhaps within the darkest depths of the black interior there was a faint glow, a glimmer of light inside – some deep, dark glow of green.

This is no normal man.

A single gem was embedded on his forehead, at the top of the helmet. It was small but it glowed, a strange greenish glow that pulsed with an unnatural regularity, the slow beating of a crystal heart. He had not noticed the gem flashing when the warrior had lain inert on the ground. Halam looked from the pulsing gem buried in the helmet to the flickering lights reflected within the eye plates of Taxarzerek. Green was one of the colours in Taxarzerek's eyes and that light now pulsed with exactly the same regularity.

Halam had assumed that the strange lights in Taxarzerek's eye plates were part of some strange method of seeing. Could it be that there was now some connection between the Arcan and the warrior? He gazed as the twinkling lights turned from red to blue to green and so on through all the spectrum. They all flashed at differing speeds but the green glimmered on, completely in time with the warrior's pulsing gem.

Taxarzerek had risen to his feet beside the warrior and stood gazing across at the rest of the party. The Arcan was tiny in comparison with his protector, if that was all he was. He looked now as if he was in charge, in command of all that stood before him. He had regained his confidence. The old Taxarzerek, the oiliness, the smooth suavity, the cunning sly man they had first talked with the down on the plain had returned

'Is he fully recovered?' Rissar asked the question rather drily, for it was obvious that the warrior was complete.

'Yes, he is quite functional,' said Taxarzerek.

Halam scowled. *Is it good to talk of a person as functional?*. 'He is quite recovered now. He was somewhat damaged . . .' He stopped. 'Wounded, I mean, and I have given him the aid required.'

'Taxarzerek of Arca, where are the other warriors? There are more than one.' Rissar spoke now with a harsh grain to his voice, a sharpness very unlike the Malasar's normal tone.

Halam hoped that this was the beginning of a break with this hateful companion. He did not like this Arcan. If he had ever doubted before, he was sure now. He was not their friend. Perhaps, at last, Rissar would not permit him to travel with them.

'I cannot know,' replied the Arcan smoothly. 'The sentinels do not speak, they protect. It is their function. He cannot . . . report, cannot talk. Normally I can trace them, but not at the moment.'

Rissar did not reply.

Behind Taxarzerek now stood a warrior he clearly felt could fully protect him. He was not frightened of them any more if he ever had been. Nothing Rissar said or did was going to faze him. Silence settled back over the scene, a confrontation without words, a soundless battle of wills. This tableau of silence was broken as, with a creak, the warrior sheathed his broken sword.

It slid easily into a slot at the top of his hip. No scabbard hung from his belt, no external means to sheathe the sword. This man never removed his sword, never stripped himself of his armour, never ceased the pursuit of war. As Halam stood looking at the warrior he turned his head slowly from side to side, surveying the party, deciding no doubt whether they constituted a threat. Halam wondered what the colossus would do if he decided that they did.

The two groups were separate now – the Arcan with the towering bulk of the warrior beside him, and opposite him, the seven of them. Halam's friends still held their weapons drawn; only Rosart and himself were not armed. The two groups considered each other, deciding whether to fight.

Breaking the silence, Rissar spoke. 'Let us make camp beside the city. Perhaps this day's journey is complete.' Rissar seemed untouched by the tension that filled the air, by the suspicion surrounding Taxarzerek. He set about preparing for the night. Insnar bounded off into the waving grasses and was lost to Halam's sight. They moved. The tableau broke.

The camp was an uneasy place, more divided than it had ever been. The wary peace that had settled on them during the past days was entirely gone and replaced by suspicion and mistrust. Taxarzerek had always held himself separate and isolated. This time it was different. The Arcan was mysterious, bizarre and puzzling, but no one had seen a way for him really to be a threat. He carried no weapons. Halam knew the power that Rissar wielded. Also, Taxarzerek had been adamant that he was no danger. But now, towering over them, was the means of his attack.

Without question, these warriors don't only defend.

He realised the Arcan had merely been an annoyance before. They had been striving to reach the Citadel without further delays. Taxarzerek had come and brought with him confusion, strange ideas and a bizarre view of the world. Now he had the means to force his cold, emotionless will on them. Surely, this was how everyone who sat around their camp thought – except for Rissar. And, it seemed, Insnar.

He had returned and sat beside the Malasar, licking himself with the air of calm only an animal can achieve.

Halam did not want to think about their peril any further. He helped Helmar and the other Offspring light a small fire to cluster around. It had to be small. The supply of wood was sparse. They found a well close to where they camped, further towards the strange ruins of the city. Rosart and Jored took the water-skins and filled them. The acrid water was strangely pungent but seemed drinkable.

As the Hardsar walked to the well, they were followed by the giant warrior. He seemed content once he assured himself what they were doing. He returned to the camp to stand beside Taxarzerek without even glancing back at the Hardsar.

Halam sat down by the fire with the Offspring. He frowned, quashing a desire to scream. He turned and considered the Offspring sitting beside him. They were not looking at him, or even the Arcan warrior. Their attention was on the city. They stared across at it with a strange air of fascination, almost of enchantment. Halam did not care what joys the city held for them. He turned and looked at Taxarzerek. He still sat apart. The warrior now sat beside him, his armour glinting brightly in the redness of the still sinking sun and the glow of the volcanic fires that surrounded their valley. They were in the last oasis of green in a land of flame and in it sat a red-glowing sentinel.

The warrior's head turned occasionally as if to catch some small peripheral movement or simply to take in the world around him. The strange green gem in his helmet pulsed on. *The warrior is as bizarre as his master.*

It was hard for Halam to believe that this man lived entirely encased in metal and never thought to remove his helmet or armour, to relax at the end of the day. Halam turned and looked at Rissar who sat, as usual, just on the edge of the camp with Insnar. He was looking back at Halam and, oddly, Halam knew what Rissar would have said to him. He would have spoken words of patience; he would have spoken of calm.

Halam turned back to stare at the Arcan. Whatever Rissar would say, he was not sure about trust when such a one sat within their camp. He drew a slow, deep breath and decided that he would walk over and ask Taxarzerek for more information about the warrior. No one else was going to do it. Perhaps the Arcan would tell him. He could try again to gain information from him.

Halam rose to his feet. Helmar, as he stood, turned and stared up at him, as if puzzled that he was going somewhere at such a wonderful moment. Halam looked down at him, wondering whether to say something. But the Offspring's attention straightaway turned back to the city – nothing else was of importance. Trioch spoke some low words that Halam did not catch.

He turned and walked slowly over towards the Arcan. The warrior's head swung in his direction and fixed him with a stare as he approached. Halam knew at once what was in the metallic man's mind. Was this a threat? Was he attacking? He rested his hand upon the butt of his sword and, drawing his breath, continued forward. The action was not lost on the warrior, who straightened and placed his great metal gauntlet on the hilt of his sheathed greatsword, broken though Halam knew it to be. Halam stopped before the figure of Taxarzerek and without speaking a word sat down before him, cross-legged.

'What does your lord wish to know?' said Taxarzerek. So the Arcan knew, or suspected, that Rissar had suggested their previous talk. Now he supposed that Halam had come for the same reason. He felt the silence of the camp behind him and knew that many eyes were fixed on his back. All except the Offspring would be wondering what would now happen. What was Halam doing? What would Taxarzerek say?

'Not just my lord, but all of us,' Halam said after some hesitation, deciding if he must be the emissary of the whole camp he may as well state it. 'Your warrior is impressive, Taxarzerek, he is a large man, well able to protect you and himself. How many of them are there?'

The Arcan hesitated. Halam felt he was remembering the details he had given them before, checking whether he was about to be consistent.

'Ten . . .' The answer was terse but trailed off into nothing. The Arcan had not wanted to say the number. Yet, he knew he could not avoid giving them some answers. Halam drew his breath in slowly. Given the confidence that had returned to Taxarzerek by the presence of just one of these colossi, what would his potential be if he found all ten? Halam wondered if that figure were even vaguely correct.

There might be many more. The thought was appalling.

Halam drew another slow breath. In his mind, he was convinced that this alliance was now dangerous to them all. He must somehow persuade Rissar to separate from this alien and his new protector. 'And why is the warrior here? This is not where you said you were ambushed. That was further into this land. Did he escape and come here?'

The Arcan pursed his lips and then pressed them into a thin, exasperated line. He no longer had reason to fear these barbarians with whom he had travelled. With the warrior beside him, he saw no reason to appease. Halam looked across at his arrogance and hoped that the Arcan would of his own accord go his own way.

After all, why does he need us?

'I do not know the answer to your questions.' He spoke brusquely. 'I cannot ask the warrior. He was damaged. His memory was damaged . . . I mean, he has forgotten. He is unable to tell me. It is of no importance. His function is to fight, to protect. What

happened is not important. I have re-established a
link . . . I mean, he has returned to me. I cannot trace
the others. They have been linked . . .' Taxarzerek
stopped as if confused about how to explain it.

Halam raised an eyebrow. 'Why can't he talk to
us – by sign language, or by writing? If he removed
his helmet couldn't we find some way to
understand?'

Taxarzerek smiled the same distant,
unconnected smile that had become normal in their
dealings with him. But this time there was more of a
sneer to it. Halam realised he had said something
stupid, so utterly inane that the Arcan seemed to be
having trouble responding without deep sarcasm.
'No. He cannot . . . will not. He does not remove the
armour.'

The answer was patronising, the sort of answer
you give to a child that cannot understand, that won't
understand until it grows. Halam scowled. This was
stupid. What use is an army that cannot speak and
cannot report back? What use was a single warrior
who can't warn you of attack? Halam looked at the
warrior sitting impassively beside his master, still
watching Halam unemotionally through the black slit
in his helm. The green gem in his helmet pulsed on
regularly, a crystal heart, reflecting some endless
rhythm. The warrior did not move, did not alter his
stance. How could he remain so unnaturally still?

Halam turned his attention back to the Arcan,
who had watched this silent exchange without

uttering a sound. Taxarzerek had the air of dealing with an innocent fool. Halam was not a violent man but the contempt of this man for him was unbearable. Halam did not understand. Why split the functions of people to such an extreme? Warriors encased in metal who gave no thought to their humanity but only to conflict. He stared across at Taxarzerek, blinded behind his eye plates. 'Very well . . .' There was no more to say, no more words to use to fence with him. The Arcan had his warrior and he did not need their aid any more.

Very well, I know what to say to Rissar. There is no other choice. The Arcan must not be allowed to continue with us. It is too dangerous. If Taxarzerek does not need us, what need do we have of him? He had only been a source of confusion and doubt.

Halam nodded curtly and rose to his feet. He bowed to Taxarzerek, letting his gaze settle for a moment on the man's twinkling eye plates. The Arcan did not appear to have noticed Halam's look, nor felt the strength of his emotions. He looked at Halam with the same unsympathetic expression.

'Thank you, Taxarzerek,' Halam said. The words came over sarcastically. They both knew no information had passed. He turned to go.

'Perhaps you will answer me one question in return?'

Halam looked back. 'If I can, I will.'

'Why did your lord order a stop? It was the middle of the afternoon. There was still time, still daylight. We could have got much further into the land before night fell.'

Halam shrugged. 'I do not know. This is the City of the Gate. Perhaps this is where travellers always rested before entering the land. If so, he might stop for that reason. There is much ahead of us, and I for one welcome the respite. We will face the fire land soon enough.'

Halam walked away without waiting to see if the answer satisfied Taxarzerek. He made his way over to the fire where Helmar still sat, awaiting his return. Trioch and Sigmor sat beside him but all their attention was still fixed on the ruins of the city. Jored and Rosart sat just a few feet away. They were gazing at Halam walking towards them over the grass. They were fascinated, interested now to learn the content of the exchange.

Halam slowed, not relishing talking, sharing his failure with them. He had gained nothing from the Arcan and he did not want to spend many minutes weighing every thought, every nuance of Taxarzerek's responses. They should be rid of him.

He stopped and looked around him, for the first time really looking at this part of the valley, the ruined city and the sun still slowly setting into the west, crimson over black mountains, congealed blood on a shadowed wall. There was a feeling here, a redolence, some echo of unremembered greatness. If he was silent for long enough he would understand, he would grasp it. Why had he worried about the

Arcan when there was this yearning cry, waiting to be found? He looked over towards the ruins of the city. He knew, somehow, that it was this place that was the source of the feeling. It was an ancient place; whilst much devastated there was still a grandeur. He gazed at it, not caring what others thought or wanted. He wanted to look at the ruins. This was what the Offspring had been feeling.

No single building was without a collapsed roof or a fallen wall. Nevertheless, he could see it had been a beautiful city, even with all the ways it had been ruined. There had been towers and halls as great as any in In Haxass. None of it remained now. At least, nothing was whole. It was all broken and smashed like the toy of a careless child, thrown down and needed no more. He wondered at the uniformity of its destruction; it was as if someone had purposely left no place unharmed, no single building undamaged. Someone had hated it so much they had wanted everything to be smashed. He wondered what it had been like when it was whole.

He imagined a city full of the Offspring, all with the power they had to sing the darkness away. How indeed had it looked at night, when they had gathered together and sang the fire into being? Would it not have glowed with a sempiternal light?

He looked at the buildings for many minutes. Gradually, he saw it repaired, rebuilt, or perhaps never ruined. The vision disturbed him, frightened him. He looked away, scared that the city was capturing him, calling him into some other existence, some other place where the world was whole, the city not broken. If he continued to look he would become one of those ancient people, the people of Arnex singing daylight into darkness.

He turned back to look at the people gathered around the fire and met instead the eyes of Sigmor. The Child of the fire smiled back at him. Halam knew that Sigmor understood what had just happened.

Did they see the same thing?

Halam walked away, breaking the spell, breaking the bond between Sigmor and himself. He walked over to where Rissar sat with Insnar. The jaksar was eating; the Malasar had given him some of his food.

The Malasar looked up at him. Halam sat down.

'You spoke to Taxarzerek?'

'Yes, lord, but I learnt very little. He said there were ten warriors. That, I admit, worries me. This one seems immense enough, unstoppable. How could we stand against so many of them?'

Rissar raised his eyebrows. 'Stand against them? Do you intend to fight them?'

'Lord, you know well the minds of the people gathered here – you know what everyone in this camp is thinking. If I can see it then you can. Before tonight Taxarzerek was strange, bizarre, an odd companion to choose for our road. Yet it was hard to see how he could be a threat or any real delay. Now he has the warrior. He is, surely you see it, fully armed. Would we let other armed fighters, whose origin we do not know, travel with us?'

'But we know his origin,' said Rissar softly, 'and I would, despite your reasonable concerns, rather know where this man is and what he is doing. His arrival is important and is linked to our enemies. People of his provenance always have ... effects when they come. We need to know where he is and what he is doing.'

'So you will allow him to accompany us?'

Rissar raised his head. 'I will not prevent it.'

'Then,' said Halam with feeling, 'I can only hope he decides he no longer desires our company and departs of his own accord.'

Insnar had finished his food; he turned from it and sat down and stared across at Halam. At once, Halam felt shamed by this animal who did not question but only followed – and with utter trust.

Halam sighed, a long, exasperated sigh. 'I asked Taxarzerek what the warrior had told him of the attackers. I thought to discover their disposition, their strength, but he claimed that the warrior had forgotten and cannot speak or communicate in any way.'

Rissar nodded but did not smile.

Halam spoke the question in his mind. 'Why do they divide the functions of a person so? It is so strange. A warrior who does not speak, who does nothing but fight for another's protection. Taxarzerek may speak and has relinquished his view of the world. Why do they live like this?'

Rissar responded slowly. 'They think that they gain . . . greater wisdom. It is . . . foolishness. They would not see it as so.'

Halam bent forward. 'Wisdom? But how does this gain them anything?'

'I cannot explain it fully, Halam, for you would need other things explained before you understood. Taxarzerek speaks better than you or me. He has a . . . facility with languages, as he said. There is little spoken that he cannot understand and replicate. He believes this skill among others is worth everything. Yet, he gains it by sacrifice. With the eye plates, he thinks he sees better, further, and sees things that you cannot see. But to do it he blinds himself. Taxarzerek, who can speak every language, is dumb, for he never communicates entirely of himself. He is not free to speak as he thinks.'

Rissar's words were inexplicable.

Halam turned and looked across at the Arcan. 'What then of the warrior? Does he gain strength and might and yet is weak?' Even to himself, the words were nonsense.

'He is different. It is not simple. He is merely unwise. The warrior is an opportunity not taken.'

Halam let the words run around in his mind for a while. He did not understand. 'Taxarzerek seemed to find my questions about the warrior strange. He seemed to think that I did not understand something very obvious. He found me comical, which is confusing, for I only asked a simple question.'

'And what was the question you asked?'

Halam looked back at the Malasar. 'I asked why the warrior could not remove his helmet to communicate with us by signs.'

Rissar smiled and Halam was immediately irritated. *Is Rissar going to laugh as well?*

Seriousness returned to the Malasar's face and he nodded. 'Yes, I can imagine that will have caused Taxarzerek amusement. He takes great delight in keeping his thoughts to himself, so he knows their import when others do not.'

'But why was he amused, disdainful? He spoke to me as if I was a child who needed to be led. He seemed to believe I could never understand.' Halam stared at Rissar. He could feel his face was taut, set.

Rissar shook his head slowly, understanding Halam's anger in his very bearing. 'Do not be angry, Halam. He found it amusing because you think that the warrior is a person.'

Halam said nothing. His surprise was too great. Rissar looked across at him and there was sympathy in the stare. Halam knew he was aware that he struggled with the concepts. He wished to help.

The Malasar continued speaking. 'The warrior is not a man. It does not live as we do. Although he could. Perhaps, once, there was part of him that was, but no longer. They deny him that.'

Halam looked back at the pulsing gem glowing in the helmet of the giant warrior, still sitting motionless beside the Arcan.

'What is he then . . . ?'

'There is no longer a word I could use that you would understand. The ancients knew of such . . . devices, but we no longer have them.'

Halam sat in silence for several minutes. 'I do not understand.'

'No, and that is what Taxarzerek discerned, and what made him scoff. The knowledge of the making of such things is . . . past. What is unclear is what their return to our world means.'

'We must awaken Arnex,' Halam said, the phrase bursting from him and he knew not why.

He saw that Rissar's eyes were burning into his. 'You are right and should remind me of such things. Remember, with all that is known by Franeus, no mystery cannot be . . . overcome.'

Halam turned, aware of a presence at his side. Helmar had walked silently up and stood now to one side, waiting patiently for Rissar and Halam to finish.

'Lord,' he said abruptly, and their attention turned to him, 'my brother, my sister and I would like to go into the city.'

Rissar looked up at him. 'You wish to greet your ancestors?'

'My lord, we wish to see the City of the Gate. We have heard of it in the tales. We have told the stories to our children for generation after generation. We would go there.'

Rissar nodded. 'I understand. There is no problem. Go, see the City of the Offspring, where your people lived for so long.' He looked across at Halam. 'Halam, go with them if you wish, for you will learn things about ancient times. They will permit your presence.' He glanced up at Helmar who nodded. Rissar continued to stare at Helmar. 'But be back before the total dark, Child of the fire.'

Helmar nodded. 'Of course, my lord, there is only a need for a short visit. We wish only to see the ruins. There will be no need to tarry. The city still holds within it much power for us. We would pass its towers.'

'Be cautious then,' said Rissar.

'Indeed, we will.'

Halam turned. 'But surely we cannot go. The Arcan would be even more able to best those who remained.'

Rissar smiled slowly, laughing slightly. 'Have no fear. The Arcan could not best me even if I sat here alone. The warrior is not as great as Taxarzerek imagines, nor does it give him the protection he thinks it brings. Great is the power of the Snake god. The imitation of power on Arca is a sorry likeness.'

Halam still hesitated.

'Go,' said Rissar, 'and learn to trust.'

Halam rose to his feet then, for if Rissar said such words, what real choice did he have? And he did wish to see the city. Despite the strangeness of the feeling that had overcome him when he had looked properly at the place before, he felt the essential nature of the city. There was no threat for him in those ruins and the buildings were very beautiful. He looked across at Helmar. The Child gazed back at him, waiting.

'I would like to see the city. It looks,' he hesitated, 'interesting.'

'Then come, brother of the circle. Let us trust.'

Helmar swung round and indicated quickly to Trioch and Sigmor. The other two Offspring rose at once to their feet and strode across the grass towards them. Halam saw Jored's head rise in interest but the Hardsara did not move. Halam caught his glance, but he did not speak.

Jored turned and muttered some indistinguishable words to Rosart sitting beside him. The woodsman looked up from the ground where he had been working on his bow, checking and tightening. He just watched them leave.

The Offspring walked off briskly. Halam rushed after them, giving the Hardsar no further thought. Helmar, Trioch and Sigmor were in a hurry, so great was their desire. The city proper lay across a stretch of dry, coarse grass and the Offspring strode across it, all but running in their eagerness to reach the place. As they hurried there Halam looked ahead of them. It was a strange place, a city without walls. There were many exits and entrances into it. From each building a door led to the outside world; between each dwelling was a street or an alleyway and its maze of streets came to a sudden stop as the city ended and the grass began. From all these exits were the faint remains of roads, long overgrown.

So, this place had been built in a happier age. This was not a place that could be defended, not a place where the inhabitants even expected attack. No enemy had ever come against this city until the final one. Unless, and the thought occurred late to Halam as he hurried after the Offspring, in times gone by there was some other defence. Walls that were invisible.

While there were many approaches, on the side of the city facing them two great columns of stone framed the widest of the entrances. It led to a broad and magnificent avenue. The columns were immensely high, and, to Halam's surprise, they were made of pure white stone. As he looked, he knew that he had seen that stone before somewhere, in a dream.

The pillars were at the beginning of the avenue – the welcoming portal of the City of the Gate. Through it, Halam was sure the travellers would pass, the visitors, the strangers entering the land of Arnex. If this place was the City of the Gate, then these monoliths were surely the gate itself. Beyond them, just inside the city itself, was a huge flat table of stone. It looked like the giant banqueting table of some great king. This was also carved from the same white stone. From where he was it seemed undamaged.

They had crossed the ground quickly, so keen were the Offspring to reach the gateway. They strode through the pillars with all the air of homecoming conquerors. The Offspring were proud, Halam could see that. As they passed beneath the towering monoliths of welcome, Halam caught the faint sound of singing, echoing around the ruins, as if their passing had triggered some ancient memory, a city remembering the music, singing again the songs of old. He turned, glancing at Helmar and the others, seeking the source of the voices. *Are there people here?* But before he took one more step he knew that there were none, just the city itself. The City of the Gate was welcoming home its citizens. Enduring, the song was light, gentle, lilting, full of joy and peace. It faded as an echo drifts away in the breeze. It seemed to Halam that, when they passed through the gate, it was as if they had plucked the string of some ancient instrument.

The voices faded away into silence.

◈ Chapter 15 ◈

They walked beyond the gate, up to the flat stone. Was it a great table? In the centre was a hollow depression, blackened by fire, and still pitted by an ancient ferocity. A flame had burned there for many years. A welcoming fire, Halam imagined, for the visitors to this land this abode of Arnex. Whatever it had been before, now this was a land of fire, though not in any way the Offspring ever wished.

Halam stepped up to the table and looked down at the hollow. What was it that had burned there? What had been its fuel? Helmar standing beside him reached out and placed his hand in the centre of the stone. He opened his mouth and spoke words in a language that Halam did not know.

When he had finished, Halam said, 'Helmar, what is this stone?'

He raised his eyes and looked briefly at Halam. Then he looked away, meeting the gazes of Trioch and Sigmor who stood silently to the side. There were tears in his eyes.

'It was here, brother, that the fire of welcome burned, always, to greet travellers as they came to our city. It is extinguished now and does not welcome. Oh, that the fire burned again that I need never leave the walls of our home.'

'Fear not, my brother. It will return,' said Trioch.

'Truly,' said Sigmor.

They walked round the great table – *an altar to fire,* Halam decided – and on down the grand avenue. This was clearly the main street of the city and as they walked they passed large dwellings on either side. They were all ruined; not a single house was without some sign of destruction – a fallen roof, a collapsed wall even, once or twice – all but complete destruction. The devastation was so uniform that Halam wondered again if it had been done deliberately. Somehow it was more than just the passage of time. Could people have come here, simply and solely to destroy this place? To break it and leave it half-ravaged to serve as some sort of reminder of their power.

It is possible; it is truly possible. But who had hated these people that much?

The city was larger than he had thought from their camp. Perhaps he had not paid enough attention to it, looked at it as it deserved to be looked at. It was great, a huge and magnificent place. They walked slowly on amid the fallen roofs and ruined houses for many minutes, and still the avenue swept ahead of them. There seemed no end to the place.

Outside each building was a small plinth, about half the height of a person, yet wide, as wide as a person's shoulder. On top of the plinth, a hollowed stone was balanced. Halam walked over to look at one of them more closely and realised that a fire had burned outside the doors of each house, atop these plinths, like the fire of welcome burned on the great table at the gate. As he walked along with the Offspring, they drank every sight in with obvious joy. Halam tried to imagine walking down this street when the city had been intact and its citizens filled it, fire greeting you at every door, and fire surrounding you on every side; the effect would have been overwhelming.

He stopped, astounded by the images that leapt into his mind. Around them was a land of fire, entered through a gateway of fire. Yet the fire of the Offspring had surely never been the same as that which filled the land now. Their fire was a refining fire of knowledge and a fire of passion. It did not wound; it did not incinerate. It was not a fire of destruction, but a fire of light, a fire of life – not the fire of darkness and death.

As he stood there, he felt there was something else strange about the city. It took him several moments to realise what it was. As he looked around there were no great houses, no palaces, no mansions of the rich merchants or the nobles. In the equivalent area of In Haxass the housing would be mixed, small and large for the poor and the great. Here there were large houses, but they were all of the same size. There were no houses of the poor, no bottom rung of society.

In the City of the Gate, each building was different from all its fellows and yet entirely similar in size and grandeur. Had they all lived in mansions? Had there been no rulers here, no lord, no merchants richer than the common? Had they all been princes? Or none of them?

It must have been a wondrous place and a beautiful society.

They reached the centre of the city. Even there, there was no great palace for the king. Beyond them, the avenue swept onwards past more houses to the end of the city. In the middle of the central precinct, a huge dais had been built. It was reached by climbing twelve massive steps and filled the great square. *It must measure a hundred feet.*

Halam walked over with Helmar and mounted the steps slowly. He imagined that at its height he would find ruins, the foundations of some great monument to the Snake god destroyed perhaps by whoever had come here in war. As he reached the twelfth step, there was no sign of ruins, no sign that the dais had held a building in the whole of its history. Instead, there was, once more, a deep hollow blackened by ancient fire. At the gates of this place, at the door of every house, and now in the very centre of the city itself, a fire had burned. *What a sight it must have been.*

He turned and looked back over the city. Towers surrounded him in every direction but never were they concentrated together to form any sort of fortress or castle. They were everywhere, surrounding him, and he knew that, strangely, even though every building was different, there was some pattern to their placement, some significance to their form and location. There was some meaning here, although he could not grasp it. Whatever it was, the whole scene before him was balanced, whole and fulfilled.

He saw that at the height of the towers, where they still stood, were blackened stones darkened by the fire. So fire had burned at their pinnacles as well as all around them. Even before the Offspring began to sing, this city would have been filled with fire. When the song of the circle began, the whole city must have been held within the flame of the song. Within this place, darkness had never come. Here, the day had been perpetual. At least, it had lasted as long as the Offspring had sung. It did not continue now, for they had left this place, and their song had ended.

Until, he realised, *I returned to stand with them now.*

Halam turned to Trioch who stood by his side, silently drinking in the city around them. 'It was a beautiful city,' he said.

'Yes, and full it was of our people in times that are gone. When Arnex returns perhaps we shall rebuild. I would wish it so, but it is not the way of the Snake god to do the same again. Instead, we must pass from greatness to greatness, from the magnificent to the glorious.' She looked for a moment as if she was both enraptured and deeply sad at the same time.

Beyond the city, Halam could see the fiery mountains. The dark and foreboding hills presaged a dark and perilous land ahead of them and on either side of them. Strange as it was, the City of the Gate was the last reminder of a straightforward world before blackness and red fire. For the first time, he wondered if this land of Arnex had always looked like this – this devastation, this destruction, this terrible consuming fire. Was the city a memory of a kinder time? Were the dark lands a terrible ruin of some beautiful land? Or had it always been like this? He did not know.

He released a long, exasperated, despairing sigh. He walked away from Trioch and back to the edge of the steps where Helmar still stood. As he reached the top step a metal figure stepped into the square below him. He came out of one of the ruined buildings. It was the warrior. Halam hesitated; what was it doing here? Had it followed them? Surely they should have seen it approach? 'Helmar . . .' he said.

The Child turned and looked down and gasped in shock.

The warrior strode forward. He stood at the head of the great avenue now, trying, it seemed to Halam, to block their exit. With a sudden fluid movement, the colossus drew his sword. The sword was whole and undamaged. *How . . . ?*

Halam backed off, drawing his sword.

Helmar came with him. 'Trioch! Sigmor!' Helmar called their names and they ran to stand alongside him. The warrior ran up the steps. His speed was amazing, the lightness of his step, stunning. Gaining the top, he stopped and swung his greatsword in a vicious arc then it stopped, silent, still, waiting.

'He wants to fight us,' said Sigmor quietly.

The Children had drawn their swords. Halam raised his blade. He felt the surge of power flow into him.

'Allam ecti tor,' he said, the words coming unbidden to his lips.

'Oram terom bir,' said Helmar, raising his sword.

'Trach tachorem,' said Trioch.

The warrior stepped forward, slowly now, apparently unsure of how the four of them would come at him. In his helmet, the gem pulsed rhythmically on.

'Wait,' said Sigmor, 'the gem in the warrior's helm is blue.'

Halam peered. 'Has it changed colour?'

'Or is it another warrior? Lost in the city.' Trioch spoke the words quietly.

The warrior swung his sword again, viciously fast, and strode forward. They separated, backing off, readying themselves for defence. The warrior stopped again and turned his head from side to side, considering them. Halam thought it looked angry, but it had no means to communicate any emotion.

'He grows impatient,' said Sigmor drily.

At once, without a word to Halam, the three Offspring ran towards the warrior. They cried out, as one, words of an unknown language. The warrior swept his sword around, parrying easily the blows of Trioch and Sigmor, thrusting them back by the sheer force of arm. Halam ran forward and, raising his sword above his head, struck at the warrior before he could recover his position. His sword hit him squarely in his chest, and it slid off without even denting it. Helmar struck last, to the side, and danced quickly away. His blow had done no more damage than Halam's.

They fell back and circled the giant. This was going to be a more difficult, more involved fight than it might at first appear. As Halam had feared, this warrior was no mean fighter. He was built only for that task. Abruptly the warrior thrust, lunging forward, trying to impale Helmar on the point of his greatsword. The Child danced away. The warrior's head turned, surveying the people gathered around him.

'Perhaps we should run,' said Trioch. 'There are many exits from the city. We could escape this fight.'

They circled again, warily, unsure who would take the initiative next.

'He is too fast,' said Halam. 'Do not let his size fool you. This thing is quick. He will catch us.'

'Very well,' said Helmar. 'So it must be.'

Halam caught a glance exchanged between Trioch and Helmar. At once, Trioch began to chant, her voice rising and falling in a strange unworldly cadence. The warrior spun, leaping forward at the same time, his sword swinging downward. The sword slashed at Trioch. She threw her sword up, over her head, parrying the blow with difficulty. She fell to her knees before the force of the blow.

Yet still, she chanted on. Now Sigmor took up the song, his voice intertwining with Trioch's. The song was beautiful. It was not the chant of warriors marching into battle, but the song of people praising beauty. For a moment, the warrior's attention was taken by the new voice joining the chant. When he turned back, an instant later, to smash Trioch to the ground, she was already struggling to her feet.

The warrior smashed his greatsword down, taking every advantage from his superior height. The blow was caught, with difficulty, by Helmar, who had moved in from the side, interposing his sword between the warrior and Trioch. The force of the blow seemed enough to break his arm.

Trioch scrambled to her feet.

The chant grew louder now as Helmar, dropping back, added his voice to the song. As he did, faintly in the background, Halam began to hear other voices singing, the chorus of a faraway choir, echoing over the hills, joining the song. The city itself, the echo of dead citizens and a memory of the past, joined once more the song of its people. The warrior struck again, ferociously, at Helmar. Halam felt he was angry to be cheated of his prize. His blade had not tasted blood. The Offspring leader fell backwards, towards the centre of the dais, where the blackened memory of fire still stained the white perfection of the stone.

For a moment the chant faltered. Without thought, without caring, Halam took up the song. He did not know where the words came from, nor the language in which he sang. As Helmar staggered before the blows of the warrior the song continued. It did not fail. Even as Halam joined the chant, Helmar, though he fell back into the very blackness of the central hollow, rejoined his voice to the song. Around them, the very air began to glow.

The warrior moved forward again rapidly, striking at the fallen Helmar. Halam, without ceasing in his song, rushed forward, swinging his sword down to strike at the rear of the monster. In that frozen moment, the light around them grew suddenly terribly bright. As Halam's sword smashed into the rear of the warrior, fire burst into being around them. The roar of the flame exploding into life and the scream from Helmar sounded together, mixing victory and horror.

The warrior staggered back, his whole body burning with yellow fire, the very air around them ablaze with a flame more yellow than seemed possible. Trioch ran forward; the warrior staggered back, his sword sweeping aimlessly from side to side, a hand raised to his head as if afflicted by some pain, finding some blindness assailed him.

Helmar lay on his back, a great bloody gash across his chest. The flesh was open, and within,

Halam could see the organs of the man inside. Blood streamed and gushed from his wound. At the sight, Halam felt bile rise to his throat but still he did not cease in the song. None who stood there amid the blazing fire ceased in the chant; only Helmar had stopped as he spat crimson blood from his lips. Halam knew that to stop the song was to put out the fire that was destroying the colossus.

Halam turned and ran at the warrior, throwing a sword blow at the colossus who staggered and reeled as the flame roared around him. His sword struck the warrior again and as it did the blade burst into flame – a white pure flame, mixing and adding to the ferocity of the yellow blaze that encircled the metallic man. The warrior fell to his knees.

Heat streamed from the warrior now. The flame consumed the metal of his armour. The blast of heat was too great to approach even though Halam stood, chanting on. He was surrounded by the same flame that was consuming the warrior, but it was not harming him. They sang on. Halam could see that the metal body of the warrior was melting. The giant fell forward, face downwards, his sword clattering from his hand and skittering across the ground. The heat and flame roared on around him, so fierce now that his body was flowing, melting away into a silvery puddle.

Halam turned to look across at Helmar. Trioch knelt beside him, still singing, not looking up, not caring what the fate of the warrior was. Her whole attention was on her brother of the fire. Sigmor stood beside her, staring down at the figure of Helmar. The leader of the Offspring was still. Blood seemed to be pouring from his wound, unquenchable, and his life was ebbing away if it were not already gone.

The chant ended.

Sigmor stopped first, abruptly and with finality, an utter end to the song. Without a moment's hesitation, both Trioch and Halam ceased. At the same instant, the fire stopped. The fading daylight of a murky day burst in upon them again.

Halam turned, stealing a glance at the warrior. The thing lay still, prone, vanquished, on the floor of the dais, never to rise. Parts of the metal of his body had melted; pools of molten metal lay around him, coagulating and solidifying. This ... device would never rise again and would kill no more. Within the warrior's body, Halam could now see, as Rissar had said, there had been no man. Inside he could see only a mess, a maze of mangled and melted wire.

Halam turned back and knelt beside Helmar.

'Is it destroyed?' Helmar's voice rattled, the blood catching in his throat, gurgling his oncoming death.

'The fire consumed it,' said Trioch.

'You will be the first Child to die in this city for an age,' said Sigmor, kneeling now, his gaze firmly fixed on Helmar before them. 'Have pride, Helmar, Eye of fire, in the death that has been granted you.'

Helmar's eyes moved over to take in the face of

his friend.

He stared up at him with a grateful look in his eyes.

'The ... fire ... is ... yours.' Struggling, Helmar reached out his hand and touched Sigmor's fingertips with his own. There was a flicker of light, a glimmer of some glowing thing passing between them. As the words left his lips, life ceased in his body. His eyes darkened and within him, the fire glowed no more.

Halam looked back; the warrior was still there, and beyond him, the sun had finally set in the black hills. They had tarried too long. The night was all but upon them. Rissar had told them not to remain there when darkness came. They could never get back before the gloom overwhelmed them. The warrior had come and they had destroyed it with their song. It had come. It had killed. It had been destroyed.

It had performed its only function and then it had died.

Victory is not always good business. He looked at the body of Helmar, the empty shell that had been a man with such life, and he remembered the man he had killed in the Fortress when he had escaped. The man had come against him and was alive no more. He rose to his feet; he did not wish to look upon the body of his friend any longer.

There was a scream, cutting the air with harshness. This was not the cry of an injured person, but that of a strange, tortured animal. He looked up quickly, beyond the towers of the city. Out of the black darkness, birds were emerging. Huge, they were, twisted and vicious. Even at this distance, he could see they were vile and repulsive. They plunged and wheeled downwards, striving to be the first to attack. Halam tensed, sweeping his sword up into the air before his eyes. The power it gave to him swelled. Trioch and Sigmor leapt to their feet behind him.

The keening scream of the birds echoed again. No one, no normal natural animal could have cried out like that, in pain, in anguish, in terrible and total wretchedness. The birds, flocking now, turned and dived for the ground. They were attacking.

'The camp,' Halam shouted.

He turned, his eyes meeting Trioch's and Sigmor's.

'We must return.'

They nodded, yet they did not turn and start to run; instead, Trioch knelt beside Helmar and, in a moment, Sigmor had joined her before the body. Trioch placed her hand directly on Helmar's chest, in the very wound that had struck him down. Sigmor, glancing up at Halam, did the same, then he spoke. 'Helmar, the fire that you gave me, I return to you.'

A flash, an orange spurt of flame, flared around them, enveloping the body within a moment. Despite it all, Halam watched in complete fascination. Sigmor held his hand within the flame as it flared and died away around him.

Halam was not surprised when he looked

again that the body that had been Helmar was no longer there. Fine black ash covered the ground, mixing with the black stain of a thousand fires, drifting already in the breeze. The two Offspring leapt to their feet. The pain in Sigmor's face was clear – sorrow, grief and distress.

'To the next fight then and for the Snake god! May we all die as our brother has, before the city of our people,' Sigmor said and the Offspring raced off.

Halam ran after them and, quickly, he was beside them, down the steps and onto the wide avenue of the gate. The three ran together down the great road. The spiteful cries of the birds echoed around them in encroaching darkness. They burst from the city without a momentary thought for the pillars or the blackened hollow in the stone of welcome, and then they saw the horrible great birds in the sky, plunging downwards. Their wings were featherless, dry, stretched skin over huge talons. Their bodies were spindly, their heads thin and sharp with vicious beaks, terrible, piercing, and from which the cries of pain and anguish came.

They were dropping onto the camp.

Halam and the two Offspring ran on, exhausted, panting now, their chests heaving. They ran on, the long grass tugging at their feet as they ran, pulling them back from their desire. Halam strained to see ahead in the gloom, to see the camp, to see Rissar or the Hardsar, or even the Arcan.

They crested a small rise in the rolling ground

and the sight burst suddenly upon him.

Rissar was standing, his staff in two hands like a quarterstaff as the birds dived at him. The Hardsar stood beside the campfire. Rosart was firing quickly, arrow after arrow into the air, and if the birds came close Jored swung his hammer.

A bird dropped abruptly from the sky and, for a moment, Halam thought it had been felled by an arrow from the singing bow of the woodsman. But, talons out, at the last moment it swooped upwards towards Rissar. There was a flash of red from Rissar's staff and the bowstring of Rosart sang. The bird keened that same horrible unearthly scream and rose again, its wings smoking, a fire burning on its back, an arrow piercing its neck, yet on it flew, up into the darkness that now filled the sky. Its cry echoed on and it disappeared into the night.

Taxarzerek was on the ground lying face down, his hands over his head, under the very feet of the warrior. The metallic colossus stood over him, swinging its broken sword whenever a bird came within range. Halam ran. The birds were circling again, dark wings against the blackness. Again, one swooped down to attack, but this time its target was the Arcan.

As it plunged down the warrior reached up with its free hand and tore the bird from the sky. The beast cried out its terror, fear and wrath. Dropping his broken sword, the warrior held the bird in both hands, a wing grasped in each. It struggled to be free.

The warrior tore the creature asunder. Black blood fountained into the air, showering the sheltering Arcan with foulness. There was a flash of some bright energy, quickly extinguished, and the corpse of the bird was gone. Halam was shocked to a skidding stop.

Every bird in the air keened together a single terrible cry and then, circling once more, black shapes against the night sky, they flew north, back towards the land of fire from which they had come. Had they beaten them off? Halam ran on, reaching the camp just as Rissar lowered his staff to the ground.

'I thought . . .' he began.

Rissar swung round to look at him. 'Ah, good, you are alive.' His eyes darted, taking in the figures of Trioch and Sigmor standing together behind Halam. 'Where is Helmar?'

Halam was silent.

Sigmor, behind him, spoke. 'He is dead, my lord.'

The words seemed to echo out. Everyone in the camp, even the warrior, turned and looked at the Child.

'How then did he die, Sigmor, Offspring?'

'We were attacked,' said Halam before Sigmor could answer, 'in the city, attacked by a warrior, like . . .' He swung around and pointed with his unsheathed sword. 'Like that.'

Taxarzerek was struggling to his feet, wiping black blood from his metallic body, grimacing at the foul mess it had made. He looked up at the words. 'Is there some problem?' he said eventually, and for those words alone Halam could have struck him down.

Rissar nodded. 'It seems there was another of your warriors in the city.'

Taxarzerek raised his head, interested, anxious to know more, unrepentant.

'He attacked us there,' said Sigmor, 'and he killed our brother Helmar.'

Taxarzerek hesitated, as if aware, at last, of the swirling emotions around him and of the potential threat it posed. There was a ripple of some unnamed emotion on his face. Had he understood the nature of the situation? Behind him, hideously, the warrior stood, silently removing the gore of the slaughtered bird from his armour, seemingly unaware of the threat. Halam understood now that it was not a person. It was an *it*.

'It must have thought,' Taxarzerek began cautiously, 'have been mistaken, it must have believed you were the same people who seized . . . Perhaps it was damaged . . . deranged somehow. It is truly very regrettable.' The Arcan paused, Halam thought, to wonder if the words had been enough to placate. 'And where is it now?'

Halam drew a sharp breath to stop himself running at the Arcan screaming. This man did not care who it was who had died. He had no interest even now in anything but the possible recovery of his monstrous warrior. 'We have destroyed him,' he said sharply. 'He will never return, Taxarzerek of Arca.'

Taxarzerek turned and looked at Halam. Even the warrior stopped his patient cleaning and looked across at the Aallesara. Halam stared back.

'Destroyed?' Taxarzerek all but shouted the word. He strode impatiently towards them. 'How can you have done that? What has happened?'

'He was destroyed by the fire,' said Trioch. Her voice was softer than Halam's had been, but her words were firm.

Real emotions crossed the face of Taxarzerek for perhaps the first time since Halam had ever known him. Testy anger swelled and then died across his features. It was replaced by disbelief, confusion, and yes, some hate.

'It is hard to believe you have done this,' Taxarzerek said; no emotion now sounded in his voice, 'for the warriors are very ... strong, very tough. There is little that could destroy one. I would like very much to see where he lies.'

'Not on this night,' said Rissar at once. 'It is already dark and we should not have divided before darkness came upon us. We will not separate again before the light is in the sky. If you go, Taxarzerek of Arca, you go alone. Whatever you wish to be done can be done in the light of day.' He turned away, ending the discussion, and grasping Halam by the arm pulled him bodily back towards the campfire. Insnar was sitting there waiting for them next to the warmth of the fire.

Taxarzerek was angry. He stood seething, motionless for several minutes. Then he turned and strode back to stand beside the warrior. From where he now sat beside Rissar, Halam continued to watch him. Trioch and Sigmor turned from the Arcan and walked purposefully towards Rissar. Sigmor came straight up and spoke without preamble.

'We called forth the fire to destroy this thing,' he said, 'and for my people that has meaning.'

Rissar nodded. 'And what is the meaning, Sigmor, Offspring?'

Sigmor crouched down before the Malasar so that he could stare him in the face. 'When the fire comes, my lord, it always attacks the warped. It does not burn the good, it consumes the bad.'

Rissar looked up, meeting the eyes of the Child of the fire.

'Yes, this is so, and what then is your thought?'

'So, my lord, it has destroyed a warrior of Taxarzerek. This man is evil. The things that he seeks to regain are evil and they will attack us again. We must not allow them to travel with us. We might call the fire again . . .'

He stopped. Rissar had looked down to the ground and was stroking the jaksar. Insnar sat, staring at the Offspring with a calm, animal gaze.

Rissar spoke. 'Son of the fire, yes, the fire comes forth upon all that is warped and wrong and it does consume. The fire burns that too. The intent of the warrior was distorted. It attacked you and wished to destroy you. This is the malevolence that the fire came forth to cleanse. From this, you cannot judge Taxarzerek. What were the powers that impelled the warrior? Did Taxarzerek command it or another? Do we know?'

Sigmor leant forward, meeting the Malasar's eyes. The Child was angry. He was firm, strong, sure of himself. There was no doubt.

'But I believe it.'

Rissar stared back at him. 'We shall see, Sigmor. The morning will be here soon. Many things may seem different then.'

Trioch placed a hand on Sigmor's shoulder. 'No more, brother, remember the words of the fire that brought us here. We must follow this lord. There is no respite in that. We will obey him, as Helmar would have done.'

Sigmor turned abruptly. He stared at her. For a moment a fire burned in his eyes that no soft words would quench. Then, slowly, he rose to his feet and walked away. He did not look back.

Silence settled on the camp like a pall, a deadening soundlessness that crushed all thought of joy. They sat where they sat, in their separate groups, and no words passed their lips. Jored and Rosart sat alone and did not even come over and greet Halam. The Lakeman gazed over at them and Jored met his eye but there was no meaning; no thought was behind it, just a nameless look of acknowledgement.

They did not eat. No one had an appetite.

Halam turned. Insnar had got to his feet and was standing next to him. At the glance, at the meeting of their eye, the jaksar padded over and lay down on the ground next to him, his head resting on Halam's knee. The jaksar made no sound; in fact, he promptly went to sleep. But Halam knew the meaning. The jaksar sensed Halam's dread and had come to comfort him. This was simply his way of bringing comfort, being there. Despite himself, Halam could only laugh, a quiet, private laugh. He looked at Rissar who smiled back.

The darkness was total now, the stars above them faint and distant. The haze of smoke and mist rising from their terrible place separated them from the stars. Their light filtered through the murk, producing a gloom of darkness not penetrated even by the moons, their reminder of the day, the echo of what had been, was lost. Would daylight ever come again?

The darkness completely overcame them. Yet, finally, silence no longer ruled the camp. People began to move around, preparing for the night, readying themselves for sleep. The meagre campfire cast some small light. Halam laid his head on the ground and let sleep take him, not caring where he lay. The days that would follow were going to be terrible, he knew it. The attack of the birds had been only a foretaste, an initiation into the terrors ahead.

He felt his heart pounding as tiredness

overwhelmed him. There was too much to worry about not to sleep – too much to comprehend. He slept without dreams, a dark, deep slumber like lying in a deep dark pit with no light. He slept without thought, without any respite from the shadow.

The singing woke him. He opened his eyes, rising to sit. For a moment, in the time between waking and sleep, he thought it was dawn, that the day had already come. Then, before him, he saw the city. A light burned over it like the echo of a distant fire from an ancient, all but forgotten age. A fire blazing without consuming the ruins, a memory of all the fires of the long past. The city was remembering those nights, long ago, so many years past, when it had been filled with fire during the day and light during the night. Or perhaps it was remembering the citizen of its towers that had died there that day. The city was singing, the voices high, sharp, pulling at his feelings, drawing him upwards, calling all to the fire. Calling to come and sing:

Come, come, come as you are.
Let go, join the circle.
Come, join.
Be free.

Halam's heart throbbed. He remembered those few days when they had sung with the Offspring, together, around the fire that they had lit. He looked around, seeking the Offspring, wishing to gaze upon them, to find Sigmor and Trioch.

Both the Offspring sat transfixed, their arms

raised. They still sat around the fire, but they were not there. Instead, they gloried in the beauty of the song. They had left that place and were in another. Halam turned to find Rissar. The Malasar sat staring at the city without motion, without visible reaction, slowly stroking the fur of the jaksar lying in his lap. Insnar's head was raised; he was gazing at the light like an animal sensing some strange thing where nothing had ever been. A mystery that he did not understand.

Halam looked at Rissar. There was something in his gaze, as if his eyes saw beyond the light, beyond the fire and into the darkness. Halam turned back to the city, to the song. As it swept over him, words came:

Terror in the air.
Fire, blood,
And vapour of smoke.
It is the new song of the day.

The camp was lit all around by the fire from the city. Halam looked at the two Hardsar. They looked as confused as he felt. Reluctantly, not caring what he saw, Halam turned his attention to the Arcan. He too was awake, if sitting up with the twinkling lights in his eye plates meant he was awake. The expression on Taxarzerek's face was one of mild interest. There was no more.

The warrior beside him was not looking at the city at all but was staring across at Halam, emotionless. Halam felt he was gazing at the one who had said he had destroyed the other ... was it a brother? He rose to his feet and without knowing why found himself picking up his sword and scabbard from the ground, belting it on. In the next moment, he drew the sword slowly from its scabbard. Rissar rose beside him.

The sweeping surge of power filled him. The sword was warning him that it would be needed and at that moment, the sound of the song was cut across by the terrible keening scream of the birds. Halam swung his sword upwards. In black darkness against the night, a shape swooped down.

He waited for it.

The birds had returned.

◈ Chapter 16 ◈

Halam's sword connected and slid into a dark shape above him. He felt it touch bone and a thin scream rent the air. Darkness enveloped him. Hot blood fell on him. It was a moment of horror, of soft leathery darkness covering him, foul blood dripping onto his face, sharp talons scrabbling at him, raking his shoulder, his face, rending flesh. The darkness that was his attacker lifted from him. The return of the night was a strange relief.

Upwards the horror swept, keening, crying out its anguish, calling out its anger at prey lost, a victim not taken. The terrible bird was lost into the blackness. Halam swung round, seeking the fate of his companions. The sound of beating wings filled the air. The camp had erupted into action. The Offspring were on their feet, swords sweeping up at the dark creatures. The Hardsar stood together, back to back, Jored keeping the birds off with great sweeps of his hammer while Rosart aimed and fired arrows at all that strayed close.

Behind there was a horrendous roar. It was different from the high scream of the birds, deeper – the throaty deep growl of some great monster. Behind the growl was another noise, the strange whining of some great engine. He turned. A huge shape lumbered into view towards the city, cutting off the way. It was a strange thing. Halam could think of no proper words to describe it. It was massive, a chariot, larger than any Halam had ever seen. Its wheels were huge and atop was a central castellation. From this turret, a massive tube thrust out, straight towards them. This was more than some simple chariot. It looked like a wheeled fortress lumbering towards them. He could not understand what it was, or what the great tube might be. But it was pointed at them. It must be a weapon – to fire some great missile like the bolt of a giant crossbow.

'To me!' Rissar screamed and at once Halam turned and ran to him.

Rissar raised his staff aloft and sang in a language that Halam did not know. The camp burst into daylight. Incandescent energy flashed out from the staff like the pulse of a lightning bolt and for a moment the world was clear to them. The light revealed horror.

Towards them, from the bottom of the valley, where the fire land began, more chariots came. There were at least eight of them, maybe more behind. They were all as huge as the first. Their great tubes were swinging round to aim. On the top these wheeled chariots stood more Arcan warriors, the lights of their helmets flashing multiple colours. They were all as huge as the one that stood with Taxarzerek. They were still far down the pass. But the birds were still swooping down, thin and vicious, diving at them. Halam sliced another that strayed too close. Utter terror, complete despair flooded Halam's mind. The chariot was between them and the city, but the rest of the force was rushing relentlessly towards them. There was but a moment before they were lost.

How can we face all these enemies?

Between them and the city, there was only the one.

'To the city, to the city!' Rissar shouted. 'There we stand against them.'

The city was the only obvious means of escape, even Halam could see. Its buildings glowed with a terrible light, fierce and all-encompassing. Could its fire destroy them? Had the fire even begun because of them coming? They ran, scattering. He was frightened.

The chariot rider was a man, but such a man. He glowed and pulsed with released energy like he might, somehow, be made of fire. For a moment, Halam thought it might be the bandit he had faced in those Hardsar forest slopes so long ago – Raczek, their chief. But, if it was, he was transformed, a man of fire, the creature of a firestorm.

Again, Rissar cried out, raising his voice over the din of screams and howls from the oncoming horde. 'To me, to me!' Daylight burst into being above him. Birds scattered back from the light as if it wounded them.

Running, shouting, and singing into the night, the whole camp ran to him. The Offspring, the Hardsar, even Taxarzerek came. Indeed, Taxarzerek was the first to reach him, his warrior close behind brandishing its broken sword. It turned as it ran up, gazing back at the oncoming horde as if hesitant to leave a fight.

The single tracked chariot still blocked their

path, lumbering slowly towards them. Within the tube was a light, a fire coming, a burning beginning.

If this is a weapon, it is about to fire.

The other behemoth vehicles were too far away. They could not block their passage to the city and not aim their strange tube weapons – not if they moved fast enough. So they raced to their one opponent. Raising their weapons in defiance of him, the Hardsar crying out their battle cries, the Offspring chanting their song, they ran.

Maybe they would all die that night. To die as Helmar had died – to die within such beauty – the City of the Gate singing fire into the night; that had meaning. If death awaited, Halam greeted it gladly. He held his sword before him, not caring now whether he lived or died. He cared not. It mattered not.

And the power of his sword filled him and took him.

They reached the behemoth. The tube on top suddenly belched a great ball of fire that flashed across the ground. But too late; they had already reached the chariot. The ball of fire flashed over their heads, crashing into the camp they had abandoned. The long grasses exploded into fire and black smoke. They leapt at the rider and on the behemoth. The Arcan warrior ran straight up onto the front of the vehicle. Smaller weapons were firing flashes of light out of the front and sides but whatever they were they seemed not to affect the warrior. Halam ducked to the side, seeking to look under the monster. Could he strike at some weak point in its underbelly? Great wheels were turning of their own accord, by what terrible sorcery Halam did not know.

He glanced up. The warrior of Taxarzerek had reached the great tube. He leapt upwards and seized and pulled it down. By the sheer force of his weight and strength, he dragged the turret downwards. The glowing, burning rider – it was Raczek! He screamed his defiance and stabbed a long burning lance at his attacker. Bolts of fire flashed from it, filling the air with energy. Rissar stood to the side and the bolts of energy swerved and entered his pure white staff. His staff began to glow. Jored had leapt onto the side of the vehicle and, swinging his hammer towards the rider, made him stop and duck.

The Arcan warrior had now got a full grip on the pipe and began, inexorably, to pull the central turret downwards. The rider shot a bolt from his lance at Jored, shouting curses in some vicious tongue. The Hardsara struck the lance from his hands with a single sweep of his war hammer. It broke in half with a flash of released light and heat. The very world around them seemed to be on fire. The Offspring were singing. Birds were diving from the skies but as they reached the fire of the song they burst into flame and retreated, smoking and screaming rage.

Halam thrust his sword into the side of the chariot, through the metal armoured plates that were like the scales of some great reptile, covering its wheels. As he pushed it inside, the sword pulsed. All the power, all the strength that the sword gave flowed out from him through the blade, throbbing into the wheel arch. The chariot wheels screamed – the voice of a wounded beast, the shrill scream of metal scraping over metal. There was a sudden and strong smell of burning, acrid and strong. Halam pulled his sword out. The chariot, screaming its rupture, shuddered to a stop.

Raczek had pulled some mace from his back and jumped from the turret. He threw himself forward. He was heading for the warrior who had now bent the great tube of fire down. Raczek had turned the mace round and fire gushed from the handle of the club. It belched over the head of the warrior who was still holding the great pipe, twisting it downward. The great metallic warrior did not even look up. Flashes of what seemed like lightning flashed and spurted from the fiery figure of Raczek, but they seemed to just bounce off the armour of the Arcan warrior. With a sudden snap, the great cylindrical tube broke. Now the Arcan warrior looked up and threw the pipe aside. Ignoring Raczek, he leapt upwards and seized the turret to which the weapon had been attached. He began to rip it from its foundations.

Rosart was screaming out some words, some Hardsar battle cry, and was loosing arrows from a twanging bow. An arrow shot across the intervening distance and took the rider full in the chest. A great ball of darkness seemed to balloon from the arrow strike, sucking the power from Raczek and dimming the glowing light that surrounded him.

He toppled backwards. At the same moment, the warrior won his battle with the turret. It snapped with a sound like a bone shattering. The death of the behemoth echoed across the valley. The warrior lifted the turret from the vehicle and threw it behind him. It clattered over the front of the chariot, and the warrior rose slowly to his full height. He surveyed the rest of them as if he expected applause. Halam imagined that, if he had been able, he would have grinned. There was a red flash where Raczek, the rider, had fallen. A great ball of light and energy rose into the sky.

'Run,' shouted Rissar.

They broke, leaping from the broken chariot. They ran onwards. There was nothing now between them and the city. The rest of the chariots and their riders had barely reached where the camp had been. They had misjudged. They had attacked too soon. As they ran, the light from Rissar's staff faded and the song of the Offspring faltered. The darkness of the night surrounded them. There was only the city ahead. Halam could no longer see their attackers. Surely none would reach them before they gained the city.

Out of the darkness, the birds came at them from the night sky. They came suddenly, without warning, snapping, biting like hunting volfs at their heels. They ran on, striking at them when they came too close. As he ran, Halam realised that he had a gash in his shoulder, deep and painful. He did not know when he had got the wound. Did he remember the terrible feeling of talons raking his flesh? He shuddered. He ran on through the pain. What else was possible? Ahead of them, the city was close. They would reach it very soon. The great fire that filled it now touched every building, every stone, and every memory of habitation within and without, glowing, flickering and flaming, filling the very substance of the place with fire and light. The singing of the city, the echoed memory of the ancient world, grew louder, more exultant, more victorious. Was the city welcoming home its ancient citizens?

Exhausted, they reached the twin pillars of welcome. They swept through them without stopping. They ran into the fire and it took them, filling their whole bodies with light. They glowed with the fire of a city long dead, such was the power of the city. He turned and looked back. Taxarzerek ran into the fire without stopping. Behind, his warrior, the protector, the sentinel hesitated, pausing before the great white columns and glancing back. Inhuman and lifeless as he was, did he fear to walk into the fire that had consumed his fellow?

Does he understand? Does he know what happened?

Can he understand enough to be frightened?

The warrior looked back into the darkness, at the hordes that pursued them. Perhaps, instead, he wanted to go back and fight. Then, after that moment, he turned and ran into the city and the fire.

Halam look at his hands and arms. They

appeared translucent, crystalline with the light and fire surrounding him. He looked down in amazement at his hands, his clothes. They were filled with light and fire. The flames licked at them. He raised his arm, fascinated with how the light and the fire penetrated and filled his very body. His hands appeared transparent in the brightness of the flames that filled the city and them all.

Was it an everlasting fire, even though the fire was sung no more? The Offspring dwelt no more in this place, but it flamed on. Did it burn forever even though there was no one to sing it into being? For a moment, it seemed to him that it was not just the memory of a song, but that every particle of dust, every rock, every stone of the city and every ounce of his flesh was singing, remembering the glory of an ancient past.

They ran on down the main street, further into the city. Now they were safe, but Rissar had not stopped. On, he led them, further into the fire, farther into the light, deep into its brightness, far into a remembered song. Halam did not look back any more. The terrible things that pursued them, the scream of the birds and their swooping cries faded into the song swelling around him. No vile attackers and no darkness could possess this place. If the birds or the chariots or their warrior riders entered this place the fire would consume them. It would not be a place of light and cool fire for them. It would be destruction and devastation. They ran on, down the main avenue to the very centre of the city, to where they had fought the blue warrior.

Where Helmar had died. The run stopped.

They stood before the steps of the dais. Rissar looked around the group. No one was missing. No one had fallen. No one failed to escape. The Arcan warrior stood there, towering next to Taxarzerek. The fire around them reflected from the Arcan's armour, filling the surroundings with more light and brightness. He shone like a torch. For this, the green warrior, there was no judgement, no destruction, and no heat of melting. He was intact, complete, and functioning, still living if any life powered that pulsing gem.

Rissar turned and gazed at Sigmor. Halam understood the glance, the meaning of the look. Without speaking, Rissar was asking him, showing him that the destruction of one warrior did not, after all, judge all.

Quietly, Rissar reached down to stroke Insnar who was standing, teeth bared, at his feet. Casting a glance around the group, he began to ascend the twelve steps to the top of the dais. Halam followed him and slowly they all mounted the steps, walking to the centre of the song. Rissar turned and gazed back over the glowing city, straining, Halam supposed, to see beyond the light and into the darkness. Halam came and stood beside him, staring back. For him, there was nothing to see, no view of what it was that now transpired beyond the towers. They were encased in daylight and no darkness could penetrate. The dark world outside was gone, invisible, lost in a deathless light. Halam turned away. The Malasar continued to look as if he could see beyond the song.

Halam looked around. Taxarzerek now stood on the far side of the dais where the fallen warrior lay. The Arcan had his back to him but he could see the dismay that filled him. His back was lowered, his shoulders hunched; he was defeated. The fire flickered and glowed off the Arcan's metal garment. It filled him with sparkling light, rivalling the glowing lights of his eye plates. As Halam gazed at him, Taxarzerek turned and looked at him. The Arcan's face held emotion. The look was not of mockery or anguish, it was amazement. Trioch and Sigmor stood some way off, watching the Arcan's reaction to the fallen warrior. Jored sat on the floor of the plinth, next to them, with Rosart at his side. Were the Hardsar tired?

The green warrior had stood at the top of the steps, unmoving. Then, as if he saw it for the first time, the warrior walked slowly over to the other side of the dais. There lay the greatsword the blue-gemmed warrior had fought with. It was undamaged. It had not been consumed by fire. The warrior bent and picked it up, discarding at once his own broken sword, which clattered to the ground.

He turned, sheathing the sword in the scabbard slot in his side. Then he walked slowly, impassively, to the body of his fellow. He knelt next to the body and stopped, suddenly preternaturally still.

Halam walked to the Offspring and Hardsar. Taxarzerek stepped towards them, unemployed emotions still crossing his face. 'You vanquished him. You really did.' His voice rang with astonishment, real honest emotion from the Arcan. 'And you destroyed that combat tank with the burning man. The photonic weaponry did not affect you.' He paused as if unable to comprehend the situation. He looked back at the fallen warrior. 'It is hard to believe that you destroyed this sentinel. We thought, I believed, that these warriors could not be bested in a fight. They are designed to be better than any barbarian civilisation can ... They are even protected against most natural disasters. There is little that should be able to disable them. Even fire, any normal fire could not consume him.'

The two Offspring, ignoring Taxarzerek, came and stood beside Halam. Halam looked over at the green warrior kneeling beside his fellow, utterly still. The eerie singing of the city still swirling around them, with a creak the green-gemmed warrior took the body of the blue warrior, like a fallen brother, into his arms. He slowly walked off across the dais towards the steps where Rissar still stood, staring into the fires of the song.

Where is he taking it?

Taxarzerek was still speaking, his sightless eyes now on Halam. 'I am sorry that he attacked you. Sorry that it is our technology that's being used against you. Sorry for your ... sorry for the one you lost. My warrior ...' To his surprise, Halam knew he meant it. 'You wield great powers, my friend. I do not understand.'

The warrior had walked across the dais, carrying the blue to the steps. To Halam the whole event had the air of a funeral as if someone had died. As if this was an actual being, a true person, and a friend. He watched the unhurried, walking warrior. He doubted then that Rissar had been right. Did the warriors live? This was not the reaction of a device, an object, a thing. This was the action of a friend. Had they traded a life for a life? The warrior walked off the dais and down into the city. It disappeared within the broken buildings.

'Where is he going?' Halam turned to Taxarzerek.

Taxarzerek glanced in the direction where the warrior had gone. 'He will dispose of him, retrieve what he can.' He turned away, uninterested.

Halam walked to where Rissar still stood. His arms were now raised, brandishing the staff, as if in supplication to the fire that flowed around him. The light and fire filled his body and his clothes. He shone back with an undying light. His clothes were white, his hair very black. Halam dared not speak to him but walked to where Jored and Rosart were sitting. He wanted to forget the sad march of the warrior.

Rosart was speaking. 'What do you think happens? Will they pursue us here? They were great in number, should we prepare?'

Jored shrugged. 'There were very many of them, but I do not think they can enter here – not while the fire burns. I think it would consume them, as it did the warrior of Taxarzerek when they fought it.' He looked at Halam. 'We are safe while the city sings. What happens when the morning comes, I do not know.'

'They will go, I think.' Rissar had appeared abruptly at their side. 'They struck too soon. They were too confident of victory. They should have brought the whole force to bear at once. Their leader tried to cut us off before his forces had arrived. That was foolish. It gave us a warning. It was our chance. He will not make that mistake again.'

Rosart interrupted. 'Did I not kill him? The arrow struck.'

Rissar shook his head. 'It is not easy to kill the makkuz. You may vanquish their form, deplete their strength, but they survive. They are merely ... wounded, discomforted. He will return.' He sat down with them. Insnar came and stood beside him as if he too listened to the discussion. 'They now fear the song of this city. They understand now that the City of the Gate, despite being ruined, holds too much power. So they will not want to face us. They will try to draw us out, move us away. I don't know if they have understood our goal as of yet. But they will wait to see where we go. They will try to catch us in some better ground and overwhelm us with weaponry.'

He surveyed them all. 'And you all know we must leave. We must enter the fire land and hide from them until we are ready. We must choose the place for our fight, not them.'

'How can we best these forces?' Halam said. 'There are few of us and they are an army. No matter what ground we find, won't they swamp us in a fight? They are too many.'

'We go to Arnex, Halam. This is the moment. The time has come for him to awaken. When we reach him there is nothing that will prevent us.'

'So be it,' said Jored, but he said it quietly, as a thing he hoped rather than knew. Rosart did not speak. Halam gazed back at the Malasar.

The Arcan warrior reappeared up the steps. He no longer carried the body of the blue-gemmed warrior in his arms. He walked over to Taxarzerek and stood impassively next to him. Rissar looked across at the Arcan.

Taxarzerek gazed back at the sorcerer and spoke. 'You wield great power, though I do not understand where its source is. Yet I see it.' Taxarzerek exhaled slowly. He looked again as if he was speaking with an equal. The superciliousness was gone. He seemed to be expressing real emotions. It was unnerving.

'That was true last night, my friend,' Rissar replied smoothly, 'yet you did not care to show your concern to Trioch and Sigmor for the untimely death of their brother Helmar. This angered them.' The Malasar glanced over at Sigmor who glared back.

Taxarzerek was silent for several seconds before he replied. He raised his head. 'I . . . I found it hard to believe that you had truly destroyed a sentinel. I did not believe the story.' He glanced at

Trioch and Sigmor standing together. 'I did not realise what power you wield, my friends.' He paused and decided before he spoke again. 'I came here, to this world . . . to this land . . . to recover a ship that had travelled here. Central thought it crashed here, lost by some error. We had lost control of it. But it was . . . diverted here. It contained weaponry. These people you fight against . . . they have taken it and made it their own. That is why I cannot trace it, recover it, apart from this unit. I could not prevent . . .' He stopped and looked across at Rissar with real regret in his face. 'I apologise, lord, on behalf of my people. It was not our intent to attack you. Our military systems have been purloined. I came to retrieve them. I need to recover them, to prevent further attacks on you. I will report all this to central once I re-establish communication. I now need some technology from . . . them to do so.'

'I know, Taxarzerek of Arca. Is there a way for you to regain control of the warriors?'

Insnar was now sitting at the top of the steps only a few feet away, watching the discussion rather wearily. Halam's attention turned to the jaksar. The little creature looked exhausted. He walked over to him as Rissar and Taxarzerek continued talking. He bent down to try to take the animal into his arms. Insnar whined faintly as Halam took him and then with animal fickleness struggled to be free. Halam released him at once, but the jaksar did not run off. He simply sat down again on the steps and looked up at Halam, who smiled and sat down on the step beside him. No doubt there were things to be done, things to worry about, but at that moment he cared only to sit beside a friend and stare out at the city. He stroked the jaksar absently. Behind him the conversation continued; it was complex and full of words and ideas that Halam did not know, but even with this, he could tell that Taxarzerek was at last being honest and straightforward and having a frank conversation.

Halam and Insnar sat together on the steps and Halam let himself be lost in the fire that burned around him and the swelling sound of the city singing, surging around him like the waves that flowed on the lake when the wind was high. He gazed out and let his mind settle at last on the vision it had tried to give him before – the vision of a city whole, a city healed, a city filled with singing and joy, a city of light.

As the song went on, he realised that he was now sitting against a great tree in a wide land, a green and succulent place, as rich as the lands south of the lake where the farmlands and the lands of the nobles lay. The heartland of the Aallesar wealth.

Am I dreaming? Is this the City of the Gate in a kinder age?

It could not be, for there was no city here, and to the west was the ocean. The sea looked calm and beautiful, a deep grey-blue, inviting him to swim in it. It was spring but warm. He looked around. He was under the branches of a great tree, protected by its leafy loveliness from the glare of the sun. Down from him, the valley swept away in its final depth, green, lush, complete in life. He looked up at the sun and the towering mountains east of him. He knew somehow, felt it in his heart, that this place would be found far to the west, beyond the hills of the Pasra. He knew that there were the narrow lands of the Istsar, the fisherfolk. There, it was said, they lived where the great mountain range reached the ocean at last and crashed down to throw itself, finally, into the sea. This land did not look, though, like the place he had imagined when he heard those stories. Of course, he had never travelled there, although he had met traders from the Baronial lands that bordered it. The landscape was somehow what he imagined it to be, poised between high mountains and the sea. But this was a beautiful place. This place was so much lusher and more inviting than he had expected. The stories always made it sound like such a harsh constricted place – the Istsar, a people struggling to fit onto the edge of the world, living on a narrow shelf of land before the wild and tumultuous western ocean. Clearly, that was untrue.

Some distance away, past the fields, was a peaceful fishing village by the shore. It looked like an idyll of a place. Behind him the mountains, taller than any he had seen in all his life, were white and capped with snow – even though, around him, the weather was warm.

He sat and knew that there was some duty incomplete, some job undone. The feeling of unease lingered, stealing the beauty of the day from him.

Nevertheless, as he sat, the peace of the place flowed over him. The grass here was deep and green, vibrant with its life, the trees healthy, strong, and beautiful just in themselves. Slowly, the thoughts of tasks not accomplished, the quest into fire lands became meaningless to him. The last he remembered was a ruined and broken city in a land of fire. He could have sat there forever. Until that moment he had never wondered about or wished for a life of solitude but now, here, he could have desired it. This was a place of total peace, and his dreams rarely held such beauty within them.

In the far distance, at the deepest part of the valley, a solitary figure was walking towards him. He knew immediately who it was, and that again, in dreams, he had been brought to her. Terras. Here he was again to see her, to comfort her and himself. To support and be supported. If, back in the blasted land of fire from which he had come, duties were required of him, it no longer mattered. Here he was now, and he was there for her.

He rose to his feet, although as he looked down he knew that he was not really there and would not be able to tell her of his presence. He moved down the side of the valley to her, through the luxurious grass, richer than the carpets of a king. She was walking up to him, and as he approached he saw that she had changed greatly.

She looked different in all respects from the last time he had seen her. Her clothes were different and she walked with an air of certainty. There was a strength and confidence that she had not had when he had seen her in the golden wood of autumn. The Terras he had met on the moors of the Wasra was back. He knew not where she had been, or the things she had seen, but he knew that she had altered and grown beyond his understanding. He stopped where he stood and waited for her to walk to him. As he watched her approach, she seemed more beautiful to him than she had ever been before. She was still the powerful and thrilling Hardsara bride, but she was bolder, warmer, and full of life and vigour. All her strength, her confidence was there, but there was something new – completeness, thriving; Terras was burgeoning with vigour. He could not understand why, but he knew it was true. *Has she learnt something that has made her thrive?*

As she walked she had one hand on her stomach, which seemed a little larger than when he had last seen her. He was pleased that she had found good food to sustain here wherever she was, and whatever had happened. She stopped walking when she reached him and for a moment he wondered, gloriously, if she could see him.

'Halam?' she said.

He stepped forward and reached out to touch her, but she spoke to the air, not to him.

'Why do I think of you again?'

He stopped, his hand an inch from her face, and then, impulsively, his desire for her overcoming him, he stepped forward and placed his lips against hers. Her lips responded to him, and for an instant they kissed, but then some reality, some brand of common sense, perhaps the very foolishness of the idea flooded her and she pulled back. He could see that she was frightened by a kiss that seemed to come from nothing, from empty air. She was confused now; he could see it in her face and he was sorry. He had not been brought here to frighten and disturb her.

'Why do I think of you so strongly, Halam? Could you be here, somehow, waiting for me?' He touched her gently on the cheek. She showed no sign that she felt his caress. Halam stood silent, knowing that he could not speak, nor help her with words.

'I have spoken with the fisherfolk and I have travelled their land telling them all that I know. Now it is time to leave and to sail south. Franeus said I must.'

He raised his head, confused now.

What does she mean? Where is she going?

She turned around and fixed her gaze on something beyond. There was a large fishing boat in the wide harbour of the village down by the sea. 'There I will find the new task to be done.' She grasped the hilt of her sword. 'I was taken from Halam and sent here and to the desert, the tomb. Why else would I feel so close to him, why else but to tell me that to find him the path leads where I must go?'

She strode abruptly away, just as she had in the wood, leaving Halam behind. He stood there and watched her go through the fields towards the sea and the waiting boat. He did not move or think, but let his eyes drink her in. She passed beyond the lush pasture.

Halam closed his eyes, just for a moment.

◎

The fishing boat cast off from the last of the fishing ports and Terras leant against the gunwale at the bow and gazed back where she had just spent the last few moments. This was the southernmost of the Istsar villages and she had now toured their whole land, from the furthest north to the furthest south. It had taken her many weeks. She had lost count, but winter had arrived and slipped away to the spring. As time went by, she wondered where Halam was and how the quest fared. The stories of Fracos said that he had found Rissar, but that was so long ago. But she did not know when the fortress had catapulted her. So was it possible that the quest was not even begun yet? Or was it already over? She could not know.

She sighed. Her thoughts returned to the moments she had just spent in the countryside. She had meant it to be a few minutes alone. Time to think before the next journey began. She had walked into a beautiful glade nestled at the foot of the formidable Pasra mountains. It was just a pretty spot beyond the fishing port. Just a place to be quiet, a moment of peace amongst these many busy days. Yet it had not been quiet. Halam had come to her mind; she had felt close to him, almost as if in his presence.

Could it be true that we connected?

Her hand went again to her stomach and stroking it she wondered again about who her womb contained – a daughter or a son? It had not been long after arriving in Haven that she had realised she had missed her monthly time. This was strange in itself. They had always come with a familiar regularity. She had not said anything to anyone for the first few days. It was the trip across the plains, the jolt of change through the megalith or and the climb in the Pasra that had caused the irregularity. It had been a tough trip, physically and emotionally. That must be the reason she missed. With such thoughts, she set it aside. There was too much else to do.

The queen, Narcise, had many questions, many queries. She had wanted to know everything, to understand everything. Not only about what Franeus had said, but who Terras's people were and how long they had lived in the Wasra. Terras had answered her as best she could, although she did not know all the answers. However, she spent enough time in Narcise's company to realise that dissembling or outright falsehood would never work. She was too clever, too precise, and too careful of detail to have a lie, or even avoidance, escape her notice. Narcise was a clever and perceptive woman and surmised much of what Terras did not tell her of her people's story. So Terras had answered and told her directly when she did not know things and even when she would not say, because they were her own people's secrets. After just a few days, Terras had begun to feel that Narcise was as close to a friend as she had ever known.

She had had friends in her village. But she had always been the Hardsare, the princess, and the men amongst her friends had always known that her choice of them could make them the next king. The women had too often treated her with wary respect, an esteem which left little room for friendship. This had, at times, been hard, especially when she had lost her mother, perhaps the one woman who had not treated her like the princess.

So, eventually, in a quiet and relaxed moment, she shared with Narcise that she had missed her monthly time. Narcise had been a paragon. She had summoned her physicians who had all, conscientiously and a little embarrassingly, investigated Terras. Of course, it was far too early to be sure, but they told Terras that it was likely. Some days later she had realised she often felt nauseous in the mornings. Then she was sure.

Narcise had appreciated everything that Terras had to say and had been, in the end, satisfied with all the answers to her questions. She had agreed then that the Seer Fracos had spoken the truth, and she believed that because Terras had been found, the One would come. The fisherfolk must prepare.

Then she told her that Terras must travel to each of the Istsar towns and villages, up and down the coast, and not only show herself but repeat what Franeus had said. Narcise had insisted that this be done. The Istsar would not be ordered, she explained. They were to be persuaded.

Terras had travelled hundreds of miles north and south from Haven to visit all the ports. The fisherfolk land was long and narrow, stretching all down the coast. The boat she went on was captained, if that was the right word, by Shiskes, the guard she had met on the first day. He was lame from some terrible accident at sea and walked with a pronounced limp. Because of this, he could not be master of a fishing vessel any longer. He was no longer fit enough to manage if things went badly, but Narcise had judged him very capable to be master of the fishing boat that carried her up and down the coast. He had left his son with his close friend, Fisk, a pleasant and kind man who loved the boy as much as Shiskes himself.

As they travelled, they were never very far from the coast and safety. Shiskes was a good master and the trip had been quiet and, largely, uneventful. Occasionally she found the motion of the boat combined with her other reasons to feel sick made her very uncomfortable. Shiskes was the soul of care. She showed a little by then and was certain that she and Halam were to have a child. A son of the warriors or the next Hardsare who would choose the king after them. The thought gave her joy and pause at the same time. She saw her life and her death. It made her emotional. What was their world going to be? Would she even find Halam again?

The Istsar ruled the coastline from north to south, a land few others wanted, to be truthful, and perhaps only useful to these fishers as a base and set of ports. Village and town Masters of all sorts had entertained her and welcomed her and questioned her. This was not Terras's area of skill. She was a fighter, as were all her people. She spoke straightforwardly and bluntly. She was no diplomat and knew no diplomats. This was the sort of effete activity of the lake city, In Haxass. Halam would have been better at this. It was not the job for a Hardsara warrior, let alone the princess. She resolved things with strength, decisiveness and surety. She was a warrior. She knew how to fight and to win. To spend days talking with people, enjoying food with them, enjoying, or tolerating their stories had been frustrating. She had endured it and it had been successful in the end. She had learnt the value of courtesy and grace. She understood what made Halam so honest in his feelings.

In the northernmost ports, it had been very cold, and they had been there in the depths of winter. She remembered the northmost village. From there, further north, the landscape became too rough, even for the Istsar. Terras was told there were no people who lived there. It was not possible. It was too harsh a place. And east of the northernmost lands were volcanic lands and lands of ice. There lay the Citadel of Arnex. She had stood in the last town and felt a deep urge to leave, to travel to it, to find Halam. To abandon all this talk and do something. But she did not. She stayed.

Sometimes, at night, there was a strange luminescence in the sky – twisting and glowing bands of light moving through the sky. One night they had been echoed by a glowing fire from the ground. It was a strange sight, as if the earth and sky sang to each other in fire and light. She wondered what it signified, but the Master of that town said it meant nothing – just a strange version of the skyfire. There was nothing there. No one lived north of them.

The small town they were leaving had been the final port of call, far to the south. The Master there had been very welcoming and indeed he had already heard most of what Terras had come to tell him from other fisherfolk who had travelled through his port and the village. This last visit had been very easy, very pleasant, and had simply been an exercise in eating marvellous fish dishes that the Master served his guests. That and listening to many stories of the prowess at sea of his village and the marvellous catch they had achieved. This had been the last night and Terras had known that in the morning she, Shiskes and his crew would set sail for the south and the stone desert. Perhaps now she would use her prowess in battle. She hoped so.

She supported herself in the bow of the fishing boat as they sailed swiftly away from that last port. She turned and watched Shiskes and his crew steering their course out into the open sea. Some of them were the guards who had met her that first day. She turned back to face ahead. This land was warm. Warmer than Haven, much warmer than the north. The boat nosed beyond the final causeway and the crew rushed around changing the sails in some way that Terras assumed would be right for their trip down the coast to the south.

Shiskes appeared, limping up the boat towards

her. 'Our final trip,' he said. 'Where is it you are going in the stone desert, my lady?'

'You know the answer to that, Shiskes, for you have heard me tell it many times. Once I gave the message to the Istsar, I am to travel south of the desert to a tomb there. It'll be some way inland, but Franeus did not say how far. He said to travel along the southernmost edge of the desert.'

'But why, my lady? You could stay with us, at least while you await the birth of your child.' Shiskes looked momentarily unhappy. 'My lady, you may not realise it, but your time among the Istsar has made you beloved of the people. We do not take many strangers to ourselves. We are a quiet and secluded people with the sea as our mother. We care not for others who live in the world. They are full of guile and trickery. But you have been accepted, lady. You tell us new times that are coming. We remember again the tale of the crystal storm. Even the Istsar will be changed. We know the words of the Seer Fracos were true.'

Terras smiled. 'Thank you, Shiskes. You have been a friend throughout this. From that first day, you trusted me. Trust me now as we travel south for reasons I do not yet understand.'

'I do not understand either, Terras. Why must you leave?'

She inclined her head. 'For the same reason I came, Master Shiskes.' He smiled back as she used his title. It was, she knew, a thing that her coming had given him back – a boat, a crew, and a purpose to life.

'My people swear oaths to obey the will of the three. So this I must do. I am sworn. I would rather be in the tents of my father, my Hardsaro in my arms, waiting together for the birth of our child. Franeus said I would understand when I get to the tomb. So, I must go.'

Shiskes shrugged, still unsatisfied. His look of quiet regret did not fade from his face. 'Do you want some food, lady? This tide will carry us to the winds further out and we will make good headway this night. The journey will be long. The fallen desert is very great.'

Terras shook her head. 'I will stay here, if I may,' she said, 'and watch the sunset.'

'You may, my lady. You will not be in our way.'

Shiskes limped away, back down the boat. Despite his injury, he walked with an easy familiarity with the vagaries of the sea. Better than Terras would ever manage. It seemed to her that he was well capable of working at fishing. But his people knew better, perhaps, what was needed in the deep. She watched him go.

Perhaps he fears this is his last voyage.
Will he be returned to the tower guard?

She watched the sunset. She hoped that the queen would grant him other work, at sea, when he returned to Haven, this task complete. They might let him keep the boat for other commissions. He mastered it with pride. Sadly, she doubted it. She had become very fond of the Istsar people, the kindness of

Narcise, the loyalty and friendship of Shiskes and his men, the love between him and Fisk. The unfailing, lavish generosity of the fishers she had met.

Did crossing the southern edge of the stone desert to some unknown mausoleum promise some more adventurous times? She hoped so. Then, automatically, her hand drifted to her abdomen. Would her child be safe if her warrior skills were put into practice? She was many weeks along now. She shrugged the feeling off. She was Hardsare. She would embrace her fate. She would serve the Snake god with all her might, whatever came.

The sun set beneath the waves of the western sea and she let herself struggle back down the boat towards the lower cabins. They would sail all night. Shiskes was at the helm. She nodded to him and went below.

◈ **Chapter 17** ◈

Halam had sat there for a few moments. But he turned and beside him, Sigmor was just finishing dressing the wound in his shoulder. Sigmor smiled. 'The song had taken you, my friend. What did you see within it?'

Halam realised that he must have sat there for many minutes. Could it be hours even? How long? He did not reply to Sigmor's question as the idea filled him. There was something, something about Terras, but he could not recall it. As he strained to catch it, the thought eluded him all the more. What had he seen?

He turned and looked around. The whole party sat scattered across the steps. The jaksar had gone from his side and sat now with Rissar on the top step. Taxarzerek and his solitary sentinel were sitting not far from the Malasar. The warrior was silent, motionless as always, gazing forwards without moving, except every few minutes its head would slowly scan the area.

Halam shook his head. 'I . . .' He looked at Sigmor. 'How long have I been sitting here?'

Sigmor grinned. 'An hour or two, my friend, no more. The day has not come. You were inside the song, brother, and lived within the wonder of this place. Have no fear, great is the power of the city. It will not harm you. It remembers the praise of the Snake god in times gone by in its unleashed potency.'

Shaking his head, Halam looked at the wound

on his shoulder, now bound with strips of cloth. He stared at the Child of the fire. Sigmor had torn his clothes to provide the bandage, and he now had a ragged edge around the bottom of his robe.

Sigmor seemed to understand his look. 'It does not matter, my friend – people are more important than clothes. I can always get another robe, but I cannot as easily find another brother of the fire.' He touched Halam on his arm.

A stillness had settled over the party. They sat on the steps staring into the beauty of the night without any thought of words. Somehow in that fire, within that memory of a greater age, Halam felt and knew the joy he had found only in his dreams of Terras. Here, in this place, was the same atmosphere, the same ambience he had found in that golden wood. This city had some connection with the bygone age and places far away. It gave one its splendour and shared its wisdom. Perhaps, within its song, one could be in many realms and see much of what was true. So he sat and watched for the dawn to come. The sun would come up to his right, where black mountains overlooked the valley of the gate.

Eventually, the day grew to be as the sky filled slowly with light. The fire around them faded, giving way to the greater song of the dawn. The song ebbed away as well, drawn inexorably into magnificence. When the day had fully come, Halam turned and looked at Rissar. 'What do we do now?'

The Malasari turned his gaze, but slowly as if he too had been lost in the new song of being. 'We go on. We must travel far this day. We must reach deep into the fire land. If we do not do this, we will be caught in the open tonight.' He rose to his feet. 'Indeed,' he said, 'the day is almost here. Let us leave.'

There was a movement to Halam's left and turning he saw that Taxarzerek was standing up as well. The Arcan walked forward and spoke, his voice stern, serious. 'Is it still permitted to accompany you?'

Rissar turned to him. His surprise showed on his face. He looked at the Arcan. 'Why do you ask the question?'

Taxarzerek took another step forward; his face was grim, concerned. 'Because one of our warriors has attacked and killed one of your people.' He stopped as if he had said enough, but after a pause, he continued. 'Our technology, our weaponry is being used against you. Your enemies have taken control of the other warriors and ATCTs that I was sent here to recover. I would understand if you did not wish my company on the road.'

Halam could not believe their luck. Here, finally, was the opportunity to shed themselves of this stranger. He and his warrior were not required. Now he admitted it himself. Halam turned to the Malasar in joy but Rissar was smiling, not only in humour but in acceptance.

'My friend, there are still warriors and vehicles to be found, are there not? And if we wield power enough to destroy a warrior then perhaps our adversaries have similar powers. Are you, despite the single warrior you have regained, not still at risk along the road? Do you not need us to protect you still? Taxarzerek, you are a practical man.'

Taxarzerek stared back at him from his twinkling eye plates. 'All that is true, lord. But then, answer me one practical question.'

'Ask it,' said Rissar, 'and if I am able, I will answer.'

'What is occurring here? What is your purpose in travelling into this land? No sane people would try to penetrate such a place if they did not have an urgent need. And why are you opposed by such great forces? When I first arrived I thought I was seeking a simple crash and lost weaponry. The enemies who attacked me were seeking you, waiting for you to arrive. Why are you here? We have kept much from each other but what happened here last night was . . . difficult for me. I do not understand.'

'Understand?' Rissar spoke slowly and they all waited to see how much he would reveal to this alien. 'When complete understanding is desired, it is always hard. Not all things are understandable in the way we wish, Taxarzerek of Arca. Sometimes one must just be. My companions and I are on a quest. How else may I describe it to you? A task? An objective? First, we go to liberate world. Some would stop us. They hold this world and others within the dark chaos they make. This is our purpose here. If this is of regard, then follow. If you seek only to be protected, then follow. If you have a concern to understand, then follow. If you have a desire to change, then follow.

Then perhaps you will grasp something you do not know. And you will learn to be.'

Taxarzerek said nothing for many moments and even then his reply was not a response to Rissar's words. 'You have great powers, or can summon them. I do not understand how such power can exist. My people are unable to summon such things without a great deal of technology, yet you carry none.'

Rissar replied, 'You have given up much to gain what you have, Taxarzerek. The course you took to achieve what you have is a barrier to you moving on.' He walked towards the Arcan. 'Taxarzerek, you worry too much about understanding and too little about being and doing. I think there is yet a task for you in all this. Embrace the goal before you. Live it. You may come with us.' Taxarzerek did not respond. The Malasari stared at him for several moments then Rissar turned and looked at the rest of the party. 'Then let us go. We must strike far this day.'

No one spoke, although Halam knew that in common with him many of them still had doubts about the wisdom of allowing this man to travel with them.

Why should we trust him when so much is at stake?

They left the city, hurrying through its ruined streets. Rissar pushed ahead, clearly in a hurry to leave the place. The buildings around them showed no signs of the fire that had raged through them the night before. As Halam walked he wondered again if the city sang the fire into being every night. Or was it possible that the fire had returned that night because the Offspring had returned to the city? Or because the attackers came?

They walked out into the valley, past the great stone altar, through the twin pillars of welcome, and out into the blackened grass beyond. The grass was trampled and burnt by the passage of the foul chariots. Tanks, the Arcan had called them. Great fires had raged here. In places the grass was bare, destroyed by some immense conflagration. Something had happened after they entered the city. Something they had not seen. Had the tanks attacked, or tried to enter the city and been beaten back by the flames? It seemed so.

They walked forward to the spot where they had fought with the tank and its rider. It was no longer there. Where the tank had been destroyed the grass was dead. The ground was barren now and bare as if some great hand had gouged it from existence. Of the carcass, the remains of the great tank, there was no sign. There were pieces of broken metal and some strange materials Halam did not know scattered around. The tank had been removed somehow, but remnants had been left. There was no sign of the fate of the rider, Raczek.

'Where have they gone?' Jored said.

'They have returned to the land of fire,' Rissar replied. 'They will have tried to assail us in the city, and they failed. They could not enter it safely. The fire will have consumed those that tried. It is not their place. Now they will not want to face us with such power to aid us. They hope to draw us out. They know our goal is further on. They will wait for us to come to them in the land ahead. They will seek to catch us in a place of their choosing.' Rissar looked at them all.

Halam swallowed. They must fight them again. Next time the full force would come, not just one chariot and its rider. They moved quickly then, breakfasting as they walked. Rissar drove the pace, forcing them to hurry after him. They moved down the valley. Black mountains surrounded them, pitted with flame, smoke curling from their peaks, rivers of fire running down their sides. Beyond the valley, beyond the fire, the mountains continued and grew, higher and higher, as if they were building a wall to the end of the world, reaching up to support the great bowl of the sky. Some peaks, high as they were, rose above the fire. Their heights were covered by ice and snow. Wreaths of steam surrounded them as the heat from below met the cool of the ice above. It was a terrible place, just as Taxarzerek had described. At the prospect of entering, Halam faltered. There was no sign of the enemies that had attacked them. As Rissar had said, they waited for them in the land of fire ahead. It would be a much better place to ambush them, far away from the city. What terrible horror was ahead? They were just walking into it.

He stepped from the fading green of the valley, half-burnt and dead, and onto the blasted earth beyond. It seemed to mark the end of life and the beginning of death. Yet, as they moved onto the rock-strewn floor of the volcanic land, Rissar breathed a sigh of relief, as if he had reached his goal. Halam felt no relief, only fear. He stared across at the Malasar and wondered why they had to reach this fire land? He knew they came for Arnex, but he had not understood the immensity of the task. When he left that poolside outside In Haxass it had seemed so easy. Terras had been correct – oh, so long ago. She had known what was ahead. He had not understood. Perhaps this would cost him his life.

A great pall of smoke and steam hung over them. All sight of the valley and City of the Gate behind them was extinguished. Rissar strapped his staff to his back and picked Insnar up, for the creature walked on the debris of the fire with obvious distaste. He did not struggle to be free as Rissar took him but patiently lay in his arms. As the day progressed the clouds of steam and smoke shifted, and occasionally a gap would appear in the mist giving them some momentary glance into the world of horror around them. Bubbling pits of redness, rivers of fire scarred the landscape and ripped all life from the world. The high mountains rumbled anger at their very presence. On they trudged. As the day reached its zenith, the mist lifted even more. Halam could see clearly. The land around them was torn by fire, ringed by smoking peaks. From the mountains ran streams of flame, rivers of molten rock, pouring slowly into bubbling lakes of fire. They were in a great deep bowl of a valley, gouged from the earth and filled with fire.

There were hills within this deep, just low hummocks and mounds, tiny in comparison with the mountains surrounding them. Atop these hillocks were sometimes oases in the desert of heat. On top of one, Halam saw the whiteness of a ruined city and on another, a single pale, ruined building. Then the moment passed, the mist billowed in. The sight was lost. Were they just some of the ruins Taxarzerek had seen? Or their destination? Why had such a dreadful desolation been wrought here? How could people have hated so much? They walked on into the smoke and steam, passing between great jagged rocks, struggling on the rubble that surrounded them. There had been huge explosions here and many rocks had spewed out onto this land from the force of the eruptions. Massive boulders had been split into sharp pieces by the ferocity of the fire. They lay strewn around the area. The sun was still in the sky, but as they passed beneath the clouds of smoke it was hidden from them. Even the disc of its brightness was lost and it became but a shadow, the memory of the sun now darkened and lost.

Rissar hurried. They followed, battling on through the rocks and debris of eruptions and fire, fighting not to fall as the sharp stones turned beneath their feet. Halam felt fear invade his whole mind. This was not a place for people. This was a place of death. He could not, at that moment, conceive of why he had come. Who was this Arnex, this Warrior King? How could they ever awaken him? Was there anything here but destruction? Rissar seemed to be seeking somewhere, or something perhaps. He struck one way and then, suddenly, he would turn and go another. Halam became lost amid the maze of huge rocks and sharp stones. The mist and smoke closed round them and he knew, was certain, that he could never find his way back to that last valley where life still survived. He had no choice now but to follow and hope that he reached his goal. Eventually, as the afternoon turned towards its end, Rissar's search among the maze of broken rocks ceased. He found his goal.

It was a canyon, surrounded on three sides by great, steep rocks – three broken mounds of hills lost to destruction. There seemed to be but one entrance and it was only wide enough to admit them in single file. No chariot, no combat vehicle would have got through. Birds would have trouble dropping into the canyon from above and be able to rise out again afterwards. They would not be able to spread their wings in the narrowness. The enemy, if they came, would have to attack on foot and one at a time.

'This will take us further in,' Rissar said as he led them into it. Halam could see that this was a safe place for them and maybe a secure way onward – a route the enemy would not have taken and could not now easily follow. However, and Halam knew this at once, there might already be enemies and metal warriors waiting for them inside. But he knew Rissar's idea was clever. If they came, Halam would far rather find himself pitted against single assailants, however many lined up, than fight the full force. They had found a place to spend the night.

They followed in silence, no one daring to

voice contrary or fearful thoughts. Jored and Rosart came forward to walk beside Halam. Rosart gave him a rueful glance as if he expected some response, and Jored smiled and shrugged. Halam was not sure what they meant.

Do they understand my fear?

Do they seek to encourage their worthless king-to-be?

They walked for many minutes and then Rissar stopped. The way had widened a little and they could walk beside each other, although the walls above them still curved inwards. There was but a narrow gap overhead to see the clouded sky. Rissar stared around for several moments and then glanced back at Halam standing beside the two Hardsar. His gaze rested on Jored and he pointed wordlessly up at the rocks.

He did not need to speak. Jored did not wait. He swung the great hammer round onto his back, tied it securely, and in moments was scrambling high up on the rock side. He was to guard, to gain some view of their surroundings. 'I will go also, lord,' said Trioch before anyone else spoke. She ran quickly to the rocks on the other side of the narrow canyon and, wiping her hand across her mouth, scrambled quickly up the rock face.

'We will be safe here,' said Rissar. 'Nothing will come upon us unseen.'

He bent and placed the jaksar on the ground before him. The creature looked down at the debris-covered earth in disgust and then looked up as if working out some way of jumping back into Rissar's arms. Halam wondered if the expression meant: *Why did you bring me here?*

'This is the nearest place of safety,' said Rissar. 'We will light no fire.'

Taxarzerek spoke. 'You knew the canyon was here.'

Rissar turned. 'I know this land. I have said this.'

The Arcan nodded. 'I too have been to this land, but I could not walk it again and find any place I sought. It is a maze. Even my navigational systems cannot properly map it. There are strange electromagnetic distortions.'

Rissar nodded. 'I know . . .'

The sun was close to its setting. They could no longer see its light above them. If it was still in the sky, it lent little of its light to this place. Whatever the truth, the gloom around them was slowly deepening to blackness. They sat there, backs to the stone, waiting for the full darkness to come. That evening was full of dread for Halam and, he suspected, everyone. They waited long into the night for the attack to appear. When the darkness was at its greatest, Halam knew that Rissar had found a good place for their sanctuary. He could not even see his hand before his face. *How, in this darkness, could attackers find us?*

He decided to sleep, or at least to try. He was sure that ahead of them was another terrible day. It seemed foolish to face it exhausted. He slept fitfully, as they all did. Rissar ordered changing of the guards regularly; to sit high on the rocks above the canyon was a terrible task and one it was difficult to do for so many hours.

Rissar roused Halam as the night was reaching its end. He woke quickly. His sleep had been fitful. He felt as if he had just managed no more than a light doze from the last time something had woken him. Rissar pointed up at the rocks to the side. He nodded. He must take a turn.

He scrambled with difficulty up the rock side and found, at last, Rosart. He was lying on the top of the canyon wall, on a narrow ledge just below the apex. The murky darkness enveloped them. The mist and smoke hid even the night from their eyes. Halam touched Rosart and indicated that he might go down. The woodsman nodded and gave Halam a strange look before he slipped away into the misty blackness. Strangely, there was respect in the look; could the woodsman's opinion of the weak Aallesar who had come to steal his Hardsare bride have changed? Rosart had looked at him as though he was his king-to-be, and he, his loyal liege. Halam felt ashamed. All he felt inside was fear. He was a worthless prince.

His was the final shift before dawn. A few more hours of waiting and daylight would come. The enemy would not have found them on this night at least. He lay there in the gloom and listened to the screams of birds cutting through the air, hunting for them. They were circling the whole land, seeking and crying out their anger that their prey was hidden.

Occasionally he heard the faraway rumble of a chariot. After he had lain there for many minutes, more than an hour, he heard the heavy tread of some hugeness. A tracked tank, he guessed. And it was close, too close. He held his breath and did not move. Slowly, the sound of its passage faded. They had evaded whatever it was the enemy had planned. He released a long-held breath. As dawn came, it was consummately dull; the light was faint, the yellowish clouds and steam billowed around him. He knew that this partial light, this murk was all that he could expect for the day. Jored came up to fetch him when the daylight had reached its full dreariness and indicated silently that he should come down.

They left the canyon as soon as they were all gathered together. Rissar led, as always. Now, behind him, the Arcan warrior trod, his metal gauntlet ready on his sword hilt. Taxarzerek followed close behind, seeking to be in the middle of the quest, where he would be safe.

The canyon did not run that much further before it opened out and they found themselves traversing more of the complex of rocks and rubble as the day before. On this new day, the maze was even more confusing because a deeper fog surrounded them. The mist and murkiness were worse, bad weather adding to the gruesome smoke of the place. There was an acrid rain, a light hazy shower mixing with the fog. Or did he only feel the acid wetness of the mist around him?

Rissar cast about, gaining his bearings,

checking that he was where he thought he was before he struck off, consistently north. At least, Halam assumed he was heading north, but he had no way of knowing for sure. Perhaps this was the error the enemy had made. Rissar had been here before and knew the ground better than them.

The fog did not lift all day. The sun was never seen, just an amorphous dullness of light above. Sometimes, far besides them, the red light of some deep fire pit would glow through the mist but Rissar would always turn aside and go round some other way. Despite all his fear, Halam could not doubt that Rissar did seem to know where he was going.

In the afternoon, when the tiredness in his limbs was seeping down through Halam's feet and making each step, each touch of his feet to the rock painful, they emerged suddenly from one of the paths into a larger, open area. As the party stepped up to the clearing, Taxarzerek hissed out a warning. 'This is where I was ambushed.'

The company tensed; the great warrior, standing in front of Taxarzerek, slid his sword slowly from the slit in his side and, stepping back, stood silently at his master's side. Jored released his hammer from behind his back, swinging the harness around, so it was easily in his reach.

They stood still for many minutes, listening, wondering if an ambush awaited them. Only silence greeted their patience. There was a creak; Halam jerked around, pulling his sword up, nervous, concerned, but it was only the warrior surveying the place with great attention.

Rissar looked round at the Arcan. 'And where did the attackers come from?'

'Over those rocks, suddenly, when I reached the middle of the ground. I was coming south, through there.' He had pointed across the clearing, at another dimly visible entrance. Rissar indicated briefly in two directions and both the Hardsar and the Offspring disappeared off into the fog. Halam, Rissar and the Arcan waited silently for their return. The warrior stood perfectly still. He held his greatsword across his body and stared impassively across the clearing. The silence echoed back at them. It seemed for a moment as if the fog had swallowed the scouts up. The mist billowed around, deepening and thickening, forming strange and fantastic shapes before them. They could no longer see the far side of the clearing.

The Hardsar returned first, stepping suddenly and silently from the fog, shaking their heads from side to side, saying not a word. Trioch and Sigmor did not come. Once more the gloomy silence settled around the whole party. Halam had just become sure in his mind that they were lost and was just about to suggest beginning a search, when they appeared, running, out of the mist. Trioch stepped very close to Rissar and spoke in a whisper.

'We ran on a little way further. Just over the hill ahead there is some sort of building.'

Rissar frowned. 'A ruin?'

'It is a strange shape. Not like any of the other

ruins we have seen. It did not seem to be built out of stone. There was a particular rock that my people used for such purposes. It is not made of that. It may be some other device. Or have some other purpose. This is a new place, a new thing. I could not tell what it was.' She paused as everyone strained to hear her. 'It is large and next to it there is an enclosure, perhaps for animals, with a high fence made of metal. There was no sign of anyone. We watched for a long time. But it does not have the look of desertion.'

Halam spoke to Rissar, also in the same conspiratorial whisper. 'Do you know this building?'

Rissar turned. 'There were many in this valley in the times before the fire came. There will be many ruins, most are lost forever beneath the ash and rock disgorged from the mountains. They were all built of stone. I do not know of this place. No people were here when I came last. But that was long ago.'

'Perhaps it was to protect it that I was attacked,' said Taxarzerek, rather too loudly for Halam's liking. 'Perhaps my warriors will be nearby or held even within the building. Perhaps they were here, so I was attacked to prevent me from reaching them and relinking to their control.' He stopped speaking and gazed upwards, his eye plates twinkling a furious pattern. Halam thought he was seeking, somehow, to contact the missing warriors.

'Perhaps,' said Rissar absently.

It was clear that Taxarzerek's warriors were not the main thing on his mind. He walked forward. They all followed after him, Trioch and Sigmor showing the way. At last, they crossed the open clearing and reached a broken hill on the far side. They clambered over the rocks that bordered it, the Arcan struggling and making far too much noise in the effort. His warrior slipped up the rocks without any discernible effort. The rocks led upward and soon they were scaling the broken hill itself. They reached the summit and found themselves looking down into an ash-strewn valley. There was no life, only rocks, sharp stones, and fine black ash.

In the bottom of the vale was a large dark grey structure.

Halam stared at it. It did not look very much like a building, or even a rebuilt ruin. The material of which it was made was nothing he recognised. It had a strange appearance, too, a sort of long thin egg-shape. It was broken at one end. Part of the perfect shape had snapped and fallen to the ground.

There was a single doorway, although somehow it did not look like a door. It was high up and reached by a metallic walkway. This ramp probably swung up to seal the entrance, like a drawbridge of sorts. It would then regain an extended egg-shape. Next to the ramp was an enclosure with a metal fence around it. There was nothing inside.

Taxarzerek finally struggled up beside Rissar and looked down at the building. He looked completely unhappy, uncomfortable. He turned his head. 'That is not a building. It is . . . the ship that I was seeking. The one that was purloined. It housed the warriors I was sent to find. Central did not inform me of the ATCTs. They must have been in the hold.'

Rissar nodded at this information but did not speak. He stared down at it for a long time. No one spoke. 'There,' he snapped. 'There are makkuz.'

A man had emerged from the doorway and walked down the ramp. He was a strange man. Whilst he had the form of a man there was a glow to him. It was not quite the fire that Raczek had when he rode the tank. It was as if light was leaking from him. He stood, a shining man, on the ramp, surveying the scene. He stared about but he did not move. Occasionally his head turned and he would peer into the gloom. He had an air of someone waiting.

Halam lay and watched. In some indefinable way, the light, energy was seeping from him. In the pale light of the fading day, the sun having difficulty lighting their surroundings, his body glowed with light and power. It flowed out from him. Halam was suddenly reminded of the night when he had stood before Raczek in the hall of the fortress. He remembered now that there was strange heat, an odd power emanating from him and his companion, Tazek. They were something else, not merely men. As he looked, he remembered the ambush in the forest and that first night in the forests of the Hardwasra when he had looked on Raczek, had seen in his eyes a terrible power, a potency beyond the norm, a force that set him apart. Raczek would destroy everything. He was Hraddas and a servant of Uknor the Destroyer. Halam stared. He already knew this.

Franeus had told him.

'They are the Hraddas,' he whispered. He knew it was stupid to say it. Didn't they all already know that?

'Followers of Uknor.' Rissar nodded. 'Creatures in the thrall of chaos from the beginning.' He spoke without turning his head. 'They cannot construct such technology from their form. They must always be a man or a beast. So they need the weaponry of others. They mean to prevent us from reaching our goal. They believe that these things will overwhelm us. They underestimate the power of the Snake god . . .' Rissar scanned each member of the group, slowly making eye contact with them all. He stroked Insnar lying beside him. He went on. 'I don't believe they know yet why we have travelled here. The idea is beyond them. They have scouted this land for centuries and found it empty and desolate. Eventually, they will discern our goal. Then they will understand their peril and desperately, they will try to prevent us from awakening Arnex.'

Halam turned back to look at the shining man still waiting outside the strange ship of the Arcans. Around the man, outside the ship, distant as he was, danger swelled. Fear shivered through Halam.

He looked around at the rest of the company, lying flattened on the rocks around them. The Hardsar were lying together, watching the shining one with an air of fighters about to go into battle, calculating, estimating what it was that stood against them. The Offspring also lay together silently watching. But they did not watch the enemy, they watched Rissar. They awaited his command. They only served. Both ways were admirable. Taxarzerek had moved further back once he had spoken his words and lay now out of sight of the ship. He awaited the actions of others. He always did. Next to him lay his protective warrior, his gigantic form as out of sight as he could achieve.

Even though he was afraid himself, this annoyed Halam. When would Taxarzerek take some risk? Halam was not a brave man but he was certainly not cowardly in the casual way that Taxarzerek was. He never aided them in anything. He simply stayed in a safe position until someone else did something. It was galling.

Rosart rose and moved, crab-like, across the hilltop to where Rissar lay. He lowered himself down beside Halam and peered across at the Malasar. 'How are we going to . . . ?' he began. Rissar cut the question off with a sharp motion of his hand, his eyes still on the ship and the man beside it. Halam quickly turned his attention back to the building.

The man had walked forward and was staring intently at them. In horror, Halam wondered if he had seen some movement, some giveaway action and knew now that people lay there, watching him from the hilltop. Halam remained motionless, and slowly he realised that the man was not staring at them. He was looking very slightly to their left. Halam turned his head and all but gasped out in his surprise.

There, at the very foot of the rocky hill on

which they crouched, one of the combat vehicles was lumbering from the mist. The rider, another glowing man, was standing in a hole within the strange turret on the top of the chariot. Sitting behind him on the back of the vehicle was an Arcan warrior. Tall as he was, his head was very nearly on the level with them. They flattened against the rock, not daring to breathe in case he saw them. But the tank lumbered by and neither the rider nor the warrior turned their heads. They looked forward, their attention wholly fixed on the strange ship and the waiting man.

As the rider passed he raised his hand, as if in greeting to the waiting guard. As he reached the ship, the rider dismounted from the great combat vehicle, sliding down its side to the ash-strewn ground.

They talked but there was no way to hear the words. Anyway, Halam was sure they were speaking some strange harsh language that he did not know. He had heard the language before when these creatures communicated. For these were not people. They were enemies and not of this world. These were Hraddas, the makkuz, the monsters from the skies. But they had never left his world. They were real.

When they had talked for several minutes the rider turned and quickly remounted the great vehicle, swinging himself up onto the back of the chariot with great expertise. He raised his hand again and slowly swung the lumbering vehicle round. The chariot began to trudge back towards them. They dared not move but lay motionless as he approached and slowly disappeared down the same rock pathway from which he had emerged.

The shining man at the ship did not wait but turned at once and went back inside the ship, running effortlessly up the ramp. The valley returned to absolute silence and emptiness. The mist and smoke billowed, their view of the ship fading as the fog thickened. It would be dark soon. They could not see the sun but surely the dusk was coming. They all gazed in terrible fascination at the scene for several minutes, unable to move.

'What do we do now, my lord?' Jored said abruptly. He had moved silently to lie beside Rosart.

'We will try to skirt around the starship,' said Rissar quietly. 'We have no reason to enter the place. There is no purpose in attacking. The fogs and mists will hide us from them until the night has come.' Jored looked profoundly disappointed at this. Rissar continued. 'There will be sufficient of these enemies to fight when we reach the Citadel.' He smiled at the giant Hardsara. Then he glanced down at Taxarzerek as if he expected some protest from him.

The Arcan gazed back at him passively. All his determination, such as it was, had leached from him. Eventually, he spoke. 'I tried to link to that sentinel. He did not respond. There has been a change made to the interface characteristic.' No one responded. 'I will try to work out what . . .' He trailed off.

So they circled back, down the rocky hill and around the clearing, taking another longer route to avoid the structure, spending the rest of the day ensuring that they were never within sight of it. By the time they were past it, the pale light that served for the day, glowing through the smoke and clouds, was fading.

They started north again.

'We must find a place for the night,' said Rissar, his grey eyes peering around in the gloomy darkness of the mist. If he had planned a place for that night they had taken too long circling the Arcan starship to reach it. They searched for some well-protected area like the canyon, but the ruined rocks and tricky paths simply led on and on. Eventually, it became too dark for them properly to see their way. A cry sounded across the black, misty sky. The birds were searching for them. In the blackness, it was difficult to make out Rissar's features but Halam imagined the concern showing there. It was what he felt; surely the Malasar would feel the same. Jored spoke from the mist. Halam turned; he could not make out his face but only hear the giant's voice echoing into the night.

'Lord, they will find us if we do not hide soon.'

He saw Rissar turn but he could not make out his features. 'Do not fear. The darkness will not overcome.'

'Truly,' said the voice of Trioch from the mist. Halam turned and looked at her gloomy form in the misty blackness. *She and Sigmor must hate trudging through this dark – they who sang day into darkness.*

The Malasari spoke no more words, but walked forward and, as always, they all quietly followed him. Even the Arcan came, silently, almost obedient, the lights of his eye plates twinkling, giving a faint light to their way. They settled themselves at last in a narrow path between great broken rocks. The track there turned sharply to the right and they made the camp in the angle of the corner so that they could see both exits and nothing could come upon them without warning. It would be hard to come at them over the rocks unless the birds came and attacked from directly above. Rosart immediately climbed the jagged rocks behind them, not waiting for Rissar's order. He mounted the first guard.

Rissar would permit no other to climb the rocks, whispering that one man exposed to the sky was all they would chance. They sat in absolute darkness, the moons and stars shrouded by the smoke and mist and the broken shards of rock towering around them. It felt like they sat in some smashed and broken megalith, the shattered memory of an ancient people, long forgotten. Halam knew it was not true. These were no ancient monuments but merely the broken and splintered rocks of a blasted land.

It was not long before the birds screamed their anger and terror across the night, searching for them in rage. Concerned that their victims had escaped, these bird-things were not going to give up. Halam wondered briefly how Raczek and the enemy had managed to get such beasts to do their bidding. He had never seen such terrible creatures nor heard tell of them. In what nether region had they been spawned? Could they be Hraddas, like the shining ones? He lay there and realised his foolishness. He understood what they were. *Why am I so slow? Why am I confused all the time?*

He worried that they would indeed work out where they were headed. Then they would hold the majority of their force near the Citadel. It was all very well hiding and scuttling their way through the mists and fogs and concealing themselves in the darkness. They would have to face them eventually. Once their destination was guessed, the shining men had but to wait for them with all the power of the Arcan weapons. Rissar was powerful but how could they, the rest of the party, stand against them all with only their swords, bows and hammers? The Arcan technology was great, their weaponry wondrously powerful. He peered into the night and trembled. Jored followed Rosart as the next shift of guard duty but no one slept that night. Doubts and fears snatched all their tiredness from them. Halam took the watch from Jored and, as he lay on the rock, the night seemed to deepen. He stared into nothingness. *When will they come?*

◈ **Chapter 18** ◈

Guard duty was useless. Halam could see nothing in the darkness. He peered ahead of him, watching the mist billowing in the night making shapes and growing his fears in its shadow. He knew that he would not see anyone or anything coming even if he lay there and stared forever. He had lain there for a long time, straining to see in the gloom, when suddenly his sword writhed in his hand as if it had come suddenly alive. It swung upwards and in his mind its power surged. Screaming out of the darkness, the bird struck. The last-minute movement, the thrust of his sword, cheated the outstretched talons of a piece of his back. He leapt to his feet, sweeping his sword upwards again, smashing aside the vicious beak that lunged for his chest.

The bird, denied his prey, let out a piercing shriek and flew off into the night. The rest of the company below him was in motion, shouting their concern, not caring now if they were heard.

'Are you hurt? Halam, are you hurt?'

Rosart reached the top of the rock a moment later and Halam had never seen anything as welcome as the woodsman's face. 'Come down,' said the forester. 'They have found us. We must move.' Halam gripped the woodsman's forearm and felt his grasp in return. It was good to connect with another human. Halam had been alone with his fears for too long. He slid down the great stone and onto the rock-strewn ground below. Chips of stone flew off into the blackness.

'It attacked me,' he said at once, 'and then flew off into the night. It will bring its friends.'

'It will,' said Rissar. 'We must go at once.'

Rosart hit the ground beside Halam. 'There is no sign of movement, no noise of their approach,' he said. 'We have time, the bird must have been alone – searching.'

Hastily, they picked everything up and ran into the blackness. No words were required. Surely the final reckoning was on them; what else was there to do? They ran on into the darkness, surrounded by it, infested by its touch, lost in black mists and smoke. To find their way as they ran they used not only their sight, dim and gloomy as it was, but all their senses – touch, vision and feeling.

Strangely it was Taxarzerek who proved the best at making progress in the dark. They hurried along, turning from path to path, losing themselves in the maze of tracks. Hopefully, they would also lose their pursuers.

The roaring of the combat vehicles came. The scorching crash of them firing at the rocks where they had been echoed around, flashing lights into the darkness. They were hunting, pursuing them in the night. The bird that had attacked had brought the forces down upon them. They saw no one, but the firing of the vehicles grew louder, closer, fiercer; flashes of abrupt light filled the blackness. Their hunters were closing in. They were on their trail. The firing of the vehicles' guns and the lumbering sounds of their movement came closer.

'They track well in the night,' said Rosart bitterly.

'They have means to see in the darkness if we are exposed,' said Rissar, hurrying on.

'How can that be?' Halam said. 'Light is light, the eyes need it to see.'

'When there is more time I will explain it to you, Halam Hardsaro. Suffice to say it is not the eye that sees. It is your mind that understands what it is the eye records. With certain aids, it is possible to see in the darkness. Taxarzerek knows this.'

Halam glanced back at the Arcan and his glittering eyes. It made a certain sense. Was that how he saw? Halam was not keen on the idea of losing his eyes and what he saw with them, not for any supposed gain.

Ahead of them, a glimmer of reddish light was creeping into the blackness of the night. At first, Halam could not be sure it was there; in the darkness that surrounded them, it was hard to see. They ran on and Rissar now headed for the faint light. It was a glow of blood-red against the yellow mists above and around. Halam realised where they were heading. They were approaching one of the rivers of fire, a bubbling trench of molten rock. Rissar hurried on all the quicker towards the dim light. The blood light of a river of death before them aided them in finding the way.

The light became brighter, redder as they got

closer to its source. They began to run, able now to see their way clearly through the dimness and to trust the placing of their feet. The roars of the pursuing vehicles firing into the night echoed around them. Yet, as they ran, their pursuers did not gain more ground.

They ran fast; now in semi-light and semi-darkness things were more equal. Then Halam saw that their way was blocked by a huge rock. But from the brighter red light shining ahead of them, he knew they must also be close to the river. *Is that the best word for what it is? But a river is a thing of life and beauty. This is a river of fire and death.*

That was not what it should be, not what it could be. It did not make sense to call them the same thing. One was existence and the other was destruction. They ran around the massive rock not even waiting to check ahead.

They ran straight into their pursuers, into the band of the shining men, fire and heat flowing from them, blood light from the river beyond them. Terrible as those who had ambushed them in the forests of the Hardwasra, these showed even more of their true form. They were alone, without mounts, without combat vehicles. But there were so many that Halam could not count them. Then he saw that at the back stood one of the giant Arcan warriors, his helmet gem pulsing red. Jored screamed out some Hardsara war cry. His war hammer in both hands, he charged. The Offspring began to sing. Rissar cried some strange words above their song. The enemies were holding the fire-mace things as Raczek had, again holding the head of the mace in their hands and pointing the handle outwards. They turned to face the sudden onslaught from their right. Jored plunged forward, swinging his hammer and screaming his defiance at the host. He toppled one fighter and such was the force of his strike that the fire-mace fell to the ash-strewn earth. The fighter disappeared in a sudden flash of red.

Halam swung his sword up and leapt into the fight, screaming out some incoherent sound, half fear, half bravery. He did not think. His sword sang its power into his hands and gave him all the strength and skill it possessed. He had none of his own. The fight was confused, both sides swinging blindly in the mixture of red light and darkness. Night surrounded them. The only light emanated from the molten river. All around them, rock, friend, and foe, were the colour of blood. The handles of the fire-maces spewed fire, yellow and red, into the night. Halam targeted the weapons more than their wielders. If the spewing fire struck, surely it would kill.

There was a moment of utter chaos. Then, in a frozen moment, Halam faced a single man, who grinned as he swung round his fire-mace towards the weak Lakeman. He aimed at Halam's chest, but something, at the last moment, moved Halam aside and the vomiting fire from the end of the weapon swept past him, its heat scorching as it went off into the night. Another inch and it would have burnt a hole beyond any healing.

The man had stepped forward as he fired his weapon, making him off-balance for an instant, Halam chopped his sword sideward and down, severing the neck of the shining man. The man toppled downward, surrounded by a red light. Halam screamed as he realised that the fire had burnt him, the scorching of the wound finally reaching his brain. He swung round, a wild scream of anger tearing from him. Beside him, the red Arcan warrior had neatly sidestepped the protecting green sentinel and was moving quickly toward Taxarzerek. The savants that remained so hidden swung into place before the Arcan, protecting him.

Is the red attacking one of his own – one of those he was constructed to protect?

Halam threw himself towards the attacking warrior. But the green sentinel had swung round and thrown his whole weight into the very mass of the sidestepping warrior. He swung his greatsword and smashed all his might, all his weight into a blow on the head of the attacker. A shriek filled the air, not from the warrior but from Taxarzerek. One of the savants had been caught in the grasp of the red warrior. It was falling to the ground, smashed, burning and broken. Taxarzerek was screeching like a wild animal caught in the trap of a hunter. He seized his head, then he fell like a stone to the ground, still grasping his head in both hands and screaming in pain. Nothing had touched him.

The enemy warrior was rising slowly as if confused, puzzled by the effect the blow had had on the Arcan. In that moment of hesitation, the green sentinel turned fast and seized him. The green metal colossus lifted his fellow from the ground. The red warrior's feet kicked out. Swinging round with him in his grasp the green sentinel threw the warrior into a great knot of the attackers. The throw was amazing, smashing the attackers to the ground. Many enemies were crushed under the weight of the warrior landing on them. Their corpses smashed bloodily to the ground. In a flash of energy, the bodies were gone. Shocked, the remaining attackers took a step back.

Halam struck another, a woman, who was distracted by the death of the others. She too fell, a deep cut to her shoulder; she again disappeared in a flash of yellow fire.

Are they dead or merely vanquished?

The green Arcan sentinel went berserk. He launched himself forward, deserting Taxarzerek to his fate, and ran into the thickest part of the remaining fight. His sword was gone, but he was holding one of the fire-maces that the enemy carried. He strode through the attackers striking bone-crunching blows with one clenched fist and firing energy bolts from the mace in the other. The night was full of war.

Halam turned to look at the fallen Arcan. Taxarzerek was rising to his feet. Inhis eye plates a pulsing red light glowed but now with the same rhythmic pattern to it as the pulse of green beside it. The red Arcan warrior was rising from the ground and at once turned and joined the battle with his green-lit fellow sentinel. Taxarzerek, Halam realised, had regained control of the red colossus. But the Arcan wasn't looking. He was tenderly lifting the broken savant from the ground, like a parent finding a dead child.

The red warrior hesitated a moment in his onslaught and then quietly, as if thoughtfully, he too picked up one of the fire-maces that had fallen to the ground. One of their enemies struck at him as he bent down but the warrior simply looked up and struck the man down with the butt of his new weapon, then turned it around and fired it fully into the chest of the one who had attacked him. The enemy fighter disappeared in a blaze of fire and yellow light. Taxarzerek, holding the smashed savant in his hands, screamed again.

The enemy retreated. But just as Halam thought they were going to scatter and run, instead they all, as one, turned their weapons on the red-gemmed sentinel. He was enveloped in a blaze of yellow fire. Then they did scatter back into the darkness. As they went they screamed out pain, shouted their anger, calling for aid into the night. At the very moment of their retreat, the terrible birds burst into being amongst them.

Or did they transform?

They screamed words as they changed, spoken in their tongue, but Halam, his sword slack, knew the meaning without understanding the words. As soon as the enemy ran the green warrior stopped his berserk hunt and threw a bloodied and broken mace to the ground. He turned back.

The red warrior was on his knees, his body strangely still burning with yellow fire. As the green warrior reached him, he slumped forward, his head swinging as if to look one last time on his fellow. Halam looked around him. The members of the quest stood, horrified, amazed as he that not one of them had been lost.

Taxarzerek was helped to his feet by the two Offspring. He rose unsteadily to his feet, still holding his head and moaning. 'I am dead,' he said. 'We are dead.' Sigmor and Trioch stood on either side of the Arcan. He looked between them as if puzzled that he was still alive. The whole scene was still lit by the blood-red light of the river of fire.

The horror of this fight slowly spread through Halam's body. They stood around in the redness and looked for the corpses of the people they had killed. There were no bodies. Everything was gone as if the fight had never occurred.

What has happened? How many have we killed?
Have we killed no one? Was it all our imagination?
What was it, who was it that we faced?

The green warrior picked up his greatsword from the ground and sheathed it noisily into its slot. He bent down and took a discarded fire-mace. Quietly, he opened a second slot in his other thigh and slid the weapon into it. He turned his head to consider the Arcan. Taxarzerek was standing on his own feet now, the broken savant still held in his hands, the smashed servant of a wrecked man. He was looking sightlessly at Halam. Pain and loss filled his face; he was devastated. The silvered surfaces of his eye plates were dull. No lights twinkled in their depths.

'We are dead,' Taxarzerek said. 'We died. I am dead. I am lost.'

Rissar stepped up, appearing from nowhere in the redness. He spoke. 'No, Taxarzerek, you still live. You are not lost.'

The Arcan swung his blank eye plates round and as he did the twinkling lights returned to his eyes. He stared up at the Malasar as a corpse returned from death. He held up the broken savant.

'I am alive. I am not.'

'We must leave,' said Rissar, his tone apologetic. 'They will return in more force. We must not be here.'

Taxarzerek nodded wearily and indicated briefly, curtly, to the green warrior. He spoke no words, but the huge metallic fighter moved forward. Taxarzerek turned and nodded again, wordlessly. The sentinel picked up the body of the fallen red-lit warrior and turned back to face them. 'We are ready,' said Taxarzerek, still grasping the broken savant like a cherished gift suddenly broken.

They ran into dim redness. The warrior ran, still holding the form of his red brother in his arms. Halam felt sick and bile rose to his throat, filling his mouth with bitterness. But now the fight was no more. All the horror of death had disappeared in those flashes of light. He swallowed the bitterness filling his throat and kept moving forward, unable to conceive what still drove him. They hurried on, amid the rocks and the cries of the vicious birds sounding through the night, hunting.

The birds screamed in the fog; the combat vehicles roared and fired their weapons. Rocks and hills exploded into light around them.

The Hraddas were coming. The host was gathering.

The red light of the fire grew brighter as they continued and the darkness itself seemed to become hot around him. Halam began to fear their destination as much as the monsters that followed. They turned a final bend and a blast of raw heat assailed him. This was the reason for the redness. This was the reason for the heat. This was the end. A river of molten rock and fire stretched before them, blocking their way, cutting into the land, ripping even the rock in its path. It flowed past them and waves of heat surged up from it, a physical barrier to prevent them from going further.

'This is a fitting place to die,' said Taxarzerek into the silence.

They were trapped.

Jored spoke. 'Where is our way?' The first sane words in a world of utter shock. 'The way is blocked.'

Rissar did not reply at once but walked forward and placed his hand upon Taxarzerek's shoulder.

'Have peace. Your grief is known. You begin to understand.'

The Arcan nodded and looked up at the

Malasar.

'Yes, I believe I do.'

Taxarzerek turned to the warrior just behind him and again without words, just a curt nod, the warrior comprehended the order. He took the savant from Taxarzerek's arms and laid it on the body of his brother. He strode towards the river of fire. With but a moment's pause, he threw the body of his red brother and the savant into the channel of molten fire. Bizarrely they bobbed in the stream for a moment, like a stick thrown into a stream. Then they melted before their eyes; they sank into the red fire.

Taxarzerek screamed again. The pain and death were his.

A bird shrieked close by, already calling the forces of the makkuz upon them. 'My lord!' said Jored.

'This way,' said Rissar quietly. 'Here.'

He began to edge his way along the side of the chasm, upstream, towards the actual source of the fire, higher into the mountain from which it issued. They followed.

Where else can we go?

If the Malasar is false, what else is there?

Halam glanced at Rosart who returned his look. His eyes had the same look of fear and doubt. The heat of the molten river surged up at them, almost knocking them from their feet with its ferocity. Beneath their feet the rocks were slippery, but not with water; they were loose as if in a moment they too would slip into the liquid fire. They struggled on, afraid at any moment that the path would cease and throw them into the fire.

As he climbed, Halam could smell his clothes searing in the flame and another strange smell, as if his flesh was cooking in the heat. This was not the fire of sun and sky or the fire of the Offspring. This was another fire, the fire of the deep earth, the fire of death. They climbed on, struggling into the night. Halam wondered where they were going. Did Rissar know the way?

Has the Malasar led us to die?

Was that the meaning of the words to the Arcan?

Halam felt the soles of his boots burning with the heat of the rock under them. At last, the path curved away from the fire and Rissar, to everyone's relief, took that way, but they did not stop; they kept climbing upwards, parallel to the fire still, but now at a safer distance. At last, in exhaustion and with fiery, useless air filling their lungs, they reached a widening in the path where they could sit down and rest.

They dropped to the ground, exhausted, with no thought of finding a comfortable spot. They wished only to stop, to cease their forward progress. The crimson light of the fire pulsed around them, waves of heat sucking every part of their strength, physical and emotional. It filled the air they breathed with exhaustion. Halam crawled, wearied and despairing, dragging himself across the ground to crouch behind a rock, hiding from unwelcome eyes.

No one spoke until, at last, Rissar's words echoed around the camp. 'The heat and light will hide us,' he said from where he sat.

Halam struggled up to look at the Malasar. He held Insnar in his lap. The animal's eyes were wide and frightened. He had carried the jaksar all this way and even through that terrible fight. Halam had given no thought to the little animal in all the horror. *How has he managed? How has he survived?*

'Just as the darkness hides them from us, they will not see us here. We will wait for the morning. The day will bring hope.'

At these words, Halam looked around the group. Everyone was tired, with faces covered in dirt and ash; clothes were ripped and singed by fire. Even the shining metal of the Arcan warrior was dulled, dirty and dark with smears of ash. This was no longer a quest, sure of its victory, an optimistic group setting out from that Hardsar village so long ago. Terras had been beside him then and his life had been a transformed and joyous thing. How long ago was it? How many weeks were there from hope to misery? He could not remember. It was an age ago when he was young and foolish. They couldn't have known that the enemy would reach this place before them. Halam turned his face away from the sight of the jaksar, pitiable and frightened.

It is hopeless.

He realised that now. They were not going to achieve their purpose. It was lost, all was lost. There was no hope. They were waiting for the morning, but when it came the fire would still burn around them and the hunters would still be seeking them. Surely they would find them soon. The vehicles, the warriors would be there and next time the birds would swoop from above. They could barely win when faced with the few. The many would crush them. Anguish filled his heart. They had failed.

◎

Dawn, as it approached, was a sorry affair, hardly greater than the heat and light of the red fire beside them – a dull light crawling into existence and almost apologetically taking some of the darkness from the sky. Of the sun itself, there was no sign. Halam lay against the hot rocks and watched the night pass away in total wretchedness. He was tired – tired, dirty and hot. The heat pulsed around them, rising from the river of fire in great waves of suffocation and exhaustion. The mountains around them rumbled in anger, their thundering wrath echoing the presence of strangers within a land of fire and death. He had not slept and the heat in the air stole away whatever rest he had torn from the short night.

He lay there, waiting for the day, the very act of breathing becoming painful. He craved a breath of cool air. Exhaustion filled his body; every muscle, every bone ached. His left arm throbbed painfully. The enemy attacker had burnt him with fire from the fire-mace. He looked down at the wound through the ragged cloth that was all that remained of his sleeve. It seemed such a very long time since he had slept.

He realised, sitting, staring into the dark and drawing the hot air into his lungs, that he was at the end of his strength. This hopelessness that filled his heart was not just emotional. It was physical. He was utterly exhausted. How many miles had they run? How long had he pushed himself onward, driving himself? And even when he was not running, he was still walking forward, always forward. *Where to?*

He remembered gloomily all those days behind them. Surely they had spent many days wandering in the lava-strewn maze of rock below them, attackers, vehicle, beast and bird hunting them, desiring his flesh in their mouths, tearing chunks from him, burning him whenever they could. Now they devoured his hope.

He bowed his head; even now, as the daylight began to fill the sky, he knew that it had ended. How could they possibly get to the Citadel? They were lost, lost and damned in the smoke, running from every shadow. It was hopeless, the enemy – the birds, the chariots, the warriors – would search for them constantly. He knew it in his bones. There would be no respite. They would not give up. He would not see the Citadel. They would hunt until they found them, and finding them, they would consume them. Here, amid the rubble of the fire's destruction the Hraddas had wrought in the ravaging so long ago There was no hope left. Their enemy of darkness and fire would come in time.

He understood now why the enemy had not waited for them outside the City of the Gate. There they could call forth the power of the city, the power of fire invincible. There the daylight had been full and the sun shone in the sky, bright and unassailable.

Here it was hard to tell day from night. This was a land of fire and darkness. Here, the enemy could reign supreme. Here, there was no hope. Here was defeat. If there had been another land here centuries ago when the Malasar ruled the world, if it had been a brighter, hopeful place, it had been lost in the years past, lost entirely. Now it was crushed beneath destruction. The City of the Gate had been the last vestige, an echo of a song long faded. Now, this was the place of the enemy, a place of death and devastation.

He stared across the hot rocks before him. Even if by some chance, some miracle, they gained the Citadel, would they not be waiting for them there – the warriors, the enemy, the strange steedless chariots? The enemy, the shining ones and the evil birds, now knew the goal of their quest. Even if they did not hunt them down they would wait for them there.

Why didn't Rissar give up? Didn't he understand that the quest was lost? When they had reached this land and found it full of the enemy, they should have known. Arnex was lost. They would never achieve the Citadel.

Rissar had misjudged, bringing so few with him. The army of the Hardsar nation could have stood against them. Rosart had been right on that day when he and Hewas and Terras and Halam had stood on the plain before the Fortress of Endless Night. He had gone back for the whole Hardsar host. They should have brought them with them when assailing the fire lands of the north.

Halam imagined it. With the Hardsar nation at his back, these people mounted on chariots, these Arcan warriors, these people who could make themselves birds, those vicious birds, would not seem so great. They would have smashed their way through all opposition in but a few days. Many would have died in the fight and the battle would have been terrible. But did the Hardsar not live for battle and war? They would have won through. Of course they would have. Against these foul monsters, their force of arms would win through. Only that.

He lay there; before him, Hewas's face rose up. The Hardsari had been humbled when it had seemed that the army would not be needed. He had returned across the plain, back to the moors of the Hardsar lands for nothing. Hewas had been right, the decision of a general and a king; he had been correct.

And Hewas had promised he would follow with the host. What was it that the Hardsara elder, Hurga, the lord of the dagger, had said? *Perhaps we might yet prove useful.* He had been right. It was Rissar who had been wrong. It was the Malasari who had made the wrong decision. He had been foolish. They should never have left the host. The very thought of it gave Halam some vestige of hope. If only they had stayed and had swept across the plain as a mighty army. Nothing could have stood in their path. It mattered not what the Torasar wished. The Hardsar would pass. That was not important beside the all-encompassing purpose. That would have been the way to awaken Arnex. A mighty army, smashing all opposition before its path.

Halam laughed and even to his ears it sounded like a strange wicked, ruined laugh. What would it have mattered when the strange Taxarzerek and his savants waited for them at the end of the plain? Before the thousands of Hardsar sweeping north, Taxarzerek would have hidden, afraid as any stranger would be in the face of an army. They would never have met him, never have been cursed by his disturbing presence.

Of course, they might not have met the Offspring of the fire and that would have been a pity. Halam liked Trioch and Sigmor and found in them something that he missed in himself. Before a great army of Hardsar, the Offspring too would have quailed. Perhaps they would not have made their presence known. That would have been regrettable, but then Helmar would not be dead. The Child would not have had to die, screaming his pain before the greatsword of an Arcan warrior. Halam winced as he remembered the sight of the man's death.

He spat on the ground before him.

No, Rissar had been wrong. He had led them badly. The host of the Hardsar should have been brought. How could the motley band of seven people and one sentinel, even as strong as the Arcan warrior, best all these terrible assailants?

Now they would die. The Hardsar host was not there. There was no way out. They must hide forever amidst this rubble of ruination or, better still, turn and run away back through the gruesome land behind them. But then the enemy would catch them. They would hunt them down and they would die, trying to escape.

He stared up at the sky. The dawn had fully come, dim, suffused with the redness of the fire, lost in the mist. The land greeted it not at all and darkness crouched in every crack of rock or billow of mist surrounding him. A choking smoke rising from the river of molten rock bit at his throat, acrid fumes stealing away his hope. He spat again, wishing that he could somehow remove the taste from his mouth. He pulled his water-skin up to his mouth and swallowed a mouthful of water, hoping it could remove the bad taste, but the fumes entered his nostrils and soured even that drink, acrid as it was. He was short of water now. He could not continue much longer. There was no water here. He lay on the ground for a long time, not rising with the dawn as had become the custom. No one else spoke; they all seemed to be waiting for the light to become brighter. Halam knew that it would not. This was the full day. There was no more. He wished he could lie there forever. Lost but hidden.

Rissar rose to his feet. Insnar, who had slept the night in his arms, jumped to the ground and looked around. There was no longer despair in the face of the jaksar, only tiredness and distaste. Rissar was staring out through the mist. Somehow the action made Halam angry.

Is he acting as if there is something to see in this

terrible gloom?

Rissar turned and his eyes caught Halam's gaze. For a moment Halam felt his heart had been cut open and Rissar could see everything within. But when Rissar spoke it was not to Halam. 'We must move on.' He spoke quietly, gently reminding everyone, but his voice cut through the silence of their despairing wait. 'The fog will hide us from their sight. We must go on – to our goal.'

Halam lay back against the rocks. They dug into his back, but he stayed there, peering up at the man he had followed this far. He had to speak. 'Rissar, what will happen when we reach the Citadel?'

Rissar turned and looked at him, but despite the tone in Halam's voice, his gaze was not harsh. 'You know the quest, Halam Hardsaro, we go to awaken Arnex.'

Halam saw nothing in the words but an accusation. The mist and smoke from the river of fire billowed between them.

Halam let his breath out slowly through his teeth, expelling the bitterness of the smoke. 'Yes, I know the quest, lord, but the enemy is here before us. We did not know, we did not expect them to be here, to be waiting, to prevent us from achieving the goal. How can we go on now that such forces oppose us? We cannot best them, we are too few and we skulk even now in hiding, running from them whenever in their hunt they find us.'

Halam drew in another harsh, bitter breath.

'Can you not see that they will be waiting for us at the Citadel? They know where we are going. They know our purpose. They will have guessed. The quest is no longer hidden – how then can we enter the Citadel, even if we can reach it? Rissar, don't you understand that they will be holding it against us when we get there? Can't you see?'

It was spilling from him now, all the fear, all the doubt, all the despair. He could not have stopped talking even if he had wished it. He continued, acid thoughts expelling themselves with each word. 'If we returned now and ran back the way we have come, lord, the Hardsar nation is behind us, we could find them. Hewas will come with an army. All the people we need at our side. No enemy could stand against us then. We could force . . .' Rissar held up his hand, but Halam could not stop. 'We are only eight, lord, even with the warrior, and they are ten times that, maybe a hundred times. We cannot win against them. They will win. They will command the Citadel.'

Rissar sat down on the rocks again. He looked across at Halam and without turning, even to glance at the others, he slowly shook his head. 'Halam, it is not their Citadel. It is the Citadel of Arnex.'

Halam met his gaze evenly. 'It was once. But now, Rissar? How will we best them? Eight against eight hundred?'

Rissar became serious. 'You do not need to go on, Halam Hardsaro, no one here does.' He looked around the rest of the group. No one spoke.

Halam looked at Rosart. This Hardsara

woodsman would understand. Wasn't this exactly his wisdom, which had been spoken as they stood before the fortress? He would know that the Hardsar host was needed now better than anyone. 'Rosart, speak to him.' Halam stared at him desperately. 'You know the wisdom of what I say. Let us return for the army.'

The woodsman looked awkward. He stared across at Halam. 'I will not make that mistake again, Halam Hardsaro. I have already learnt this lesson. If death awaits me, I will welcome it. Such is the way of the Hardsar. We fight for the king. If it brings us death, we accept it. There is honour in such a death, freely given. I forgot that before.' Rosart looked across at him, his gaze unwavering. 'You are my prince. I will follow you. But perhaps you must learn the lesson I learnt. I understand the way of the Trish harga more than I ever did. Truly I do. If I go to my death then it will be at the side of my prince, my lord Jored and my Malasari.' He looked up at Rissar. 'I will die with you, for you, my lord, if you will it.'

Rissar nodded. 'I do not, Rosart Hardsara. And you have found the way of your people.'

Halam let out a tired breath. He knew what the forester had said was right. It was, oddly, a thought that filled him with a strange peace. To give your life for a thing you believed in, a person you believed in. Perhaps Rosart was right. Halam stood now where the woodsman Hardsara, son of Herfa, had been on that day when they stood before the greatness of the fortress. The woodsman had decided wrongly then. Now he disavowed it and took the path Halam had chosen.

Halam felt his face flush as he realised. Even in the heat, his face grew hotter. Rosart was right, of course he was. Halam had spoken so many brave words. He had sworn on that day long ago, ages past, it seemed, when he had wanted Terras more than he wanted his own life. Now here was the point of what he had sworn. This was what it truly meant. He was not worthy. The promises were all meaningless; he had meant none of it. These thoughts should never have entered his mind. He could not possess what Rosart already had, what even the little forest creature Insnar already had. He was a Lakeman, a weak, effete Aallesar, not worthy to be king of the mountain people.

'This conversation is pointless.'

He turned in surprise. It was Taxarzerek.

'Why is that, Taxarzerek?' Rissar replied, turning to face the eyeless man.

'Because there is nowhere else to go. I heartily wish that I had never even thought of returning to this awful place, never thought of reclaiming our technology, our warriors. We can always make more weapons. We did not need to recover them. We did it, I came because we could. We did not understand who had taken them or why they had crashed here, so I came.' He looked around, his eye plates sparkling. 'I wish when I saw the fire you had lit and saw you all sitting within it, I had simply walked past. I saw some advantage in travelling with you, to come back ... here.' He swept his arm around the surrounding devastation. He glanced down and, to Halam's amazement, there was real emotion in this man. His lips were quivering.

'But I came. I thought I could not leave the weaponry, the warriors, the vehicles. I could not go home without them. So I walked here on my own two feet, without compulsion. I even lied to you to ensure it. If I had told all the truth, perhaps you would not have helped. If you had realised the strength of my warriors you would not have helped. But, perhaps ...' He stopped, seeming confused by his thoughts. He was silent for many moments. No one spoke; they waited silently for him to continue. He raised his head and spoke again. 'But now, there is no escape. We have no choice. If we split the party, we will all be lost. They will hunt us down, one by one, without mercy. Do not think, Halam, that by returning you will now escape their wrath. We can go on together or we can return together. And either way, they will catch us.'

Halam looked over at the warrior. The metal fighter simply sat, silent, his hand on the haft of his sword, the other holding one of the fire-maces. There was no thought, no worry; he was simply waiting for them to finish the conversation and move. Halam stared at the metal visage, the helm of the warrior, and wondered again if there was indeed anything in that thing which lived, had ever truly lived. If he did live, he, like Insnar and Rosart, was simply going to follow.

Taxarzerek was still speaking. 'I do not believe

that you, my lord Rissar, will turn back.' The Arcan spread his hands, indicating them all. 'And you alone know where you are heading and why. We have all followed, perhaps for a variety of reasons, but I have seen much of the power there has been in this journey. I will not separate from the strongest of the company at this, the worst point of our journey. We must go with him. I follow.'

'Yes,' said Trioch now, 'it is as you say. It may well be that death awaits us all, but the Offspring have faced death before and Helmar my brother was given it. He died in the land of my people and in the city for which we yearn. I will not turn back. I will die in his obedience. Perhaps my death will be as my brother's was, an honour, a testimony to why my people live.'

Sigmor nodded his agreement. 'Truly,' he said, 'I will follow. To die in this land that was once ours is fitting. If it comes, I will welcome it.'

'Neither will this Hardsara be false,' said Jored.

'No,' said Rosart, 'the Hardsar cannot be and remain the people of the guard. Yet it is I who choose this way of my own will. I care not for the vows all the people have taken – that Hardsar are born to take. This is my choice. I have learnt this thing. I will die within it.'

Rissar looked at Halam. There was no demand in his eyes but only concern, concern and commitment. 'Halam, speak.'

'I am sorry, I am truly sorry, Rissar.' There were tears in his eyes. He felt them rolling down his cheeks. 'I feel lost. I do not know the way. I am not worthy to be the Hardsaro. These people are greater than I. I am not worthy of the Hardsare. I am nothing.' He looked at the two Hardsar. Jored smiled back at him. Encouragement from such a man at that moment was more than he could bear.

Halam did not know what he was saying until he said it. 'I cannot see the way forward. If I must follow into death, I do not want to. I am afraid.' He looked across at the Malasari.

Rissar sat in silence. The jaksar, at his feet, was looking at Halam. They all were.

'Yet I will come.'

◈ Chapter 19 ◈

Rissar rose to his feet. He bent and offered Halam his hand; he reached up tentatively and then he grasped it firmly. The Malasari spoke. 'Then come. We will awaken Arnex.'

Rissar pulled Halam to his feet. Then he turned, looked down briefly at the jaksar and spoke some muttered growls to the animal. Insnar walked forward and Rissar picked him up, settling him between the crook of his arm and his shoulder, half within his cloak and half out. In his other hand, he took the Staff of Ages from the ground. He looked out, surveying the mist before them. The whole quest waited as he gazed into it. He was the only one who knew the way.

'We must be cautious as we go.' As if to punctuate his remark, the cry of a bird echoed out of the mist. It was far away, but it was hunting. Rissar turned and continued to climb up the mountain. They all followed him in silence.

What else is there, but to follow?

Halam took the place directly behind the Malasar. For him, there was no other place. Behind him, the giant metal warrior came and then Taxarzerek. The Offspring and the Hardsar followed in the rear.

They fought their way up through the mist. The way was difficult, hard and hot. As the climb grew higher it grew steeper and the rocks they climbed looser and more easily dislodged. The climbing became very difficult. They worked around great pits of fire gouged from the earth and once, turning north, crossed a huge river of flame bridged by a narrow and perilous span of rock.

Then, to everyone's relief, Rissar turned down, away from the fire that raged down that mountainside and back into cooler areas below. They were returning to the base of the valley, yet their detour was bringing them to an entirely different point from the one from which they had ascended. Their pursuers would, hopefully, not discover where they were. They would hunt in the wrong place. How long would it take them to find them? He did not know, but the tortuous route they had taken would delay them. At worst it would confuse them just enough. This was the hope that filled Halam's mind.

When they reached the bottom of the mountain, they had descended beneath the worst of the mist. The air became cooler, less acrid, almost breathable again. Halam took it in great lungfuls. On another day he would have found it too foul. Today it felt clean. They circled for a while until, unfailingly, Rissar turned back to the north, towards the Citadel. At least Halam hoped that was where they were headed. They travelled quickly, trotting in their haste, driven. At every opportunity they turned north, whatever the obstacle; whatever maze of rock prevented them, back they would turn. Halam heard birds screaming their rage and anguish into the gloom but they kept heading northward. The mountains rumbled on. Did they disapprove of the invasion? But which invasion were they protesting about, theirs or the enemy?

Tiredness flooded Halam in ways that he had not thought possible. How did someone this tired keep going? The wound in his arm was throbbing. He had not tended it at all during the night. Looking around, they all had untended, uncared-for scrapes and burns. Why should he be any different? No one bothered. Halam walked without thought. If he'd had time to think, to consider his position, to do anything other than putting one foot in front of another, he would have collapsed. He was lost in the mist. He would never find his way out. Now he walked after the retreating backs of the Offspring. He had fallen behind, letting the Offspring take his lead. He did not care where they were. He did not care where he was. He wanted only to stop, to finally reach the goal and cease. Sometimes the idea of death was a relief.

They struggled on all that day, through the noon when the day reached its crescendo of dimness. They trudged on into the dingy half-light of the afternoon. When it was late, the sun was briefly visible, touching the horizon. The mist cleared and the view opened to reveal an awesome sight. Ahead of them, built on a great round hill, was a large city. Halam stopped walking and stared at it. It was so distant, so far away. There still was such a way to go before they could reach it.

The city was white, but broken, ruined, and spattered with ash. It broke out of the landscape like teeth protruding from a blackened jawbone. The hill on which it stood was surrounded by fire. Many molten rivers running down from the volcanoes surrounding it fed a lake of fire. The rivers all settled, seething, bubbling, into an enormous moat filled with flame. From this mass of molten stone, the hill thrust like the whitened bones of some ancient awesome animal, buried in black rock.

He stared at it. It was their goal. He knew it. There could be no other. It was fearful, ringed with fire, a place of darkness and devastation. The sort of place where a person might run, unswerving, to meet his death head-on. It was a place of death and death surrounded it.

Death protecting death from ... what? Who could assail such a place?

He knew that he would die there. He knew it with a vehement knowledge beyond understanding. This was the gate of death. He had come to it. He was here to die. He had walked to the Hardsar village. He had sworn foolish oaths. He had claimed a woman. He had found love beyond his understanding. He had lost his love, abandoned her to a lonely, unknown destiny. He would never now see the great places of the world. He would never again wonder at their beauty. He would never hold his beloved in his arms.

He had walked here from the mansions of his father, the palaces of the Aallesari. He had walked here from the comfort of his childhood. And he had come quickly, without delay, without stopping to live a life worth having. He had come of his own will. He had walked to this, his death. He had left his father's house with anger. Now, he would not see the City on the Lake again. He thought of his father, his beautiful sister Jasada, and his nervous and warm-hearted mother, Misaneer. He would never see them again. They would never know where or how he died. They would not even know where he was.

He gazed forward at the lake of fire surrounding the city. The city would have been unreachable but for a narrow bridge that arched across the gap, linking the cool ground on their side of the world with the white buildings beyond the ring of death. It was a strange bridge, eerily white, curved like the broken rib of a long-dead leviathan. It would be hot on that bridge, unbearably hot, and they would be out in the open over a river of fire and exposed to attack, not only from behind and in front but from above as well. The foolishness of the thought occurred to him at once.

What does it matter how hot it is when death awaits?

The birds, the vicious birds would be able to strike at them without anything to stop them. Again and again they would swoop, and but a single blow would topple you from that bridge to die in the molten lake beneath.

And they would be waiting. Of course they would be waiting.

He stared on. Between them and the bridge was a great, empty plain. There was no cover on it. They would not even reach the bridge before they were killed by the monsters that would wait there. The Hraddas had come, the monsters from the skies who destroyed – the makkuz.

They had all stopped. 'We shall not reach it today,' said Rissar, 'it is too late, but we will cross that bridge before another night comes to the world. Now, we must find somewhere to spend this last night.'

Halam put his hands to his head. *Last night? Yes, this is our last night.* They would never reach it. They would not survive.

They sought for some cover. They searched until night had fully come, finding a place at the last minute before darkness. It was a canyon of sorts, like the one they had found that first night they had entered this foulness of a place. It had only one entrance, but the rocks around it were low, too easily seen over. Nevertheless, it was all there was. Rissar led them in.

They crouched down to keep their heads low in the hope of hiding their position from the eyes of the enemies. The darkness enveloped them. They sat and no one thought of sleep; no one even moved. An attack was bound to come. It was obvious. The nearer they drew to the Citadel, the smaller the area the makkuz must search. They would find them. They would find them this night. It was just a matter of time. This was the end, bent forward in the darkness, hiding. Halam would die as he lived, in fear.

He drew his sword and laid it across his knees. If he was to die, he would die with the sword in his hand. He would kill before he surrendered at last to his death. He looked down at the blade that had given him so much strength. He dared not even glance at the scabbard for fear of what it might say, what might be written there. He stared deeply into the blade but not a glimmer of light came from it. Was there no power left in it for him? Had he cast aside all it had to give? Would it never return to him now?

When the darkness was at its deepest, they came. They cascaded over the rocks, coming from all directions. They were many. It was confused. They were terrible in their anger, men and women armed with the fire-maces and other wand-like spears of light. They had found them. They had crept up, attacking together and in force. These enemies would not again strike when they weren't prepared. They had not hunted in small groups that the quest could beat. They came in force. They came to kill.

Halam leapt up. At once exhaustion rose with him from the ground. He almost fell back to the ground in weariness. An enemy lunged at him, cackling her joy – an easy kill. Halam lifted his sword but it was swept aside by the enemy's great spear of light. Despair held Halam's arm back. He was going to die. His antagonist hesitated for a moment then she smiled a terrible smile, lifted the great spear and pointed it quietly at his chest.

Halam was truly dead, he gave himself up.

This was the time. It was over.

Without his willing it, his sword began to glow. It shone at once, terribly bright. It glowed as it never had before. It shone as bright as the sun they had lost forever beneath this darkness, this land of fire and night. The enemy quailed, but still she fired her great spear. A burgeoning funnel of power streamed from it, but it was claimed by the sword, taken from the very air to make his sword even brighter, even more dazzling. The enemy staggered backwards as if the light from his sword was sucking her very essence from her. Halam stared down at the sword. He had not even wielded it and yet it was killing the makkuz. The night was chased away by the brightness of the sword. Daylight had come. He looked up. The mist was swept away and as he stood the canopy of stars exploded into being above them. Great ribbons of light filled the sky and coursed across it. The gloom and mists of the land were gone. Halam stared up at the stars as one might welcome the homecoming of a long-lost brother or sister.

Attackers streamed across the low hills of the canyon and beyond, across the plain they had gathered. Tanks came in such numbers that he could not count. On them, Arcan warriors stood or shining ones, the Hraddas. They were too many. In moments they would arrive. Above, the vicious birds keened, sweeping across the sky towards them. Halam fought with the others of the quest but here there was no escape. Here they must fight to the end.

Halam tightened his grip on his sword; its power was fully present. *Why did I never trust it?* He gave himself to his sword. The sword fought as it had never fought before. It took him. It drove him. It pulled him. It dodged and weaved him through the spewing fire all around him. It struck. It parried. He struck. He parried. He dodged. Now he would never let it go. Now he would not release its power ever again. He gave himself to it. He gave the battle totally to his sword. There was no Halam. There was only the weapon. There was only a dagger spinning into a fire. There was only the freedom of a sword given – as he sat before the fire with his Hardsara princess.

He was the sword.

The sword and the man were one.

He cared not for death or life.

The enemies fell back before the light streaming from his sword. He lunged, stabbing the sword, grazing the side of one of his enemies. The man stared back at him. The wound was not fatal. Yet the light itself spreading upwards from his wound was what was killing him, not the edge of the blade. The Hraddas fell, his whole body filled with light and surrounded by light streaming from Halam's blade. The fighter dissolved into nothingness as some energy in him, some power, ebbed and eked away, wounded and broken by the power of Halam of the sword.

In that sudden moment of calm, Halam glanced round. The Arcan was cowering on the ground just behind him. The warrior stood over him, fighting, simultaneously, at least eight attackers. His greatsword was in one hand and the mace, reversed, firing in the other. His skill was great, his prowess was mighty, but in another moment he would be overcome and dragged to the ground. Halam stepped back to aid the metal sentinel. What could he do against eight, even with his sword? He turned, seeking Trioch and Sigmor, knowing what was needed. He saw them. They fought together, alongside each other, against another five of their attackers. They were singing together as they fought.

He met Sigmor's gaze and the Child of the fire seemed at once to understand. This was the time. Taxarzerek understood. He had won a place in the circle. Halam joined his voice to their song. He began to chant. The song they sang was a slow song, a distant song, a song of life and strength. It was not a song of their victory. It was not a song of their power and strength. It was a song of silence and peace. It was a song of what was not, but could be, a song of what they were not, but would be.

Jored joined the chant as well. Then, hesitating, Rosart began to sing, the woodsman, the humbled fighter, the would-be worthy to stand beside the Hardsare.

Taxarzerek leapt to his feet behind the warrior, screaming his accompaniment. His voice was not strong. He had forgotten how to sing. Yet the song took what he gave to itself and made it a part. The song of the Arcans was joined with theirs. The fire sprang into being around them. Halam's sword burst into flame. How could it be brighter? And yet it was. Rissar swung his staff, quarterstaff style, and hit one of the attackers. The Staff of Ages burst into flame. Lightning shot out from it in every direction.

'At last,' the Malasari cried, 'the new song

begins.'

The fire of their song grew vast and burned as if it would never stop.

The vicious birds in the air burst into flame.

The fire roared out from them.

The makkuz scattered back, burnt, taken, absorbed, overcome, screaming in rage. The fire sprang outwards. As the light caught the beings and things of metal they did not all perish in consuming fire as Halam expected. Two sentinels stopped and threw down their weapons. Casting them away, they seemed no longer to know why they stood there or why they sought to destroy. They ran, screaming, into the night. Their chariots stopped. The fire hit the other combat tanks and they melted before it. Other Arcan warriors leapt from the collapsing ruins of their chariots and as they hit the ground, their legs gave way and melting they fused into the earth. Birds and the makkuz threw themselves at them, screaming in denied anger and fear. But they fell back, burnt by the fire, screaming in pain and anguish. They were swept backwards, cheated, frightened, defiant and angry.

'Now,' shouted Rissar, 'we are complete. Follow me to the last fortress.'

He walked forward into the darkness, holding his staff flaming before him, the symbol of a forgotten people, the ancient way of the Malasar and long lost to the knowledge of the world. Halam strode after him and did not even look back to see who followed. The awesome joy of a moment had seized him and would never let go. He did not care if he walked to his death or his life. He would follow. There was no longer a choice. There was only what was. There was only whatever would be.

They burst from the detritus of the rocks and onto the open plain. They sang. They broke into a run. Fire flowed around them. The flames were sweeping back from them, filling the land of death with life, like a torch held in the wind fills the night with light. The mist billowed again around them. The darkness of the sky was deep, but they ran into it. The quest ran and they sang. They ran on. The plain thudding beneath their feet, they came where the Citadel lay.

The heat from the rivers of fire was great, its redness overtaking the night, rivalling the fire of their song. They ran for the bridge across the lake of fire. It would not be long before they reached it.

The fleeing enemy turned then and before the last Citadel; they attacked again, despairing, desperate. Did hundreds of the Hraddas stand before them? As they watched, some burst into flame, turning shining fighters into globes of fire and pillars of light. Above them were many of the birds, vicious and ready, their prey before them. There was no hesitation in Rissar's pace as he saw them. The party followed behind him. He continued until he stood right before the bridge. There, at last, he stopped.

'At last,' Rissar cried, 'the time has come, and now that I stand before the city of Arnex, you cannot prevent me. All here is mine. In it and them, there is nothing of you. The new song has begun. The time is done. The whole is complete. Arnex will be awoken.'

He held his staff aloft, two-handed. Insnar stood at his side. When had the Malasar had put him down? Halam did not know. Now the creature stood where they all stood, beside the magician king. Did the song of the Offspring falter? Did the fire around them cease and the darkness sweep in? Was there no song to be sung before such might? Yet they could die, and love, and be forever this.

The world seemed to shimmer. For a moment Halam thought it was only one of the mind-tricks, the false worlds of thought that Rissar had used before, but as it developed he knew for sure that it was not. The world around him did not change. It did not become something else. It leapt into greater focus. It was becoming more real, not less. The world was showing a reality that had waited there, beneath their poor and limited vision.

A scream sounded from the throats of the fiery riders and birds, though Halam knew not why. Halam looked down and gasped in surprise. It was Rissar who had changed the greater. Now in his hands he held the finely carved Staff of Ages that Halam had seen only in his mind before. He was dressed in flowing robes and his black hair cascaded back from him. He was very great. This was no wanderer, no itinerant. This was no stranger.

This was the Malasari, the magician king of old.

The chariots, the warriors, the birds screaming, wavered and the riders ceased to laugh. Light flowed out from the magician king. It did not flash like lightning in the darkness might, nor burst like sunlight from behind a darkened cloud on a summer day. The light flowed, as water streams down from a hidden stream, running across the ground to cascade into being – a blazing waterfall of light.

The makkuz who could not surrender threw up their hands. The Arcan warriors who could not speak screamed. The light had swept over Halam and his whole body glowed. He looked down at his hands, which were almost transparent in their brightness. This was the truth that the City of the Gate had sung but a memory. This was a remembrance of the true light, true fire. This was what the future called forth to the now.

Halam realised that this new song, this music that would be, had been the source of all the power that had flowed to them throughout the whole of the quest. It was this that had given the fire that shone around the City of the Gate. It was this that had given Halam his sword. This was the source of all the light and power, courage and bravery they had ever found. This had given them everything and was everything they needed to reach this point. The song that was to come had brought them here by its power. They had done nothing that had not contained it. Halam welcomed the power that flowed from it and to him. With the light came a feeling of incomparable joy and peace beyond imagination. In his total inability, it was something he could not go on living without . . . He stopped.

Without what . . . ?

The beings of fire scattered before it, screaming. The fire had stolen their energy, sucked their power from them. They retreated, beaten. They cowered. They ran. The remaining birds rose screaming into the sky, streaming fire behind them. Rissar walked forward, the pool of spreading brightness moving with him. They all followed him. They came slowly, unhurriedly. Nothing stood against them. On they walked, across the final space and onto the single white bridge across the lake of fire.

Before them lay the Citadel. The bridge was steep and now that he stood upon it, Halam saw that it was bleached but very beautiful. It was made of the pure stone from which the pillars of welcome in the City of the Gate were carved. It was magnificent. As they crossed it, Halam heard the screaming birds still swooping down at them from the night, crying out in pain and fear as they struck the light that surrounded them all. Not a single vicious claw or beak came near them and no sign was seen of their enemies. They crossed the lake of fire and atop the huge bridge, Halam stared down at the city that awaited them.

The bridge had once ended in a single massive white archway. The centre of the arch had fallen now, leaving two strange curved pillars marking the entrance to the Citadel of Arnex. They walked down, their feet treading the way passed by many a king, many a prince coming to the Citadel of the Warrior. As they passed through the curved pillars, the light around them faded, dying back into the staff of the

Malasari.

Halam turned; the rest of the party still followed. Trioch came and Sigmor walked behind her. For it was known; Trioch led the Offspring of the fire. She was the Eye. Then the warrior came. He walked proud, upright, with the greatsword grasped in two powerful hands. Taxarzerek came behind him. His eye plates were blank and yet Halam knew that he could see. The Hardsar, Jored and Rosart came last. Rosart looked like a man completely made, Jored like a man who had fulfilled his whole reason to be.

'Trust in the new song,' said Rissar. 'There is only life and it is all. This is the truth. We have found the song.' He turned and looked at Halam. 'And you, my companions, you have come too.'

Halam nodded. 'So be it.'

'Truly,' said Trioch.

A last dark vicious bird swooped at them from the night. It screamed its horror, bared its talons and Rissar glanced up at it. As it plummeted it looked as if, for a moment, it could strike the Malasari down, but at the last moment, just before it entered the Citadel itself, it turned and screamed off into the night, cheated. Perhaps, after all, fear had been its only weapon.

'Are our foes not in the Citadel?'

'No,' said Rissar, answering Jored, Lord of the Hammer, 'the Citadel would not permit it, as with the City of the Gate. This is the place of Arnex. This is his throne. He is the Warrior King.'

Halam examined Rissar. Did he see him for the

first time? He was dressed in flowing robes. The staff at his side was white and carved with intricate writing. This was the Malasari. Beside him, Insnar stood, the faithful companion. The jaksar was no longer the tired, dirty and wearied creature of those last few days. The jaksar was the beast. This animal lived and life itself glowed from him. He was the king of his species, the greatest of all the beasts. He was unsurpassed, for he lived.

Halam looked down at his arm. The wound that had been there was no more. He pulled the bandage with which Sigmor had dressed his first injury away from his shoulder. He stared down at the flesh of his shoulder. That hurt was gone.

Rissar turned and walked on into the city. They followed, walking inside the white buildings. As he walked Halam realised that this was not only a Citadel, a fortress and a castle. This had been a city of palaces and mansions. Once they were great, but now they were ruined and lost. Ashes lay strewn about the streets and on the roofs of the palaces, where roofs remained. It lay in great drifts, like black snow on some terrible winter morn of shadow. The ash was jet black, complete in its darkness, and the walls of the buildings were white. All would have been white on black but for the glow from the lake of fire that surrounded them. It deluged the scene with red. The Citadel was a pure place of contrasts, black on white, white on black, and yet that straightforward simplicity was shattered, for it was covered in blood. Halam was lost in the strength of it, lost in its beauty, lost even in its destruction. It was hard to believe that this place existed in the same world as the house of his father. Somehow, somewhere, they must have passed beyond the world into a nether region, a terrible realm, where there were only those three colours. He walked after Rissar and he felt like he inhabited a dream, without any ability to turn aside from its course.

The ash was piled up in the streets and sometimes, as they trod, it came as high as their knees. They walked on, sweeping it before them, like men wading in the shallows of a huge black ocean. In the centre of the Citadel was a single building that was not ruined. The roof was on and although ash lay around it in heaps, it could still be seen for what it was. It was beautiful yet simple, formed of two massive structures overlapping at their centres. It was huge beyond belief.

'Lord, is this where Arnex lies?' said Sigmor. The fire of his life was fulfilled. He was an Offspring, one of the people of Arnex.

'It is,' said Rissar, turning to look at the Child. 'This is where he has awaited us for many generations.'

The building had no windows, but two great stone doors marked the entrance before them. They were black and hard to see for the darkness that was in them. They took the light into themselves but they did not let it out. The Hardsar came forward at once and they all struggled to open these great portals of the Citadel. They had begun to move slowly aside when the Arcan warrior, without prompting, bent forward and lent his strength to the task. The doors opened before them.

Inside there was complete darkness. Halam hesitated, fearing what they would find. At once he remembered that all people, all the Aallesar, were taught that Arnex had been slain. What if they found within this place only his corpse, or his skeleton, or nothingness for he had rotted away centuries before? Rissar entered without hesitation and spread his arms. A light seemed to grow from the ground, spreading up from the black ash. It was a red light, crimson as the blood of a freshly slain man.

It crawled up the walls of the place.

They walked forward, the light filling the interior of the Citadel. Walls dissolved away before them and they discovered what had been for so long hidden. They went up the great corridor that was revealed, and came to the huge inner chamber where the two great buildings intersected. Before the entrance was a great wall of fire. As they approached, it dimmed and was swept away. The room they entered was immense and the roof above them was cavernous in its vastness.

The red light spread outwards from Rissar and as it reached great ancient lampstands standing in a circle around the room they burst into flame, filling, at last, the chamber with new light, a yellow light, fresh light, the light of the sun. Halam blinked his surprise that another colour but red and black could exist. A huge hall was open to their gaze. In the centre of the chamber, lying on a marble slab, like the ancient, forgotten tomb of a king, was a man. They walked forward. Halam looked down on his face. He was surprised. This was a young man. His face held no sign of age, no blemish of the passing years. He could not be more than ten years older than Halam himself, fifteen at the most. Yet the more Halam looked, the more he knew that this was a face beyond time. It was a face without time and on which time's effect was completely lost.

The Warrior King was dressed in a pale robe, and a long white cloak hung from the marble slab in folds. Across his chest was a golden sash and on his feet he wore armoured shoes of burnished bronze or gold. Was there golden armour beneath those robes? A sword lay on him. It was immense, stretching from his mouth to his feet. The cross-guard almost touched his shoulders. It was colossal, and on the haft of the sword, there was writing. The pommel was a white gem, which touched his lips. The whiteness of the gem was so great that it seemed, even there, surrounded by the yellow, red and the black, to glow faintly with its light. In his right hand, Arnex held nine gems flickering with light, all different colours, some bright, some dim and some almost extinguished. But none were dark.

It was Arnex, truly Arnex at last.

Halam could not believe it. He was really here.

He was everything that Halam had imagined and more. His hair was so white, his face so young, his sword so beautiful; he was without comparison and no words could describe his beauty. Halam looked upon the face of the Warrior King and he knew he had not been not complete until this moment. His whole life, and all that he had been, was as ragged clothes and broken shards before this. Rissar walked towards the figure of the sleeping man. He was a man sleeping without breath and without the taint of time. Rissar looked back, for a moment, at his friends, and then he placed his staff on the sword that lay on Arnex's body. They matched, the same in length and span. The whiteness of the gem flared to life.

'Awake, Arnex, my brother, my friend, myself. The time is upon us. Behold, I have come.'

The world broke apart; light exploded from nowhere, the world was shattered and lost and could never be remade. A wind blew out from that joining, a wind more powerful than any hurricane or storm that had ever filled the lands. It swept out from the vault on which the Warrior King lay, and all flame fled before it.

Halam felt the wind come. He felt it surge up to him. He tensed for it to throw him against the walls and destroy him. Annihilate him and sweep all that was broken from the world forever. Yet it did not destroy. It came and it did not. It swept through him as if the barrier of one man was not enough to stop it. He was not moved; it took him and caught him in its power. As it passed it sucked from him everything that he had ever feared and disliked about himself and from him all feelings and knowledge of worthlessness were gone. Could they ever return?

A part of him would fly with that wind forever and whatever he did after this, whatever place he went, whatever he said, there was always some part of himself that would be flying, riding free with the wind above an endless land of absolute beauty. A thousand colours swirled into being around him and he could not see for their brightness. He did not care. He wished only to die here and live forever within the wind. As the moment faded he looked again and saw that Arnex stood now.

The Warrior King spoke. 'I am he. I am Arnex. I am awake.'

The words thundered out with a power like the cataracts of the mountain lakes near Halam's home. Such was their strength that Halam lost all sense of the world around him. The power of his words subsided and Halam saw before him once again. Arnex stood beside Rissar and he held his two-handed greatsword before him, upright.

'Let the praise of the Snake god be on my lips, a double-edged sword in my hands. Let the power of the Snake god be with us. Let our enemies fear. For we are his. I am Arnex.'

His sword burst into flame and all the other lights in the Citadel went out. It was a joy that this light above all had been lit and he, the King of the Warriors, was returned to the world. What other beauty was there, but this sweet benison?

The Malasari spoke.

'Let us go forward then and do the will of the

Snake god.'

'It is why I am here,' said Arnex.

The Transformation of Wind
Book 3 – An Excerpt

The sea journey had been long. As Terras, Shiskes and the crew travelled south the mountains of the Pasra descended slowly lower, mountains became hills and eventually came to a rolling land before the mouth of the large river that flowed from the lakeland. There was a port there, the last port. The country there was ruled by a baron who possessed all the lands down the coast to the stone desert. He was in allegiance with the lakeland king, but they did not make land there. Shiskes said the baron was not friendly and his loyalty to the lakeland was more name than reality. His people did not permit the fisherfolk to sail up the river without high tolls, thereby forcing them to trade what they brought in his port and at poor prices. The Istsar only passed inland when they had business with the Aallesar. The farmer people that the baron ruled had little time for fisherfolk, except when it was in their interest.

Shiskes explained. 'We do not like the baron or his people either. He is an arrogant man and thinks himself far enough away from the Aallesari to act however he wishes. He would declare himself independent if he dared.'

And so they passed by.

Yet, as Terras gazed from their boat to the shore she could see that the port was busy with traders from Aallesar and Istsar, as well as other dark-skinned people she did not know. At the end, whatever the politics, this was the one place they could all safely meet, trade, and make money. Money swept politics aside.

It had taken them days to reach this far and Shiskes said there were many days more of travel to pass the lands of the stone wilderness. The landscape of the shoreline south of the port was rocky, a shattered and torn place where centuries of tide and storm had broken the stone and the heat of the day had cracked it. The weather, even though it was still spring, was warm and pleasant, and grew warmer still as they continued south. Here, there was no place to trade or even a beach to land on that they might hunt – if there were any animals alive on such a shattered coastline. Their food was what the Istsar drew from the sea, but such was their skill that they never went hungry. Indeed they were often embarrassed by the quantity.

The ruined coast of the baron's lands became the melted stones of the desert itself. As days went by the broken and ruined coastline stretched onwards, ever south. The temperature grew hotter and the sun grew stronger. The heat of the sun and sea had smashed these rocks too, but as the desert stretched on, she comprehended what a truly barren, lifeless place it was.

In the days that followed, as they sailed past

the desolate coast, Terras understood it was a wrecked land, a land devastated and empty. It seemed hard to understand why Franeus had sent her to this place, even to the southernmost tip of it. What could be there? A tomb, he had said. Why go to a tomb? To mourn a forgotten people? Was there something there to understand? And what could a tomb teach apart from the death of a people of long ago?

Eventually, after their long journey, they reached the end of the land of barren deserts and broken stones. The first signs were some soil and grasses on the coastline. Stubby trees of some strange type Terras did not know grew in small and shallow oases in the stone. No people lived there in these small gnammas, full of struggling life on the edge of the land of death.

The day eventually came when they reached a wide circular bay; the landscape of barren stone had finally dropped away into a parched and baked land. The bay was finally a place where they could consider sailing in and anchoring out where the water was at its deepest. A small dinghy would now be sufficient to get Terras to the shore.

Shiskes was not happy. Beyond the bay, south, they could see that the land was no longer completely barren. Life struggled here too, but here it was winning. Was this the end of the desert or should they go further?

'Lady Terras, you must not leave us here. It does not look like the beginning of a good journey.

Stay with us, let us return to the land of my people. Have your child with us and let us care for you.'

Terras hugged him. 'I know you care, Master Shiskes,' she said, 'but this is my task, the goal lies ahead. Franeus would not have sent me if the journey were not possible. I am sworn. I will travel to this place and see what it is that I must see.'

Shiskes did not prevent her, but he insisted on her taking more of the dried fish stores than she felt she could comfortably eat for many weeks. She wondered if he had left enough for themselves, but he assured her.

'Lady Terras, we can fish for more if we need, have no fear for us. We are content. Mother sea is rich this far south and we are returning to our home. Mother will feed us. We will travel, happy.'

Terras understood the implication. She was not travelling, happy. But they dinghied her to the shore and she stood there on the rocky, sandy beach and watched them scull back to the fishing boat. They departed quickly. The evening tide was ebbing. She stood and waved them away. It was sad to see them go; Shiskes particularly had become a friend. As she waved, she thought of her other friend, of Narcise and her kindness. Would they meet again? She did not know.

Now she was alone again. So much of her time since losing Halam she had been alone. The worst had been that trip over the heights of the Pasra. It had been lonely. But it was good now too. It was a relief that she did not have to explain herself to another group of Istsar. Now, at least, her path was one she knew – to travel, to hunt and to camp. To make her way through another of the difficult, arduous places of the world. The Hardsar trained to live in such a way – as all warriors must.

She lit a fire on the beach that night for that was what the Hardsar always did. It was already late in the day. She would make her start in the morning. It would be a better one for waiting. It was hardly necessary to have a fire; the temperature here was warm. Whilst it must be, at the best, spring, there was little sign of it here. This was where the world was warm and the weather full of sunshine. She sat and wondered when Franeus had intended her to reach her goal. He had set no timetable. There was therefore no sense of urgency. It disturbed her, not to have a target to reach. What should she aspire to? As the evening grew dark she walked along the beach, watching the sun drop quietly, almost apologetically, into the ocean beyond. There was a ruin nearby, a long-abandoned place built of white stone, but long ago broken and destroyed. There was nothing to learn from it.

The next day she travelled further south before striking to the east. As she suspected the land was a little more pleasant the further she was from the desert itself. There she found a land of stony hills and sudden valleys. At the tops of the hills, there were rocky formations. It was as if the stone desert could not quite let go. But it allowed, in the valleys, a little fertile land to return. Despite the constant climbing up and down, it was an easy place to travel. Yet, it was always full of surprises as she came upon some beautiful little hidden valley between two rocky outcrops. It was dry land, but not arid and dead. There were the remains of farms, some more recently made and abandoned, and then the remains of more ancient places, white and broken. Once there must have been more people living there. A long time ago it might have been easier, it might have been a rich land. There was water, lazy little streams flowing from the south towards the sea. The climate and the land had been richer before the stone desert came. Then there had been water from the north too, now lost. This land had not always been as it was now. She knew it.

She came upon some people the day after, making their living from a farm watered by a listless stream from the south. She spoke to them. They were few and she was fully armed. They were not, she judged, any danger to her. They were wary of her, but not aggressive. Sadly they did not speak much of the common tongue, only their own language, which she did not know and of which she could make little sense. She guessed that they did not see many strangers but just lived their lives without anyone bothering them. There was an attraction in that.

She spoke the words 'mausoleum' and 'tomb', and that seemed to spark some interest; despite their limited knowledge of the sacred tongue, these words they knew. They nodded sagely to each other and pointed further to the east. If that meant what it seemed to, she was at least heading in the right direction. Though there was no way to get them to tell her the distance. She tried to use her hands and a great deal of waving to ask, 'How many days?' but they either didn't understand or didn't know the answer. Terras suspected the latter.

They might know of the place but, never having gone there or seen it, they did not know anything. Maybe among their people it was just some ancient memory, a story told over the cooking fire at night. The other word they seemed to know was Willsar. They became quite excited then, exuberant even. Perhaps once, long ago, they had thought of themselves as Willsara.

She set off again and let herself swing a little more south for there the land was easier and the water even more plentiful. She hoped that this would not cause her to miss her goal. She could still see the edge of the stone desert to the north – there, before the horizon dipped down. If she was careful she should not miss anything.

She walked without hurry. She still knew of no urgency to bring her to this place. Franeus had wanted her to persuade the Istsar people of what was happening in the world and she had done it. And, by the Snake god, what a long time it had taken. To travel easily now wasted only a little more time than those Masters of the Istsar had. And she did not need a strenuous and harsh journey. She did not want to threaten their child.

It was the third week of travel that she saw it.

It nestled on the horizon where the stone desert ended and this dry land began. A large building, it was entirely alone on the landscape. It could have been a temple or perhaps a tomb, but it was exactly where Franeus had said it would be. It must be her place, the mausoleum.

She turned slightly north-east, back towards the edge of the desert, and headed as directly for it as she could. A day ended and she camped, realising as she did that this was the last camp before she reached it. It took her a good way into the following day to even approach it. It was further away than it seemed. It was a taller, larger place than she realised. Three streams ran up to it and she had to ford one of them at a shallower part. But none of these rivers were deep, as she had come to expect in this languorous land. The stone desert began just north of her. A precipice of broken stone marked where this habitable land ended and the inhospitable and deadly desert began. No streams flowed down from the promontory. The desert's edge was a place forgotten by water, bereft of life.

It was late afternoon as she reached it. A great archway marked the entrance to a massive courtyard, but the top of the arch had fallen and she needed to climb and thread her way through the rubble to reach the courtyard. There had been a huge square pool in the middle and steps led down to it from the archway, but there was no water in it. It had dried up or failed long ago. What looked like great faucets lined the bottom of the pool. These, she decided, had filled it once. Perhaps the lazy shallow streams around the place had once been the source. Whatever the truth, they had ceased to work long ago. There were more steps on the far side of the pool so that people could, as needed, descend from either end.

At the sides of the courtyard of the pool were rooms and outbuildings, but it was hard to see or imagine what they had once been. The place had long ago been ransacked and everything of use or value taken away. They were but empty shells of places that had once been important and no doubt thought vital. Many of the roofs had fallen in too, which made deciding the use of any of these places quite impossible.

At the far end of the courtyard was a great temple. It was the highest and grandest of all the buildings and was almost entirely intact. The doors were broken, but the roof was in one piece and there was no damage to its walls. Surely, this was the place to which she had been sent.

Why had she been brought here? The mausoleum, if that was what it was, seemed deserted and empty. The people who lived in this land had probably forgotten the use of the building centuries before. They only remembered it now because of its size and faded grandeur.

Blown down from the desert, sand and pebbles covered everything. It was a truly dismal place and as she walked to the temple she thought about what she would do next. Returning to the shore seemed like a fruitless exercise, for no Istsar boats were waiting to carry her north. She could not cross the desert, surely, for she had never heard of anyone who had. People moving between the north and south of the land did it by boat either in the far eastern lands or here in the far west. What would she do if she found nothing here? What would she do and where could she go? South? She had banked the whole of the last few months of her life on coming to, on reaching this place and now it was nothing but an empty shell.

Terras walked over to the broken doors.

She passed through the ruined entrance of the temple. Two statues guarded the doorway, although since they were not armed, perhaps they were meant as welcoming heralds. She stared at them for many minutes. They were beautiful statues of strong and capable people, one man and one woman, dressed in long flowing robes. They did not look like guards or greeters either. They were inside, so couldn't, even representationally, be keeping people out. It seemed bizarre to her.

There was no furniture inside the temple. Great steps headed down into some basement and beyond that there was nothing, except a great carving of the Snake god coiled around its stone staff. It would have been taken, she was sure, if it had not been carved out of the far wall itself, a great bas-relief. It would have been impossible to prise even a stone from it without bringing the whole wall down.

It was very late now and the sun was heading for the horizon to the west. Its light streamed in through great broken windows. Windows they had been, but now they were just gaps, slashes in the wall. In the morning the sun would light the place from the east through great slits of windows on either side of the relief of the Snake god. As the morning sun crept into the sky the temple would fill with light and in the afternoon the sun, heading to the west, would fill the temple again with the light of a setting sun, through the doors and windows of the west.

Why am I here? Must I wait?

She should make camp, perhaps in one of the side rooms, where the roof was still intact. It rained rarely here, but it might protect her from any weather. It felt odd to camp in the temple. She stood there as the sun made its dusty way to dusk. She wondered about descending the stairs before leaving. Perhaps there would be very little light down there, but the light from the western windows convinced her, at least, to walk down the steps to see what was there. She could then mount a more thorough exploration in the full light of tomorrow.

As she trod on the first step, a great wind came down off the desert, warm, dry, and dusty, yet full of strength and emptiness. It blew the sand and leaves that covered the floor into a swirling tornado. She walked down the first step as the wind swirled around her. There was a creak.

It was not the sound of the stone step on which she walked. She knew that at once and instinctively. Her sword leapt into her hand and she spun around, a great sweeping motion that took all the space around her, seeking the enemy.

There was no one. The tomb was as empty as it had been before. The two statues stood framing the door. Everything else was the solemn emptiness that it had been before, had long been. The last light of the day was odd now. Tinged by the colours of dusk, the statues seemed different. The colours of the setting sun coloured them brown at the top where the rays of daylight touched them. But they had not moved. They had not changed. They were not the source of the noise. There was nothing.

Had the doors moved in the sudden wind? She paused. *That's it.* She nearly gave up and went off to find a campsite. But then, as she had intended, she instead slipped quickly down the steps. There was a great room below, with a huge bas-relief of warriors marching to war at the far end. Each side of the room there were even more statues, at least a dozen. She stared at them in the quickening gloom and was just about to turn and retreat up the steps when a hand quietly touched her on the shoulder.

The Singer Series

of

Fantasy novels

If you'd like to receive information about future books in the Singer Series, please sign up on our website:

https://snaedeendeavours.com

Next is:
The Transformation of the Wind

Then look out for a prequel
The Quintessence of Shadow

J Andrew Evans, December 2020

Printed in Great Britain
by Amazon